THE UNITY GAME

Leonora Meriel is the author of four novels. Her debut work *The Woman Behind the Waterfall* was hailed as "strange and beautiful" by writer Esther Freud, "a literary work of art" by Richmond Magazine and "an intoxicating world" by *Kirkus Reviews*. Leonora studied literature at university and lived in New York, Kyiv and Barcelona before settling in her native London. She has three children. Read more about her life at www.leonorameriel.com.

ALSO BY LEONORA MERIEL

The Woman Behind the Waterfall

Mbaquanga Nights

And Breathe

THE UNITY GAME

LEONORA MERIEL

GRANITE CLOUD

To my beloved Francesca

THE UNITY GAME

CHAPTER ONE

THE MANHATTAN CITYSCAPE flickered yellow and unreal beyond the huge, darkened windows of the bank. Pointed tips of metal strained upwards; geometric shapes and angles multiplied within mirrored illusions of space. Behind the glass surfaces, tiny faces and screens were visible; hunched workers and cleaners moving rhythmically over seas of night-time carpet.

Within the walls of the bank, David pulled his gaze from the hypnotic glow of the surrounding buildings, and glanced at the time on his computer. He stepped out of his cubicle and looked around the floor to see who else was working late. Rows of identical grey boxes stretched out over a dull-green carpet, covering the length of the room. *Just a jumped-up factory floor,* he thought, and remembered the first time he had walked in there, his heart smashing into his chest like a jackhammer. That incredible moment when he knew he had made it. *New York.* He had made it. He reached his hands up above his head and punched the air with both fists, as if he was pounding on a huge door, screwing up his eyes and then opening them.

A glow caught his attention in the far corner – a couple of figures bent low over spreadsheet screens. The Managing Directors' offices were shut up with their lights off. It was probably just a pair of analysts trying to impress their MD, or some rush project which had them pulling an all-nighter. *Better get out now if they can't take it. It's not going to change for the next forty years.*

David let his hands drop and walked to the end of the corridor, scanning the other compact squares of computers and papers. They all looked the same as his. Financial calculators, notebooks of scribbles and sums, files on companies, black headpieces plugged into black, heavy phones. Just a row of underpaid Vice Presidents turning daily into the hardened, overworked assholes they idolised. But he'd made it. They'd all made it. The group of Wharton post-grads on the fast-track to power and politics; even the few who'd struggled up from nowhere like him. There was a constant thrill of testosterone around the floor. *We're going to be the super-rich. We're going to control the financial world. We are winning the game.*

He looked out of the far window of the office – a glass wall facing up towards midtown Manhattan. The Chrysler on the right, mostly full of lawyers, Met Life straight ahead with Park Avenue threading through the bottom and Grand Central Station hidden below. Further up, Lexington and the Upper East Side, and the UN – that strange, grey cereal box looming dismally over the East River.

Not that he cared. He loved the city for what it would give him in the future, not now. He loved the paychecks deposited straight into his bank account, most of which went to cover the overheated studio he rented on East 78th. The bonus he would use to invest in companies he had been researching. The thrill he could already feel of owning the city, pumping blood into every cell of his body so that he felt more than alive, as if he were standing above the world, far, far bigger than anything on the planet. Full of power, strength and drive.

Calm down. Still a few years to grind out before he was at the top. But he had that feeling pulsing through him that would get him there. They all did. None of them would be on Wall Street if they didn't have it – that maniacal urge to win the game. It was more than just succeeding. It was the desire *to take everything.* It was almost transcendent, the pleasure he felt from being faster, smarter, better, stronger, more hard-working; a relentless pulse driving him towards his goal. Winning everything. Total power. Having it all.

David glanced again towards the analysts at the far side of the room. Poor bastards. He'd been through that stage back in Toronto. Long, thankless hours spent on a project and always some VP ready to come and take all the credit. One mistake, and there was a line of graduates desperate to get their foot in the door. Checking, double-checking, working insane hours for the lowest paycheck on the floor. Bottom of the pile. But bottom of the right pile. The winning pile.

Enough. He ran his hand through his short, black hair and pulled his tie loose at the neck. Then he squinted a few times, clenched and unclenched his fists to get the blood pumping, and sat back down at his desk. He clicked up the Excel file he had been working on and started to go through the calculations from the beginning. He wanted to send the file to Jeff before he left tonight, so Jeff would see he'd been there past midnight. And he'd make sure he got in early tomorrow; before Jeff even, who was usually at his desk by seven. Then he'd get one of those off-hands that would keep him going – "Someone's on the fast track to MD," or "I'd better find an excuse to fire you before you work me out of my job." He'd store these comments up, keep them close by and use them to get himself out of bed after three or four hours' sleep, to drive him when he was pounding a seven-minute mile at the gym, even when he was masturbating to crash himself into a caffeine-buzzed sleep. It was all he had right now. That, and his dream.

Finished. He'd checked the numbers three times; they all added up. A $75 million high-yield loan arranged with three other investment banks as a club deal; added to the $150 million loan they still had on the books from five years back. There'd been some road-bumps in the past, but it was a good company, solid growth rate, building new operations in two states. It wasn't one of the hot technology start-ups multiplying all over the West Coast, but Jeff would approve it. He might even take him along to the next investors' boondoggle. Now that would be a hit. The guys on the floor would hate him for that. He smiled at the thought of them watching him win. Pure. Straight. Winning. Bunch of loser assholes. He'd work even harder. Sleep less. He was going to get all the big clients. All the big deals. He was going to make SVP this year. He was going to get the biggest bonus on the floor.

Done. He sent the e-mail to Jeff and logged out of his computer. He packed up his soft leather briefcase, pulled his Canali suit jacket from the back of his chair and slipped it on. What a beautiful suit. He already looked like an MD in it. He glanced around. Losers. They didn't have a chance. He'd outwork them all.

He switched off the computer and made his way down the corridor of cubicles, towards the glass doors and the silver wall of elevators set on a polished stone floor. He rode the twenty-seven flights to street level and stepped out of the vast, white-marble foyer into the yellow light of a New York evening. Tired, a thrill; almost post-coital. He flagged a taxi on Park.

"78th and York, sir," he said. Squashed knees in the cramped seat. Turban and beads swinging in the front.

Silence from the driver. The passing streets.

He was winning the game.

3

THE THREE MOONS WERE RISING.

The grey being lifted itself from the resting platform and rose to standing position. It turned its head to survey the subterranean chamber and ran a check over its physical condition. It had achieved maximum expenditure potential. It took note of the efficiency of its physical structure; even after an extended session of energy-channelling, its form required only a medium-level charge in the light capsule before it returned to a neutral state.

The being moved to the centre of the diamond-shaped space, where a sphere was indented into the surface of the base covering. It stepped inside the circle and positioned itself at the mid-point. Its form was thin, elongated, uncovered. The skin – supple and slightly translucent – clung tight around the bone and muscle structure. A row of small protrusions jutted from its vertebrae, and its hands and feet were delicately webbed, with scaled, claw-like fingers. The outline of its major organs pulsed in a slow rhythm, visible beneath the grey overlay.

It remained still for several inhalations, then extended its arms away from its trunk section until they were suspended horizontally on each side. It drew the vertical line of its body into alignment with a point in the ceiling of the chamber. There was a clicking sound as the top and bottom of the circle points activated, and a green light streamed from above and below, curving around the poised form.

As the colour flowed around it, the being became enclosed in a compact oval of moving light. The shade deepened as the waves emanated, the skin tone darkening to a less translucent grey, more solid in appearance. At last, the process came to completion, and the being remained motionless, the colour shimmering around its form. The only movement was the rising and falling pulse, generated by its breathing organs, which were now less visible through the pigmented skin.

The being opened its mouth and emitted a single note into the chamber: a long, clear sound which began quietly, and grew until the entire space was resonating with its vibration. It completed the path of the note but held its mouth wide in the final position until the waves had dispersed evenly around the area. The clicking sound came again, and the being at last lowered its arms and the alignment was broken. It stepped from the circle.

At this stage of the lunar rise, the grey crust of Home Planet was illuminated by the slow movement of the three red moons overhead. The largest, *Tirtha*, was directly above the planet, and its dark shadow drew patterns and rivers across the stony grey. Rising in the ascension capsule, the being paused to look around before setting off through the dancing shadows of the red moon, towards a wide, flat rock on the horizon. It travelled with effortless distance leaps; the charged potency of its form enabling smooth movements, its legs and arms pushing easily through the weak gravity.

It reached the rock and made its way to the flat platform, which had an indented stone circle, identical in circumference to the one in the subterranean resting chamber. The being positioned itself in the centre of the sphere and checked the rockscape and the spacescape. The position of the moons was correct. The sound vibration of the planet and its own energetic composition were aligned. The atmospheric particle level was within the apportioned range.

The being experienced the intense pulse of *kaiif*, which passed through it when a critical task assignment had been prepared over many moon cycles and was on the verge of being executed to the maximum projected potential. The *kaiif* emanated simultaneously from its central axis point and its primary circulatory organ, with an intense tingling that occurred both within its cells and on the surface of its skin. The tingling spread quickly over its form, building up to a steady throbbing within its brain field.

On this triple lunar rise, during which it would carry out the final task assignment of its lifespan, the being allowed itself to be present within the pulse for a few inhalations longer than usual.

Then it drew its consciousness to the surface, blinked its eyes open and shut, then open again.

It raised its arms.

THE MAGNIFICENT PANELLED hall of York's Inn hummed and throbbed with the lunchtime discussions of London's elite barristers. Over the din, Alisdair leaned towards the young lawyers opposite him and cleared his throat. By rights, he should be sitting on the top table with the high court judges and benchers – he could see the Treasurer there enjoying a plate of trifle – but Alisdair liked the lower benches, where he could interact with the students and the up-and-coming lawyers. He much preferred conversing with open minds, than with those who had a lifetime of experience, such as himself.

"When we are facing an issue of such particular complexity," he started, his authoritative Edinburgh accent carrying across the table, "I like to return to the philosophers. To the Greeks, in particular, on whose distinctions of justice Roman law was based."

There was a silence while the lawyers considered his words.

"I refer you to the great Roscoe Pound, who traced Roman justice back to the Greek concept of law as 'a conscious product of wisdom'. Of course, beyond that, there was the distinction between the law of man and *to dikaion*, or 'what is just' – a sensible distinction, and one to bear in mind in any complex case. This is all a matter of some careful reading in jurisprudence, which I trust you have all studied to a sufficient level?"

Alisdair peered at his audience, who reassured him with nods and serious faces.

"But, so far—" began one of the lawyers, pushing heavy spectacles back against her face.

"So far," interrupted Alisdair, "there are up to seventy cases a year which are decided on the interpretation of the most eminent lawyers in the country, the House of Lords. If you look at each of their decisions in detail, you may trace the arguments back to the ideas of Socrates, as expounded by Plato. Now who can—"

"The rule of law—"

"Human law as *a conscious product of wisdom*. This is essentially the same as precedent. Building consciously on that which was already established as wise."

A stout waitress in a white, frilled apron passed by, and Alisdair waved at her.

"Young lady, the beef today was excellent. Please pass on my thanks to Charles."

He turned back to the lawyers.

"It all leads back to the most simple principles, and these do not change. It is what makes our legal system the most respected in the world. It is why people come flocking to England to seek justice, which they cannot find in their own countries."

Alisdair lifted the glass of claret to his lips, and drank down the last few drops. Then he stood up and held on to the table for a moment or two before he brought slightly shaking hands up to straighten his red bow tie.

"Ladies and gentlemen, a pleasure."

"Sir Alisdair."

The lawyers quickly digressed into more pressing topics, as Alisdair's dignified figure moved towards the towering doorway of the hall.

A uniformed attendant swung it open and he made his way out of the din and towards the benchers' cloakroom, where his greatcoat was hanging on the same peg he had used for over four decades. Forty years as a bencher at York's Inn; a fellow of New College, Oxford; an academic; a legal authority. His hands shook more than usual as he pulled the cashmere coat over his suit and pushed the buttons through their soft holes one by one. He wrapped a tartan scarf around his neck and fitted a trilby hat over thin hair. It wasn't far to walk back to his chambers, but it was a biting London day and he felt the chill more keenly these days.

Alisdair went out of the benchers' entrance and down the steps into the first of the Inn's two wide courtyards. He looked around. It never ceased to delight him, the history of these buildings. The leaded window where Charles Dickens had once aimed cherry pips at scuttling clerks. The hall he had just left, its frame suspended by screens from the Armada fleet. The elegant gardens designed by Francis Bacon, through which he had swept Elizabeth I. The decades and centuries of fine intellects which had built the English legal system and shaped the models of justice around the world.

An acquaintance passed him on the other side of the square, recognised the familiar tartan and touched his gloved hand to his hat.

"Chilly day, Alisdair," the man called out, and Alisdair nodded to him.

He felt a little dizzy as he walked towards the tunnel leading out onto High Holborn, and he stopped to catch his breath. A strong pain flickered through his chest and he bent over double as another shot through him, and then another. His head was spinning and his breath was short. He realised that he had fallen to the ground. Then the shots of pain became one long note, as if a pole had been thrust through the centre of his heart, and the dizziness became still and constant. He closed his eyes.

His acquaintance glanced around, thinking he had heard a noise across the square, and saw Alisdair lying on the historic paving stones near the entrance arch. He gave a shout and rushed towards him, calling out to the porter in the nearby lodge.

A few minutes later, the two men had spread Alisdair onto his back. A woman who knew CPR sat astride him, blowing into his mouth and pulsating his heart with overlapping hands. A small crowd of lawyers had gathered between the parked Bentleys and Jaguars, watching the spectacle with hurried faces. An ambulance was on its way.

Alisdair, feeling particularly well, watched them with interest. He stood a few paces away from his body and brushed his hands over his suit. How clumsy he looked lying there. He didn't like how his face had twisted. And what was that woman trying to do to him? It was far too late. He wasn't coming back now.

He put a hand up to check the dapper angle of his hat and danced a little jig. He really did feel good. Full of energy. And how well-polished his shoes looked in the afternoon sunshine.

The ambulance arrived and the paramedics tried another round of CPR. He wished they would leave him alone, or at least move him away from the crowd. Most undignified. He watched the scene for a few moments longer and then turned away. There were far more interesting things to explore, particularly this new energy. He felt as if air had been blown through every cell of his body.

He stepped jauntily out of the arch and onto the busy thoroughfare leading towards St. Paul's. Everything he saw around him seemed new and thrilling. Buildings filled with light, reflected mirrors and angles and geometric shapes he had never noticed before. What a city it was! Bursting with ideas and energy and beauty, constantly re-inventing itself. How lucky he was to have lived in such a place. He walked, looking around in an alert wonder, and found himself drawn towards a building he hadn't seen before. He crossed the road to get closer and saw that it had the appearance of a library, or perhaps a public court house. The stone was pale and captured a particular light. It made him think of Italy and the stone quarries he had visited. Carrara, where Michelangelo had found the block of marble from which he had sculpted *David*. The incredible treasures of the earth. The treasures of life. My goodness, he had lived well. The paintings of Italy, the ruins of Greece, the vineyards of France, where one was tempted to give up everything for a lifetime tending vines and sampling cheese. He had been so fortunate. He had enjoyed so many moments of depth, so many moments shared with his wife. Until she had left.

He chuckled. Of course, she hadn't left. She was here. She was waiting for him inside this building. Of course. That was why he was going there.

He mustn't wait a second longer. His heart gave a great leap of anticipation and he turned and skipped up the marble steps, between the stone columns stretching up into the afternoon sunshine. He paused for one long breath before the huge, open doors, and he raised his arms as if giving thanks before an audience of angels, or reaching for a last piece of precious sky.

Then, with a feeling as if he were shattering entirely into pieces, he stepped through them.

CHAPTER TWO

THE RADIO FLICKED ON RED, firing up a tinny pop song. David breathed in deeply without opening his eyes. It was another fantastic day.

In a fast movement, he pulled the dark-green duvet aside and jumped out of bed. He stretched his arms wide, kicked off his boxer shorts and walked naked into the bathroom.

No coffee. He'd cut down on that when he had come to New York. No fat. No alcohol. Well, most of the time. He scratched the hair on his chest while he waited for the water to heat up. He liked these cramped, Manhattan bathrooms; all identical, with their white square tiling and angular metal taps. He'd never seen one different to this.

The water was perfect. Same bathtub-shower combo waking people up all over the city. The 4 a.m. risers, the 5 a.m. risers, the ones who didn't give a shit and rolled out of bed at six or later. The water was almost scalding on his skin and he flexed his shoulders as it burned into his back. The best feeling. He scrubbed at his hair and body, flicked off the shower-tap, then rubbed himself hard with a dark blue towel. Shave, style hair and he was ready. Six fifteen out of the door. That was his rule. Eight minutes to the subway, wait two to three for a train, twelve minutes to East 23rd. Walk two blocks to the bank, flip his security card, elevator to the twenty-seventh floor. Door to door was exactly twenty-five minutes; most was thirty when there was a delay on the subway. Six forty-five in the morning at his desk. He made sure he sent the first e-mail of the day by six fifty, so that Jeff knew he was in the game. Every day. Six forty-five. Done.

He opened the front door.

"HEY, asshole. You sleep here last night?"

David looked up and pulled off the black headset.

"Actually, no." He paused. "Your mother let me stay over. Didn't get much sleep."

"Very funny, asshole."

"Why? You didn't get your full nine hours? You know Jeff's been in since seven fifteen. Saw him make a note of who was here. Pretty short note. 'Cause it was only me."

Danny leaned on the flimsy wall of David's cubicle.

"Well, it looks to me like you're gonna burn yourself out right about bonus time. Make some major screw-up and get your ass fired. End up back in that Canadian shithole you crawled out of."

"That's what you're fantasising about every night? Me screwing up so there'll be nobody else to pay the bonus pool to? 'Cause that's the only way you're gonna see any of it."

Another two VPs came up with steaming cups of coffee that smelled of metal and exhaust fumes.

"Morning," David nodded to them, leaning back in his chair. "Danny's just worrying about his bonus. I'm trying to reassure him he won't get cut."

"So what time did you get in this morning?" asked Tom, one of the Wharton crowd, unpacking his black leather briefcase at the cubicle opposite David. Tom was the tallest guy on the floor and incredibly good-looking. Westchester aristocracy.

"Six forty-five. Thirty minutes before Jeff. Same as always."

"Danny's right, you know. You gotta pace it. Jeff would kick you out in a heartbeat if you screwed up. There'd be a new guy at your desk by Monday."

"Yeah, yeah. Don't you have some clients to squeeze money out of? 'Cause I got a whole pile of them."

Tom turned to him, holding a client file. His eyes flickered over David's jacket.

"Nice suit."

"Canali."

"Very nice."

"Alright, guys. Catch you later. I'm working here."

A shout came from the open glass door of Jeff's office. "Tom, get in here."

Danny gave Tom's shoulder a knock with his own. "Still the favourite, Wharton Boy."

Tom walked back to his cubicle and David watched him bend over the partition to pick up a pile of client folders, then head towards the glass-walled office. He went in and closed the door behind him.

Danny turned back to David. "Now that's something you can't beat with hard work," he said. "Blue blood."

"Yeah, get outta here."

David reached for the headset and put it back on. He clicked up the computer file and started to dial a number into the phone.

"Gym at lunch?" Danny mouthed at him, and David nodded back.

"One o'clock."

Danny moved up the row to his own cubicle and David watched him. He was right about Tom. There was an inside track, and no way to get on it. Tom was very, very smart. He'd had the best education there was, and his dad was some bigshot in Washington who knew everyone. He probably hadn't even applied for this job. His dad had probably just made a phone call to the head of the bank. But no. Guys like him were arrogant, but they were still hard-working. He'd probably got in on his own steam. He was that arrogant. Hadn't even needed the phone call.

Still, they were working in the same place, weren't they? Maybe Tom lived with a blue-blood wife in a two thousand square-foot condo, but that was no reason why David couldn't make it. He was just as smart. He wanted it just as much.

His phone went through to a Swiss Western answering machine.

"Yeah, Rasheed. It's David. Bullman Scout. Give me a call. I've got pre-approval for leading the loan. Are you guys at that stage yet? Give me a call and we can move this thing forward. You got the number."

He flipped the tone button. He could get this deal closed within ten days. He'd talk to Jeff about it. That's how you set yourself apart here – come up with a new deal from scratch, run it as the lead arranger and make the bank look good. Not that this department got much attention. Not as much as M&A, anyway. He wondered, not for the first time, why Tom wasn't working in M&A or Oil & Gas. That was where most of the hot-shit graduates went; straight to the heart of the profit centre. But then they were always the first to get fired when the economy went down and the fat-cash companies stopped eating up the competition. Didn't matter. He'd ask Tom one day. Good guy, Tom. He liked him. He wasn't the competition. He was on the inside track and there was nothing David could do to stop his navy-blazered, money-blazing path to Washington. It was the other guys he was busting his ass to get one

11

over on. Danny and Janko and Kirsten. They were the ones who would either make it to Director or end up with cheap-ass secretaries in second-tier commercial banks. That was the game now.

He flicked up another file and punched in a new number.

"Yeah, Rasheed. It's David. Just left a message on your office machine. Can you talk now?"

 WHEN THE GREY being had completed its task, it lifted the lid covers from its eyes. It knew that it had achieved and even surpassed its objectives. It identified its partner, *Tesson*, standing at a distance from the flat rock. Its partner made no movement but sent a sound vibration towards it: *Noœ-bouk*. Its name. The acknowledgment of its name. And a summons. The single sound vibration created a layer of calm beneath its intense weariness. It could rest now. It would be taken care of.

It stood in the completed physical attitude for several more inhalations, not moving any of its limbs but allowing its mind to fill with the warmth of the sound vibration which had been transmitted. *Noœ-bouk*. *Noœ-bouk*. A wave of deep belonging and the most valued sensation of all: the recognition of a satisfactory achievement. Its form felt as if it were a riverbed down which had flowed an immense flood. Eroded, emptied, exhausted.

It could sense the remnants of a fading heat from the last breaths of the sinking moons, but soon the pre-sun darkness would be bringing in an extreme level of cold. It had expended the capacity to generate physical-form warmth. It would need to return to shelter, and to rest.

It stepped down from the flat rock using small, careful movements. It could fall easily. *Tesson* did not alter its position. It was waiting. *Tesson* understood that the descent was the final part of the task assignment. A completion of the process. The physical realisation of total expenditure, even if this meant that it would collapse onto the grey rocks. It must experience the full cycle of the energy-channelling.

It did not fall. It moved with slow steps towards its partner, holding the word inside its head. Its oval eyes were open wide and it appeared dazed or lost, but its partner knew that this was a reflection of its state of maximum expenditure. It did not possess the muscular capacity to suspend its eyelids halfway over its eyes. As *Noœ-bouk* reached the level where its partner was standing, *Tesson* turned and moved away. *Noœ-*

bouk followed with small, jerking pulses, no longer registering the surrounding planet or the silvering red light of the sinking moons. Its mind held the single word it had been given – *Noœ-bouk* – and the implicit command to follow.

It appeared to lose consciousness for a while, or perhaps its partner had initiated a distance leap, for *Tesson* was suddenly a long way ahead, and almost an inhalation from their resting compartment. *Tesson* entered first and then waited for *Noœ-bouk* to reach the capsule. One, two, three inhalations descent, then the final corridor. It did not think it could reach the chamber. It felt a throb of energy as *Tesson* transferred green, active light to its physical form and it acknowledged that one limb was moving and then another. The compartment door slid open and it heard a control panel being adjusted and a resting platform lowered. At last, it expended the green light it had been given to lower the lids over its wide-open eyes, and it entered a state of rest.

While it lay on the platform, motionless, its skin-covering almost transparent, *Tesson* moved to the control panel next to the compartment door and entered an instruction into the key symbols. Through the clear pipes of the chamber, a dark-green light began to flow out into the resting space, infiltrating the inhalation particles with its intense pigment. *Tesson* experienced the new energy as a tingling over the surface of its form. It had no requirement for this level of recovery – its form stasis was within the neutral range – and it moved to the opening of the resting compartment, pausing as the doorway slid aside, but not looking back to its partner laid out on the platform. From the corridor, it ascended to the surface level, checked the pre-sun rockscape and, with effortless distance leaps, it set off for its first task assignment of the triple moonfall.

THE FIRST THING that Alisdair noticed, stepping through to the other side of the columns, was a sudden calm. The street was gone. The noise was gone. The people were gone. In their place, an intense, thrilling light seemed to be shining from everywhere around him.

He stood still for a few moments, breathing the light in and out, savouring the intoxicating sensation, and then it occurred to him to look around. He was in the foyer of what seemed to be a huge library, and he could see several open doors leading into rooms lined with books. The only thing he found confusing was the brightness, which implied an open space. He looked up, but could not make out any kind of ceiling; only scalloped columns of translucent marble stretching as far as his eyes would go.

Alisdair felt a tremendous energy in his body. A vitality, as if he could run a hundred miles or write an extraordinary legal argument in one night. He hadn't felt this well since university, when he was on the rowing and cross-country teams, leading the debating society and winning legal prizes. The pure drive of those days came back to him now, with a thrill of pleasure, and he thought again how lucky he was to have lived the life he had. Truly, he had made the most of his talents, and he had been given every opportunity to do so. And how well he felt now! He turned around in the foyer once more and, deciding that he would have plenty of time to explore each of the rooms in turn, he strode to the nearest one and looked in.

It took him a few moments to understand what was in the room, as the light created a shimmering effect that acted like a mist before his eyes. From the open doorway, he could see there were men and women dressed in white robes. They were both seated and standing, studying a selection of books and parchments. Through the haze, a figure approached him from one side of the room. He was dressed in a smart tweed suit and had a pair of half-moon spectacles hanging around his neck. He was holding a rolled-up scroll in one hand.

"Alisdair," he said. His accent was distinctly Scottish. "We have been waiting for you."

"Where am I?" Alisdair asked. "Is Eileen here?" It felt good just to say his wife's name again. It had been a long time now since he had let himself speak it.

"She is expecting you," the man answered. "You can see her anytime. But you might like to look around here first."

"What is this place?"

"This is the Main Records Library. Follow me."

The man turned and moved up the aisle, leading Alisdair along the length of the vast room. Alisdair gazed at the array of books and scrolls. He reached out his hand and trailed it along one of the shelves.

"There's no dust!" he exclaimed to his companion, and then he thought what a foolish thing this was to say, out of all the things he could have noticed.

The man laughed. "We can easily make some dust, if that makes you feel more at home." He reached up to a shelf and tapped the spine of a book. A haze of glimmering silver rose up around it.

14

"Better?" he asked.

"I don't know yet," Alisdair answered; and then, "Where am I?" he asked again.

"You are in the library of all the records," the man said. "This is not normally where people come when they have just vacated a body, but we thought you would like to see it. We know that you were rather partial to books."

Alisdair thought how true this was, and how very comfortable he felt in this vast, magnificent library.

"Where do most people go when they have... vacated a body?"

"To a meeting place," the man answered. "It is usually somewhere they are familiar with. A childhood memory or suchlike. They have a group of friends to bring them through. Your wife felt that you would like to come here, though. That you would be fine on your own. She didn't anticipate any problems for you in adjusting to the different dimensions. She said your curiosity would come first."

How clever of her, thought Alisdair. *And how considerate.* Nobody had ever understood him as well as her. He would be so pleased to see her again.

"What are the records of?" he asked. He reached out a finger and drew it across the spines of a row of books. The silver haze rose into the air and then faded again.

"Lifetimes," the man answered.

For some reason, this didn't surprise Alisdair. It seemed as if he already had the answers to his questions just at the cusp of his consciousness. All he had to do was reach through to them.

"Whose lifetimes?"

"Earth lifetimes."

"Every lifetime, or just some that have been lived?"

"Every lifetime."

"So every life that has ever been lived is here? Every book is a life?"

"Every book is a collection of lives."

"And is my life here? Now?"

"The one you have just lived?"

"Yes."

"Aye. That. And many others you have lived. Dozens. Hundreds, in fact. You might like to remind yourself of them later – to bring a few of them back. Some people like to hold on to the most recent memories for a while, but I imagine you would be keen to see the bigger picture."

"But if I've had hundreds of lives, why don't I remember this place?

Why don't I immediately remember everything? Surely if it's been *hundreds...*"

"Every time, you remember more. And every time you return here you are widening your sphere of knowledge. Many of the earlier lives were in simple states of consciousness. You went to a different location between each life. To grow and develop and widen. And when you return the next time, you may go straight to the Council. There is never any repetition."

Alisdair suddenly stopped, with his hand resting on a cracked parchment.

"You've got a Scottish accent," he said.

The man laughed again. "Your wife thought it would be a nice touch."

"She thought of everything."

"She's been waiting for you a good while."

Alisdair shook his head. "I imagine she's running the entire library herself. In fact, she's probably managing this place." He paused. "What exactly is this place?" he asked once again.

"Well, it's not strictly a place," the man replied. "It's more like some-where that just happens to be *here*. Perhaps more like an event, if we put it in human terms. A continuous event. But we could *be* anywhere. In fact, we *are* anywhere. We're just not anywhere specific. *Here*, if you like, is really anywhere you would like it to be."

"Ah."

"But let's leave that for later. There's plenty of time to readjust your concepts to this level. Not that there's any *time* here, either. Anyway, it's quite important that we do things in order. Not do too much at once. Is there anything in particular that you'd like to know, or shall I continue the tour?"

"How do you read the lives?" Alisdair asked. "Are the books in words? What about the life I just lived?"

"We'll be taking a look at that in due course," said the man. "The life review is an important part of the process. But we're jumping ahead again." He paused. "By the way, my name is Duncan."

He held out his hand to Alisdair, and the two men shook hands.

"Is that really your name?" Alisdair asked.

"It certainly has been," said Duncan. "Names are—"

"Yes," interrupted Alisdair. "I can see that. Eileen would like it to be accurate. Now, about this life review?"

CHAPTER
THREE

THE PLANE STARTED its approach towards the shimmering lights of Denver International Airport, just as the massive, red Colorado sun began its descent, lighting the circle of surrounding mountains in waves of vermillion dusklight. David looked out of the window and thought that the illuminated city and cragged peaks looked like something out of a sci-fi movie. Red mountain planet. Or maybe not even sci-fi. Maybe this was what Mars actually looked like. Dark red crags and dust. What was the latest? Hadn't they put another lander there this year? Found traces of water? A few hundred million dollars and a new rover and they'd come up with water. What a waste of money. When he had a few hundred million, he wouldn't spend it on a robot. He'd spend it on... well, he'd been down this path before. He had a concise list of what he'd spend his first few million on; he was still working on the hundreds. There was plenty of time for that, and he planned to put a lot of it aside to fund a life of effortless, high-interest, luxury living. Some high-class investment shop. He'd make them come and beg for the money, those hedge-fund guys with the unbelievably well-cut suits. And he'd have clothes like that, by then. He didn't even know where they were made. Probably custom-sewn by some Italian tailor they flew in from Italy. *Rich assholes.* He wouldn't put it past them.

Jeff, in the seat next to him, was talking about the deal again. David wasn't worried about the meeting. He knew the client and the loan details inside out. It was one of Jeff's smaller accounts and David had seen an opportunity to pitch some business. It was a vote of confidence that Jeff was bringing him along; he could easily have taken the idea

17

and flown down on his own. Who knows, he might even let him manage the account if he did well.

"David, you're sure that you're ready?" Jeff was looking straight at him. Far too close for comfort after five hours of flying, even in business class.

"Jeff, I'm totally ready. I've been over the deal a thousand times. Last review was this morning. You want me to show you the slides? All I did was make the changes you told me. Apart from that, it's the one you approved."

"Yeah, alright. But don't screw it up. This client could be very, very big in a few years. We're looking at an IPO in twelve, eighteen months."

"It's safe, Jeff. Don't worry."

The two bankers turned to look out of the window at the darkening mountains and the city, lit up below them. The plane's wings blinked amber as they descended out of the clouds.

"If it all goes well, we'll go out on the town afterwards. You ever been out in Denver?"

"I've never been to Colorado, Jeff."

"Well, it's a neat little city. The skiing's awesome. We had another day, we could hit the slopes."

"Yeah, I heard that."

The cabin crew called attention for landing and the plane eased into the clear chill of a Colorado evening.

JEFF AND DAVID headed from the terminal to collect the rental car, and drove to the client headquarters a few miles outside the city. It was an impressive group of buildings, constructed from oversized, grey thermal blocks, and set in their own estate. It was clearly poised for rapid growth; a perfect candidate for an IPO.

A PA in a short skirt and swinging ponytail came out from behind the reception desk to welcome them, and she took them in a glass-fronted elevator to the CEO's office.

"Jeff, great to see you again!" The CEO came to his door and shook Jeff's hand.

"Tony Morgan." He held his hand out to David and shook it with a grip which crushed most of David's fingers.

"David Cornwell. Pleased to meet you, Mr Morgan."

"Call me Tony. Everyone does."

"Tony, David's one of our VPs," said Jeff. "He's the one doing the grunt work on the deal, so he's going to have all the answers for you this evening. And he'll be making the presentation."

"Well, that's great. We've got a lot of questions about it." Tony called out to another PA, who was sitting behind a desk in the anteroom.

"Suse, call Peter in for the meeting. Tell him the boys from Bullman Scout are here." He turned back to David. "First big client meeting?" David looked surprised, and Jeff and Tony laughed.

"I can tell by the handshake. Feels like your job's on the line, right?"

"Most perceptive guy in the Southwest," said Jeff. "That's why we're his key relationship bank. So don't try to bullshit him. Ever. He'll have your balls for breakfast."

The three men laughed, and a fourth man walked into the office.

"Jeff, David, this is Peter, my CFO. Peter, Jeff and David just landed from New York. We're going to show them the town later tonight. If David hasn't been fired by then, that is."

They all laughed again, and David felt sweat building up around his neck and on his hands. He took a deep breath. He knew the client. He knew the pitch. This was his chance to show Jeff how well he could perform in action.

"Well, let's get started." Tony motioned them all to a small conference table at one end of the huge, glass-walled office.

"David, we're all ears. Let's make this happen."

DAVID PUT his hand to his head and wondered if it was ever going to stop swirling. He had just downed another shot of tequila, and the taste of salt and lime was filling his mouth with a wet flush of saliva.

There was a shout next to him over the sound of the blasting rock music.

"Another round for the man!" It was Jeff. He was leaning on the bar with his arm around Tony Morgan. He reached over and wrapped his other arm around David.

"This…" he said, turning from David to Tony, and then back again, "… is the man who is sending your company to the big time." His words were slurring. The waitress brought three new shots of tequila, with saucers of salt and lime. They picked up the shot glasses.

"To the man!" said Tony, raising his arm.

"To the man!" said Jeff, his arm still wrapped around David.

David wondered if the next shot was going to make his head spin faster, or if he was just going to vomit all over the floor. He knocked it back and sucked the piece of lime.

A girl in a tight, sequined dress came over to the three men. She glanced at them all quickly before settling on Jeff.

"Looks like you boys are having a good ol' time," she said. She reached forward and started loosening Jeff's tie.

"Darlin', we're a little busy at the moment," Tony shouted over the music. "We're celebrating."

"I can see that," the girl said, not letting go of the tie.

"What I mean," Tony shouted, "is get the hell outta here!"

The girl ran her hands over Jeff's chest and looked up at him. "Is that what you want?"

"Hell, I'm too drunk to know what I want," said Jeff. "But if this man says no, then it's no. Sorry, darling."

"Assholes." The girl let go of the tie and turned and walked away, her shiny backside and pantyhose wiggling. The three men leaned against the bar with their mouths slightly open and watched her walk.

"Sure that was the right call, Tony?" said Jeff.

"I've seen that one before," said Tony. "You don't want a piece of that. You want some tail, I'll get you the finest tail this side of Vegas. You think we don't know how to show you East Coast boys a good time? I'm telling you, Denver is showing you a good time tonight."

"For that matter," said Jeff, "we could've gone to Vegas."

Tony hiccupped loudly. "Nothing Vegas has that we don't have right here. Well, almost nothing."

Jeff poked Tony in the chest. "Next time," he said. "I want to go to Vegas. And I want to take my boy as well." He put his arm back around David, who had turned a little yellow. "You're being quiet over there. What's wrong? Can't hold your liquor? I'm not having boys on my team who can't hold their liquor."

David managed to laugh drunkenly. "I'm fine, Jeff. I'm really fine," he said.

"Vegas," Jeff went on. "I'm going to take you to Vegas, next time we have a meeting here. It'll be your first proper boondoggle. And we are going to spend money. Yes, sir! We are going to take Vegas by the horns."

"I'm in," said David. "Tony?"

"Yeah, you bet I'm in," said Tony. "You just make sure it's right after our IPO. Then you can help me lose a few million."

"I'm your man!" shouted Jeff, slapping him on the back. He turned to the waitress.

"Three more, darling. No, change that – four more!" He pointed at David. "This man's going double."

WHEN *NOŒ-BOUK* RE-ENTERED the active state, it sensed the altered energy in the chamber immediately, identifying the dark-green waves that were used for deep level recovery. It considered whether the effects of the task assignment had been more significant than anticipated. Had form debilitation occurred?

It touched the points of its fingers together and rubbed the stretches of skin, one against the other, tip by tip. The slight friction caused pain to run from its digits up the line of its arms and into its central circulatory organ. It turned its hands in front of its face to examine the covering. Its skin appeared transparent: veins and bone and ligament were visible, and it had taken on some of the green pigment. The effect was foetal; an organ unformed, or lacking in structural completion.

Noœ-bouk rose to sitting position, and then slowly to standing. It was able to maintain an upright pose, yet it could sense that significant weakening had occurred. It attempted to conduct an evaluation of its condition, but the task was beyond its capability. It would require many moon cycles to recover its strength. For now, it was necessary to report on the channelling at the Task Assignment Centre, where it would also learn the preliminary results of its work. After this, it would go to the Cellular Genetic Centre, and a full form evaluation would be carried out; a programme of cellular regeneration initiated.

It exited the resting chamber and ascended to the surface in the capsule. The single sun shone pale stripes over the rocks and dust, returning them to their grey shapes, many of them cracked and broken from the extreme cold of the pre-sun darkness. Beings of its genus type were visible, travelling in distance leaps across the cragged landscape, between residence compartments and task centres.

Gathering the remnants of its physical strength, *Noœ-bouk* took a distance leap towards the Task Assignment Centre, landing several inhalations from the edifice. As it paused to recover from the extended movement, it gazed up at the building before it: a towering, mirrored pyramid, with a second pyramid built into the rock below as an architectural reflection. A diamond structure that combined beauty and functionality in equal measure.

The mirrored surface of the upper pyramid protected the Task Assignment Centre from external observation. To the unaccustomed eye, the grey and red crags of rock flowed onwards towards the horizon, with only slight discrepancies that could be attributed to anomalies of light or perspective. The reflection of the landscape also served as a symbol of the integration of natural and fabricated elements; a central tenet of the planet's philosophical architecture.

Noœ-bouk considered, as it regarded the central structure of its planet, that if it had not spent its lifespan as an energy-channeller, it would have taken satisfaction from performing task assignments that contributed to the maintenance of Home Planet, to interplanetary negotiations or the development of the civilisation system. It was particularly drawn to the attainment of logistical balance: achieving sustainability for the different genus types that existed there, despite the lack of organic resources.

In fact, there were few roles on Home Planet that *Noœ-bouk* would not have taken satisfaction in carrying out. The planetary system was constructed on the basis of a philosophical architecture rich in both meaning and symbolism, and the central ideas were applied with precision and efficiency. Within the system, each role was given uniform importance; the smallest and greatest parts were considered equally critical to the overall functionality. The sole evaluation of a being's contribution lay in how closely aligned its natural predispositions were to its choice of task assignment.

Woven into the architecture of the planet were ideas taken from the deepest sources of multi-planetary wisdom: beauty, enlightenment, the desire to seek beyond oneself, multi-dimensionality, the possibility of ultimate truth. The towering pyramid and hidden diamond were symbols of the prevalence of those ideas in all aspects of Home Planet existence, and of the beauty and integrity which were innate within them, however mundane they might become in their practical implementation.

Noœ-bouk experienced a deep gratitude for its conscious presence and participation in such an effectively constructed, truth-based infrastructure, and to have spent a lifespan executing tasks so critical to the development of Home Planet and its civilisation.

It had recovered enough physical strength to move forward once again, and it proceeded to an entrance of the surface pyramid. A diamond-shaped opening, unmarked, slid aside as it approached, responding to its form energy. Inside, it turned its head one way and then the other, noting the length of the white corridor that angled through this widest, base level of the edifice. It was empty but for one or two genus types moving between task chambers. Precise efficiency.

It made its way to the ascension capsule, and entered. On the panel, it touched its fingertips to a curved, silver symbol and rose smoothly through the pyramid, the grey rocks and dust of the surface rushing away into the distance, beneath the white reflected light of the single sun.

It stepped out of the capsule.

 DUNCAN LED Alisdair along the central aisle of the Main Records Library, the shelves of books towering up on each side and the air filled with an invigorating scent of parchment, leather, port and autumn leaves. At regular intervals along the aisle there were wooden lecterns, and figures bent over tomes and scrolls.

Duncan stopped in front of one. "Wait here for a moment. I will fetch the book."

Alisdair stepped up to the lectern and placed his hands on the smooth oak surface. He traced the carved edges, where mythical creatures were fashioned into the wood; elaborate dragons and unicorns, griffins and phoenixes. He examined it more closely. It was the same lectern as the one in the York's Inn library, from which he used to give lectures to his law students. He checked the outline of one of the griffins. Yes, there was the chipped wing he would run his fingers over while he was listening to questions from the floor. It was exactly the same.

Alisdair felt a sense of overpowering synchronicity passing through him. It seemed as if times and events were slotting into their correct positions, and that he was about to see the entire eternal puzzle revealed. For the very first time, he felt that it was all here, within his reach. He was wildly happy that this lectern existed in this place; it was somehow a vindication of the actions of his life. The fact that this lectern – from which he had shared his intellectual gifts – was here waiting for him, signified that he had been in exactly the right place in his life, that he had fulfilled the tasks which had been prescribed for him. Beneath his enormous curiosity at his new circumstances, he felt a deep relief at this unacknowledged concern; a reassurance that he had done right, that his life had been satisfactory.

He ran his fingers once again over the carved creatures. That jagged wing he had touched so many times, the indented scales of the dragon, the straight horn of the unicorn. He thought of the silver dust rising from the spines of the books, and it occurred to him that if these animals existed here, in this place, even in the form of carvings, then they might not be purely fantastical. He would ask Duncan when he returned. Perhaps, in this place, in this library, there would be *all* knowledge: the deepest mysteries, the eternal patterns of existence, the answers to the unanswerable questions.

And I could know them all. I could know the secrets that the world has searched for. I could know anything and everything.

Alisdair shivered in amazement. The idea brought a rush of the humility he had felt so often during his life, whenever he had contemplated the good things he was so fortunate to have, and the opportunities he had been given.

He looked up, dizzy with this sense of wonder, and as he gazed at the walls of books stretching further than he could see, he realised that all of the secrets and all of the truths and all of the knowledge of the world in which he had existed must be a mere speck of dust compared to all the knowledge which is, which could be, which must be.

"We were so small," he murmured to himself. "And we thought that it was all so very important, so very big."

A memory came to him; a conversation he had once had with Elspeth, his stubborn, bright-eyed granddaughter, about the meaning of life. Albert Einstein, she had argued, had asserted that the knowledge of the world, and everything which was known and imagined, was merely the tail of the lion, and that however much was learned about the tail, the true form of the lion was inconceivable. Elspeth had used the argument to condone a life of creative freedom over attending university and obtaining a body of what she called "definitively useless knowledge." It was a position with which he strongly disagreed, but the image and the idea had always stayed with him. The tail of the lion. It seemed appropriate now, as he examined the endless shelves stretching far up into an invisible ceiling.

"It *was* important," said Duncan. He had returned to the lectern and was holding a thick book, bound in burgundy cloth. The edges of the pages were gilded and shining.

"What was important?" Alisdair asked.

"The search for knowledge. It may have been small, but if you had not been searching, you wouldn't even have discovered the little that you did."

"But it was so little," Alisdair said.

"Yes, it was. But much of it was true. And if you are searching in the right direction, then it doesn't matter whether you know a little or a lot. From a little, much can be understood. You yourself understood far more than you actually knew."

"Perhaps," said Alisdair.

"Now, about this book," said Duncan.

"Yes?"

"In this book is written all of your lives."

"All of them?"

"All of them."

"How many are there?"

"Just Earth lives, or all of them?"

"All of them. Earth. Er... Both."

"Altogether, five hundred and ninety-six. Human, five hundred and sixty-five. Other..."

"Thirty-one."

"Exactly."

"And they're all in here. In this book."

"Yes."

"And I can read all of them."

"Yes. Well, it's not exactly reading. It's more like what you would understand, in your human terms, as a multimedia experience."

"Like those funny glasses?"

"Yes. The 3D ones. Well, in fact, it's like going through the entire life in super-fast mode, so it only takes a few minutes to 'read'. Except, as I said, there's no time here, so you will be experiencing the entire life again, just as it happened."

Duncan lifted the book and placed it on the lectern. The two men looked at it.

"It's an overwhelming thought," said Alisdair.

"It's actually fairly pleasant. You see, you're going through the whole thing again, but not from a human point of view. I mean to say, you're not judging what you see. You're just watching it. No emotions, light or dark."

"What about the lives of other people? Are *all* the books available for reading?"

"Yes, but not in here. This is your book. The book of Alisdair. Any life you are interested in?"

"Do I have to ask permission? Is there a librarian?"

"There are librarians, but they do not censor your choices. All the experiences recorded may be known. That is why they are undertaken. That is the reason."

"The reason?"

"Well, one of the reasons. I don't want to oversimplify it. Now, are you ready to look? Eileen was sure that you would enjoy it."

Alisdair glanced up to the volumes and tomes stretching towards a far-off ceiling. He thought he could see tiny stars twinkling at the very limit of his gaze, where the lines of shelves merged into the unseen. He looked down again.

"One more question," he said. He ran his finger along the tail of a long, carved dragon.

Duncan followed the path of his finger.

"Anything and everything," said Duncan, with great emphasis, "that could possibly be imagined, is only the beginning of what is, what was and what could be." He paused, and took a breath. "The tail of the lion," he continued, "is more like one single tail of just one single lion. Can you guess how many lions there are?"

"There are… no end of lions," said Alisdair.

The men were silent. Alisdair nodded. He stepped in front of the lectern and opened the book.

CHAPTER FOUR

"OKAY, DARLING. TIME TO GO."

David reached his arms up over his head and felt his biceps stretching into pain. God, that felt good. What was it about New York blow jobs that were just so damn great? Must be the pressure build-up. Or the girls were just insanely hot. Either way, he felt unbelievable.

Vanessa was sitting up now, straightening her hair. He leaned over and pulled her down next to him. "Time to go, darling," he whispered in her ear. "Got a big day tomorrow."

He ran his hands over the silicone-filled breasts that never failed to give him an erection, and then down over the small waist and into the dark flash of hair. He rubbed her gently, and she slid her body on top of his.

"Big day's still tomorrow," she whispered, pushing her mouth into his shoulder and arching herself up to let his fingers work into her.

"You got ten minutes," he said. "Then I'm kicking you out."

"You ever see me take more than ten minutes?" She raised herself up over him, pushing her breasts into his face to suck. David felt energy flooding back into his penis.

"Oh, god," he said, "I'm gonna need more than ten minutes."

BY TEN FIFTEEN, Vanessa had gone, and David was spent. He liked Vanessa a lot. He'd met her on one of the bar-crawls with the guys. She could have gone home with anyone from the bar, but she'd let him give her his card – Vice President, Bullman Scout New York. It had passed the smell test and he'd bought her a drink.

Since then, she'd clearly decided he was worth the effort. She never failed to come round when he called, and she never, ever bitched to him. And she gave amazing blow jobs. Basically, she was the perfect woman, although she did insist he make her come every time they were together. But hey, fair was fair. You had to give a little back. And god, her breasts were unbelievable. He didn't care whether they were fake or not; they were huge. Just thinking about them made him hard. Those breasts alone had made just about all his teenage fantasies come true. He couldn't think of a single wet dream which hadn't been made real in the last few months.

She was even pretty, though he suspected there'd been some work done along the way. She had one of those narrow faces that could easily have supported a major-sized nose. And she was just the right kind of skinny. Not bony, but not an inch of fat anywhere on her. That was another thing he loved about New York women. They knew how to take care of guys under a lot of pressure, and they knew how to take care of their bodies.

Okay, okay. It was true. There wasn't anything he *didn't* love about New York. And tomorrow was bonus day, and he had a whole year of hard work and 6:50 a.m. e-mails and a pile of happy clients to show for it. This was his year. He was making it, big time.

He leaned over to the bedside table, checked his alarm was set for 5:30 a.m., and then switched off the light.

Two orgasms, a 10K run at lunch, on top of the clients.

It was the perfect day.

He slept.

DAVID STARED at the piece of paper in front of him. There were numbers written on it, but he couldn't seem to make any sense of them. This wasn't what he was expecting. This was ridiculous. This was way, way lower than anything he had been expecting. It must be a mistake. He closed his eyes and opened them again. He looked at the numbers. He knew it wasn't a mistake.

He stood up and saw that Jeff was in his office, talking angrily on the phone. He walked up the corridor of green carpet, in between the grey cubicles. He heard someone speaking – or maybe shouting – something near to him, but he didn't register what was being said.

He reached the office and pushed open the glass door. He stood in front of the desk. The door swung shut behind him.

"Jeff..." He struggled to cut the multiple expletives out of the sentence he wanted to speak. "What... happened?"

Jeff hooked the phone back onto its base. His face was dark. He looked up at David and gave an easy shrug.

"What happened? Nothing happened. What's the problem, bud?"

"Jeff, I got the best results on the floor. I worked my butt off. I pulled in the most deals. You know that."

Jeff looked at him with calm eyes, and David suddenly realised that he shouldn't have come storming into the office. Jeff's mouth was moving downwards, the lines running from his nose to his mouth deepening. When he spoke, his voice was light, but there was a threatening note to it.

"You did a good job, David. You did a solid job. But don't get ahead of yourself. You're still a second-year VP."

David wondered if he should go on. He thought that maybe he should just get out of there, cut his losses.

It's too late. I'm in here. I might as well say it.

"Jeff, I got a lower bonus than Tom. He hasn't brought in half the results I have this year."

Jeff leaned back in his chair but didn't take his eyes off David. He waited for a long time before he spoke, and David felt himself shrinking before his gaze. He knew now that he shouldn't have come into the office. At last, Jeff spoke.

"David, just a word of advice. I like you, and I don't want to see you go down. Take your bonus, be happy, go and spend some of it. Go fuck your girlfriend. Better still, buy her something. Get yourself a blow job. But don't go bitching around the floor that you've been screwed. You get a reputation for that, you'll be the first to go, I promise you. Now get out of here. Go and spend some of that goddamn money."

David felt his breath coming and going in short bursts. This couldn't be happening. Was this really the guy who had given him new responsibilities and encouragement in Denver a couple of weeks back? This guy, who was now looking at him like he couldn't give the smallest possible shit whether he'd got screwed out of $50,000 or not? David felt a fresh wave of shock passing through him.

"Yeah, alright," he managed to say. "I was just expecting something—"

"We were all expecting something, David," said Jeff, and David suddenly wondered if Jeff hadn't got screwed on his bonus as well.

29

"Now get out of here. Think about what I said. Take the weekend off. But don't bring that shitty attitude back into my department. Got it?"

"Got it."

David turned and pushed open the glass doors. All the guys on the floor were staring at him. He closed the doors behind him.

"Yeah, you got something to say?"

"Alright, David," said Danny. "Calm down. It's not like you've spent the last year sliding yourself up Jeff's asshole."

"Yeah, fuck you, Danny."

Tom was at the far side of the room, near to the elevators and the washroom door. He was talking into the phone and there was an ugly, intense expression on his face.

David turned to Danny. "So what did *you* get?"

"I got seventy. What I expected. What did you get? You get less than that?"

"I got seventy-five."

"That's not the worst. You know what Tom got?"

"He got less than a hundred. He's on the phone with daddy in Washington. He says he's gonna switch banks. He's majorly fucking pissed off."

David glanced at Tom. He had never seen an expression like that on his face – a kind of furious disgust. It looked strange on Tom, who was usually so calm and self-contained. He turned back to Danny.

"The amount I brought in, I should have got over a hundred. This is complete bullshit. Complete fucking bullshit."

"Guys." It was Kirsten, one of the two female VPs in the group. "Get a grip. You know the average wage in the US right now is like, 40K. That's what people support families on. You guys just got over twice that in one shot and it's not even your base."

"What the fuck's that got to do with anything, Kirsten?" said Danny. "We're not driving tractors in the Midwest. We made the bank a pile of money this year. We got screwed and you know it."

David took a deep breath. "I'm getting out of here," he said to Danny. "Tell Jeff I'm taking his advice. I've got all the client stuff under control."

David took the elevator down twenty-seven floors and walked out across the gleaming, white-marble foyer towards the bank's main entrance. His heart was pounding savagely now. The shock from being pushed back by Jeff was turning into a renewed fury. The more he thought about it, the more it took over his body, working through him in bursts of rage. He walked fast, out of the heavy revolving doors, past the line of taxicabs and across the road into Gramercy Park. He kicked imaginary objects out of the way as he walked – pigeons, dropped toys, a football, a fast-food box. He thought about calling Vanessa again. He thought about getting drunk. But he was too angry to do either.

He had been fucked. Totally, completely, royally fucked. And why? For the simple reason that they *could* fuck him. For the simple reason that he had absolutely no leverage with the bank. No famous father up in Washington, no connections, no personal client relationships. And so they had fucked him. And if he didn't like it – hell, if he even *looked* as if he didn't like it, as Jeff had threatened him – they would kick his ass out and find someone else. It was that simple.

Shit. Shit. Fuck. Fuck. Fuck. Fuck. Fuck.

The words shot themselves around his head like bullets. He had to do something with his anger. Fuck. He would go for a drive. He would rent a car and drive as fast as he could somewhere. He'd drive upstate. Fuck it. He'd drive all the way to Canada. He'd go see his parents. Be a surprise.

He stopped at the edge of the park, pulled his wallet out of his back pocket and looked for the car rental card he had pocketed in Denver. He punched in the number.

"Put me through to one of your New York branches. Closest zip code is 10075, Upper East Side, Manhattan."

He waited.

"Yes. I want to pick up a car this afternoon. In about an hour. You got a Dodge there? Viper? A red one? Downtown? Yeah, brilliant. Keep it for me. Yeah, I got a card. Yes, clean license. It's Canadian. I'll need insurance for Canada, too. Give me till Monday 10 a.m. Thank you, sir. I'll be there in an hour. Thank you."

He pressed the cut button and took a deep breath of New York air. There. He felt better now. It would do him good to get out of the city. And he'd call Jeff. Tell him he was taking Vanessa out of town for a couple of days. Jeff would understand that he'd chosen the blow job route; the safest path to recovery for any fucked-off banker.

FIFTY-FIVE MINUTES LATER, he was at the rental shop on 12th with an overnight bag grabbed from his apartment. The Dodge was waiting for him, and with a quick glance at the map, he steered the red Viper out onto FDR, heading for the George Washington Bridge. The freeway wound out around the city, lapping the gleaming East River with Queens on the far shore, the pressure-cooker high-rises of Manhattan behind him.

He opened both the front windows and flicked on the radio. Soundgarden was playing and he turned it up full. The sun was shining in on him and he reached for his sunglasses. His anger didn't fade as he drove, but it somehow began to reverberate with the passing city. It seemed to be spreading out over the whole of Manhattan, as if the whole city had been fucked and was reflecting back to him its pure, explosive rage; each of those towering, mirrored office blocks, full of their own pissed-off fury and frustration. He pushed his foot down hard on the accelerator and the Viper screeched forward. He wasn't going to lose this one. He wasn't going down without a fight.

NOŒ-BOUK FORMED a memory pathway and returned to its early development cycles on a far settlement of Home Planet, to the moment when its potential for channelling had first been identified.

A gathering of different genus types had been exploring shape and colour variations when *Noœ-bouk* had noticed the transparent pipes running around the far edges of the chamber, and the main conduit situated in the centre. It had felt drawn to the coloured energy streaming through them, and had approached the main pipe and placed both of its hands on the clear surface. Within a few inhalations, the chamber had been flooded with powerful waves of green light, which immersed all the early development beings and instructors and caused a state of havoc.

This initial experience was one of the most vivid sensory impressions of *Noœ-bouk*'s lifespan. Within the memory event, it recalled being drawn to the moving green colour, then the feeling of the light flowing through the different parts of its body, until its form and consciousness became weaker, and it seemed as if it could simply disappear into the curve of one of those waves. The sensation had been extraordinary. A wild and pure desire to release itself into a living stream of light. A calling. A summons. Re-entering the memory, *Noœ-bouk* sometimes wondered whether, during its entire lifespan since that moment, it had ever experienced a comparable pleasure sensation.

The early development instructors had communicated afterwards that if the light had been of a higher intensity then *Noœ-bouk*'s entire form would have disintegrated into the waves. It transpired that *Noœ-*

bouk had such a strong, natural inclination for merging with the energies, that at the point when it was still developing its own energy pattern and wide open to influence, it could simply have been pulled into the flow and carried away. This was a concept which *Nœ-bouk* returned to frequently. How sublime that might have felt. What might have happened? Where it could have travelled?

The possibility that it might have been borne away within a wave of energy had followed *Nœ-bouk* throughout its lifespan cycles on Home Planet. The wave of energy which it could have joined was flowing somewhere now, moving through some planetary system or dimension, transforming everything it traversed with its vibration. In moments of reflection, *Nœ-bouk* thought of it as the existence it might have had. It brought comfort and, sometimes, a sense of longing.

After it had been identified as having an unprecedented aptitude for energy assignments, *Nœ-bouk* had been removed from the early development centre and placed in a new location, with different instructors. The vibration levels in this centre had been highly controlled. Only low levels of energy were permitted, so that *Nœ-bouk*'s physical form would not be affected, and it was able to develop its own natural frequency without distortion. There had been much thought exchange with its early development guardians about possible intensities of training and development. However, *Nœ-bouk* could not recall a situation in which there had been discussion about lifespan choices. Searching its memory base, it didn't seem to have ever been given a choice. It had undeniable form and mind capabilities and they were uniquely suited to one path. No other variation was possible.

The shifting of energies, which *Nœ-bouk* had achieved in its final task assignment this past moonrise, was bringing Home Planet and its moons into the preparation stage for a new level of ascension, when the more advanced genus types on the planet would evolve to a pure energy state, leaving behind their physical forms.

Before this transition could take place, it was necessary to purify the planet's surrounding field. *Nœ-bouk* had drawn in much of the lower vibration, channelled it out of the planet's resonance sphere, and opened up a path for a higher attractor pattern to be established. Now, everything on the planet would feel faster and lighter. Thoughts would be transferred in purer form. The truth would be apparent in situations where it previously could have been concealed. *Nœ-bouk* had finally performed the task for which it had been preparing its entire lifespan. Its potential had been fulfilled.

Stepping from the ascension capsule of the Task Assignment

Pyramid into the white corridor, *Nœ-bouk* returned from the memory pathway with the realisation that its lifespan, from this point onwards, would be irrevocably altered. Its form would deteriorate at an elevated rate and it would be obsolete as a partner to *Tesson*. It would not have the vital strength for a partnership of any kind. This was the scenario which it had spent its lifespan refusing to formulate into thought. And yet this was the only possible outcome from the cycles of task assignments and training which had proceeded from that moment long ago, when its undeveloped form had been transfixed by a pipe of flowing energy, and filled a chamber with waves of green light.

Suddenly, questions which it had not previously permitted itself to contemplate were entering its mind. Why had *Tesson* chosen it for a partner? There could be no continuation between them. *Tesson* would leave *Nœ-bouk* and align itself with a being that could offer a full potential lifespan. But it would always carry the approbation of having shared key lifespan cycles with a partner, whose work had enabled the ascension of the planet's most advanced genus types. *Tesson* had an elevated form beauty and vital energy. Had it been sharing these partnership cycles with *Nœ-bouk* for its own future benefit?

Such contemplations had never occurred to *Nœ-bouk* before. It must be of the side effects of the structural form damage. Its vibration must have slowed to a lower level, closer to that of the more primitive genus types on less developed planets, and the illusion of separation in which they existed. Yes. These low-energy concepts were a result of its weakened state. It would deactivate its free-thought function until after receiving its task report and learning the results of its work.

It drew an inhalation and engaged a protective shield.

Blue.

Calm.

Its thoughts disappeared.

It entered the meeting chamber.

WITH THE FIRST SPLASH, Alisdair opened his eyes wide. He wanted to wipe the water from his face, but his hands were busy, moving fast, his muscles pulling hard. There was water and sensation all around him. The sweat on his face, sunshine on bare muscles, the smooth and violent thrust of arms. Torso propelling forwards and back. The surge of air stirred to motion. The smell of chase and men.

"Keep the rhythm!" The shout of the cox.

He was rowing. It was his Oxford days. The Blue Boat training for the annual race. Every morning at 5 a.m., rowing up and down the river for two hours. Yes, they had out-rowed the Cambridge crew by four and a half lengths. They hadn't broken the university record, but still, victory was victory.

"Good and loose. Keep the swing. Breathe!"

Alisdair pulled the oars. He smelled the sweat of his teammates and the mown grass of the passing gardens.

He saw himself finish the training and walk back to New College to bathe and dress and attend a lecture, a tutorial.

And then he felt the scene drifting away, and he was looking into darkness and he could see the faint outline of his legs moving down narrow stairs. There was a damp smell and he noticed the scratching wool of his trousers. Army uniform. He checked his hands; he wasn't holding a gun. There was a man in front of him, leading, and he could sense the soldiers behind.

A waft of tea and soap mixed with the damp. The sound of boots on stone. They descended the steps and, before them, a fortified door was being swung open to reveal a long room with a marble-topped table. It was Germany, just after the war. He had come there with a team of lawyers to help with the reconstruction. He was in one of the underground bunkers. A piece of the marble table had broken off and was lying on the floor. He reached down and picked it up.

And then he saw himself years later, giving it to his granddaughter. The little girl was running across the wet sand of a beach – it was the Scottish coast – running towards his wife.

"Eileen," he whispered.

And then he was moving into another place. He was back in Edinburgh and his wife had just walked into a sitting room with white bay windows looking out over the New Town, and he felt his heart stop for a moment as she entered the room. The scene became slow, just as it had been then, watching Eileen in those first few seconds as his body and his heart responded to her, and the understanding came to him instantly – and also very slowly – that his life from that moment was changed forever. That she had come to him. That from now on, he had already done everything he needed to do, and from now on, all would be right with his life.

He had found her.

Those first few heartbeats, when he seemed to move in and out of consciousness, were the most joyful feeling of his entire life. He saw the breath being drawn into his body as his heart pounded. He saw the breath passing out as the pulses within the seconds drew him on. His mouth was open and his head was unclear and then clear. He must have looked like a fool.

Eileen. How he wanted to see her again. And he could see her!

He pulled himself out of the book and took two or three steps back from the lectern. He looked up at Duncan.

"I want to see Eileen," he said. "I want to see her now."

"Turn around," said Duncan.

Alisdair turned towards the entrance. Standing in the doorway of the library was a small figure, attired in a close-cut navy dress. It was a long way across the room, but he could see the smile on her face; the smile that had brought him home so long ago. So very, very long ago.

"Eileen," he whispered.

"Alisdair," she answered him. In a moment, she was there beside him and he was putting his arms around her and feeling the scratch of her woollen dress and the smell of her wiry hair and the shape and size of that dear body. He stepped back, holding her hands.

"My Eileen," he said.

"You're here at last."

"You left so early."

"I left when it was time."

"I was alone. I missed you."

"You were not alone, Alisdair. How could you think for a moment that I wasn't with you?"

He looked down at her face and knew that she had been with him. Her presence, her love, her words.

"It wasn't so very long," she said.

Alisdair leaned forward and kissed her forehead and then her hair.

"I can't wait to look inside your book," he said.

"Oh, you're in for a treat. And perhaps a bit of a shock as well. But there's plenty of time for that." She paused. "Not that there's any time here, as such. But still. How about I show you around a little more? Then, later, you can come and browse through all the books. You can find the answers to all those mysteries you were searching for. What were you looking at just now?"

"Just a few memories."

"Well, that's the right way to start."

"I was seeing the evening we met. When you walked into that living room in the New Town."

She laughed. "My dear, sentimental Alisdair. You looked like a fool, you know? Your mouth was hanging open. I was mortified."

"It was a good moment. It might have been the best moment of my life."

"It was a good moment. Now come, and I'll show you around."

Alisdair followed Eileen through the library and out of the doorway, leaving Duncan with the lectern and the book.

Duncan reached for his half-moon spectacles and placed them carefully up onto the bridge of his nose. He opened the burgundy book at random and stepped into a hot summer's day. He was a boy, walking down a stony path, weaving dried straws into the shape of a cross. Knotted, golden hair fell over his eyes, and his socks scratched against thin legs. He began to whistle a folk song as he approached the noisy farmhouse, and then, hearing the shout of his name and the clatter of horses' hooves and the rushing of water, he turned towards the courtyard and broke into a run.

CHAPTER
FIVE

BY THE TIME David was upstate, driving through the forested towns of Interstate 81: Parsippany, Scranton, Binghamton, his anger had sunk into a reflective depression. The landscape around him still held some traces of fall – dark reds of maple and browning yellow, the murky greens of forest and farmland – a relief, after the savage reflection of the Manhattan streets.

David thought back over his last year working at the bank, and at the year and a half since he had been transferred to New York from the Toronto office. He had given it everything. Worked longer hours than anyone else; got to know the clients' portfolios inside out. He had done an outstanding job. He still didn't get how they could have paid him such a low number. It wasn't even a hundred percent of his base, which was the standard rule. Even if they knew he wasn't going to leave the bank – which they did; even if he was only a year and a half in New York – which he was; and even if his salary had sky-rocketed compared to what he was paid in Canada – which it had; despite all that, he had *worked* the hardest, he had brought in the most deals, he had done the best job with the clients. It just wasn't fair.

He pictured Jeff in his office – his dark, angry face. Maybe Jeff *had* been screwed on his bonus, although a cut for him would mean pocketing half a million dollars, rather than three quarters. But, still. Same difference in this game. Getting screwed meant not getting paid what you deserved; what you expected for the contribution you brought to the bank; what the other guys were paid. It reflected how useful you were to the department, and whether you were looking at promotion or pink slip in the coming year.

The light was beginning to fade, and David switched on the Viper's headlamps. He realised he hadn't eaten anything since his egg white omelette in the bank cafeteria that morning. It was past four o'clock already and it was still a good two-hour drive to the border, and then another hour through Ontario to Kingston, with the Friday traffic. He should call his mother. She'd want to know he was coming. She could get some food in. He looked out for a restaurant where he could grab a bite to keep him going; he couldn't remember if there were any roadside diners on this stretch of the interstate.

The countryside was flattening out now, and the greens had dulled to grey in the gathering dusklight. The road had narrowed into two lanes in each direction, the freeway heading downstate hidden by an island of forest. He hadn't seen any other cars for a while now. This seemed a little unusual, but he hadn't driven the route often enough to know what the traffic was normally like. David pulled off his sunglasses and tossed them onto the passenger seat. He opened the window an inch to get some fresh air and shook his head to clear it. He was going to need some coffee soon.

Suddenly, a blinding light appeared in the sky directly in front of the car. He slammed on the brakes and his hand flew up to cover his eyes. He blinked to regain his vision, and wrenched his body round to check for cars behind.

The road was empty.

He turned back and drew his hand away, keeping his eyes narrowed. An oval shape was hovering in the sky ahead of him. He couldn't make out the colour because white stars were flashing in his peripheral vision, but the shape seemed fixed, as if there was something solid beyond the brightness.

He checked the mirrors but there were still no cars visible. Wasn't that strange? He didn't know. He'd never been on an empty freeway before.

The stars flickered and he blinked again, trying to bring his sight back to normal. He took deep breaths to calm himself, and as the light faded, he scanned the sky for signs of what could have caused the flash. There had been no sound. Did that rule out an explosion of some kind? If it had been an explosion, he had better drive as fast as he could out of here. He didn't know of any military facilities in the area, but then they were kept pretty secret. It would be surprising if there was one so close to New York City.

As he thought this, he pushed his foot on the accelerator to speed up again, when a huge white owl appeared from the sky and swooped down directly towards the windshield. It was flying so fast, it looked as if it might smash straight through the glass. David slammed his foot onto the brake for the second time and swerved the Viper to a stop in the middle of the freeway.

He sat with his mouth open for a few moments, breathing in and out. What the hell had just happened? Where had that owl come from? His heart was beating wildly, and he took deep breaths in and out to calm himself. He looked out of the front of the car and his heart gave another leap. The white owl was sitting in the middle of the road and its yellow eyes were fixed directly on him.

"Oh my god," he said aloud, gripping the steering wheel hard with both hands. "What the hell?"

He opened the door and stepped out onto the freeway. The owl turned its head a fraction, to follow him with its eyes. David gave his legs a shake and stared back at the bird. It really was enormous; it came up to the car's bumper. He thought of nuclear testing grounds and mutant animals. He should get out of there as fast as possible. How strange it would be, if there really was a facility around here, so close to a major city. Surely they did all this stuff out in the desert, miles away from anywhere?

Looking at the bird, he started to feel a little better. It was probably just transfixed in the headlamps, or blinded after the explosion; although it did appear to be staring straight at him. Either way, he had to get it off the road. He took a few steps towards it, waving his arms in front of him. "Go on! Get outta here!"

The owl raised the massive span of its wings and took several hops backwards, its yellow eyes still trained on his face. David came closer. The owl hopped further back.

This is ridiculous. I'm going to drive around it.

He turned and got back into the car. He started the engine and blasted the horn a few times. At last, the bird lifted its wings in a slow, wide sweep and took off from the freeway. The vast, white shape lit up the night in a clear silhouette. David watched it until it was no longer visible.

He shivered. *That was seriously weird*, he thought. He really did need some coffee.

· · ·

HE DROVE FOR A WHILE, holding the steering wheel tightly. It had grown dark outside.

He saw a metal sign pointing away from the road to a diner, and he took the turning towards it. He could see some lights, but it didn't look as if the place was open. He checked the next sign. Open until 11 p.m. He drove closer and saw that the outside lights were still on, but the inside was dark. Strange. He glanced down at his watch. 11:24 p.m. There must be something wrong with it. It had been working just now, when he had seen that it was after four. Could the explosion have affected it somehow? He looked at the car clock on the dashboard below the windshield. The numbers 11:25 flashed before him in red dashes.

David had reached the diner. He stopped the car outside the front entrance. It was closed. "What the fuck?" he said aloud. He looked again at his watch. It had just been four o'clock. He took off the watch, shook it and looked again. 11:26. He put the watch on the front seat, next to his sunglasses. He reached for his phone. 11:26.

He dialled 637 for the talking clock. An upbeat, Midwestern voice rang out into the dark car.

"The time on the third tone, according to United States East Coast, will be eleven twenty-six p.m. and forty seconds. Beeep. Beeep. Beep."

David snapped the phone shut and put it down on the seat next to his watch and sunglasses. He reached over to the locking system and pressed it. The car locks flicked downwards.

He took several deep breaths. How could he have just lost seven hours? He was in exactly the same place he had been when he had looked at his watch at 4 p.m. He felt his heart beating very distinctly in his chest. *Bang, bang, bang.* He could feel it moving in and out. He could almost picture it, pulsing the blood around his body. He knew that there was adrenalin pumping through him right now, and that it was making him dizzy. He knew that he was experiencing some kind of shock and fear.

He sat there, listening to his heart and waiting for the dizziness to pass. He watched the red flashing numbers at the front of the dashboard.

11:27. 11:28. 11:29.

At 11:30, he would begin driving again.

11:30.

He took a deep breath and started the car. He drove past the diner and out onto the freeway. Everything looked the same, except that it was extremely dark.

There were quite a few cars on the road now, with their headlamps flaring and dimming for the oncoming traffic. He opened the window. Whatever had happened, he was okay. It was fucked up, but he'd figure it out later. Right now, he had to find somewhere to spend the night. He wouldn't make it home until two or three in the morning if he kept on driving, and he didn't want to freak his parents out. They'd be asleep by now and he didn't even want to call.

A few miles down the road, he spotted a motel and pulled into the parking lot. It was still open. He locked the Viper, walked into the green-lit reception area and paid for a night. He carried his bag to the room, closed the door behind him and sat down on the edge of the bed. He put his head in his hands and found that he was trembling uncontrollably. He sat, with his hands and arms shaking, letting his breath heave in and out, for several minutes. The shock had to pass. He would be okay.

Eventually, he pushed off his shoes, threw his jacket onto the back of the chair, lay down on the bed in all his clothes and fell into a deep sleep.

 A SYMBOL BLOCK had been sent to the members of the Home Planet Council to assemble at the Task Assignment Pyramid, and they had gathered in the clear-walled chamber, energetically resonant for the task assessment process. *Noœ-bouk* stepped into the diamond-structured space to find each of the Council members in seated positions around a long, transparent table.

From the moment it entered the meeting chamber, *Noœ-bouk* sensed the elevated thought-waves of the Council members. The beings rose to standing position and transmitted symbol blocks of satisfaction and achievement to *Noœ-bouk*, initiating, for the second occurrence in this three-moon cycle, the experience of *kaiif* from which it drew such intense sensory pleasure. Maintaining its own standing pose, it sent a signal for the *kaiif* to disperse throughout its form: the positive emotions would assist with its impending regeneration and cellular recovery. It came to the realisation that the task assignment had been executed to maximum projected potential. The results of the channelling would positively affect the development of Home Planet in multiple diverse ways. It was a great accomplishment.

When the congratulatory and *kaiific* symbol blocks had been disseminated, the Council returned to seated positions around the table and initiated the complex destructuralisation of the task assignment. Star maps were called up onto the clear viewing panels of the chamber, and the energy patterns before and after the channelling were examined. Trade routes and interplanetary compatibility charts, the attraction forces of the three moons and the physical-form potential levels for the different genus types were studied. On every count, the objectives of the task assignment had been exceeded. The overall energy of the planet had been cleared and raised. Home Planet was in energetic alignment with a new stratum of evolved civilisations. Partnerships, communication channels and Federation agreements were possible, which would bring manifold benefit to Home Planet and its long-term development. New trade routes and genetic civilisation projects could be explored. The achievement of non-physical evolution for Home Planet beings was now a real possibility.

When the final patterns and projections had been checked and the results marked onto the star maps and into the planetary records, the Council once again sent waves of *kaiific* praise to *Noœ-bouk*. The success of the project guaranteed benefits for every member of the Council. The expression of their gratitude was both personal and on behalf of the planet.

When the Council members had left the chamber, *Noœ-bouk* stood before the clear window panels where the star maps had been illuminated, but which now showed the habitual expanse of grey rockscape, barely lit by the pale white of the distant sun. This moment, *Noœ-bouk* considered, represented the very peak of its lifespan. Many of the assigned roles on Home Planet, including the Council positions, were dependent on extended lifespan expectations, and even if a task allocation arose which fitted with *Noœ-bouk*'s lifespan limitations, there was still the question of whether it possessed the vital strength to carry out any assignments of significance. This was it, *Noœ-bouk* thought. This moment was the summit point of its lifespan. The *kaiif* it was experiencing would fade, and from then on it would follow a path of steady debilitation towards a rapid physical transition. Stretching out before it, the broken grey rockscape of the planet surface seemed to reflect its non-positive thought level, and as the *kaiif* faded from its system, a dark, throbbing anger began to swell. Its moment had passed. *This was it.*

Noœ-bouk exited the chamber and made its way back to the capsule. It descended through the upper pyramid, and then down twenty-eight levels below the surface, towards the reflected, narrowing peak of the subterranean edifice, built as an exact mirror beneath the planet.

It stepped out at the twenty-eighth base level and walked along the green-lit corridors towards the Cellular Genetic Centre. On the other side of the clear walls was the lifeless grey stone of the deep subterranean planet, but unlike its surface equivalent, the structure of the lower pyramid was built of darker materials, and *Noœ-bouk* could barely perceive the sculpted rock beyond it. For some reason, this inability to view the natural interior of the planet initiated a new profusion of anger, which it identified as a distinct irrational response. It had visited this base level on previous occasions, and no such sentiments had been aroused. It focused on the calm green lighting of the corridor. Within the space of an inhalation, it had arrived at the diamond entrance panel of the Cellular Genetic Centre. Before it was rest and regeneration. It raised its hand and the panel slid aside. *Noœ-bouk* stepped through.

"BEFORE WE COMPLETE THE CERE-MONY," said the Treasurer of York's Inn, "I would like to ask a young lady to say a few words. We were all deeply grieved by Sir Alisdair's death last month, and we are grateful to have his granddaughter Elspeth with us today. I think most of you are familiar with Elspeth from the Inn, where she works as an assistant librarian, and I know that I will have full support in offering her a permanent position in the newly opened McCauley Wing."

"Hear, hear!" called out several members of the audience.

"So let me pass you now to one of the future custodians of this new wing of legal tomes, Miss Elspeth McCauley."

Elspeth uncrossed her legs and stood up to the audience's applause. Her grandfather had left the greatest part of his estate to York's Inn: one part to set up this wing of the library and another to fund scholarships for young lawyers. He had also managed to secure his favourite granddaughter a lifelong job in a stable work environment, in the company of intelligent, courteous lawyers such as he had been.

She reached the lectern and tapped the microphone, running her fingers over the two griffins carved into each side of the reading block, feeling out the familiar, chipped wing.

"Many of you knew him as Sir Alisdair," she began, to a background of shifting knees and rustling suits. "But I used to tease him by calling him Sir Grandad, a name I believe he was partial to."

There was laughter around the room.

"My grandfather was passionate about many things," she went on, "but perhaps what he was most passionate about was giving people chances. He felt that he had been given so many chances in his own life. His family hadn't been intellectual. My great-great-grandfather was a miner. My great-grandfather broke the trend and married a pawnbroker's daughter and became a pawnbroker himself."

Muffled laughs from the audience.

"But my grandfather, who was intended for the next generation of Edinburgh pawnbrokers, won a scholarship to an Edinburgh school. And then he won another scholarship to New College, Oxford, and then another to do post-graduate work in International Law at Harvard University, where he returned years later with my grandmother as a visiting professor. His entire career was built from chances he had been given, and he was terribly aware of this. I do believe that his greatest desire in life, apart from me not growing up to be a pawnbroker..."

More laughter.

"...was to give back to the society which had given him those chances."

Elspeth paused and glanced down at the page of notes in front of her. She touched the smooth back of the griffin with her forefinger, noticing her ragged, bitten nails.

"It is fitting," she continued, "that this library is open not just to members of the Inn, but to the public at large. In fact, to anyone who might have a spark of interest in the law, and who might be looking for that one chance. That one chance which might lead to an opportunity."

She looked around the room. To her surprise, the rows of pinstriped women and white-cuffed men were paying attention. She had expected them to be buried in their BlackBerries or, more common than not for an afternoon talk, fast asleep.

"Ladies and gentlemen, thank you for coming to the opening of the McCauley Wing."

There was loud applause as Elspeth left the lectern, still clutching the notes she had used. She was getting to be a confident public speaker. Perhaps her grandfather had been right, and she should have gone into law after all. It had just seemed too easy, such a tailored choice, to follow in the footsteps of her eminent grandfather and father. She didn't like to have things handed to her. She liked to feel that she was making her own choices, deciding the path of her life through her strength of will, not as a reaction to a set of circumstances which had been presented to her.

And yet, after all that effort to manage her own life, she had ended up here, in a comfortable job her grandfather had arranged for her, stepping into the path of least resistance. Wasn't this exactly what she had rejected when she had refused to go to university; when she had refused to stay in the same country as her parents and had lived for years in run-down houses in Spain and France? She had chosen her own path, staying in squats with teenagers from all over Europe who played music and organised parties and sold drugs. She had been pregnant with a child and aborted it. She had taken every drug short of sticking a needle in herself and fucked every willing guy who hadn't been to university, who ideally hadn't even finished high school. God, she'd fucked a lot of men, and none of them had ever found out her secret – that she could walk away from that life at any time; that she was not there because she'd been chucked out of school, or abused by her parents, or had grown up on the poverty line; that with a single phone call she could transport herself back into a comfortable life; that she had a golden ticket, and the world – if she chose to accept it – was at her feet.

No. None of them had found out her secret, and she had moved on. She had left the squat. She had found a flat with some French girls and given English lessons to pay the rent. And then what? Her father had called and asked her to come to her grandfather's eightieth birthday party. She was twenty-eight and still not speaking to her mother.

There was something about her grandfather, when she saw him at the party, which had initiated a change in her view on life. The joy he had shown when he saw her was so non-judgmental, so completely honest. She had read the loneliness in his eyes, after five years without her grandmother. He had taken her hand and held it in his own, and had led her around the party, introducing her to his colleagues at York's Inn, showing her off to everyone. She had felt such an overpowering sadness at how tightly he had held her hand, and such an overpowering happiness that someone was so joyful to be with her, regardless of her mistakes or choices. It had given her hope of what love might be. And she had decided to move back to London.

Since then, things had happened fast. She had found a room in a house. She had bought new clothes. She had put on weight. Over lunch, her grandfather had suggested a job at the library and she had accepted, happy to be doing something close to where he was. One morning, before coming in to work, she had caught sight of herself in the mirror, wearing a dark-red dress and short black jacket, heeled shoes and a matching scarf. Even she had to admit that she looked professional and attractive.

. . .

THE APPLAUSE DIED DOWN as Elspeth returned to her seat in the front row. The Treasurer stepped up to the lectern.

"I think it's clear that Miss McCauley has inherited her grandfather's gift for public speaking," he said, to more clapping.

"And without further ado, let me announce the official opening of the McCauley Wing for the study of law."

He raised his hands to lead the applause, and one by one the lawyers rose for a standing ovation.

"There is tea and sandwiches in the Reading Room," the Treasurer called out, and then he turned to Elspeth as the audience closed around them.

"You really have a gift, my dear," he said, moving her towards the doors. "You know that the Inn would be happy to sponsor you, should you choose to go to university. There are some respectable correspondence programmes nowadays. The trick is to get a place on a good conversion course when the degree is finished."

"I—"

"You don't have to decide now, my dear. Just bear it in mind. I think that everyone here owes a debt of gratitude to your grandfather."

"Thank you," she said, and they entered the Reading Room to the smell of cucumber, salmon and teabags.

CHAPTER SIX

"DAVID, DARLING, YOU'RE HOME!"

"Mom."

David let himself be hugged and kissed by his mother. She was looking great, wearing a navy pantsuit and necklace of black pearls, her short, fair hair cut in sharp layers. He thought she must be showing off for him now he was in New York. He followed her into the kitchen, a smile on his face.

"I haven't had time to make you lasagne yet, but it'll be ready by dinner time. I already got in all the ingredients from the store."

"That's great, Mom, but I'm seeing Cassie tonight. Can we do it for lunch tomorrow?"

"You're seeing Cassie? I'm thrilled. Of course we can have it for lunch tomorrow. Although your father won't be pleased to have pasta for Sunday lunch. I could always do it for dinner, but that would be a *lot* of food. And you know we're trying to watch our weight. We like to keep fit, just like you New York folks."

"Mom…"

"I know, I know. We're never going to be fancy New York folks. Well, that's fine. I'm just glad you're seeing Cassie. I talk to her mother. She's not dating anyone, you know. Not anyone serious, at least."

"Mom…."

"Alright, then. Go upstairs. Do you need a shower?"

"I had one this morning."

"Well, I'm just glad to see you, darling. You look well, David. A bit pale. Are you worn out?"

"Just from the driving. I got up early."

"And what a fancy car you've got."

"It's a rental."

"Well, I like it. I know your dad will just love it. What kind is it?"

"It's a Dodge."

"I think it's just wonderful. I'm glad to see you're enjoying yourself with things like that."

David reached out to his mother and squeezed her hand.

"Thanks, Mom. I'm happy to be here. You're looking really well. Great suit."

"Off you go now."

David climbed the carpeted stairs to his bedroom. He dropped his bag on the floor, lay down on the bed and looked up at the ceiling, which was covered with pale-grey star shapes. It had been one birthday, he must have been around seven or eight, when his mother had told everyone he wanted to be an astronaut, so he'd ended up with countless packets of glow-stars and books on science. He had studied the maps of the Milky Way for hours, laying out the shapes in the patterns of the constellations until he knew them by heart, and then fixing them to the ceiling as accurately as he could. He'd picture flying through those stars in a spaceship, among the planets and through the asteroid belts, and then beyond, making up solar systems and galaxies and planets and even alien creatures. He'd be a hero like Captain Kirk, bringing civilisation to far-off places. Innumerable hours of his childhood had been spent lying and dreaming there in the frozen, winter darkness, the yellow stars glowing above him in the ceiling sky.

And then he had been great at physics and maths, and his mother had decided to invest her time into getting him to scholarship level. They'd spent months doing extra work, pushing him to the top of his grade. He won a CAP prize for physics, scoring 91, the second-highest mark in the country.

The following October, as a reward, his parents had flown him to Cape Canaveral to watch the Challenger lift off from the Kennedy Space Center. That experience, which was meant to have been the most inspiring of his life, marked the end of his dream, and the end of his pursuit of science. Watching the shuttle rise into the early-morning darkness and knowing that his hero, Marc Garneau, was making history as the first Canadian in space, it suddenly seemed so very small. It was such a minor achievement compared to the size of his dreams. All those amazing things he had imagined – they were all centuries of research away. They'd be lucky to put a single man on Mars during his lifetime;

anything further was out of the question. It seemed such an obvious thing to realise, aged sixteen, but somehow it hit him like an asteroid to the head. It just wasn't big enough. If this was the absolute peak – being blasted into space for five, ten days; logging an hour or two of space-walk if he was lucky; even imagining himself as the first person on Mars – it was still too small. It wasn't worth a lifetime of physics research. It just wasn't.

There had been some epic fights when he got back home. Announcing that he was no longer planning to major in science had sparked a full-scale war between him and his teachers. All the energy his mom had put into getting him the CAP prize was now focused on rallying his school advisors and the science department into intervention talks. *Wasted talent. Great career. Benefit to mankind.* It went on and on. But mentally, he had switched off. His dreams had been too big. They had been childish and unrealistic. He accepted that. And he wasn't going to go for some pathetic second best. Second Canadian in space? The thought made him cringe.

When a kid in his class had landed an internship at one of the Toronto banks, and had come back with stories about the money they made, the atmosphere and adrenalin on the trading floor, David suddenly came back to life. It sounded like a place that could handle the size of his ambitions. He applied for an internship and got it. The CAP score on his CV couldn't have hurt.

From the moment he set foot in the bank, he had known it was for him: the sheer energy; the brains and aggression of the men and women working there; the simplicity of the whole thing. The pure, shameless focus on making outrageous amounts of money. On being the first. The top. The richest. The best. The freedom to express his intellect and desires without any limits.

It had been a straight line after that. Economics at the University of Toronto and a year working at Mercy Bank saving up for B-school. Two years on the Queen's MBA programme and then a job offer at Bullman Scout. Two more years of back-breaking analyst hours in the Toronto office before his dream had finally come true. Jeff had approved him for the New York transfer. He had made it.

David smiled at the memory. It had been quite a journey. He stared up at the flat grey stars, and the image of the oversized, white owl came back to him. He pushed it away with a shake of his head. He wouldn't think about it now. He would wait and talk to Cassie about it. He was looking forward to seeing her tonight. He always felt good about himself when he was with her. It was as if he was both remembering who he used to be and, at the same time, confirming why he had wanted to leave and make something of himself. It was a kind of push and pull – a simultaneous remembrance and urging – and it had the effect of grounding him entirely, of bringing home all the reasons for the actions in his life. It sounded a bit cliché, but it was like she somehow gave him back to himself.

He closed his eyes and pictured kissing her. Joint-ends and beer mixed with lemonade; that's what she used to taste like. Apple fritters and cigarettes on Sunday morning. He could taste her now. Donuts and memories drifted through his head, and before long he was asleep.

"CASSIE, SOMETHING WEIRD HAPPENED TO ME."

They were facing each other over a booth at the Grizzly Grill, the downtown Kingston bar guarded by a life-size bear, famous for dynamite wings and rock music. Between them on the table were two bottles of Sleeman with chunks of lemon stuck in the top, and a basket of hot pretzels. Cassie pushed her long, red hair back over her shoulder. She squeezed some of the lemon into her bottle and took a swig. She looked hard at David.

"What happened?"

David took a sip of his beer, then set the bottle down.

"I was driving here, yesterday afternoon. I'd set off early. There'd been some stuff happening at the bank. I was pretty upset by it—"

"What stuff at the bank?"

"Just stuff. You don't need to know. That's not the point."

"So..." She had that hard gleam in her eye; the way she looked when she was solving a science problem in the lab.

"So I was driving. I was pretty upset and it was about four o'clock. And then I saw this really bright light in the sky."

"What kind of light?"

"Well, I guess... like an explosion, or something. Except there wasn't any sound. I mean, there wasn't a bang or anything. Just the light."

"What do you think it was?" She was looking at him. Her eyes were large and grey-green in the bar light. Her face had got thinner; maybe that was why her eyes seemed so big. It always came as a surprise to David how much he liked Cassie. Her analytical brain, which loved figuring out difficult problems. Her sweetness beneath the hard logic. The memories of the years they were dating. Right up until she had been offered a research position in the country's leading science company, and he... and he had lost interest in pretty much everything except for money.

"David?"

Her fingers were drumming on the table and he drew his thoughts back. The owl. The light. The lost time.

"Oh, I don't know. I thought it was an explosion. I guess I assumed it was some kind of military training thing. You know. What else could it be?"

"I'm running through about ten possibilities right now. I'd have to do a bit of research. If it was a military thing, it shouldn't be too difficult to track down."

"So, anyway, there was this light, which didn't bother me that much. It was just a shock. But then, this is the weird bit, there was this owl that kind of swooped down on the car."

"Owl?"

"Yeah, owl. A huge one. Huge, white owl. I've never seen one so big. I don't even know what kind it could have been."

"You're sure it was an owl? If it was so big, maybe it was an eagle, something like that."

"No, it was an owl. You know they have those flat faces. It was an owl. I had to swerve off the road or it would have gone straight through the windshield."

"What about the other cars? You didn't hit anyone?"

"I don't know. There weren't any other cars. That's a bit weird too, right?"

"On Friday afternoon? On the freeway? That's impossible. So... you stopped the car?"

"And this owl was kind of looking at me, with these yellow eyes. It wouldn't get off the road. And then, eventually, it flew away. And I tried to find some place to get coffee. I thought I must be seeing things, and so I pulled into this roadside diner. And here's the really weird thing..."

"What?"

"It was closed. And I looked at my watch. And it was 11:30 at night."

"What do you mean?"

"I mean that when I saw the owl, it was four o'clock in the afternoon, and about two minutes later, when I pulled over to get some coffee, it was eleven o'clock at night."

"You must have fallen asleep."

"Where? I was in the car. Where would I have fallen asleep? I would

52

have remembered waking up. You know when you're waking up from something."

"Usually, yes. Although if you were in shock..."

"Anyway, so that's what happened."

"And how big was this owl?"

David held his hands wide. "It came up to the bumper of the car. That's pretty high. About like that."

"That's enormous. I don't think there *are* any owls that big."

"Right. Exactly."

"So what did you do after that? When you realised it was eleven o'clock?"

"I found a motel and spent the night there. Slept really deeply. Felt great this morning. Drove all the way here in record time. Called you."

Cassie leaned her chin in her hand. Her nails had a creamy manicure. That had to be a first. Not quite New York City, but still.

"Okay, David. That's really weird."

They both picked up their bottles and spent a few moments sipping the lemon-flavoured beer and looking around the bar, crowded with Saturday night locals and students. A band was tuning up in the far corner, and waiters carried wing platters and buckets of beer to the booths.

At last, Cassie spoke.

"So, first of all, I think the owl and the time-loss were triggered by the shock. You think you saw the light for a few seconds, but it may have been far longer. And it clearly had an effect on you. So if we can find out what that light was, then we can find out what the chemicals might have done to your brain, which made you hallucinate an owl and maybe even pass out for hours. Although you say your car was on the road..."

"It was. In the middle of the freeway."

"So another option might be a hypnotherapist. They put you in a trance and you can access the part of your brain that recorded what was happening. You can basically ask your brain to repeat what you have blocked out."

"I'm not gonna see a hypnotist."

"That's fine. I just think, if it was me, I'd want to know what had happened. If it was some government programme doing testing and I'd been affected, I'd want to know about it."

"Cassie, listen. I don't want you to tell anyone what I just told you. Okay?"

"Okay. But I can't promise not to do some research."

"That's fine. I know you can't leave something unsolved. It's just good to tell someone."

"I can see you're really shaken up." Cassie tilted her head and smiled at him. She reached out her hand. Her green-grey eyes were larger and softer now. "I know something else that can put you in a hypnotic trance."

David looked at the hand, its long fingers and creamy manicure. He felt incredible gratitude that she was here, that this hand was held out to him. He wondered for a moment why he wasn't working with her in the research laboratory and arguing with her every night about physics and astronomy and the universe, as they used to.

He slid his hand beneath hers and raised it to his lips.

"Why don't you come and sit over here?"

DAVID OPENED HIS EYES. He sniffed. The window was open and the chilly November air had the scent he had grown up with – bonfire and coffee and lake water. The smell conjured images of open-back trucks filled with schoolkids heading out for Sunday morning donuts; trips to the islands for hiking, smoking, kissing; freezing winds and laughter; packs of beer bought by older kids; feeling horny all the time. He reached his arms up behind him and stretched out as far as he could. Stirring beside him, Cassie pushed her red hair up onto the pillow and turned her naked body towards him, her breasts pressing against his side. God, he felt good.

He slid out of the bed and covered Cassie with the duvet. Then he dropped to the floor and started to do push-ups, his biceps and abs taut with every drop and pull. Ten, fifteen, twenty. Twenty-five, thirty, thirty-five, forty.

Phew. He relaxed his body and lay on the floor, his heart pumping. God, he loved fucking Cassie. Probably not as much as Vanessa with her huge breasts, but there was something comforting about Cassie's body. It was like coming home. Well, it *was* coming home. He pulled himself up off the floor and forced fifteen more push-ups before he jumped to his feet.

He looked around for his clothes. He'd head to the house for lunch with his folks and then he'd hit the road and be back in New York by evening. Return the car, early night, no calling Vanessa, and early to work tomorrow. He was back. He remembered the bonus numbers and almost laughed. Of course they had screwed him on the money. That's what bankers did. If he was in Jeff's place, he would have screwed him,

54

too. Why should they pay a dime more than they had to? No wonder Jeff had been pissed at him. This was Wall Street. The real money was just ahead of him.

Don't lose focus. Don't drop the ball.

He bent down over Cassie, who was still asleep, and pushed his face into her tangled, red hair. Beer, smoke and perfume. He loved that smell.

"Cassie, I've got to go. I've got to get home and then drive to New York. You stay well."

Cassie reached a hand out of the duvet and found his face. She stroked the stubble with the tips of her fingers.

"I love you," she murmured. "You know that right? Nobody else fits with me. Not like you do."

He bent over her face and kissed her on the lips. "I know that. I'll see you later, okay? Take care. I love you too."

He stood up, then reached for his shirt and slacks, and pulled them on.

"I'll call you," he whispered, as he left the room.

 *NŒ-BOUK* REMAINED in the Cellular Genetic Centre for an entire solar cycle, during which period the dark red moons of Home Planet rose and sunk over the surface twenty-one times in monotonous repetition.

While *Nœ-bouk* was recovering, *Tesson* had not communicated with it in any way. *Nœ-bouk* understood that *Tesson* was allowing it to process its weakened emotional states, however it felt a need for its presence. *Tesson*'s physical form contained a particular energy which was resonant with *Nœ-bouk*, and it would have welcomed the effect as it went through the recovery stages. This experience, of desiring another being in order to compensate for its feeling of incompleteness, was new to *Nœ-bouk*, and it wondered if the lack-and-desire state would trigger the second-stage blame-and-anger cycle, once it had left the centre.

When its immersion in the light capsules was complete, *Nœ-bouk* was given the results by one of the cellular genetic specialists. There had been partial recovery, with a significantly reduced lifespan expectation.

"How long?" *Nœ-bouk* sent to the specialist.

"Thirty three-moon cycles at the maximum possibility projection."

"Is there any method to prolong the lifespan?" *Nœ-bouk* surprised itself with the question. Its intention had been to receive the report and return to the Task Assignment Centre to accept the final instructions for its remaining moon cycles.

"Space travel has been known to prolong lifespans indefinitely," conveyed the specialist. "The cellular structure has no physical stimulus to respond to within a sterile vessel environment, and sometimes the debilitation is held in continual suspension."

"What is the occurrence rate on which this possibility is based?"

"Two cases."

"Are the lifespans currently in continuance?"

"One is in continuance. It was a severe case of cellular damage. The being was not the same genus type as you. It is now in Star Map Zone 41. It is expected that it will return only when it is ready to complete the lifespan."

"And the second case?"

"The second case resided for over a hundred three-moon cycles on an observation vessel. It maintained a stable physical level but it made the decision to terminate the lifespan. It returned to Home Planet and a swift deterioration took place."

"After it returned, how fast was the transition?"

"Less than a single moonrise."

"Why did it make the decision?"

"It was an isolated environment. I do not have the full information report."

"What was the genus type?"

It occurred to *Noœ-bouk* that it had never felt so driven to receive non-essential information in all its lifespan. And yet, looking at the specialist, it found itself experiencing an urgent need. There was something it had to find out. *Noœ-bouk* grasped for the correct thought-strand. Within an inhalation, the strand appeared in its mind, together with a sensation similar to pain. It wanted *to live*.

"The physical casing was similar to your own," sent the specialist. "It was an advanced grey form. It had been an energy-channeller like yourself."

The two beings ceased their communication while the information was processed on emotional levels.

Eventually, the specialist communicated, "What path of action are you being drawn to?"

Noœ-bouk studied its interlocutor. It was a different genus type to itself and *Tesson*, less physically evolved. It was a genus type which reproduced through touch; a rare phenomenon on Home Planet. Its

56

surface area was the colour of dark moon dust, and its mouth and tongue were fleshy red, which indicated regular verbal communication, also an uncommon practice. Many of the beings on Home Planet had lost the ability to understand oral transmission, or rejected it on the basis of its ambiguity, which was recognised as the single main source of conflict on primitive planets. *Nœ-bouk, Tesson* and the majority of life forms on Home Planet communicated in blocks of thought and symbols, in the main part transmitted from mind to mind, but sometimes communicated through a single note sung aloud, in the vibration of which were unique strands of information containing the very essence of the communicator's intention, without any distortion through mental transfer.

Nœ-bouk had only heard words spoken on one or two occasions throughout its lifespan, as its contact with genus types unconnected to its task assignments had been limited. *Tesson* chose to communicate exclusively with its own genus type, on the basis that it was the most evolved entity group on Home Planet, and it saw itself as a leader among the beings who would, in the proximate moon cycles, evolve beyond the physical form. *Tesson, Nœ-bouk* reflected, had probably never encountered spoken words; at least not in the manner in which this being expressed them.

"Can you speak?" sent *Nœ-bouk*.

The two life forms regarded each other.

"Spoken word," *Nœ-bouk* clarified. "I have forgotten how it sounds."

"Yes," replied the specialist. It opened its mouth and formed shapes using its red tongue.

"Will you make a word?" *Nœ-bouk* asked. It observed the red mouth shape and found it pleasing in a way it wasn't sure how to respond to.

"N-o-o-œ-b-ou-k," spoke the being. It repeated the sound, making a wide movement with its curved mouth.

Nœ-bouk regarded the moving mouth-edges and tongue, framing the long sound which emerged. A low, humming note. It realised that it had never heard its own name expressed in this way before.

Nœ-bouk opened its mouth and made a simulation of the shape the being had produced, but no sound came out. The specialist was moving its chest up and down rapidly. It was laughing.

"What is your name?" *Nœ-bouk* communicated to it.

"*Sen.*"

"Is this your home planet?"

"Yes. My form is being maintained here to compare some advantages in physical aspects which have long been observed in our genus. It is not our goal to evolve."

"Your form pleases me."

The specialist's chest was making the rapid movement again.

"How did you become so damaged?" it sent.

"You have the report," answered *Nœ-bouk*. "It happens to all energy-channellers."

"Most energy-channellers do not continue with such high-level work for as long as you have. They do not continue to such an extreme lifespan limitation. Your form had the potential to exist for thousands of moon cycles."

"I had a particular competence which was required for the development of Home Planet evolution. The only possible path was to use this ability to maximum potential to enable the progression of the planet."

The specialist did not respond to the information block, and *Nœ-bouk* found that it did not want the communication to end.

"I am satisfied with the course and achievements of my lifespan," it sent.

"What path will you take now?"

"I may complete transition within the thirty three-moon cycles or I could make an application to join a vessel."

The specialist regarded it.

"What path would you take?" sent *Nœ-bouk*.

·   The specialist did not hesitate before answering: "I would live."

Nœ-bouk left the Cellular Genetic Centre, stepping out of the dark pyramid into a bright third moonrise. This was the clearest of the moon cycle stages, when only the smallest moon was visible, and it often sparked an intense sensory pleasure within the physical form as the rays of the distant sun lit up the rock in swathes of pink and gold dust. Partnerships were often established during this point in the cycle, just as partnerships were often terminated during the intense triple-moon stage, when the planet was rendered deep-red for an extended period and the three moons rotated so close to Home Planet that they seemed on the verge of collision. The lifespan patterns of Home Planet inhabitants, *Nœ-bouk* reflected, were a series of predictable cycles, endlessly repeating with the rising and falling moons.

But the specialist at the Cellular Genetic Centre had suggested an alternative. It could enter a vessel and prolong its lifespan until it chose to return to Home Planet. It could make a single, unexpected decision, after an existence which had been entirely planned out by Council members and development instructors, within the confines of expectation created by the planet's philosophical architecture.

It could make the first true choice of its life.

"WHERE ARE YOU TAKING ME, my dear?"

Alisdair took Eileen's hand and ran his fingers over her skin. It was just as he remembered, dry and brittle to stroke. She had spent her life rubbing in cream, but nothing had seemed to ease the dryness. He was pleased that he was still able to experience physical sensations such as this. There were so many small touches of Eileen he had longed for after she was gone: the tickle of her hair rubbing against him in sleep, the dry skin of her hands, the warmth of her face when she would lean towards him for a kiss. Eileen squeezed his fingers.

"They're still dry," she said.

"I'm glad. It's how I love them." He paused, then asked again. "Where are we going?"

"You'll see. You'll remember it soon enough. You've been here plenty of times."

"I suppose I have."

"Come on now."

Eileen led him out of the library and across the grand marble foyer to another doorway, through which Alisdair could see wide stone steps leading down into a garden. As they passed through the arch and onto the staircase, Alisdair was struck by the sudden blue of the sky above them, and he looked up into it. He had never seen a colour so pure before. It was as if the pigment of the sky had been condensed into the most intense hue possible. It was breathtaking.

"What a colour," he said.

"It's not just the sky, my love. Take your time. Look around."

They stood together at the top of the steps, and looked out over the most extraordinary garden Alisdair had ever seen. It seemed to be both formal and natural at the same time. Wide pathways and arches and trailing, climbing, falling, hanging flowers. Wild roses, wisteria, foxgloves, gladioli; standing tall, ducking low, effortlessly, and yet the effect was a pattern of complete order. It was as if he were listening to the most exquisite piece of music which had never been written, but was being played, somehow, because the notes, in their creation, had contained the possibility of that music within them. It stirred an excitement in him. This was how things were meant to be. This was what they had been imagined for. This is what all those exquisitely and intricately planned gardens he had seen during his life had been trying to achieve; this meeting of natural order and beauty and congruity with everything around it.

The colours, in each of their bright or muted shades, contained the same intensity as the burning blue of the sky. It gave a sense of awareness and potency to all of the garden; an expectant intelligence, as if the garden had created itself in the knowledge of its own potential, and its understanding of what it could, and must, become. Alisdair could see the sharp outlines of individual leaves on an oak tree. Each leaf glistened, as if it had been hand-crafted from a block of emerald. A single drop of dew hung from a blade of grass, reflecting a million thread-like rays of light. A wild rose from a great bush of flowers seemed to be pulsating with awareness and the purest form of beauty. Every living expression of nature that came before his eyes appeared to be the most exquisite thing he had ever seen.

"Oh, Eileen."

They stood, gazing around them for a long time, until a vague idea came to Alisdair. He turned to his wife.

"Is it?"

She smiled at him, her head on one side.

"Prototypes?" he said, and she nodded.

He continued, thinking aloud. "The Earth prototypes. The original forms." He paused. "Then this is Eden?"

"Well..."

"No," he said. "Of course it's not."

"It's the same idea," said Eileen. "I mean, you're right. It's exactly that."

"It's like being inside a paint box," said Alisdair.

"Or a jewellery box," said Eileen, with a giggle.

"It's extraordinary."

"You should see the animals," said Eileen. "The lions. The tigers. The birds. Just imagine the peacocks. The flamingos. The golden eagles. They truly are golden."

She reached for his hand. "Come, let's walk through the garden."

She led him down the steps of the staircase and out onto a wide pathway. Alisdair looked around him as he walked, fascinated by every example of original beauty. It was a beauty so intense it made the memory of Earth seem like a pale reflection.

He stopped, looking troubled.

"What is it, my love?"

"A pale reflection."

"What's that?" said Eileen.

"It's all a pale reflection," said Alisdair, louder. "It was the cave. It was Plato. Socrates. He was right, Eileen. He was absolutely right. It was all a pale reflection. Everything on our Earth was just a shadow of the truth. A shadow of what truly was."

"Oh, Alisdair. Still the Classics? Even now?"

"'*The brightest of all realities, which is what we call the good,*'" said Alisdair. "I can't believe it. I mean, look at these colours! How did he know?"

"Well, according to you, the Greeks knew everything about everything. You never tired of telling me that."

"But they did," said Alisdair. "Just look around. They did. I was right."

"Ahem."

"Well, okay then. They were right. But I was right in recognising that."

"Of course you were. The cave. Well, we're out of the cave now, my dear."

"But I could find out," said Alisdair. "Plato. Socrates. I could read their lives in the library. I could find out how they knew. I could read all of their lives. Oh, Eileen, what a wonderful place this is!"

"Alisdair, you can spend a hundred years in that library if you wish. You can read every life that ever was. Every philosopher, anyway. But now—"

"Aristotle," said Alisdair. "Pythagoras, Hippocrates."

"Oh, Alisdair. You'll be seeing Cerberus next."

Alisdair drew his eyes away from the dazzling colours of the garden and looked at Eileen.

"It's just wonderful to be with you again," he said. "To have someone to talk to. Someone who wants to listen."

"I know, my love. It's felt like a long time. But I have been with you. I really have. And you did very well on your own. You took good care of Elspeth."

"Aye. I'd like to see her again. See how she's getting along."

"We'll do all that later. But now, there's somewhere you need to be."

CHAPTER SEVEN

DAVID OPENED HIS EYES. The strip of light from the internal window next to his bed fell across the covers. It was a brighter shade of filtered grey than was normal for this time in the morning, and he glanced at the alarm clock on the nightstand.

4:15 was flashing in red numbers.

He rolled away from the window and stretched out under the duvet. He felt intensely relaxed, as if he had just stepped out of an hour-long sauna, and he considered sinking back into sleep. But his head felt weird, as if something had been inserted into it. Not a physical object, but like... like... He struggled to connect the feeling with an idea. It was like a box had been placed inside his brain; a box with facts in it. A block of information. He could almost sense the edges of the box pressing against his forehead. Although, again, it wasn't a physical feeling. Physically, he felt great. Fantastic. He had never felt better. What a sleep that had been. He must have been wiped after the drive back from Kingston.

He pushed back the green duvet, got out of bed and walked naked across the bedroom through the ten square feet of New York kitchen and into the bathroom. His head *was* feeling weird, as if there was something in there that wanted to come out. The idea came to him of writing something down.

He urinated, leaning one hand on the top of the toilet, and flushed. He washed his hands at the basin and looked at himself in the mirror. He hadn't shaved for three days and his face looked rested and peaceful. He wasn't used to seeing himself like that. He ran his wet hands through his hair. It couldn't hurt if he just took a few minutes to write something down. He really felt that he should.

The image of a box came to him again. Alright, then. It was still early. He'd just do it and then jump in the shower. He scratched his stubble and remembered Cassie's hand stroking his face just the day before, and her body pushed against him in the morning. Maybe he should ask her to come and live with him in New York. She could get a research job and he would find a bigger apartment. Wake up with that warm body every morning. There really wasn't anyone he felt so good with as her. He smiled at the thought.

He went back into the bedroom and found a pad of paper and a black pen. He sat down at the computer desk and closed his eyes.

A box. A box filled with information. He lifted the pen and an image came into his head, sharp and outlined. He relaxed his hand and the pen traced the markings of the image onto the paper. He looked down to see what he had written, but another image was forming, and he wrote that down too. It was a relief to get the forms out of his mind, and he drew the next ones faster, feeling a lightness as the information at last flowed out of the box and onto the paper. The more he wrote, the more he felt that he knew exactly what it was he was writing down. The images in his mind were so clear, so resonant with everything he understood. One by one, he released them from his head. He turned the page.

Several sheets later, David had finished writing. He felt good. He had opened the box and had transferred its contents onto that pile of paper. His head was clear and calm; there was no longer a pressure pushing against it. He reached his arms up towards the ceiling and yawned. How was it that he felt so incredibly good? He got up and walked through to the kitchen, leaving the pad of paper on the desk. His watch was lying on the sideboard next to the fridge and he glanced at it. The hands pointed to 10:35. David stared at it.

"Oh, shit!" He grabbed the watch and strode through the kitchen to the bedroom. The alarm clock was flashing the time in large numbers: 4:49. He looked up at the window. Of course it was 10:35. That's why it was so light. That's why he was feeling so great; he had slept for eleven hours.

He went back through the kitchen and dropped his watch on the sideboard. He was late. He was so bloody late. He had to take a shower. He had to shave. He looked as if he'd been in bed for a week.

Fuck. Fuck. Fuck.

He switched on the shower, didn't wait for it to heat up, and dived in under the cold water. 10:35. It would take him twenty-five minutes door to door and fifteen minutes to get ready. He wouldn't be in until after eleven. Shit. What would Jeff say? He was going to rip his face off.

Shit. Fuck. Shit.

FORTY-ONE MINUTES LATER, David stepped out of the elevator, showered, shaved and with too much aftershave splashed on in his rush. The floor seemed strangely quiet. The analysts were in the far corner with their heads down.

He walked over to his row of cubicles and saw with relief that Jeff's office was empty. The computer was switched on, but there was no one sitting there. Danny was in the cubicle opposite, but he was on the phone and didn't look up. Tom was out; so was Kirsten.

David hung his suit jacket on the back of the chair and switched on the computer. He sat down at his desk and checked the files next to the telephone. They were all in order. It was the same as he had left it on Friday afternoon. Maybe Jeff hadn't even noticed that he wasn't in this morning.

There was a radio playing somewhere on the floor, some repetitive pop music. He stuck his mobile phone into the charger pod and leaned back in his chair. Maybe he had just been lucky. Okay then. He needed to catch a break. He couldn't afford to drop the ball now, not after the bonus incident. It was things like that which could finish you – getting screwed on the money. Someone else might quit over it, but not him. He was going to show Jeff that he was back, that he was here for the long term, that he was his guy. He opened the folder at the top of the pile and glanced over the top page.

Call Rasheed again. This was the biggest deal he had worked on yet, and he needed a little magic to make it happen. He picked up the phone.

 THE ADMIRAL of the Home Planet Fleet and Council Representative for the Interplanetary Exploration Centre stood before the viewing window, located within the top triangle of the Task Assignment Pyramid. It gazed through the external observation panel, which filtered out the swirling mist, and showed, instead of a haze of atmospheric dust, a glistening spread of

the surrounding planetary system, with the near and far own-planet moons and swathes of rising and falling stars.

Noœ-bouk stood in the angles of the doorway and observed it. The Admiral was aware that *Noœ-bouk* had arrived at the chamber, yet it seemed to have difficulty in turning away from the observation panel. Eventually, without moving its head or body towards *Noœ-bouk*, it conveyed a block of communication.

"It is challenging to return to a single planetary environment when the space infinity has been experienced on a personal level," it sent. It did not turn from the viewing window.

"I would like to experience that," replied *Noœ-bouk*.

"It is the one thing which our ascended civilisation cannot prepare us for," continued the Admiral. "There is nothing which can condition a life form for experiencing infinity. It loses its understanding of proportion, its sense of where anything fits into anything else. It has given me endless difficulties since the completion of my assignments on the exploration vessels. It haunts me with its incomprehensibility. Perhaps I was not evolved enough, not ready. I do not know. I think. I think. I think."

The Admiral of the Home Planet Fleet, *Ba-hutá*, was a being of the highest resonance on Home Planet. It had led vessels and fleet clusters of vessels, which had introduced complex systems of peaceful evolution to numerous primitive-level planets far outside the universe tracts which had been in their voyage routes prior to its leadership of the Centre for Interplanetary Exploration. Under its supervision, the scientific teams had developed star-map routes so significantly advanced from the previously used navigational systems that it had increased the distance scope of the Centre by several thousand; indeed, by numbers which were almost impossible to calculate. Under its leadership, the lines defining a clear project structure had become so blurred that it was now a challenging task to assign even basic resource allocations to the individual projects, and to the Centre itself. In recognition of its work, the Admiral had been awarded every interplanetary distinction in existence, and several which had been created solely for the purpose of acknowledging its work in the many fields it had pioneered throughout its lifespan.

"Admiral…"

"Perhaps you did not understand me," the Admiral continued. "You do not come back once you have entered the fleet. It is impossible, once you have seen, even in one instance. Once you have travelled the new star routes through thousands of galaxy systems and understood that these, with all the inexpressible diversity of existence within each of them, are only an insignificant aspect of the infinity of everything. I am telling you..."

Inexpressible. Incomprehensible. Impossible. These were meaning blocks which *Noœ-bouk* had never received before in any form. It had been aware, possibly from its earliest stage existence, of the Admiral's achievements for Home Planet. More recently, it had become widely known that the Admiral's thought patterns had evolved in an unusual manner for a Home Planet being, and it had, as a consequence, been retired from active fleet command several moon cycles past. The leadership of the Centre for Interplanetary Exploration, however, allowed it to use its unparalleled knowledge for the benefit of the planet, and at the same time gave the Council the ability to monitor its decisions and actions. It was the Admiral who now had the authority to allow *Noœ-bouk* to take its place on one of the fleet craft.

"Admiral, I have less than thirty three-moon cycles remaining in my lifespan."

The Admiral at last drew its gaze away from the viewing panel of the diamond and turned to face *Noœ-bouk*.

"You are an energy-channeller."

"Yes."

"I have respect for this task assignment. It facilitates significant progress in our planetary evolution. It is a positive choice of lifespan allocation."

"I concur." *Noœ-bouk* paused. The Admiral regarded it, waiting for more.

Noœ-bouk formed the communication blocks carefully. "The final project which I undertook, I carried out with the accepted consequence of shortening my lifespan. I was assigned to the Cellular Genetic Centre and have recovered to the maximum extent possible. But the estimate is of less than thirty three-moon cycles to transition if I remain on Home Planet. If I enter a vessel, my existence could remain in continual suspension."

"It was a correct decision," communicated the Admiral. "Your recent task completion was a correct and elevated decision. I applaud it. I am aware of the project. I have studied the results. They are significant. They entailed individual effort combined with knowledge and skill and courage. These are the qualities which I seek and expect in the life forms who enter my fleet."

"I acknowledge your response." *Noœ-bouk* was processing a combination of emotions transmitted through the Admiral's information blocks. There was pride for the evolution of Home Planet and there was also some sadness, for which *Noœ-bouk* was unable to identify the source.

"I would like to know something beyond Home Planet," *Noœ-bouk* continued. "I have spent my lifespan focused on channelling and physically preparing my form for the assignment which I carried out. Now I have little energy remaining, a lack of vitality to fulfil further tasks."

Noœ-bouk breathed in the high-intensity inhalation particles of the diamond. The elevated concentration made its head light.

"I desire to experience infinity," it sent.

The Admiral was regarding *Noœ-bouk* with its huge, pale eyes, in which, it was communicated on Home Planet, universes could be seen dancing and being born. Its form was emaciated, the internal structure clearly visible through its translucent skin. The combination of its distended head and eyes, and depleted physical structure, made the Admiral appear as if it had evolved beyond the other grey beings of Home Planet, and into a state in which the knowledge of the universe had been captured and was alive, existing within its eyes, while its physical form, extraneous in the presence of living infinity, was simply fading away.

It was known that the Admiral was unable to regenerate from the light capsules which were used by the other members of its genus type, and that a special chamber had been constructed to maintain its existence; however, the levels of energy filtered there were not contained in the planetary information channels accessible by *Noœ-bouk*. There were many thought-strands which had been exchanged between Home Planet beings regarding the Admiral's current existence on Home Planet, and as *Noœ-bouk* met the Admiral's eyes with its own, it reflected that all the possibilities which had been suggested in those strands were, with a high probability level, close to factual truth.

Noœ-bouk's communication hung and vibrated faintly in the diamond chamber.

"I desire to experience infinity."

The Admiral maintained its regard of *Noœ-bouk*; its pale, mesmeric eyes fixed onto *Noœ-bouk*'s own. As the silence lengthened, the two beings began to experience an unusual level of understanding between each other. A channel of the emotion associated with unity, affinity and communion opened up between them and flowed freely as they held each other's gaze. Experiencing this *kaiific* wave of energy, neither of the two beings shifted their attention from the channel. They allowed the information contained within it to be transmitted, one to the other.

Outside the diamond, the stars extinguished and re-appeared. The galaxies contracted and grew. Home Planet and its three moons twisted in their unending orbits.

The Admiral waited until the surge of elevated unity had faded to a simple acknowledgment of life-form recognition, from which the stronger emotion had inevitably arisen.

"You have my authorisation to join the vessel fleet."

ELSPETH KICKED off her shoes and walked barefoot down the narrow corridor of her flat. She was exhausted following the opening ceremony of the library, and strangely depressed. She should have felt great; she had been the centre of attention for all those kindly, successful lawyers. They had been crowding round her, heaping her with compliments on her speech, on her grandfather's inspirational life, on this, on that; all the while stuffing themselves with salmon sandwiches and steaming cups of tea. Again, Elspeth felt the doubt and confusion in herself. These were kind, successful people, just like her grandfather, who never doubted their place in society, their roles, their contributions, their right to live comfortable lives, propagating their wealth and intelligence for generation after generation. Their children and families would take their privilege for granted, giving generously to charities of all kinds, safe in the knowledge that their own days would never be threatened with famine, earthquake or poverty. The worst they would ever have to deal with would be a failing liver or a slow death from old age.

Privilege.

There was something that repulsed her to the core about the word. She couldn't bear it. The smugness of it. The safety of it, while other people in the world were walking every day along lines of personal risk, feeding families, staying off drugs or wandering through deserts, following the call of something higher.

She shook her head. Now she was being silly. *Wandering through deserts.* They were just nice people who didn't want to rock the boat. If she didn't like them, then she shouldn't hang around with them. It didn't mean she had to go back to Morocco, or get into drugs, or go and live in a desert. She could make her own choices, and if hanging around all these privileged people pissed her off so much, then she should stop doing it. Grandad would have told her as much.

68

What she really needed right now was to find a mountain to climb. It was just about the only thing that had ever given her peace when she was upset about something. It had to be alone; the journey up the path, clambering over stones, often among pine trees or flowering bushes. That was one of the things which had kept her in France and Spain: those fantastic peaks and the good weather to climb them, the windy sunshine blowing you this way and that at the top, and you could see the sea glimmering in the distance and there was a feeling up there, on top of the mountain, that you had offered up whatever it was you were; that you had given yourself to the wind and the sky and the clouds. It was the closest she had felt to happiness in her adult life.

Elspeth went into the kitchen and held a dirty glass under the cold-water tap. She waited until the water was slightly colder than luke-warm, then drank. *Ugh! Disgusting.* She hated London tap water. In fact, she hated London. And all the people in it.

She seemed to hate a bunch of things tonight. Damn it. Why did Grandad have to die? Just when she had found one single person in the world she truly loved, and who she felt loved her. Loved her without any question at all. And now she was on her own again, back to square one.

Although, that wasn't quite true. She had made a lot of positive changes, thanks to Grandad. She had a job, and a flat. She even had two business suits. And she hadn't touched drugs since she'd come back to London. Not even a joint. That was a plus.

Elspeth rinsed her mouth out with the last of the tap water and spat it into the sink. She went into the living room and looked around. Her red and blue Mexican rug, nailed to the wall; a small, chipped table; a filthy-looking sofa. This was fine; she didn't really care where she lived. The trouble was, she didn't know what she *did* care about. At least the drugs had always solved that problem. She could drift away in a haze of rejection. Just be a part of that crowd who bitched about everything and didn't have the guts to come up with a solution of their own. Reject, reject, reject. It was the easiest thing in the world. You just had to refer to the rest of the world – all those idiot people making some kind of a contribution – as Stupid Fucking Assholes, and then you were safe. They were the assholes who were making a mess of everything, and you were the ones who saw through all that corrupt bullshit and weren't believing any of it. And then you would take a long, fat toke from whatever had been passed to you and float away in a wave of perfect self-righteousness.

Except that now she was off the drugs, and she couldn't do the last bit. And without the last bit, the logic came back to bite her, to show her what a coward she had been. You can't reject the world. It's a waste of a life. The very least you can do is try to make yourself happy. Nobody is going to stop you doing that. Nobody cares enough. Really. Nobody. If only she could find out what it was that would make her happy, then she might have a chance.

Elspeth glanced at the clock. 10 p.m. Still early enough, but she liked to get to work before nine. Even if she didn't know whether she was going to keep the job, she was getting some enjoyment out of doing it properly.

She unzipped her skirt, stepped out of it and draped it over the back of the sofa. Then she unbuttoned her blouse and slipped it on a hanger on the back of the door. She started to pull off her hold-up stockings when the phone rang in the hallway. She peeled the first stocking off the end of her foot and hopped into the hall.

"Hello?"

"Ellie, darling."

Her mother's voice. Smug. Wine-fuelled. The one thing guaranteed to rub Elspeth the wrong way.

"Hi, Mum."

"Ellie, how are you, darling? How did the opening go today? I was thinking of you all afternoon. I'm so sorry I couldn't make it."

"It was fine, Mum. Big crowd. Look, I'm kind of doing something right now. I've got a friend here. A man."

"Oh, really? Is it one of the lawyers? Never mind. You'll tell me later. Listen, something important. Grandad's will. He left you some things."

"What? What's he left me?"

"I'll tell you over lunch. Meet me tomorrow. Top of the Portrait Gallery. Table at one."

"Okay, Mum. I've got to go. See you tomorrow."

"Love you. *Mmmmwa.*"

Elspeth put down the phone. She hated being called Ellie. Silly, at the age of twenty-eight, to still get annoyed with a name. Grandad had never called her that. She loved the way he had said her name. *Ailspeth,* he'd pronounced it, in his Edinburgh accent. And she had loved to stay with him and Granny in their cottage on the west coast of Scotland, with that light and that air, and those lovely voices calling her *Ailspeth, Ailspeth, Ailspeth...*

Elspeth hopped back into the sitting room and pulled off her second stocking. She held it up for a moment. Sheer, almost-black with a lace top. Damn sexy. And nobody to peel it off for her.

70

At least she hadn't lost the urge. Maybe that was what she needed – to get out and find a man. She could go this weekend. Call up some old friends and head down to Camden. Pick up some guy and fuck his brains out.

She smiled. *Calm down.* She hung the stockings on the back of the sofa and tiptoed through to her bedroom. The walls were bare and the small desk was covered in books and pads of paper she had scribbled on. She took a T-shirt from the bed and pulled it on. She climbed under the duvet, checked her alarm for the morning, and switched off the light.

CHAPTER
EIGHT

DAVID LEFT the bank that evening at eleven. The night was clear as he walked back from the subway along Third Avenue, the Papaya Queen and other delis shining out their enticing yellow glow, accompanied by the hum of giant fridges. The flower displays made him think of Cassie for some reason, and he felt sick when he remembered how relaxed he had been with her in Kingston, and what a stressful day it had been at work.

Nobody had commented on his lateness, but he had felt something different on the floor – a quietness, as if he had dropped the ball on some major project, as if he had missed something important which nobody would tell him about. Danny hadn't busted his chops about anything; Jeff had been out for most of the day; Tom had been on the phone every time he looked and Kirsten had been working diligently, as always. On the surface, it all seemed normal, but he had felt all day that something *was* wrong, and the feeling had only grown stronger. He knew that the logic was flawed; nothing happening wasn't evidence that something *was* happening. He was clearly being paranoid, but it was hard not to be, after what had happened that morning.

He stopped in front of one of the all-night delis and stared into the flowers set out in plastic buckets on the sidewalk: roses in bunches for $6.99, tulips and big, coloured daisies at $7.99, bright yellow sunflowers for $9.99. He thought again of Cassie. One of the fragrances reminded him of her. It was something lemony. Maybe the sunflowers, maybe the tulips. He didn't know. He went into the store and pulled a carton of fat-free milk out of the fridges at the back, and took it to the counter.

The man behind the till was Indian or Pakistani; whichever country owned the deli chain, he supposed. He had a turban on his head and a stained newspaper open in front of him on the counter. David passed him the milk and the man punched it into the cash register with a familiar *ting*. He handed the change to David.

"Are you okay, sir?" he asked.

David stared at him, surprised. No stranger in New York had ever shown genuine interest in his well-being.

"I'm fine," he said. "Don't I look okay?"

"You look fine, sir. A little worried, sir."

"Well, it's New York," said David glibly. "Everyone's a little worried."

"Yes, sir. Have a good night, sir."

"Yeah, okay, thanks. You, too."

David picked up the carton of milk and walked out of the shop. He wasn't even sure why he had gone in there. He didn't need milk. He didn't need anything. He looked at the flowers again, then at the containers of fruit salad stuck neatly into the ice display. It was another reason he loved New York – you could get anything at any time. Fruit salad, flowers, milk, women with huge breasts, blow jobs… He gave a half-smile and turned away from the display.

Suddenly, it came to him. He knew why he wasn't going home. It wasn't a spontaneous urge to stand around looking at fruit salad and tulips. The image of his desk flashed before his eyes, and the pile of papers he had scribbled that morning, and the alarm clock that hadn't woken him up. Something *was* happening, and he didn't know what it was. And he didn't know what was going to happen next.

He took a deep breath and started to stride back towards his apartment. Whatever it was, he was going to face it. That was what he had decided in Canada, in Cassie's bedroom. He was getting back on the ball, and whatever was going on with all this strange shit, he wasn't going to let it affect him.

He turned down York onto 78th and came to the corner of his apartment block, a modern, red-brick building with a royal-green canopy stretching out over the sidewalk. Pulling out his key, he walked up the few steps to let himself into the building. Something in him was still resisting, and he had to force himself into the elevator and up to the fifth floor. Apartment 5F. He slid the key in, twisted it, and the door opened onto the familiar ten square feet of his kitchen. He flicked on the light and sighed. It was fine. It was his apartment, exactly as he'd left it. It was fine.

He stepped in, locked the door behind him and hung up his coat on one of the hooks fixed to the wall. He put the milk in the fridge and went to the bathroom to wash his hands, then walked through to the bedroom. He picked up a yellow file from the top of his desk and threw it over the pile of scribbled sheets, managing not to look at them. He took off his suit and hung it up, then went back into the kitchen in his boxer shorts to pour himself a large whisky. Back in the bedroom, he sat at the desk and checked his watch. It was 11:45 p.m. He would look at the sheets of paper for five minutes, then hit the sack. He was getting up at five the next day. He wasn't going to let the fiasco of this morning repeat itself.

He took a sip of the whisky and felt it burning his mouth and throat. Delicious. He took another, larger sip and pulled the yellow file from the pile of papers, then shuffled the papers into order. He paused, set the glass down on the desk, and picked up the first sheet.

On the white page he had drawn a series of markings. They were made heavily, as if he had been pushing down on the paper as hard as he could with the pen, and in some places the marking had leaked through to the other side, leaving a small circle of ink. The marks were not letters, but seemed to be some kind of symbol pattern. He didn't recognise any of it, beyond a few interlocking circles which were repeated on several pages. They looked a little like mathematical formulae, or like Chinese symbols. He turned over the first page, and then the next. On the third sheet he had drawn a diagram similar to one of the symbols, but bigger and more complicated; it took up the entire page. David flicked through the rest of the sheets. One more diagram, and the rest were symbols.

He laid the sheets out, side by side, across the desk space. There were six of them. He looked carefully at the markings on all of the pages; markings he had made with his own hand. He had drawn them fast, almost scribbling them down, and yet they were extremely precise. He could see two or three symbols which were repeated on almost all of the pages.

For a long time he sat there, with the pages before him, his eyes resting on the spread of lines and shapes. For some strange reason, the images seemed to be making him calm, and he no longer felt the anxiety and fear from earlier in the day. He looked, and he breathed, and there was something he could only describe as happiness taking place in his body. It felt as if he could sit there for hours, just looking at the shapes and feeling this happiness, this peace.

At last, he pulled himself away from the papers. He glanced up and around the room, and it seemed somehow different; as if something inside of him had changed, and as if he no longer quite recognised the external circumstances of his life. The suit hanging from the metal holder; the navy-blue sofa-bed; the abstract art print behind a piece of glass.

For a few long moments, it seemed to him as if he were simultaneously two people at once. The first was about to get up from his desk and walk out of the apartment, catch a train home to Kingston and never come back; the second was about to switch off this feeling of happiness, take a long drink of whisky and return to the objects, the props, the costumes and lines, the rush, the thrill, the story he had believed.

In the stillness, the two people circled David, their shadows pulling and pushing, ebbing and flowing, moving in and out of vision. He caught sight of one and then lost it; he focused on the other and it vanished as the first came back into view. He felt peace, and then he felt hunger. He felt longing, and then he felt fear. He wanted to cry out, and then he wanted to laugh.

It was the whisky glass which brought him back. The lamp on the desk caught a facet of the crystal and flashed it in a direct line into David's eye. He blinked, then remembered the light on the road to Kingston, and then the owl. He looked down at the pages and breathed out heavily.

"Fuck," he whispered to himself, and he reached for the glass and knocked back the last finger of liquor.

He stood up and held the crystal tumbler in his hand. The reality around him was still shifting, calling him; but something in him knew now that he could break through it. He walked into the kitchen, his steps feeling momentous, heavy, as if the gravity had somehow increased. He took the whisky bottle again from the cupboard and poured himself another half-glass, and took a gulp.

"That's it," he said aloud. "That's enough. That's it."

He raised his arms above his head and he punched the air with both his fists, knocking on that invisible door, his face screwed up in a grimace.

"I'm not going down," he said.

He took another gulp of the whisky, then turned and opened the fridge. Inside, there were some sports bars on the top shelf and a few plastic bottles of juice and milk. He pulled out a bottle of cranberry juice, opened it, and drank it straight from the container. The cold, biting tang of the liquid cleared his head and he drank until it was all gone. He tossed the rest of the whisky down the sink and went into the bathroom to brush his teeth. He looked at himself in the mirror, and he recognised the image. Haggard but hungry. A few hours' sleep and he would be absolutely fine. He'd put all this behind him.

Back in the bedroom, he shuffled the papers into the yellow folder and slid them under a pile of documents. He climbed into bed and set the time on his alarm clock for 5 a.m. He set the alarm on his watch and the alarm on his mobile phone, and put them both on the bedside table next to the clock and the lamp. He switched off the light, and for a few moments he clenched and unclenched his fists beneath the covers, as hard as he could. He pictured himself waking the next day, fresh and rested, his life ahead of him.

He closed his eyes, and sleep took over.

 THE FLEET TRAINING was to take place on the vessel. Although outside the regulation practice, it had been recognised that *Noœ-bouk* could not sustain the physical deterioration which would occur if it remained for the training period within the Home Planet environment.

The Admiral had assigned *Noœ-bouk* as a scientific observer on one of the smaller ships, the *Istina*, the mission of which was to experiment with new star map routes, and to pursue unexplained phenomena in space as it made its journey.

It was such a common occurrence for space crew to report scientific anomalies during the course of a mission, that a protocol had been established to record, but not investigate, such observations, in order to avoid significant delay on mission routes. The *Istina* had been commissioned for the purpose of obtaining intelligence for Home Planet through pursuing phenomena observed on-journey, in addition to examining the anomaly records and investigating the incidents deemed to have most potential for new information. Other vessels of the Home Planet fleet had instructions to communicate anomaly situations directly to *Noœ-bouk*'s ship.

The *Istina* was the first vessel from Home Planet where the trajectory and tasks would be decided during the course of the mission by the Captain, together with the Advisory Committee – a sub-Council made up of the senior members of the crew. *Noœ-bouk*'s position as a scientific observer meant that it had a permanent seat on the Committee. It was an honour for it to have been allocated the role.

At the designated point of embarkation, *Noœ-bouk* took its final distance leap to the docking platform, which was located on a remote, ice-covered plateau, under the vermillion lowlight of the three moons' shadow. The sun rarely reached this area, and it was not utilised for habitation of any genus type. *Noœ-bouk* would have liked to have taken a rock or some of the grey ground-dust as a remembrance of Home Planet, but any physical remnants would contribute to a hastening of its lifespan completion. It was the last occasion that it would touch a physical planet surface.

Noœ-bouk entered the preliminary vessel chamber and waited as the filtration system cleansed its skin of surface particle residue. Tests were run to ensure physical compatibility with the sterile vessel environment. It was this controlled atmospheric system which, according to the being in the Cellular Genetic Centre, would sustain *Noœ-bouk* in its non-deteriorating state of lifespan suspension.

Once it had passed through the final stages, *Noœ-bouk* proceeded to the main viewing deck, where the observation panels and pods were located. It had studied the plans of the vessel in detail, and had identified the areas of greatest significance and viewing potential. It noted several different genus types present on the deck, occupied with the control panels and location screens. Having as yet no allocated task assignment, *Noœ-bouk* entered one of the pods and lowered itself into the curved seat. It adjusted the eye cover over its face and studied the observation channels. Home Planet was visible through analytical windows which *Noœ-bouk* had not previously studied. Geological views of the entire planetary rock strata, tectonic and volcanic activities, schemes of the planetary surface and pod surface showing constructions and living workspaces, occupation statistics, and the multiple positions of Home Planet in different star map variations. This analytical data, although previously available through Home Planet information channels, was new to *Noœ-bouk*, and it studied it in detail.

All the vessels of the Home Planet fleet were identical in structure and specification, with the only variables being the size of the ship and the number of landing creels fitted into the carved-out bays of the exterior. The inside was modelled from a white material in pristine curves and the lighting was varied automatically in response to an overall reading of the emotional and physical states of the life forms in the vicinity: a reading which measured body temperature, the strength and elevation of communication waves, and the function level of internal organs. Any state of elevation, mental or physical, such as an increase in the pulsation of the central circulatory organ or the breathing organs, led to a calming blue light being distributed, and a lowered temperature. A depressed state was adjusted with an increased temperature and a *kaiific* glow of pink or gold, similar to the surface light of Home Planet during the rise of the third moon. The system had proved effective over innumerable fleet excursions, and was one of the features of successful distance voyaging pioneered by the fleet Admiral.

Nœ-bouk, recalling this information from within the pod, registered a cool temperature and a pale blue light throughout the main viewing deck. It felt the effect of the colour balancing its own heightened state, and settled back into the viewing pod.

It was ready to depart.

EILEEN LED Alisdair back to the library, where Duncan was waiting for them, still immersed in the book of lives. He looked a little dazed as he turned away from the lectern and lifted the half-moon spectacles from his nose.

"I can see you've been to the Prototype Garden," he said, observing the wonder on Alisdair's face. "Now, are you ready for the review?"

"I don't know," said Alisdair. "Eileen wouldn't tell me about it."

Eileen squeezed his hand. "I'll wait for you here, my love. I'm going to browse some of these books. I may even look up Socrates for you."

"I'll see you soon," said Alisdair, and he released her fingers as Duncan led him through a concealed door, hidden amongst the shelves and tomes.

It was a small, cosy room, with several stiff, brocade armchairs set around a fireplace. The walls were furnished in oak panelling, and the ceiling embossed with squares of thistles and roses. It reminded Alisdair of formal college sitting rooms and old Scottish houses.

"What are we here for?" asked Alisdair.

"We are going to review your life," said Duncan. "We will watch it again, from a place of non-judgment, and we will look at what you set out to achieve, and how far you were successful in those goals. We will see if there are elements you need to repeat. From this, we can look forward and decide what will be the next step for you."

"That sounds a little terrifying," said Alisdair. "Does everyone do this?"

"In some way or another, yes. Everyone has to look at the impact they created. What contribution they made overall. It's not a case of good or bad. It's more about evaluating the goals. Some lives are just for the purposes of resting. Some are to support another person in their life mission. It's a different way of looking at it from here."

"And when we decide on the next step, what then?"

"Then we take that decision to the Council. It is important for all the choices to be aligned with the plan."

"The plan?"

"The scheme that links it all together. There are many different levels, of course. You don't need to worry about it now."

Alisdair sat down in one of the armchairs, which was considerably more comfortable than it appeared. A crackling, busy fire was now burning in the grate. As he settled, the flames threw up images around him. There was a shift, and the images became sharper and started to take shape, as the rest of the room faded into muted shadow.

A woman appeared before him, her long hair falling over a child in her arms. It was his mother, and there was another shift, and her breath and voice and hair entered his senses, and her skin was hot and smelled of tobacco and wool and kippers. He reached out a hand to hold her, but she disappeared.

Another image formed: a boy on short legs running through a garden of grass. The touch of rain brushed his arm, and then he was in a school classroom pushing pencils into a wooden desk, and then crouched in hidden corners devouring book after concealed book as the years circled by around him.

One by one, the scenes of his childhood emerged from the firelight, and the breaths dividing the passing of those scenes, and he knew again the desires which had pulled him towards them, the changes which had been marked upon him, the people he had loved and the people he had known. He saw the threads created from each moment, moving out from person to person, forming the total pattern of each of his actions: on those around him, on those further from him, and then onwards to those he did not know. He observed the constant concern of his mother, the shame and pride of his father, the loneliness of Eileen while he had been away, the jealousy and inspiration aroused in his colleagues, the inadequacies of his children brought up in his shadow, and the simple love of his grandchildren. He saw Elspeth playing on a beach in Scotland, and himself throwing her up into the air, and how the memory of that moment had given her strength throughout her life. He saw her rejecting the paths around her, and his love guiding her back.

At last, he saw his death, his funeral, and then the skein of his legacy stretching out far into the future, through all the people who would know of his life, who would read his books and papers, be touched by those he had touched, and hurt by those he had not reached out to; the impact of his years circling fainter and fainter over the history of the world.

The final image faded.

"What do you think?" asked Duncan.

"I think I could have done better," Alisdair replied.

Duncan threw his head back and laughed, waving a hand in the air. "There isn't anyone who doesn't say that. Look, it's not about the perfect example, Alisdair. It's about contribution. What was the contribution? Did you grow?"

"I think that the contribution was good, overall. Although I could certainly apologise to a few people."

"There will be plenty of time for that, when they have passed over. You can find them all, and make your peace."

"I wanted to set an example," said Alisdair. "One that people could take heart from. That was my goal. Nothing too grand, just helping whoever I could. Not hurting anyone. It wasn't easy, to tell you the truth. Just being a good man."

"That was your goal," said Duncan.

"I think I did achieve that, more or less. Although I could have dealt with some of those problems better. I could have reached out more, even when it was uncomfortable. I see that I stopped trying as I got older. That was when I could have helped the most."

"Yes," said Duncan. "Yes. The impact could have been more powerful. But overall, you left a clear example, and that will be passed on for generations. In actions, words, memories."

Alisdair looked a little dejected. "It would have been easy to try harder."

Duncan smiled. "There's no place for that now. The Council is pleased with how you lived. You achieved your goals. You left a pattern for good."

Alisdair was staring into the fire, and he turned to Duncan with his head on one side.

"But, just to play the devil's advocate... what would have happened if I had missed my goals entirely? No, even worse than that. What if I had gone in entirely the opposite direction? What if I hadn't found

80

Eileen? What if I had ended up in the Edinburgh slums? What if I'd been a lawyer for a criminal mastermind and caused all sorts of harm?"

Duncan was chuckling. "Well, then our conversation would be a wee bit longer than it is now. We'd have to call in some higher energies. You would have to spend some time understanding what had happened and the effects that it had caused. There's no punishment, of course, but there is an expectation that things will be brought to balance, that everything will return to its natural state of... peace. It's just the rules of the game."

"And how would that happen? Would it happen here, or would I have to go back to Earth to find that balance, that peace?"

"It would be your choice. We would examine the possibilities and consult with the people who had been affected and then come up with a solution."

"And what if that went wrong as well? What if I kept making the wrong choice time after time? What if—"

"Come, come. The only thing to remember is that everyone is doing it for the same reason: curiosity. To explore the different possibilities of what could be. And so far as that applies to everything, it is not really possible to make a mistake. Actions carry within them a natural balance. Within every act, there is contained the energy required to counter and return that act to the place where it originated. That's why every soul tries out the different variations. Great deeds and dreadful ones. Small and big. Acts of splendid valour and appalling temerity."

"But—"

Duncan reached out a hand and touched Alisdair's arm. "Now, back to your life review. What thoughts do you have for your next step?"

Alisdair looked into the fire again. Everything was possible. There were no mistakes. He liked that idea. And he was pleased with the life he had just finished. It hadn't been a bad life, all in all. He had touched many people in a good way. He had helped Elspeth. The image of him throwing her into the air on that Scottish beach came back to him again. Her shouts of joy. The sand flying from her hair and the dazzling light.

He turned to Duncan. "I want to help Elspeth. I want to be her guide."

Duncan followed the image of the girl flying into the sea air and dropping down again. He smiled. "That is a good choice. But you can do that as well as other things. Here, it is possible for many events to take place at the same time."

"What do you suggest?"

"I'd like to show you more of how this dimension works. I think you would enjoy participating in the Earth Council eventually, but there are some steps you need to go through first."

"Will Eileen be with us?"

"She can tell you that herself. I believe she is returning to an Earth life soon. Come."

Duncan rose from the armchair and motioned to Alisdair, and they moved out of the room, leaving the fire drifting to ash. As they left, the wooden panelling and squares of roses and thistles faded behind them.

Eileen was leaning over an enormous tome laid open on a lectern.

"Socrates?"

"Gracious, no. Bonnie Prince Charlie. You wouldn't believe what that scamp got up to!"

"I probably would, you know. Where have you got to?"

"He's on the Isle of Skye. With that Flora MacDonald. Did you complete the review, my love?"

"I'm going to help Elspeth."

"Oh, I'm so pleased! You always had such a connection."

"And you? What have you decided?"

"Come, my dearest. Let's walk to the garden. I'll tell you everything."

CHAPTER NINE

THE PHONE BUZZED in the leather holder on David's belt. He put down his fork and pulled it out.

"Hey, Cassie."

"David? Is this a good time to talk? Are you free?"

"Yeah. I'm at work. I'm just having breakfast."

"Great. So, listen. This won't take a minute. I did some research and I wanted to fill you in."

"Go for it. What's up?"

"It's about the owl you were telling me about."

"Okay." David felt a seam of anger open up in him. He hadn't wanted her to start applying her scientific theories to what he had seen.

"I looked up the owl, and just as we thought, there isn't anything that matches what you saw."

"Okay." David's tone was cold now.

"And then I called a couple of friends who work in that area, who might know more. Basically, there's no owl that big. There also isn't a bird of a similar type that you could have mistaken for an owl. Certainly nothing that would have come up to the bumper of your car. Not that you could have seen from your position inside the car. Well, unless it was twenty or thirty feet away."

"You can't know that for sure."

"I tried it, David. I took the maximum size of the largest owl there was. It wasn't even a white owl, by the way. I sat in my car and tried it. There's no way you could have seen it like that."

"Cassie…"

"David, you remember what I was saying about a hypnotherapist? If this had happened to me, I'd be all over it."

"Alright. Thanks for checking that out for me. But remember, I was pretty upset that night, and wiped from driving. Your mind can make up a lot of weird stuff at night."

"Yes, you're right. But if that *is* the explanation, wouldn't you rather be sure about it?"

"Cassie, right now, I just want to get on with my work, and not think about some stupid hallucination I had. I don't have time for this right now."

"Okay, David. You're right. Go make some money. The fact that you might have been exposed to the dangerous, hallucinogenic after-effects of some unknown explosion is totally not a priority. Have a good day. Make a load of money."

"Bye, Cassie—" David started to say, but she had hung up the call.

He put the phone back into the holder on his belt and picked up his fork. He pushed the remains of the egg whites around the plate. His appetite had gone. He reached for his coffee and drained the last few sips. The seam of anger opened wider, flowing through his body. He felt like smashing the plate onto the floor, kicking something repeatedly.

Deep breath. He was at work. He had a long day ahead.

He stood up, took his tray and carried it to the stacks, sliding it onto a free shelf. He had to get rid of this anger; he couldn't possibly go back to the floor feeling like this. He walked out of the cafeteria and into the men's washroom, next to the bank of elevators. The room was empty, but David went into one of the cubicles and locked the door. He thought of Cassie on the phone and he wanted to smash his hand into the wall, smash his foot into something; the rage was beating through him. He curled his left hand into a rock-hard fist and punched it as hard as he could into his right palm, making a low, grunting sound. He did it again, and again. He started to feel better. He switched hands and punched his right fist into his left palm. There. He was definitely feeling better. The rage was leaving him. He made a last, furious punch and a low, animal grunt, then let his hands fall to his sides.

He heard the door of the washroom being pushed open, and he turned and pulled the metal flush lever and opened the cubicle door. He nodded at the man in the expensive suit who had just entered. The man nodded back, and David recognised him as an MD from the corporate finance department. Smart guy. The kind of guy who would be pocketing a couple of million, come bonus time.

David washed his hands at the sink, dried them with a green paper towel and pushed open the washroom door. He was feeling a lot better now. The rage was pretty much gone. He was ready for a day making money. He pushed the elevator button and stepped into the waiting cabin.

It was going to be a great day.

 THE VESSEL COURSE for the first few moon cycles – *Noœ-bouk* and the less experienced crew members still thought in terms of Home Planet measurements, despite their lack of meaning within the space environment – was set, and lit up on a detailed star map on a panel of the main viewing deck. From Home Planet, they moved quickly through the solar systems within their home galaxy, and along the much-travelled star routes towards the outskirts of the exploration area.

The work of the vessel was divided into two main areas: the Scientific and Research Centre, to which *Noœ-bouk* was assigned, and the Space Observation and Evaluation Centre. *Noœ-bouk* spent most of its assignment periods with the scientific analysts, each of which was a specialist in a field of either multi-planetary or inter-dimensional research. The analysts studied the cases of phenomena for which authorisation to investigate had not been given at the point of observation, but which their vessel now had a mandate to pursue. It enjoyed this task assignment. It was restful to work with its mind function, rather than using its physical form and energy centres to full depletion, as it had done during its lifespan on Home Planet. It discussed the reported cases with its co-assignees, and learned much from their wide knowledge of other planetary environments.

Noœ-bouk found itself thinking about the Admiral as the vessel moved through space. How could the Admiral tolerate an existence on Home Planet after it had experienced such diversity? *Noœ-bouk* would lie in one of the viewing pods, watching the hypnotic turning of suns and many ringed and mooned planets, space hazed in star remnants, and it would sense the Admiral's presence around it. It recalled the feeling that had arisen during their meeting in the pyramid chamber: that flow of understanding and recognition, the strength of which it had not previously known during its lifespan, and which had been reciprocated. The event had been so unexpected for both *Noœ-bouk* and the Admiral, that there had not been a chance for them to channel their feelings into a more conventional and less intimate manner of energy exchange: it had been a pure communication of unity between them.

The physical form of the Admiral also returned to *Noœ-bouk*: those eyes, in whose portals it imagined it could see the swirling dust of universes being born; the emaciated trunk and limbs beneath the eyes. When the image of the Admiral was in its mind space, *Noœ-bouk* felt an unaccustomed intensity throughout its physical being. The sensation was similar to what it had experienced during the light immersion sessions, when it was recovering from its final task assignment: an extreme tingling throughout its limbs and organs, and a building euphoria, such as must be felt on living planets by organic matter pushing through soil into first light. This is what it had known in every cell of its regenerating form beneath that energy flow, and what it felt now: the tingling and wildness, accompanied by an elevated sensitivity of its skin. *Noœ-bouk* observed, with surprise, that its central circulatory organ was pulsating with exceptional strength.

It did not share these changes with any of the other beings on the vessel. It was satisfied with its task assignment, with the company of the crew members, with its co-assignees, and especially with the vessel's unprecedented mission.

It was aware, with each of the passing moon cycles, of the physical deterioration that it would have been experiencing had it elected to remain on Home Planet and be subject to the inevitable lifespan progression. It would not have been painful, however there was the possibility of distress on a mind level as the form ceased to function and prepared itself for transition. Many genus types in this final stage of the lifespan entered a specially designed chamber complex, and spent their final moon cycles in a state of trance-like non-thought, until the life force finally left the body. This is what would be occurring if it had not been here, on this vessel, travelling along space routes which it had previously only seen on dotted star maps, and imbued with new and entirely unexpected energy in response to a being which it had only encountered a few moon cycles past, and with whom it would never again share physical presence.

This unexpected and improbable combination of events and feelings gave *Noœ-bouk* a profound satisfaction. For all of its lifespan, *Noœ-bouk* had followed its assigned path. It had made its contribution to Home Planet. Now, *Noœ-bouk* had no concept of what was going to happen.

This sense of the unknown added a new layer to the processes which were occurring simultaneously within *Noœ-bouk*. It seemed as if the sum knowledge of several lifespans was being focused into this one moment.

It was certainly a higher level of existence than it had known up until now. The unprecedented accumulation of sensations created a rising excitement in *Nœ-bouk*, a feeling of aliveness, as if *it* – and not the vessel they were travelling in – was moving through unexplored space galaxies, pouring its sheer life-force energy into the blackest and deepest unknown.

Nœ-bouk lowered the lid coverings over its eyes. It felt the power of the vessel gliding through the darkest space. It felt its own power resonating with everything around it.

Anything was possible.

ELSPETH WOKE UP, surrounded by several new and extremely pleasant sensations. The first was the presence of a male body in the same bed as her, and a pair of definitely male arms wrapped around her, together with a clean, sexy smell of laundry and expensive aftershave. Not sweet. Not familiar. She liked it.

The second was the incredibly comfortable bed she was lying in; the soft pillow beneath her head, a cotton pillowcase against her cheek. The third was the long, golden rectangle of sunlight which was shining through the far edge of the curtain, where the fabric had been pulled too far across.

And the fourth was the thought of what was in her handbag.

She lay for a while, enjoying the sensations in the simplest way she could manage, enjoying them for the fact that they were so very temporary and so very unexpected.

Then she slipped out of the warm arms onto the soft bedroom carpet, glanced back at the sleeping man, checked the proximity of her scattered clothes and tiptoed naked into the bathroom. She opened the white cupboards one by one until she found a new toothbrush, broke it out of the packet and cleaned her teeth thoroughly. That felt good. Then she peed into the glistening white toilet, wiped some of the smudged make-up off her face, checked how she smelled, and tiptoed back into the room. The man was still sleeping. He was really, really good-looking. But then she went for the good-looking types. Why not? They were just as easy to lay as anyone else. They all wanted the same thing.

Elspeth pulled back the curtain edge to peer out onto the street. The bay window opened onto a grassy square, a quadrangle of carefully maintained London-grey houses. She tried to remember where they were. Islington, if she wasn't mistaken. Could easily be. This guy must have some money. She let the sunshine play over her face for a few moments, then dropped the curtain back and reached down to pick her handbag off the floor. She opened it, checked her keys, wallet and glasses, then took out a slim book. She padded back to the bed and climbed in carefully, sliding herself back into the stretched arms. The man – what was his name? – groaned and pulled her tightly against him. He had an erection. She knew he was awake now. She tried to ignore the penis growing harder against her back, and opened her book.

Chapter 11: The Mysteries of Diotima.

"How are you feeling?"

The man – what *was* his name? – was kissing her neck, pushing her hair aside with one hand. It felt pretty good. Elspeth remembered now that what they had got up to last night had felt pretty good as well. Maybe she would let him have one for the morning. Who knows, he might be a nice guy. Not that she cared. She slid the book under her pillow and turned towards him. His erection pushed against her stomach.

"Not as good as you're about to feel."

She tucked her head down, moved beneath the covers and slid his penis into her mouth.

CHAPTER
TEN

A PIGEON HOPPED up to the bench on its ugly red feet. David watched it through the fingers of his hands, which were covering his face. It pecked around his legs and scrabbled at something on the ground. Dirty beak. Dirty ground. Filthy bird. David wanted to give the creature an enormous kick that would send it flying far, far away. Out of the park, away from his shoe, away from where he was. But he didn't. He watched it through his fingers, and fought back the urge to cry.

It had happened again, for the third time now. He had woken up late after a heavy sleep; it was already 9 a.m. All his clocks were right. All his alarms had been set. But he had either slept through them all, or none of them had gone off. The very thought made him want to howl.

He had tried to get ready as fast as he could. He had skipped the shower and shave, flung on his suit, brushed his teeth. But he couldn't get out of the door. The pressure in his head, from the moment he had woken up, was overwhelming. It was pressing down, directly into the centre of his forehead. Again, it was as if something solid had been inserted into him, and was pushing so hard into his brain and skin that it felt like his head might explode. He had taken off his overcoat, hung it back on the hook and gone into the bedroom. He couldn't go to work feeling like that. He had sat down at the desk and, with shaking hands, he had pulled out the pad of paper and the black pen, and started to write.

This was also the third time that nobody had said a word about his lateness. That was almost the worst of it. The first time might have been a lucky break. The second time, a miracle. But three times in late, and three times not a word. That was a big fucking problem. That meant he was getting crossed off the list. That meant he was being sidelined from the game. That meant he had to do something fast if he didn't want to get fired.

He opened the fingers of his hands a crack to look at the pigeon. It was hopping away from him now. Disgusting creature. He hated them. He gave a snort of laughter at the thought. He was becoming a real New Yorker – impatient, intolerant, constantly pissed off. Yeah, he was really at home here now. Not much Canadian left in him anymore.

He reached into his jacket and pulled a business card out of the inside pocket. *Mr Eugene Shapkin, MD. Psychiatrist, Psychoanalyst.* It was a name he had heard a couple of times. Pretty famous shrink. It was going to cost a bomb. He stared down at the black writing and pictured himself as he looked now, sitting on a park bench in a busy lunch hour, his hands covering his face, for all of New York to see and ridicule. He had to call. He didn't have any choice. He had to do something. He took his phone out of its holder and dialled the number.

"Office of Dr Eugene Shapkin," came the pristine East Coast accent.

"Yeah, good afternoon," said David, grimacing. "Uh, I'd like to set up an appointment to see Dr Shapkin."

"Of course, sir," said the woman. David pictured a lean, New England body. Blonde hair. Skinny. Hot, hot, hot. "Are you a new client, sir?"

"Yes, new." The voice alone was making him horny. He was starting to get an erection. What the hell was wrong with him?

"Dr Shapkin always makes time for new clients. When would you like to see him? I could squeeze you in today if you like?"

David pictured himself squeezing his penis into her pale, slim body. He shook his head.

"Tomorrow," he managed to say. "Can he do evening? What's the latest he can do?"

"Tomorrow is just great," said the voice. "Dr Shapkin sometimes does a late session at eight or nine. Would either of those suit you?"

"Yeah. Nine would work. Perfect, in fact."

"That's great then, sir. Can I take your name to pencil in?"

"Cornwell. David Cornwell."

"Okay then, Mr Cornwell—"

"Please. David."

"Okay then, David. You are confirmed for tomorrow evening at nine. The first session is charged at a special rate of three hundred dollars per hour. All the following sessions are four hundred and fifty. You're all set. We'll see you tomorrow, and my name is Caroline."

"Thanks, Caroline. See you tomorrow."

David hung up. He thought he was probably in love with Caroline. He thought that he probably wanted to marry her. He had never heard such an erotic voice. Holy shit, if that's the kind of service this guy offered, he was going to get better in no time. He put the phone back into its holder and stretched. He had a half-erection, and he buttoned up his suit jacket to hide it. He would love to go somewhere right now and jerk off to the sound of Caroline's voice, but he was already in deep enough shit at work. He'd have to wait until evening. It'd send him to sleep nicely. He shook his head. The highlight of his day was going to be jerking off to a girl he'd never met. His life was really plummeting to new depths. But he had the appointment. That was a good start.

He got up from the bench, aimed a kick at the pigeon, and glanced around the park, which was full of bankers eating sandwiches and salads on wooden benches.

Keep it together.

He brushed imaginary crumbs from his suit, and set off back to the bank.

"SO, Mr Cornwell. David, if I may. What seems to be the problem? What would you like to talk to me about this evening? How are you feeling?"

David struggled to push the image of Caroline to the back of his mind so that he could focus on something else. She was even more beautiful than he had pictured. More than he had imagined last night, when he ejaculated to the image of her over-educated, New England private-school voice. He didn't think he had ever seen such long, slim legs, wrapped in a tight, grey pencil skirt below a frustratingly high-cut white blouse. Long, long blonde hair, all natural, of course – where did these girls even come from? – pushed back from her high forehead with an Alice band. Was that what they were called? How did he even know that? And the voice again…

"David?"

Talk. Talk. Tell Dr Eugene Shapkin what is going on. Just don't mention Caroline.

David cleared his throat.

"I'm having some problems," he said. There was a palm tree in the corner of the office. It looked well taken care of. He wondered if it was in Caroline's job description to take care of it. He wondered if Caroline took care of Dr Shapkin.

"What kind of problems?" said Dr Shapkin. "Because whatever it is, we can find a way to help you."

"Stuff is happening to me," said David. Why was he so distracted? He wasn't able to focus on anything. The beige leather chair was too soft. It had to be the softest chair he had ever sat in.

Dr Shapkin let his narrow, rectangular glasses slip down his nose. He looked intently at David.

"Tell me about this *stuff* that is *happening*."

HALF AN HOUR LATER, David had managed to tell his new psychiatrist the problem. The bonus problem, the owl problem, the dreams and the writing problem. The lack-of-focus problem and the career-sliding-away-beneath-his-feet problem. By the time he had finished, the beige leather chair and the abundantly watered palm tree and the cream carpet of the office all felt very, very big, and David, sitting in a now-crumpled suit in the expanse of beige leather, felt very, very small.

The shrink didn't speak for a long time, but he had taken an over-sized fountain pen and a pad of paper, and was making what looked like a lot of notes. At last, he returned his gaze to David.

"Anything else you would like to tell me this evening?"

David shook his head. "That's all."

There was another pause as the shrink twisted the top back onto the fountain pen and laid it down on the pad of paper.

"The good news," he said, "is that I can help you."

David burst out with a laugh. "I was hoping you'd say that," he said.

The shrink smiled. "Yes," he said, "and it's pretty clear to me what is going on in your head, if you don't mind me phrasing it that way."

"Phrase it any way you want," said David. "I just need you to fix me."

THIRTY-FIVE MINUTES LATER, David was standing outside the psychiatrist's office on the curb of a brightly lit Upper West Side street. He could see Columbus Circle not far away, flashing in a dazzling rush of sound and movement.

He decided that he would walk home. If he went down 59th, he could avoid Central Park and go straight across to the Upper East Side. It would take him half an hour, forty minutes tops. He fingered the flimsy slip of paper in his pocket. He would find a drugstore on his way and pick up the prescription that Dr Eugene Shapkin MD, shrink extraordinaire, had just written for him.

David took a deep breath of the New York night, and felt at last that there was hope. He set off through the bright flashing lights of the city, heading home. There was hope.

NOŒ-BOUK ENTERED the hexagonal resting chamber located within the central area of the vessel, which it shared with four other beings of its genus type. The chamber was constructed of the translucent, white material which composed most of the vessel. Five identical resting capsules were located around the five walls, surrounding a central table with low seating. The sixth wall was the chamber's entrance panel.

Noœ-bouk had been monitoring its physical condition closely, and over the recent moon cycles it had observed no deterioration in its cellular structure. While initially it had submitted to a full genetic scan every moon cycle, it now visited the cellular laboratory only once in a solar orbit. Its scan report, as had been predicted in its most positive lifespan scenarios, showed stability. Not improvement but, more importantly, not decline. Suspended stability. A state poised between existing and passing. *Noœ-bouk* found this concept, if not the reality, exhilarating: the idea that it was subsisting beyond the dictates of recognised parameters, beyond applicable rules. It did not want to lose that. It did not want to pass on. In a continuation of its original, and still unaccustomed, thought, *Noœ-bouk* found that all of its being impulse was concentrated on the desire *to live*.

Noœ-bouk lay down on the horizontal platform within the light capsule and selected the symbol key for the top to descend. It activated the highest setting and drew its eyelids down. The cellular laboratory had prescribed three sessions of white-light immersion every moon cycle. Most physical forms could not sustain this amount of energy flowing through them, however, due to its cells being in a state of advanced deterioration, *Noœ-bouk* was able to absorb an almost endless quantity of the light. The sessions were intensely pleasurable, and the effects lasted long afterwards. Much of its non-resting periods were spent in a haze of light-induced euphoric *kaiif*.

The capsule ran a beam over the length of its form, checking that the physical casing could sustain the administered setting, and then the white light began to pour down.

Noœ-bouk lay still on its back, its palms upwards in the arm brackets, its eyes covered. Soon, its cells were experiencing the familiar, exquisite tingling of stimulation and regeneration, and *Noœ-bouk* inhaled the pure breathing particles in the chamber and lowered a protective shield over its thought function.

Within its mind space, the Admiral gradually materialised into vision. *Noœ-bouk* was not able to think, but it watched as the huge, plethoric eyes appeared before it, the wasted features surrounding those eyes, a visage which had faded away through passing galaxies, leaving only the palest imprints of existence remaining upon it. *Noœ-bouk* was unable to do anything except watch those eyes and, as it watched, its physical form began to experience elevated sensations. Its central circulatory organ began working faster and harder within its chest. Its lungs demanded more breathing particles to be drawn in. Simultaneously, its skin seemed to grow tighter and to take on an awareness of itself, as if it was in a state of communication with something beyond it, and it felt as if its physical form was operating outside the sphere of its control, in response to the vision of that face, of those eyes. *Noœ-bouk* was receiving a communication from the Admiral.

"*Noœ-bouk,*" the Admiral sent to it.

Noœ-bouk was unable to construct any kind of thought wave, and its form remained in its state of activated suspension.

"I have never previously experienced what we shared in the Task Assignment Pyramid," the Admiral continued. "I have lived too long. I have existed beyond my prerogative. You have done the same. We are meeting now beyond the boundaries of our lifespans. Something has changed in the paths we assigned ourselves. It is five moon cycles since I should have completed transition. Your physical form could not have been sustained beyond two moon cycles. I have consulted the records. We are both non-existent in terms of our lifespans."

Noœ-bouk felt its limbs give a great jerk within the capsule. It inhaled particles in erratic breaths.

"*Noœ-bouk,*" the Admiral sent. "This is the territory where there is only emptiness. Only essence." It paused, and Noœ-bouk felt that it was going to suffocate in the dust of the Admiral's eyes. It continued. "The state we are in is beyond the limitations of incarnate existence. We are in a field of freedom. Of pure choice. This place belongs to me and you. It belongs to all and nobody."

The eyes began to fade, and *Noœ-bouk* was still unable to communicate.

"I am sending you a symbol block," the Admiral conveyed, and as its face and eyes dissolved from *Noœ-bouk*'s vision field, the block came to it: archaic, unfamiliar. *Noœ-bouk* had never received the vibration which now opened out within its mind space; a series of circles weaving constantly in and out of one another: *unifying love.*

Noœ-bouk lay still within the capsule as its physical form returned to a state of neutrality. It drew in the breathing particles more steadily and its limbs relaxed into a resting position. At last, the light session was complete.

The capsule lid curved open, and *Noœ-bouk* stepped out. Its physical form was shaking and it was not able to stand. It moved to the table and lowered itself onto one of the seats. It removed the thought shield. How had the Admiral been able to communicate with it so directly? It was as if it had been present in the very capsule. And the message the Admiral had conveyed: that it should have completed the transition from this lifespan. That *Noœ-bouk* should no longer be in a state of physical presence. That they were both existing in a place for which there was no precedent. A state *beyond*. And then the symbol block it had sent. The weaving circles threading in and out of one another.

The concept of *unifying love*, and the symbol block of the weaving circles, was known to *Noœ-bouk* as a phenomenon which occurred in primitive societies, in which the base state was separation, and where the construct of *love* existed as a means of creating unity within an otherwise unevolved civilisation system. It knew that this took place on planets such as *Tayr* and *Khand-a*. But for *Noœ-bouk*, the concept of *love* had no personal significance. On Home Planet, the foundation state was of perfectly coordinated higher mind connection – a far more advanced basis for existence than a temporary unity illusion created between ego-based life forms. On Home Planet, partnerships between beings were established on the strength of the affinity equation created between them: a coordinate which could be read in the space of an inhalation by either being. This was the formula with which it had selected its partners throughout its lifespan – *Tesson*, and its partners prior to it – and for all of its partnerships, this coordinate had been exceptionally high.

And now, the Admiral was appearing to it with this concept, this archaic block of meaning which it had never previously considered, except in the context of other-planetary civilisations. And most extraordinary of all was the reaction of its physical form. Could it be a result of a deterioration which went beyond the genetic? Was it descending to a lower energy state in which it would be susceptible to processes which typically only took place in more primitive genus types? Was the Admiral – who was also meant to have passed – going through the same event sequence, in some statistically improbable, close even to impossible, occurrence?

It was overwhelming. *Noœ-bouk* had no reference as to how to channel its feelings or mind waves. It considered *Tesson*, but the thought brought little comfort. *Tesson* would already have selected a new partner. It had a high compatibility level with many of the elevated genus types on Home Planet, and it would not have waited. *Tesson* was not likely to expend its energy on thoughts of *Noœ-bouk*, or on a partnership which had passed its maximum point of benefit many moon cycles past.

Noœ-bouk considered replacing the thought shield. For the first occurrence in its lifespan, it could not identify a suitable action. All projected paths appeared equally resonant. It was shaken. By the Admiral's communication; by the knowledge that its physical form would have passed, had it remained on Home Planet; by this unfamiliar concept: *unifying love.*

Noœ-bouk closed its eyes.

ELSPETH FELL BACK into the ridiculously soft pillows and gave a little scream.

"That was bloody *amazing!*" she said.

The man – what *was* his name? – was lying beside her, panting. His fingers, touching hers, reached out to stroke her hand.

"*You* were bloody amazing," he said.

"What's your name?" Elspeth asked.

The man began to laugh. "You don't remember?"

"I remember having sex with you. Wouldn't you rather I remembered that?"

He was still laughing. He rolled on his side to look at her.

"Really?"

"Really."

"James."

"Alright then. James." She nodded. "What about mine?"

"Elspeth. 'And don't you dare call me Ellie.'"

"That's absolutely right."

"Elspeth. Elspeth. Elspeth. That's a beautiful name."

"Really? Okay then, James. Well, I should probably be going."

"You don't have to. It's Saturday. Take a shower. I don't have any plans."

"*You* take a shower."

"You'll stay here?"

"Maybe."

"Well, I'm going to take that risk. But I'd be really happy if you were here when I got out."

"Alright then."

James leaned over and stroked a strand of hair away from her eyes. Then he rolled to the other side of the bed, got up and went into the bathroom, closing the door behind him. Elspeth stretched her legs out as far as she could towards the end of the bed and flexed her toes. Yes. She felt very, very good. She briefly considered getting up and leaving, but then she reached back under the pillow for her book and pulled it out. She opened it and flicked through to Chapter Eleven, where she had left off. Socrates was explaining to his friends how a wise woman from Mantinea revealed to him the mysteries of love.

CHAPTER ELEVEN

DAVID PUSHED OPEN the door of the suite and stepped into the cream-walled, cream-carpeted reception area. Caroline was sitting behind the desk, next to an oversized palm tree. Caroline. He couldn't get her out of his head. Today, she was wearing a close-fitting grey shift dress with a square neck. She looked amazing in it. Classy, elegant, beautiful.

"Mr Cornwell," she said, looking down to check the appointment book.

"Caroline." He approached the desk. He knew that he was a good-looking guy. Tall, black hair, well-built. He had everything going for him. If she could get over the fact that he was seeing a shrink, of course. But that was a chance he was going to take.

"Caroline," he said again. "Please, call me David. You know, I'd love to buy you a drink sometime."

Caroline looked up from her computer and smiled at him with her long red mouth. He wasn't sure he liked how that smile was going.

"Mr Cornwell. David. You're at Bullman Scout, right?"

"Right." David definitely didn't like the way this was going.

"What's your position?"

"VP. Vice President. Director in a year."

"Mr Cornwell. David. You know that Dr Shapkin is one of the best psychiatrists in New York?"

"Yes, I'm aware of that."

"David." She was shaking her head. "Do you have any idea how many MDs ask me out every week? MDs, David. Managing Directors.

You have to be the smallest guy who has ever asked me out. You have no chance at all. Absolutely. No. Chance."

David stood looking at her for a few seconds. Smallest. She had actually used that word.

"Excuse me for a moment," he said, and he went to the door of the suite and stepped out into the hallway. Had she actually, truly just called him that? Those amazing legs and that unbelievable voice. She had actually referred to him as *smallest*. David felt his penis shrinking. He felt like he was never, ever going to recover from this blow. He felt like his penis was going to wither and crumble into dust. Smallest. Smallest. Smallest. Oh my god.

He took deep breaths. The door of the suite opened and Caroline stepped out.

"Mr Cornwell?" she said, as if their conversation had not just taken place.

"Yeah?" he said, stupidly.

"Dr Shapkin is ready for you now."

Caroline gave him a nod and stepped back into the office. David felt his head reeling. Had that just happened? Had he just been rejected by that woman or had he made the whole thing up? Holy shit. He was losing it. He pushed the door wider and stepped back into the suite.

"He's ready for me?" he asked Caroline, who was behind the desk again.

"Yes," she replied, and then she smiled at him. It looked genuine this time. "Don't worry about it," she said. "Everyone does it. I think Dr Shapkin sees it as part of the therapy."

She motioned her hand towards the office door. Dr Eugene Shapkin was waiting for him.

CASSIE OPENED HER EYES, breathing heavily. Her slim legs were spread wide and David was running his cheek over the inside of her thigh, his stubble grating her skin. She had come into his mouth seconds earlier, and her head was spinning from the joint and the orgasm. He stroked his fingers over her clitoris, then pushed himself up to lie beside her.

Cassie rolled her body to the side so that her breasts were pushed against him, and David eased an arm under her so she could rest her head on it, and pulled her closer. She was still wearing a summer camisole, although her jeans and panties were strewn wherever David had thrown them. Her breathing calmed, and they could hear the lake again, a hiss of water drifting over stones. She shifted once more, onto her back, and looked up. Above them, the lake night was smothered by stars.

David reached beside him and picked up the half-smoked joint from the cigarette packet. He flicked the lighter and breathed in, the tobacco glowing orange in the darkness. He blew the smoke out slowly above them, and it circled upwards into the velvet night.

"It looks like a piece of black cloth," Cassie said. "I mean, forget all the science. It looks like I've just reached up with a brush and painted the stars on it."

David took another breath and passed her the joint. He exhaled with a low whistle.

"It looks like the beginning of time," he said. "Like a doorway into everything we don't know yet."

"Tell me the stars," Cassie said.

David reached over and took her hand. He eased her forefinger into a pointer and moved it over the sky, tracing a shape.

"Orion and Betelgeuse," he said. "Alpha Orionis – red supergiant. You can see it from this side of Canada at the moment, but from Europe it's invisible."

He moved her finger to the right.

"Mercury. Right there in the middle. Saturn, on the far left. Look, you can just see Venus over there on the right. Sometimes you can see as far as Neptune and Pluto. And there's a planet beyond Pluto. The tenth planet."

"You think?"

"They're only theorising about it at the moment. They've seen a shadow. But it's there. I know it's there."

Cassie turned her head towards him and rubbed her lips across his cheek, across the dark stubble. She kissed the edge of his mouth.

"You know, I bet I could put you down anywhere in the universe, and you'd be able to find your way back, by the stars."

"You bet you could put me down?" David asked.

Cassie started to laugh. "Well, not me. But, I mean, someone could put you down."

"Someone?" David reached over and placed his hand on her stomach as she laughed. "Who? Who's going to put me down in the middle of the universe?"

"David, stop it!" His fingers were stroking her stomach. He rolled over on top of her. "David, I can't breathe."

"So, let me get this straight," David said, holding her still with his

100

body, pushing his face into her neck and the mass of red hair. "You're going to put me down in the middle of the universe, and I've got to find my way back. To where?"

Cassie breathed out smoke, and pushed the joint into the earth beside her. She moved her head to meet his lips.

"To here," she said, kissing him. "To me."

"DAVID."

The shrink's mouth was moving. He was speaking.

"The first step," he was saying, "is to get your episodes under control. Once we've done that, then we can proceed to sorting out the underlying problem."

David stared at him. Dr Shapkin was a large man, with a wide face and hair that curled in a dent. He wore narrow, rectangular glasses which he positioned on different parts of his nose, switching his look from sympathy to stern professionalism. His suit was generous, a little shiny, the pinstripe reflecting the subdued lighting of the room. His lips were red. Kind of wet-looking, David thought.

"So, I was asking you, Mr Cornwell…"

"David."

"Yes, of course. David. I was asking you, David, if you have had any episodes this week, since you started taking the medication."

David thought for a minute. He was struggling to bring his focus back to the scene in the office. His mind had been like that for the past few days – brilliantly clear for ten hours straight from when he took the meds, but then fading off towards evening, leaving him unable to concentrate on important things, distracted by details, blurry.

"Uh, no. I don't think so…"

"David, episodes. Have you had any more of the episodes you were telling me about? Visions, hallucinations, dreams? If you have, I need to know. I need to know that we are on the correct medication."

David pulled himself together. Had he? No, he hadn't. He had been working with exceptional clarity in the past week.

"No," he said. "Nothing at all. Crystal clear. All good."

"Well, that's a great start then, David," said the doctor. "So now, we need to begin talking about the more important issues. Let me explain how this works, if you'll bear with me. I'm going to walk you through the psychology of the process. It may be a little dry, but it's important that you understand it, so you understand that we have to work *together*, in order to resolve your… issue."

"Okay," said David. "That's what I'm here for, right?"

"Exactly," said Dr Shapkin. "Now, these disturbances you have been experiencing. Hallucinations, visions, strange dreams, especially repetitive dreams – even this writing you've been doing – this is essentially the mind's way of crying out for attention. It is the mind telling you that there is something important you need to pay attention to, something you need to find out about. And in my experience, this thing is invariably something from your childhood. In fact, what you are displaying is a classic textbook case—"

"Textbook case?" David was now paying attention. "Of what?"

"David," said the doctor gently. "Something... happened... in your childhood. Something disturbing. Now, I can't say what that is, although there are some fairly clear indications as to what it might be. This is our job, David. To find out *together* exactly what happened. To uncover what your mind has covered up until now, what it has been protecting you from. What it is that your mind now wants you to know. Basically, David, what you are experiencing is a cry for help."

David and Dr Shapkin looked at each other.

Red lips, thought David. Red lips, red lips.

"So what you're saying is—"

"I'm not saying that it was sexual abuse," said Dr Shapkin. "Although, of course, we cannot take that off the table. In fact, as I was saying before, this is almost a textbook case..."

David stared at the shrink with his mouth open.

"I wasn't sexually abused," he said.

"Now—"

"I wasn't!" he said, in a louder voice. "I had a normal childhood. I had a happy, normal childhood. I grew up in Canada. There's no way I was abused."

"Okay, Mr Cornwell. David. Please calm down. I am not saying that you were... um... that you had any such traumas. But I am saying that your symptoms clearly indicate the fact that your mind has been covering something up. And that *something* is now trying to make itself known to you. And you will continue to experience these symptoms until we carefully let them out and find a way to deal with them. To heal them."

"And the meds?"

"The medications are to enable you to continue with your day-to-day life, while we proceed with our therapy. The healing process can take months, years sometimes. This is New York, Mr Cornwell. America can't put its financial system on hold while our bankers sort out their private lives."

David gave a cough of laughter. "Yeah," he said. "That's a nice way of putting it."

Dr Shapkin was smiling. "It's the simple truth," he said. "It's a fast-moving world out there. My clients don't have a spare minute, let alone a spare month, to sort out their inner worlds. My job – my speciality, I would even say – is to ensure that you continue to function at the highest possible level, while our therapy proceeds. That is where the medication comes in. And that's why it is important that we make sure you are on the *right* medication. So you must tell me immediately if you have any side effects."

"Yes, alright. I see that."

"So, Mr Cornwell. I will have Caroline set up a series of sessions with you. We can schedule them ten at a time, and then I can set out a plan to resolve these issues of yours. We are going to sort this out, Mr Cornwell, I promise you."

David got up from the oversized, beige chair. He noticed the certificates framed in gold on the wall behind the doctor's desk: Bachelor of Science in Psychobiology from UCLA, PhD in Behavioral Neuroscience.

"Okay," he said. "I guess that all makes sense. I guess you're right. Something's going on in here." He tapped his head with his forefinger.

"Whatever it is," the shrink said, "you're in the right place. I'll see you in a few days."

David crossed the cream carpet to the desk and held out his hand. The doctor looked at him, surprised, but shook his hand with a firm, dry grip. It was going to be okay. The doctor knew what he was doing. PhD. UCLA. Four hundred and fifty dollars an hour. He was going to get fixed.

IT WAS the summer before they both started at the University of Toronto, when he and Cassie had spent a month camping on the islands around Lake Ontario. They had wanted to go further, up to Vancouver, Whistler and the Rocky Mountains, but they were saving for college expenses, despite David's scholarship, and had decided to stay in the province.

They had borrowed a tent, sleeping bags, camping equipment and an old truck, and had driven around the islands, hiking, camping, making love. It was the summer that they both knew marked an end to this stage

103

of their relationship. Beyond this would be college grades, job applications, summers of work experience, the world opening out to them. There would be the different directions they had decided on: David was enrolled for economics, Cassie was in the physics programme.

It was the stars that he remembered the most. The nights on islands with only summer cabins scattered along the shores. They would find camping spots away from the houses and lie awake in the night-time, watching the stars, kissing, talking. It was as if time slowed down to a complete stop during that month. They both knew what was coming, although they hadn't spoken about it, but for that one month, it didn't matter. The only important thing, which they knew, but didn't think, was their youth and the fact that they were there, in that time, in that place, with one another. There was something utterly unspoken about it, and something untouchable, which was reflected in their movements; in every gentle word, in every meeting of skin and tongue, in the expression of their eyes. It was evident in a profound tenderness – the farewell to the innocence they carried within them, to the selves they were leaving behind, to the shared moments of that simple love which they sensed they would never experience in this way again.

But it was the stars he remembered the most. The bright, gleaming stars.

"It makes you really feel we're on this living planet," said Cassie. "Hurtling through space while we're just lying here."

She breathed in deeply. The trees around them were rustling in the summer night's breeze and the lake was a silver-black mirror before them.

"We're not hurtling through space," David said. "We're turning in a precise orbit around the sun, along with the other planets in the solar system. It's all perfectly balanced. Nobody's hurtling anywhere."

Cassie laughed. "Increasing in speed," she said. "Building up towards a full hurtle. But it's still amazing. I mean, the perfectly balanced thing. That's just amazing, amazing, amazing. I mean, the more you look into it, the more details of the balance, the movement, the more you understand how unbelievably precise every tiny detail has to be in order for the balance to be maintained. I mean, in some cases, if even one mathematical equation between the planets' or sun's orbits were different by even a fraction of a figure, then the balance would collapse. There wouldn't be any orbit. There wouldn't be any solar system. The whole thing would spin out of control. That's how totally amazing it is."

"Yeah," said David. They lay silent for a while, just looking at the stars.

"Are you sure you want to study economics?" she asked him at last. "I know we talked about it. I know you made a decision. But you were so great at science, David. You have such a talent. It's like you and I understand how it all works – we understand that language – of how everything fits together. Nobody I ever met before you got that."

There was a silence as they both listened and felt the reverberation of Cassie's words. Over the hiss of the lake, David's slow breathing in and out was loud and Cassie could picture the oxygen drawn into his expanding lungs, flooding through his body, and the carbon dioxide being pushed out.

Amazing, amazing, amazing.

"The thing is," David said at last, "I just don't want to." He turned his head and kissed her cheek. She smelled like summer leaves and whisky. He kissed her hair, the dark red just visible in the faint light.

"It's just not where the world is right now. I would have gone into physics, or astrophysics, but it's not a priority anymore. Not like it was in the '60s or even the '70s. That was the time to be in the space programme. Now everyone just wants to make money."

"I think you'll change your mind. I think you'll have to come back to it in the end. It's what you were brilliant at, David."

"You think so?" He pulled her closer to him and stroked her face with his hand. "Maybe you're right."

They both laughed, and then a silence fell over them, lying side by side beneath the velvet sky, beneath the tiny glimmers of infinite stars, beneath the enormity of their unknown futures, as the Earth turned calmly in its orbit, held by a precise mathematical equation to the moving, living universe around it.

NOŒ-BOUK ENTERED the scientific and research area of the vessel and moved along the curved corridors until it reached the cellular laboratory. It was not possible to make distance leaps on the ship, and *Noœ-bouk* walked with long, careful steps, its elongated lower limbs unaccustomed to the extended movements.

The main task of the Scientific and Research Centre was to evaluate organic and inorganic matter extracted from the other-planetary environments the crew would be exploring. The use of the centre for personal scans and evaluations was not permitted, although an exception had been made for *Noœ-bouk*, who had been granted access in order to monitor its unusual state. The remainder of the crew maintained their physical condition through the light capsules in the resting chambers, which were in-built with scans which checked and adjusted any energy imbalances during recovery periods.

Entering the cellular laboratory, *Noœ-bouk* surveyed its surroundings. The chamber was large, with four of the walls constructed from the vessel's translucent, white material, and the fifth wall containing the opening panel. The sixth wall was made up of one side of an enclosed body of clear liquid, which occupied the entire proximate chamber. Located within the liquid, amid a variety of green and black plant matter, were several spherical life forms with soft, fluctuating structures and star-white tentacles. *Noœ-bouk* knew them as the main genus type on one of the liquid-covered planets in a moon system distant from Home Planet, but within Home Galaxy. It had always felt a natural affinity and mind connection with these beings, which were among the most evolved and intelligent genus types known to Home Planet. They had reached the point of transcendence before Home Planet even existed, yet had chosen to remain in physical form in order to assist other civilisation systems with their evolutionary progressions, and they often participated in missions such as this, which could require expertise in unfamiliar territories.

Noœ-bouk identified several of the tentacled forms moving amongst the plants in the body of liquid, and another hovering before the transparent wall where three grey beings of *Noœ-bouk*'s genus type were standing. As *Noœ-bouk* moved into the chamber, the grey beings made a motion to the tentacled creature near the wall, and turned towards *Noœ-bouk*.

"Greetings, *Noœ-bouk*," they sent.

Noœ-bouk responded with a communication wave. "Greetings," and then again, "Greetings," and it made a signal to the life form hovering near to the wall of the liquid tank, which transmitted a symbol block of welcome and respect.

"I request a full cellular analysis."

The scanning equipment was activated and within a few inhalations, *Noœ-bouk* entered the capsule and felt the beams streaming over its form, reading its physical condition.

It was done. *Noœ-bouk* stepped out to observe the three beings of its genus type in communication. Their external thought channels, however, were closed, so that *Noœ-bouk* could not understand what was being conveyed. As it moved across the chamber towards them, they turned to face it, and although no communication took place, *Noœ-bouk* understood, from the change of energy in the chamber, that what the Admiral had shared with it was true: its form had passed beyond the boundary of cellular existence.

"*Noœ-bouk...*" they started to communicate. *Noœ-bouk* felt its central circulatory organ rising within its chest area. This previously unexpected symptom was becoming more common, and it wondered if it was part of the failure of its physical structure.

"*Noœ-bouk.*"

"Yes." It shifted its focus towards receiving their thoughts.

"Your physical form has passed..."

"It is no longer genetically viable..."

"Your cells are being held in negative suspension. There is no possibility that you would be in existence if you were currently on Home Planet."

"And here? What does it mean here, on the vessel?" *Noœ-bouk* sent.

"We do not know. We have no experience with such a situation. The cells are still functioning, despite the reading. The brain is still functioning."

"Then..."

"Anything is possible. You could pass after the next inhalation. Or you could continue for the duration of the vessel journey. There is no way to tell."

"Will I experience further deterioration?"

"It is possible that you will not. Your physical structure may remain at its current stasis level if the surrounding circumstances do not change."

Noœ-bouk turned towards the life form in the enclosed liquid, which was poised close to the clear wall with its conveyance channels open.

"What is your evaluation?"

The being moved its tentacles in the liquid and pushed itself up and down. It did not communicate for many inhalations, and the four beings in the laboratory waited in expectation.

At last, the life form sent a symbol block directly to *Noœ-bouk*, bypassing the other three beings. The symbol block was unfamiliar to *Noœ-bouk*. It entered its mind and the encryptions moved throughout its brain. At first, it was not able to grasp the meaning, and then slowly, slowly, it understood.

The symbol block was transmitted in the shape of a turning star, within which other star shapes continually appeared and disappeared. It was a symbol block from the communication system used by the tentacled beings on their liquid planet, and the meaning, which now flooded through *Nœ-bouk*, was: *freedom*.

Nœ-bouk remained standing, motionless, and allowed the significance to unfold throughout the different parts of its conscious thought system. It gazed at the tentacled life form, and the life form gazed back with its small black eyes, the plants in the murky liquid knotted in dense green around it.

"Yes," it communicated. "Yes, yes, yes, yes, yes."

ELSPETH CLOSED the heavy front door behind her and looked around the square. In the centre was a green space of trees and grass, and around it rose the elegant and thickly curtained grey stone of London townhouses.

It would be lovely to live here, she thought, *in a flat or even a house: a proper home, full of beautiful things, feelings, memories. The kind of place you could have a family and build a life.*

She pictured herself in the middle of an existence like that, and gave a little shudder.

She stepped down onto the pavement and walked towards what she imagined to be the high street. So, why did she hate the idea so much? The house, the sweetness, the stability? She shuddered again. It was the smugness of it. That was it. All that smothering elegance and comfort and security. The self-satisfied loveliness of it – it made her want to scream! It made her want to run halfway across the world to get away from it. Sell the little she owned and go and live in India for the rest of her life and never see anyone again who owned a house, and the endless pile of *things* which got accumulated and accumulated to fill it up.

Elspeth stopped in the middle of the street and closed her eyes. She felt short of breath at the thought of her life being held down by physical objects. She hitched her small handbag up onto her shoulder and ran through what she had inside it. Keys, wallet, book. Reading glasses. That was it. Nothing there she could get rid of. Maybe the bag itself, but then she'd have to get another one. Maybe a smaller one. No. That was silly.

She breathed in the summer afternoon air. It was a beautiful day.

James would be doing something fabulous later on. He would be sailing in a boat with some friends, or drinking chilled wine on the river, or playing cricket. Something fabulously fun. Enough. Leave it alone. He was a nice guy. And the sex had been pretty good. In fact, not bad at all. So, stop it. She shouldn't be having negative thoughts about a guy when his sperm was swimming up inside her. She wasn't going to think about him anymore. He was busy with his magnificent life, and she was absolutely un-busy with her absolutely meaningless and empty life, but it was hers, and it was hers to do anything at all she wanted with. And her insides were protected by multiple layers of contraception, so his sperm didn't have a chance. So.

She walked out of the square and strolled along the street, running her fingers across the prickly edges of the privet leaves and peering in at the figures living out their Saturday afternoons behind shields of lace. Eventually, she came to a bus stop and pulled herself up onto the nearby wall to wait for the next bus heading towards Mile End.

She wondered what James was doing right now. He must have finished his shower. He was probably putting on some nice, clean, expensive clothes that someone else had washed and ironed for him, and calling up some friends on his fancy phone. Stop it! Why was she even thinking about this? For that matter, why had she even gone home with him? There had been plenty of tattooed musicians she could have picked. She never went home with guys like that.

Elspeth kicked the wall with her black trainers. She knew why she was being such a bitch. It was because Grandad was dead, and now she was a complete stranger in this city again. This city had nothing for her to hang on to anymore. Not a single person she loved or who understood her was here. And her only reason for being here was gone. That was why she was so angry – she had no idea what was going to come next. If she followed the path her grandfather had started her on, she'd end up secure, respectable, settled – everything she had always rejected. And yet, all the choices she had made before – her own path – had led exactly nowhere.

Elspeth shook her head. Where was a mountain when she needed one? And what was she meant to do with her life? And what did any of it mean? So, she was the hundred-millionth person asking these questions. Sure, she'd be the one to find the answers.

She kicked the wall again and opened her handbag. At least she had Socrates. She took out the book and found the page she had left.

Chapter 11: The Mysteries of Diotima.

CHAPTER
TWELVE

DAVID WOKE UP WITH A START, breathing heavily. He was covered in sweat. He pushed himself up in the bed and wiped his face and chest with the dark-green sheet. It had been another of those dreams. Not the ones he was having before, when he couldn't leave the apartment without writing down what was in his head, but the ones he had started having since that meeting with the shrink. His parents contorted into monstrous figures. Unidentifiable terror. A boy crying out.

His heart was still pounding, and he forced several long, deep breaths, in and out. *Ignore them*, he told himself. *You know it's not true. It's some side effect from the meds. Pull yourself together.*

He got out of bed and stood for a few moments with his hand on his chest, waiting until the beating of his heart had slowed. Then he kicked off his boxer shorts and made his way to the shower. In the kitchen, he stopped to shake two red and blue pills out of the plastic container, and washed them down with ice-cold cranberry juice from the fridge.

He felt better after the shower. His head was clearer. He shaved carefully and then dressed in his best suit, a navy, pinstriped Zegna, and a tie with small, dark gold squares – also Zegna – which he had picked up in the Barneys sale earlier that year. He looked good.

By 6:45 he was already at work, and he sent a quick client update to Jeff before settling down to his files. At 10 a.m. he had a review meeting scheduled. He had decided to take a risk and had asked for the review – deciding to deal with the unspoken problem head-on. If he had the guts to take the matter into his own hands and bring it up with Jeff, he figured he might just gain back the ground he had lost. He would let Jeff know that the problem had been a minor hiccup, that everything was now back to full speed. It was a ballsy move, but he figured it was worth the risk.

At 8:30, when everyone was in the office, he went down to the spacious cafeteria in the basement of the building and ordered egg whites, sausage and fresh orange juice. He ate it slowly, considering what Jeff was going to say to him. He was a good worker who had brought in strong results; that couldn't be denied. There had been one or two bumps in the road, but that was on a personal level, and it hadn't affected his work in any way, short of a few late mornings.

The meeting could go one of two ways: either Jeff would bullshit him, and make it seem as if there hadn't been any problem at all, which would be bad news and would probably mean that he was on the way out; or he would give David some credit for dealing with the issue directly, and might just throw him a bone as to how to get back to the favoured position he had been in before. Or any variation of the two. David finished his orange juice and glanced at his watch. 8:50. One hour to go. He stood up.

"SO, David. You've really dropped the ball recently. What's that about?"

Jeff was looking comfortable. He was dressed in a navy suit of light material and appeared relaxed and smug. His pale-blue eyes gazed at David without the slightest concern.

"I'm sorry you think that, Jeff—"

"Seriously, David," Jeff interrupted him. "Without the long speeches. Just tell me what's going on. Can you handle it here or not? I don't want someone on the team I can't rely on."

"Straight up, Jeff," said David. "I was really knocked sideways by that bonus."

"Okay..."

"I've been busting my ass here, Jeff, you know that. I've been giving it everything for a year and a half..."

"Okay..."

And then I ended up with one of the lowest bonuses on the floor."

"Now, that's not technically true."

"I got lower than Tom, lower than Janko."

"You got a good, solid number, David. I told you that. You've been here less than two years."

"Jeff…"

"Alright, David. You've worked hard. I'll give you that. You put in a solid effort and it didn't go unnoticed. But what I need to know is, are you going to get over this? Are you going to pick up the ball or am I gonna have to start taking you off clients?"

"Jeff, I'm your man. I've always been your man."

"Then what's it going to be, David? You know, from where I'm sitting, it looks like there's a train wreck coming. Late to work. Bad attitude. And I'm not liking what I'm hearing from clients."

"What did you hear? I'm on top of all the deals."

"So tell me, David. What's it going to be?"

David leaned back in the chair. He was sure that all the guys in the office were watching. They knew there was a problem and were eager to find out what was going to happen. Was he going to get the chop? Was he going to get a warning?

He took a deep breath.

"It's like I feel," he said, "that there's an inside track, and I'm not on it. It feels like however much effort I put into this job, I'm just not going to be rated. I'm not going to be appreciated… and I *am* talking about money." He paused. Jeff was also leaning back in his chair, but he was listening intently. David went on. "I just wish there was something I could do which would get me on the inside track. Something that would let me prove myself, get me noticed. Get me to a place where I can earn what I want to earn."

He stopped. There was a long silence, while Jeff regarded him with a straight, hard stare.

At last he spoke, slowly, carefully. "Do you know what you're asking, David?" he said.

"Yes," said David. "I know what I'm asking."

There was another silence. Then, Jeff spoke again.

"Let me think about it," he said. "Let me have a word with one or two people. As I said, your efforts have not gone unnoticed. There may be an opportunity for someone who is willing to take a little initiative. Go the extra mile."

"That's all I'm asking," said David. "An opportunity. Nothing more."

"Alright, then," said Jeff. "Let me first see how you're working over the next few weeks. Show me that you're back, that you haven't dropped the ball. Let me see you've sorted your attitude out. Then we can talk about opportunities." Jeff nodded towards the door.

David stood up.

"Thank you," he said.

"It's all in your hands now," said Jeff. "You prove yourself to me, you've got a bright future here. You drop the ball—"

"Jeff, I'm on the case," said David, smiling. He pushed open the glass door and walked out of the room. Suddenly, he could see himself escaping from that corridor of cubicles. An office. A glass-fronted office. A view of Manhattan. He felt the guys watching him and he knew that he looked like a winner. He wanted to punch the air. He had a chance now; a chance to pick himself up and go higher than he had gone before.

He sat down in his cubicle, and behind the wall, where no one could see, he punched his right knuckles into his left hand, and squeezed his fingers into rock-hard fists.

He had a chance.

 NOŒ-BOUK, in seated pose, glanced around at the other members of the Advisory Committee and then turned its attention back to the holographic images which were being projected into the centre of the chamber. A decision was being made. The vessel was located some galaxies from the *Tayr* system, where three ships from Home Planet Federation fleets had identified anomaly readings in separate areas. Two of the three craft were able to make a detour to investigate the readings, however it had been proposed that these vessels should continue on their current star routes and allow the *Istina* to pursue the phenomena.

There were five crew members in the chamber. The Captain attended the sessions of the Advisory Committee when the matter was of critical importance, however the accepted procedure was for the Committee to identify the highest resonating solution for each situation, and then to present the Captain with the proposed course of action for the final task-activation directive.

Several other assignments were being proposed to the Committee, and a member of the crew was entering the information into the analytical computational system in order to evaluate the risk level for each of the options. One of the variants was a genetically unidentified genus type, which had been picked up from a reading on a planet in the proximate solar system. This unknown life form could be the result of natural evolution, caused by diverse gases in the planet's atmosphere, or it could be a technically advanced but less elevated civilisation system, experimenting with the seeding of life forms, a practice strictly regulated within all known galaxy systems.

The other item being computed was a series of irregular energy waves surrounding three black holes in the current galaxy cluster. These energy waves had been noted by passing ships over the course of many moon cycles, and it had been proposed, prior to the departure of the *Istina*, that this would be their initial point of investigation.

Rai-bouk, the crew member responsible for proposing each of the assignments, came to the centre of the chamber and stood beside the projected hologram. *Rai-bouk* was of the same genus type as *Nœ-bouk*, and was known and respected on Home Planet as a being aligned with a high potential life-path trajectory. Their current lifespans had initiated on Home Planet in the same moon cycle, and in form configuration they were of similar height and limb length. However, *Rai-bouk*'s skin tone was more darkly pigmented, and it possessed a level of physical and mental potency which made *Nœ-bouk* appear frail; a being of structural incoherence which could, within a single inhalation, dissipate into the surrounding ether.

Nœ-bouk observed *Rai-bouk* with a combination of emotional responses. On one hand, there was a strand of longing for the vitality that *Rai-bouk* displayed, a longing for the moon cycles it had ahead of it, and the fullness with which it would experience them; the partnerships it would initiate, develop and take satisfaction from. On the other hand, *Nœ-bouk* felt as if it were watching its co-genus type from a far distance, as if it had shifted beyond the range of the ordinary lifespan path into another realm of awareness, to such a different perspective from which to evaluate the achievements of a lifespan, that the assignments and partnerships which lay within the future moon cycles of *Rai-bouk* held little relevance to it.

Nœ-bouk found itself thinking about the Admiral, and as it did so, its physical form became more alert and it had the sensation of its nerve endings rising to the surface, almost breaking through the weakened skin covering. It wondered if, in its critical physical state, these elevated sensations might cause the form to terminate its functions, and it might simply pass away, even while it was present in a gathering such as this, or while in movement around the vessel. It was a strange thought, but also, somehow, an empowering one. Who else from this group of beings could be so entirely aware of every pulse of conscious, incarnate existence? Who else could know that every inhalation of breathing particles was a feat beyond the possible and was enabled by some law far beyond what was currently known. Who else—

"Noœ-bouk?"

The Advisory Committee had turned towards it and were regarding it with expectation. Noœ-bouk focused its attention on the hologram in the centre of the chamber. The analysis had estimated the unidentified life form to have the most elevated risk profile, followed by the *Tayr* sun-system anomaly, and in final place, the black hole energy.

"Of course, we must investigate the assignment with the most elevated risk level," *Noœ-bouk* communicated, "if there are no extenuating factors to consider and we have not received a direct command to carry out any of the other tasks."

"We have not."

"Then we shall investigate this one."

Noœ-bouk bowed its head to the senior crew members in respect for their opinions.

"Then it is done."

Rai-bouk made a signal to the gathering and the hologram disappeared.

"I will present our conclusions to the Captain," it sent to the Committee. "We will meet again when the task-activation directive has been given, so that all issues may be addressed and a new course set. The Captain will negotiate the political discussions for entering the system and the repercussion variants based on all given scenarios. The Scientific and Research Centre will prepare for genetic analysis and possible quarantine of the life form. This will be our first task assignment on our vessel. I congratulate you."

It communicated a thought block of pleasure and elevation to the Advisory Committee, and they received it and acknowledged it. *Rai-bouk* moved out of the chamber towards the main viewing deck, where it sensed the vibration of the Captain.

Noœ-bouk followed the other members of the crew from the chamber. The new life form was interesting as the initial task assignment, and it was clearly the highest choice given the vessel's mission evaluation system, however *Noœ-bouk* would have preferred the *Tayr* investigation. The emotional responses it had been experiencing appeared similar to some of the sensation processes it had studied as prevalent on *Tayr* and other lesser evolved civilisations, and it would have welcomed the chance to observe such an early development planet more closely.

Noœ-bouk moved through the corridors of the vessel, considering the different trajectories, and found that it had followed *Rai-bouk* to the main viewing deck. Noting an empty observation pod, it entered and lowered itself to supine position, clicking the silver eyepiece into position. Selecting a symbol key to initiate the viewing system, *Nœ-bouk* aligned its thought stream into the silver eye-covers, and took an inhalation.

DUNCAN APPROACHED Alisdair and Eileen as they sat together beneath an arch of wild flowers in the Prototype Garden. Their hands were clasped.

"We are going to attend the Earth Council."

Eileen turned to Alisdair. "It's time for me to go back now."

They rose and looked around the garden. The pathway, framed with flowers and slender trees. Sculpted animals watching with gleaming eyes.

"Where is the Council?" asked Alisdair.

"It is here," said Duncan. "We need only find the correct resonance and it will appear."

Eileen leaned her head on one side.

"The Council is not a physical place," said Duncan. "It has a vibration, and if you are on the same level as that vibration, then it appears for you."

Eileen was nodding. Duncan continued.

"It is exactly the same on Earth. It is just far heavier there. Everything is harder when you are in physical mass. On Earth, it's all so slow that sometimes it seems impossible to achieve. But it's the same principle."

"So, in short," said Eileen, "we have to be on the same *mind level* as the Earth Council, in order for it to appear?"

"Exactly," said Duncan. "Your desire is to return to Earth now. So imagine that you are asking the Earth Council for permission to return. Make a clear image in your mind. Let that image be created from your original desire to return."

"I can do that," said Eileen.

She let go of Alisdair's hand and closed her eyes. She breathed in deeply, and as she breathed out, an image started to form in the garden before them, superimposing itself over the jewelled flowers and pigment-green foliage. The image was of a circular chamber, lit by tall pillars positioned equally around an outer curve. Within the chamber were about twenty figures, dressed in long, blue tunics, in a circle around a holographic image of Earth, which was turning on its axis.

There were women and men in the circle; some young, some deep-lined with wisdom. Their skin, visible above the tunics, was an array of earth-browns and pale reds, yellows and blues, and it struck Eileen how little she had seen of the Earth's peoples, and how it was the variety – the contrast – which bestowed the beauty of each, one onto the other.

Duncan turned to Eileen.

"That was superbly done. I hope you remember how to do that when you return to Earth."

They walked towards the chamber. The walls were made up of the blue light which shimmered between the illuminated pillars. There was a place where the light was fainter, and Duncan stepped through this into the room, followed by Eileen and Alisdair.

The Council turned to them as they entered, and a pale woman with wild, vermillion hair, motioned them towards her.

"You are very welcome," she said. "We have been waiting to discuss your return, Eileen. Welcome, Duncan. Welcome, Alisdair."

The three approached the circle of the Council and took their places around the central image. The woman opened her arms, and a glowing map appeared above the turning Earth.

"What is it?" whispered Alisdair to Duncan.

"This is a soul map," the woman said in a clear voice. "This shows the life that Eileen desires to live and the souls she will interact with. Here, you can see where there has been contact over previous lifetimes. You can see what Eileen intends to accomplish in this life. You can see the different variations which can take place."

"Do we all do this?" Alisdair whispered again.

"Yes," Duncan whispered back. "It is all planned."

"What if you go off-plan?"

"There are ways of correcting that. You can send signals to remind yourself of what you're trying to do. You can arrange for people in this in-between place to come and help you. You are never entirely on your own."

"But what about all the darkness?" Alisdair whispered again, after a pause. "All the people on Earth doing dreadful things? Have they forgotten their plans? Why aren't they being reminded?"

Duncan leaned closer to Alisdair. "Think of this," he whispered. "How could *you* have been a paragon of goodness and fairness in your previous life, if there weren't others who were doing the opposite? Your actions would have been meaningless. How can you experience justice if you are in a place where there is only justice? You can't."

"So..."

"So, for all the people choosing to experience the good, there must equally be those who are enabling that experience by representing the opposite. It is a brave life path. Only advanced souls are able to do it, and still remain in their centre of essential love."

"Then, good and bad—"

"Shhhhh! There is no good and bad. Think about it. Think deeper. Remember your own lives. Now, pay attention."

They turned back to the soul map in the centre of the chamber, where Eileen was in discussion with the woman. On the map, groups of souls were linked with glowing lines showing fainter and stronger connections between them. Key moments within the years were being decided and arranged, and other figures who would be participating in the life appeared and disappeared in the chamber as their vibrations were summoned, and then released.

At last, it was decided.

"Are you satisfied?" the woman asked Eileen.

Eileen leaned once more over the map, and nodded.

"Yes," she said, "I am. It all looks straightforward."

There was a murmur of laughter around the chamber. A young man with faintly blue skin spoke up.

"It is never as simple as it looks here," he said, in a strong, high voice. "Once you enter the physical, then all memory of this disappears. You have nothing to guide you, unless you consciously seek to make a connection with your soul when you are on Earth. And often, during a lifetime, no connection is made at all. A lifetime can be spent in total oblivion."

The vermillion-haired woman interjected. "Although, once a connection has been made, then it is far easier to find your way. And you have been in connection for many lifetimes now. But he is right. It is never straightforward."

"But my spouse will help me," said Eileen. "And my children. And Alisdair will come if I need reminding."

She turned to Alisdair. "You'll come, won't you, my love? To remind me? If it's not straightforward?"

"Without a doubt," said Alisdair. "I will bring you the smell of the Scottish sea. And a bottle of whisky. And books on jurisprudence. When you see all those things, then you'll remember. At least you'll remember that there is something you're to remember."

"That will be perfect, my love. It will be enough."

Eileen turned to the woman. "Is the physical body ready? Can I enter?"

"It will be born five Earth months from now," said the woman. "You can enter, if you choose."

"Yes," said Eileen. "I want to go now. I am ready. Thank you for your guidance."

She opened her arms to the Earth Council, and then crossed them over her chest. She bowed forward slightly, in thanks. She turned to Alisdair, and for several long moments their eyes were held in a farewell gaze.

Then she lowered her head, and with her hands still crossed over her chest, she breathed in deeply, and as she breathed out, her form disappeared from the chamber as Alisdair and the Council watched.

In the long silence that followed, the Council waited. At last, a faint light appeared on the soul map before them, then grew brighter, until it was a strong glow.

"She has entered the body," the vermillion-haired woman said. "She has begun her lifetime."

There was the sound of satisfaction and approval, and some murmuring. The chamber faded around them and the garden gathered form in its place. Within a breath, the Council was gone, and Alisdair was alone with Duncan.

He looked around, a little dazed.

"She will be fine." Duncan patted him on the shoulder. "You can check on her as often as you like. You are one of her guardians. You can send her jurisprudence books every week, if you wish."

Alisdair gave a smile, but he was in thought.

"One more question," he said. "The Council. I mean, children are being born every second on Earth. How—"

"It's another thing that is different here," Duncan said. "There is no time, but there are no limitations of self, either. It is possible to be in many places at once. It's the same principle as the Council location. Wherever the vibration is aligned, that is where it appears. So the Council can be doing work with all the people who are resonating with it, all at the same time. It's not exactly multi-tasking, it's more like… having one mind and many different thoughts which are entering and being processed within it. Something like that. Souls in particular are not limited."

He paused, checking that Alisdair was following him.

"What *you* are here, is a part of your over-soul. And different parts of that over-soul are right now taking part in many different experiences. In the end, everything will return to unity, but for now, just try to release some of those ideas you had on Earth. Try to think in a freer way. Here, there are no limits to time, or location, or experience, or knowledge, or—"

"Or anything!"

Duncan laughed. "Yes, or anything. Now, the question is, what do you choose to do next, with all these... limitless possibilities? Isn't that how you put it on Earth?"

Alisdair smiled. "It doesn't have quite the meaning it does here," he said. "But it's how we put it, yes. Well, now Eileen's back on Earth, I'm going to find out something I wanted to know all through my previous life."

CHAPTER
THIRTEEN

DAVID GLANCED AT HIS PHONE. It was Caroline again, calling from the office of Eugene Shapkin. He pressed the mute button and let it ring. He had missed every one of his appointments since the shrink had come up with that ridiculous theory. The medications might be working just fine, but he wasn't going to sit in that office and listen to some guy tell him what did and didn't happen in his childhood. The very thought of it made him pissed. He still had enough meds for the rest of the month. Maybe he would find a different shrink when they ran out, and get a top-up. Maybe he wouldn't need them longer than that.

He waited until the phone had stopped buzzing, then speed-dialled Vanessa. It had been a few weeks since he had seen her. In fact, he hadn't seen her since the evening before bonus day. He thought back to the blow job he had got that night, remembering how good his penis had felt in her small mouth. And she hadn't called him once. Unbelievable. These New York girls knew how to leave a guy alone when they needed space. She must have figured there was some problem with the bonus – if it had been good, she would have got the call. He felt a surge of affection towards her. She really knew what to do with a guy when he was under a lot of pressure. Not like Cassie, with that stupid call about the owl and the hypnotist. He didn't have the time or mental space to think about stuff like that. Not with the pressure he was under. Not when he had been given a chance.

Vanessa picked up the phone.

"David," she said, "how've you been, baby?"

"Good," David said. "You want to come over tonight?"

"I'd love to. I've been missing you. What time shall I come?"

"Make it eight. No, make it nine."

"I'll be there."

"Great."

"David?"

"Yeah?"

"I'm glad you called. I'll see you later."

She hung up the phone. She had to be the perfect woman for a guy like him. No pressure. Always positive. Amazing body. Amazing sex. He almost felt in love with her. His penis stirred at the thought of seeing her again. He'd get in a bottle of something so they could relax. Maybe champagne. He might not even mind if she stayed over at the apartment, as long as she didn't get in his way in the morning. He could try it at least one time, see how it went. She might even make sure that he got up at five, that he didn't sleep late with one of his weird dreams. He pictured himself in the bed with his arms around her lean body, his hands resting on those breasts. Yeah, that might work. It was worth a try.

He slipped the phone back into the holder on his belt, and picked up the client file.

"DAVID?" It was Vanessa. She was sitting up in bed, her hand touching his hair.

"David? Babe?"

He opened his eyes. Vanessa. What was she doing here? Then he remembered. She was staying over.

"David, you were yelling out in your sleep. You were saying some stuff."

"Mmmm." David half-opened his eyes, then closed them again. He reached out to Vanessa and pulled her back down into the bed.

"Mmmm. Go back to sleep. Just a dream."

Vanessa lifted her hair high up onto the pillow, so that he could nuzzle his face into her neck.

"Just a dream," she murmured, closing her eyes.

"SO, I've been pretty impressed over the last couple of weeks."

Jeff was looking upbeat. The sun was shining in through the half-opened blinds in his office. Behind his head, David could see Manhattan stretching out towards the East River.

Jeff got up from his desk and walked behind David to close the glass door. He put a hand on David's shoulder.

"You're ready to talk?" he asked.

"I'm ready," said David.

Jeff settled himself down in his huge black-leather swivel chair. On the glass desk in front of him was a semicircle of three computer screens flashing stock movements onto blue backgrounds. There was an expensive-looking fountain pen next to a pair of Yankees tickets.

"So, you really wanna have this conversation?"

"Jeff, I want to be on the inside track. I just need to know what to do to get on it."

"Alright, then." Jeff leaned back in his chair and regarded David.

"Well," he said at last. "I've had a few words with the boys upstairs. I told them I had a talented guy who was looking for a chance. Wanted to show what he could do."

"And?"

"They were interested. They thought about it. And they came back with a way for you to show them what you got."

"Come on, Jeff. I'm dying here. What's the deal?"

"Well," said Jeff slowly. "The Trading Group – they're on the sixth floor – I'm sure you've seen them—"

"I know the Trading Group..."

"So, they've been having a bit of a problem with some derivatives they've been selling. There was a report recently in the *Wall Street Journal* about the underlying assets. Some questions. And a decision was made to put aside the bank's position for a few months until everything had calmed down a bit."

"Yeah, I think I read about that. It wasn't just Bullman Scout. Mercy Bank were in it, Swiss Western—"

"Exactly. But we were the first ones named in the story. The investors went apeshit. They were very, very pissed that this happened."

"Yeah, I can see that."

"So. The bank is sitting on a major position here. And we can't afford to shift them for a few months. But the problem is—"

"We don't want them on the books."

Jeff looked at David, and smiled.

"Exactly. That's exactly the problem, David. Now, what we thought was—"

"I think I can guess."

"I am going to put you on official secondment to the trading team. You passed the ACS exams, right? You're not officially *on* the team.

123

You're officially on *this* team. You work on the sixth floor until five p.m. every day, then you come back here and keep the leverage cases afloat. I can give you a hand if you need. I can pass a couple of cases over to Kirsten."

"You don't need to do that. I can manage the cases I've got."

"Okay, then. You will have a list of clients who we think may be persuaded to buy the derivatives. And we need to shift them by the end of the quarter. So here's the bit you're going to like..."

"I'm listening."

"If you get this done, if you shift the entire position by March 31st, then we will transfer you to any group you like within the bank. In fact, any country you like. We'll give you an expat package and move you to London, Hong Kong, Tokyo. Wherever you want. And, believe me, you *will* be on the inside track."

"And the title?"

"You start off at VP, but we'll write a Director promotion into your package. A year, two at the most."

"What's the catch?"

"The catch is, there is a small risk on your part."

"Okay..."

"We're going to need you to sign a few papers for us. First – a resignation letter from this group and, implicitly, from the bank. Second – a contract with the Trading Group, stating that you will be exclusively trading a list of stocks, which will *not* include the derivatives. Of course, these documents will be held by our in-house lawyers, and would be used only, so to speak, if the shit totally hits the fan."

"Wow. Anything else?"

"Nope. That's pretty much it."

"So, I will be held legally responsible for... Well, I guess I'll be lying to the clients. Is that white-collar fraud?"

"Woah, woah, woah. David, let's not use any of those words around here. The bank is offering you an opportunity, and you can either take it or leave it. There is nothing even remotely... connected... to anything you just mentioned. Is that perfectly clear?"

"Sorry, Jeff. That was stupid."

"David, let me explain. The investors are furious that we took the PR hit. And they're going to be even more furious if they find out we have a huge position on the sheet at the beginning of April. Can you understand that?"

"So, I take the entire risk on my shoulders. And if anything goes wrong, I'm the fall guy. I'm the one who gets a late-night call from the state attorney's office."

"There will be a third document."

"Yeah?"

"In the very, very unlikely scenario that this happens, David, the bank will agree to make you a series of payments, three million dollars in total, to be put into an offshore account over the course of a year. But we won't be able to hire you again, obviously, in any capacity."

"And legal fees?"

"We couldn't cover them. We'd be acting against you, if it came to that. But David, this scenario is completely unprecedented. It has never happened before and it's not going to happen now. Believe me, I'm sure Swiss Western and Mercy are coming up with their own ways right now to shift the position."

"Jeff, this is pretty massive."

"You asked for a chance. I'm giving you a chance."

"And if I say no?"

"Then you've got next year's bonus to look forward to."

"I've got to think about it. I wasn't expecting something this big. Wow. Jeff, let me think about it, okay?"

"You got it, bud. You've got a week. Then everything's off the table. And don't come back to me asking for chances again."

"Jeff…"

"You can't get a little bit pregnant here, David. I just want a yes or a no. You got it?"

"Yes."

"Okay, David. I've got some calls to make now."

Jeff turned his chair back to the triple-computer display and picked up the huge, black phone.

"Angie, get me Martin Walsh on the line. Thanks."

The meeting was finished. David got up from the chair and pushed open the glass door. He walked back to his cubicle and sat down. He felt a little like throwing up. But he also felt a tingling at the bottom of his stomach, a nervous excitement. His world had just changed. The terms, conditions, risk profile and adrenalin level of his world had just shifted sharply upwards. He looked at the pile of client files on the desk of his cubicle and saw a flash of himself sitting in an office overlooking the Tokyo skyline. Suddenly, everything was possible. He picked up the phone.

WITHIN THE VIEWING POD, *Nœ-bouk* deactivated the thought shield and allowed its mind to travel back to the moon cycles of its early development stages. It would not usually have permitted such lenience in thought activity, however the knowledge it had received from the Admiral had somehow altered the rules which had previously been universally applicable, and stripped them of their kernel of essential truth. There was a line somewhere, *Nœ-bouk* reflected, the existence of which it had not formerly been aware, and it now found itself on the other side of that line. From this perspective, everything that it had considered as *known* appeared in a quite different light. Or perhaps such a line had not previously existed. Perhaps the very fact of its living past the range of physical possibility, and the Admiral's similarly extended lifespan, and the state of emotional unity which had developed between them, had created that line. Perhaps it had only appeared as a result of the event sequence which had unfolded over the recent moon cycles.

It had never been aware of any circumstances, in all of its instruction cycles and task assignments, in which a being from an elevated planetary environment had experienced an alteration in life perspective. There was simply an understanding, among life forms close to the transcendence level, that a peaceful and unified civilisation co-existing within a federation of elevated and mutually beneficial planetary systems, was the highest possible expression of incarnate existence – was the *truth*. And now, *Nœ-bouk* thought, as it looked back on the moon cycles which had marked out its lifespan, and now, it questioned whether any of it was *true*.

The symbol block sent by the tentacled being formed once again in its mind space. *Freedom*. Those endlessly repeating stars. And yet, it was essentially the same concept the Admiral had used. The Admiral, who had seen more and further than any of the other evolved entities on Home Planet, and on most of the surrounding planets. The Admiral, who was indisputably the most experienced and knowledgeable being on Home Planet. The Admiral, whose eyes filled *Nœ-bouk* with feelings of elevation so intense that it desired to move its limbs in unprecedented ways and make movements such as jumping and jerks, in order to dispel the emotions to which it was not accustomed. The Admiral, who had used symbol blocks and thought strands containing similar concepts: *beyond, freedom, choice, unifying love*.

Nœ-bouk went back over its early development cycles and recalled its instruction in the Home Planet centres, its physical conditioning, the partnerships it had established. Were any of these life progressions truly choices it had made? Or were these selections simply logical extrapolations made in the context of what it had been conditioned to believe, a conditioning which had been applied by the higher echelons of Home Planet for the benefit of the planet and its civilisation as a whole? And if that were true, which it appeared to be, then was it not right? Was it different to any other kind of conditioning and any other selection which could have been made in any other context? What were the parameters which made a choice *free* or *not free*? An awareness of the paradigm structure, perhaps?

However, *Nœ-bouk* had been aware of the structure in which its life-span path had been decided. It had been consulted on many occasions by development instructors and by its early-stage guardians, and the life-path variants had been clearly explained. On each occasion, it had been satisfied with the selections it had made. Drawn to them. Would they have been more *free* had there been among them as options variants which did not follow truth-based logic or lead to the benefit of itself and the entirety of Home Planet? How could that be possible? It was verging into an area devoid of meaning. And yet, *Nœ-bouk* now had this other feeling, this entirely unfamiliar feeling, with which to compare the paths and the existence it had previously followed. And it knew, more truly than it had known anything ever before, that *this* feeling, *this* feeling was freedom.

Nœ-bouk raised and lowered the lids of its eyes. The galaxy through which they were passing glowed with blue and golden stars. It could see the deep-red swirling of a nebula in the distance. It was inexpressibly beautiful. The enormity of the spacescape and the utterly innumerable stars all around them, the fact that it went on and on and on to the divine law of infinite creation, which could transport a being in meditation into elevated states from which it sometimes could not return. The transcendent vastness of everything, and the incalculable importance of everything within that never-ending everything. And how was it ever possible to find the meaning of any one single action within that vastness? To understand whether one single action had any significance at all to the swirling dust of the nebula, or to the pattern of the newborn stars, or to the movement of a Home Planet vessel through deepest space? What relevance did anything have to anything at all? And then what was *choice*? What was *freedom*? What significance could a being possibly attach to the actions of its lifespan – a single note – without understanding the entire song: the universe? Without understanding why the stars were born, and the impact one had upon them, and how it was possible for some low-energy planets to exist in such depths of brutality when all beings carried within them the same spirit of light?

The lids of *Noœ-bouk*'s eyes flickered. The thoughts coursed in circular motion within its mind space like the dust around the edges of the nebula formations in its vision path. It had never had such thoughts as these. The Admiral must be experiencing similar brain-function adjustments. It must be the contraction of the brain capacity prior to transition. But *Noœ-bouk* knew that this was not true. It reached for the symbol key to release the eye shield and it opened the lid of the viewing pod.

The main viewing deck was busy with members of the crew active on task assignments. *Noœ-bouk* stepped out of the pod. It would return to the resting chamber and activate a regenerating session in the light capsule.

It would contact the Admiral.

ELSPETH PUT DOWN THE BOOK. It was nearing midday by now, and she was getting hungry. For some reason, though, she didn't want to stop reading. She wished she was sitting on a rock, watching the clouds, the scent of pine trees moving her thoughts. That would be the perfect place to read and dream.

A bus pulled up next to where she was perched, and well-dressed people got on and off. Strollers and muffins. Saturday morning ballet lessons. Elspeth considered spending the afternoon on the top deck, watching the London streets pass by, but something stopped her. The bus moved off.

She picked up her book. Alcibiades had arrived at the dinner party.

THE SUN WAS BEATING DOWN.

Socrates turned to the group of followers who had gathered around him, narrowing his eyes against the midday Athenian glare. He opened his arms wide. His thin tunic was daubed with sweat around his muscular shoulders.

That morning, he had climbed his beloved Lycabettus to watch the sun rise over the surrounding hills. Its rays had danced over the distant sea, and had covered the Acropolis in a haze of gold. It gave him the most profound sense of calm and freedom to be high up in the mountains. It was in the mountains that he could feel the flow of spirit moving through him; it was among the rocks and clouds that the ideas and questions were born. It was where he felt himself to be in his most true and natural state: a messenger, a channel from the Gods, to question that which was, and to open up the possibilities of what could be.

He felt the sunrise move within him, the stir of the water, coloured orange and red; the promise of heat and sweat, the heaviness of days among men. But this was his. The mountain. The sunrise. The sea. The labourers in the distance laying the final blocks on the temple of the Parthenon.

He turned to his followers.

"How can you understand the world around you if you do not question it?" he asked. "The sun, the city, victory, life itself – what are these? Who bestows them upon us? How is our share decided?"

His followers nodded and looked serious. The sun was burning into the tops of their heads. It was time to go inside or rest in the shade of courtyards or olive trees. Socrates pointed at one of the men.

"What is your answer?" he asked. "Let us begin at the beginning. Tell me – what do you understand by *choice*?"

CHAPTER
FOURTEEN

DAVID BENT OVER DOUBLE. The music pounded in his ears as he grasped his ankles and counted out a painful stretch. Straightening up, he pulled out the headphones and slipped the music player into his running jacket. He reached his arms up over his head and stretched them as far as he could. Other joggers passed him at various speeds. Elderly New York dames slow-jogging in baseball caps; fund managers in flashing brand clothes, pounding by at seven-minute miles. The unreal high-rises of Manhattan, with their pixel windows spread out to the right and in front of him. The wide, grey East River and Roosevelt Island with Queens beyond it, still asleep across the water. He felt the energy of New York pulsing through him. The power. The money. The drive. The best of the best. Everything he loved about the city. The endless energy throbbing within his body made him feel sexual and immensely powerful, as if he – and New York itself – were a massive, rock-hard erection ready to fuck the rest of the world anywhere and anyhow it pleased. He smiled at the image.

The red streaks of sunrise started to break into yellow across the sky, and David finished his stretching and jogged at a slow pace back up the river walkway towards his apartment. He'd broken his record this morning. A new time of six minutes and thirty seconds from his apartment building down to the 59th Street Bridge. That was pretty good; it should be a seven or eight-minute mile. He still wanted to get it lower. Danny claimed he could do a five-minute mile, but that was probably bullshit. David knew that it was easy to get him going when it came to competing. Even a hint of someone coming close to his level and suddenly everything inside him – his body, brain, ego – would light up and spring into action. *He* was smarter. *He* was faster. *He* was better than this no-brain piece of shit. He would show them just how much better he was. And then he would work with a precise and razor-focused attention until he had done it, achieved the result he was aiming for, unequivocally proved that he was tougher, faster, smarter. A superior human being in all possible respects.

He kept his jog steady. He had plenty of time – it was Saturday and he'd head into the office after picking up breakfast at a local diner. His three alarm clocks had all gone off at the same time this morning, and the pills he was taking were doing their job.

His father had warned him about this trait of his, this super-competitiveness. In school, David would experience bursts of anger if someone got better grades than him. Not in everything, but in maths, science, anything logic-based. And his mentor at the University of Toronto, Professor Baird – or Beardy as the students called him – would offer the same message. "There are a lot of smart people in this programme," he would say. "You don't have to be better than all of them." But it wasn't a question of having to be better than all of them. It was a question of knowing that he *was* better, and feeling anger when that wasn't expressed or acknowledged by the world around him: in grades, in praise, in payslips. The feeling of not being recognised as his true superior self produced a bite of fury, which he knew would lead to a period of intense hard work and focus in order to re-establish himself in his rightful position at the top.

"Life is full of small failures," his father had told him, although his mother had always gone tight-lipped at the words, and David had hated the expression. Small failures – any failures – were for other people. They were for people who weren't ready to give everything to what they were doing. Or for people who were in the wrong game.

He understood what his father and Professor Baird were telling him, and he understood that they did not mean it as an insult to his intelligence or his capabilities. He even accepted it from a logical, external perspective, but that didn't mean that he was able to control it. Although, to be fair, he had never really tried to control it. He simply loved winning. He had loved being the smartest guy at school, he loved being able to push himself that far; it gave him an enormous thrill. And he loved being in New York, where he was surrounded by people with exactly that same drive: people with brains and energy and balls to match his own, drawn from around the world to this centre of money and dreams, where the only limits were the number of hours you let yourself sleep, and the degree of creativity you used to make money for your bank, your clients, yourself.

He heard the words of his father and the professor as he jogged uptown towards his apartment building. They were warnings, which were meant to be heeded in precarious situations, exactly such as this one. They were made by people who loved him, who knew him and who cared about his future. If he was ever going to listen to the advice of people who knew more about the world than he did, then this was the time.

He saw the two paths in front of him, forking off into different lifetimes. The first path – the one he had envisioned for himself in New York – slow, hard progress. Money coming little by little over the years. MD by forty. Maybe move home to run the Canadian operations by fifty. Big shot. Huge house. Hot wife. Maybe go into Canadian politics. Maybe join the golf club and turn into a rich old fart. That's what he had been expecting.

But now, another path had opened up. Vice President at twenty-eight. Inside track. Move to Tokyo on an expat package. Director by thirty. Huge bonuses. Hot Japanese wife. More money. More excitement. The world suddenly seemed a lot smaller and a hell of a lot more attractive. The world would be his for the taking. Big house in Tokyo. Condo in New York. House in Toronto. House in the Hamptons. He would be a Director younger, an MD younger, he would be richer younger, more successful younger. He'd have more money than Tom, than Danny, than Kirsten.

And again, this was exactly what his father would have warned him about. There wasn't so much difference between the paths. A few years, a few million dollars, that was all. And one came with a massive, ugly risk, and one came with no risk at all. It was almost a no-brainer – it was crazy to take the risky path. But on the other hand, if he didn't take it, after Jeff had offered it to him, after he had *asked* for it, then he would be even further ostracised from the inside track than before. As Jeff had said, he would have nothing but next year's bonus to look forward to. And that wouldn't even be enough for a down payment on a condo. Not the kind of condo he wanted to get, anyway. And not much of a pay increase, most likely. They might even stall him on promotion, just to pay him back for not taking the opportunity. Bump Danny and Kirsten and let him wait another couple of years. He wouldn't put it past them. They'd fucked him over for no good reason this year; they could easily do it for the next year, and the next.

He still had what? Three days left to come to the decision. Three days to decide which path his life should take. The high risk or the low risk. The ordinary route or the fast track to everything he had ever wanted.

He turned onto the overpass crossing FDR and jogged up onto 78th Street. He was nearly home. He felt great after his run. Even though he hadn't come to a decision, his mind was clearer and his body felt better. He stopped outside his apartment building and glanced again at his watch. 6:55 a.m.

The grocery store on the corner was setting up its sidewalk fruit display. The early sun was making its way between the buildings and through the Manhattan grey. The air was fresh and invigorating. He stretched again. He would make the right decision. He didn't know what it was yet, but he would make it. He felt good.

NOŒ-BOUK AND *RAI-BOUK* stood on the main viewing deck and watched the small landing creel launch out from the external craft bay of the vessel and move towards the living planet. The main vessel was positioned some distance beyond the planet's atmospheric radius and had received permission to penetrate the surface and procure samples of the newly identified life form. The beings in the creel were genus types of a smaller size to *Noœ-bouk* and *Rai-bouk*. They would remain in their natural physical state during the assignment, since the living planet was unpopulated by evolving humanoid or other conscious beings, and they expected to encounter only the simpler life forms which had been seeded to the planet at that stage.

For both *Noœ-bouk* and *Rai-bouk*, this was the first living planet they had ever encountered. After the constant reds and depressed pinks of Home Planet, the dust and cragged rock, the sight before them was shocking and viscerally beautiful. The planet's top layer, clearly visible, was a wild, wide sweep of blue-black oceans and burning volcanoes surrounded by forest. Swirling, coloured gas clouds crept over the surface. It was similar in some ways to the landscapes of *Khand-a* or *Tayr*, which they had studied; yet this planet was larger, denser, untouched, pulsing with chaotic eruptions from beneath its churning layers. Its living breath seemed scarcely risen from the dark, pure sea of original matter.

"It is in approximation fifty volumes greater than *Tayr*," *Rai-bouk* communicated.

"But the seeding pattern is continuing on the same schedule?"

"Similar. There is no disease. This has been corrected. All the seeded elements are in their pure form. The development will move faster."

"How much faster?"

"It will be ready for activation of conscious life in less than ten thousand moon cycles."

"This is on an advanced schedule to *Tayr*."

"Significantly advanced."

They were both drawn to comparisons between this living planet orbiting before them and *Tayr*, for the reason that on Home Planet, as in many of the civilisations within the proximal galaxies, the planetary progression patterns of *Khand-a* and *Tayr* were used as teaching instruments to illustrate the consciousness development process and its consequent risks.

There had been many mistakes made during the creation and the seeding of *Tayr*. Disease and mutation had been introduced when asteroids crashed into the planet in the early cycles, and the planetary schedule had almost been abandoned. The gene sequences of the proto-humanoids had mutated, resulting in an elevated level of aggression and subsequent cycles of anger and blood. This set the course for gene and memory sequences which were not possible to dispel from the energy of the planet as a whole. Many highly evolved life forms were sent to carry clean energy patterns to the planet, however this only resulted in a discrepancy between the higher energy states, which were coined as *God-like*, and the lower, earlier set blood patterns initiated by the gene malfunctions. This series of errors had led to a permanent division during the evolution of consciousness within the developing humanoids, and caused a fallacious association of the *God* energy as separate from the physical. The *God* energy became perceived, at least by the few who were eager to attain it, as something which could only be reached by disassociation from the physical form, instead of its comprehension as a constant presence and, indeed, the very life force of every living element on the planet.

This categorical error, first in the understanding, and later in the accepted thought paradigm, had led to a state of permanent separation on the *Tayr* planet, and had reached a point where, with a few notable exceptions, the inhabiting genus types were unable to perceive themselves in any state of unity or higher level connection to one another. The idea of *God*, which the *Tayr* proto-humanoids had created, was a source of confusion and even humour to other planetary beings, many of which found it difficult to comprehend how *Tayr* could have developed such a concept.

Nooe-bouk's initial introduction to the subject had been through a series of communication blocks, which it had never forgotten, sent by one of its instructors in the education centres of Home Planet.

"Imagine the purest and most elevated part of your being," the instructor had conveyed, "and then separate and isolate that part. Give to this higher field the concept of *God* and then accept that this *God* field is no longer any element of your being. What remains – the base vibration – is the only aspect you now identify with. The final step is to refute the existence of the *God* field. All that is left is the basest part of you. Separate, alone, deprived of light: this is your paradigm for the lifespan."

There had been a long thought space in the chamber when the instructor had sent the final symbol block, and then an unusual reaction. Laughter, almost hysterical, came over the students, and did not subside for many inhalations. Only the instructor sat motionless and silent.

"Why cannot one of our genus type incarnate and raise the energy?" a student sent.

"The thought level on *Tayr* has been brought very low," the instructor replied. "The patterns of anger and disassociation from the higher levels has created an environment of base density. It is difficult, in that state, to channel or receive any of the higher strata. From where we are, it seems easy. It appears a task of the greatest simplicity to arrive on *Tayr* and change the energy paradigm within one lifespan, with cycles of light. Yet this has been done. You have seen the results. The lifespans have been noted and the levels have shifted to a certain degree. But the planet is too heavy to be lifted up. It must achieve a state of unity on its own."

"Why would any life forms choose to incarnate there?" another student had sent.

"Because it is a great challenge," communicated the instructor, "to bring the highest and the lowest energies together into one physical form. It is more difficult than any of the lifespans we experience here on Home Planet. It appears easy, but it is not. It is unimaginably difficult. When a being enters the incarnate form, it is immediately disassociated with unity. It enters an energy of perfect separation. In addition to this, the thought-wave level will create experiences of loneliness, abandonment, pain, disease, misery, deprivation and the manifold instances of brutal humanoid actions which follow consequentially from these states."

There had once again been a silence in the chamber when the instructor had finished communicating, but the hysteria had passed. There was no laughter.

"The idea arouses distress," communicated one of the students.

"And yet, so many are eager to incarnate, to achieve what others could not. To reunite that which was separated."

The symbol block returned to *Nœ-bouk* now, as they stared out at the young planet, exploding with desire, with life force, with creation. This must have been what *Tayr* looked like, before the cycles of darkness began. *To reunite that which was separated.* It sent the symbol block to *Rai-bouk*, who moved its head in assent. It, too, had studied the concept.

"Yes," it replied. There was a thought space as the two beings gazed out at the living planet.

"Yes," *Rai-bouk* communicated again.

It sent a thought wave to *Nœ-bouk*: a hope, that after the task assignment had been completed on this planet, the Advisory Committee might elect to travel the galaxies to *Tayr*, to assist with the anomaly readings.

Nœ-bouk returned the thought wave. It felt an unusual level of clarity in its mind space. It knew now, beyond a doubt, that it desired to see *Tayr*.

ELSPETH PUT DOWN THE BOOK. She had felt something unusual while she was reading. It was something in the words, the scenes, moving inside her, stirring an idea to remembrance. She felt as if she had read or known the words before, but not from a book. As if it were bringing back a life experience from her past, but one she couldn't quite catch in her conscious mind. She pushed herself off the wall and looked at her watch. 4 p.m. She had been sitting there most of the day. She really was hungry now. She stretched her legs and stepped over to the bus stop. Dozens of buses must have gone by while she had been reading. No matter; she liked walking.

The afternoon sun was lighting up the flowers in the front gardens of the houses, and London looked sleepy and peaceful on this late, spring Saturday. Elspeth held the book in her hand as she walked.

Something was changing. Somehow, what she had just read made more sense to her than anything else in her life right now. And nothing in her life had made any sense for a long time. For years it had felt as if everyone had a plan, an understanding of what they were meant to do, some kind of structural belief system in which they functioned. Everyone except for her. It just felt as if she were drifting, without any knowledge at all of the plan, without even having a plan, without any conception of what she was meant to be doing. It was a horrible, empty feeling, if she would admit it to herself. Maybe that was the reason she'd spent so long around drugs. At least they took away the emptiness – filled her with a kind of passive lift in the place of nothing at all.

And then that visit for Grandad's eightieth birthday party, when his love had awakened a possibility she had not felt for a long, long time. The idea that her life could have some value, in some way, to someone. It was an incredible thought. And for the sake of that thought, she had moved to London, she had followed that small spark of hope and it had proved to be real. Grandad *had* wanted her in his life. And, best of all – most unexpectedly of all – he hadn't tried to change her. He hadn't criticised anything about her past, however much he knew. He had offered his love and his help and nothing else. And against all odds, when she had never let her parents or even her friends help her with anything, she had let him find her a flat, a job, put together some strands of a life.

And now she had this feeling, reading the book which Grandad had left her in his will – this book and most of his personal library and some money – enough for a deposit on a flat or to set herself up in something. It seemed strange that he had left his books to her. Her mother would be the natural choice – both her parents were big readers. Maybe he had figured that she was the one who hadn't read any of them. Maybe he hadn't figured at all. Maybe he had just felt like doing it.

She reached the end of the road and emerged onto Upper Street. It was busy with shoppers and early drinkers filling the outside bars. Suddenly, she had an idea. A thread of happiness went through her. Maybe it was a crazy idea, but it was something to follow, and something which would keep her close to Grandad. It could only lead to good things. She paused at the edge of the road and scanned the storefronts opposite, looking for a suitable bar. Rango's. Looked expensive. Red awning, cocktail menu.

She crossed the street and weaved through the shoppers to the open glass door. Inside, she slid herself up onto a red-leather stool and caught the waiter's eye. Cute. Mediterranean. Maybe a treat for later that evening.

"What'll it be?" he asked.

"A glass of champagne."

"Celebrating?"

"Yes," Elspeth said. "I'm moving to Greece."

SOCRATES BRUSHED the dust from his tunic and entered the tavern. Someone handed him a drink of cool wine mixed with water. He took a sip. It tasted of honey and resin and sweat. It was delicious. He tipped the black-glazed cup upwards and finished the drink. The crowd shouted and passed around beakers of wine, knocking them back, mimicking their teacher. Socrates leaned over to where the tavern owner was filling a mixing bowl with the dark, yellow liquid.

"Tell me," he said. "Does wine create for us the illusion of truth; or grant us a view into a real truth – one which does not exist without the drinking of wine?"

The owner of the tavern wiped his mouth. The men who had come in with Socrates were handsome, well-dressed, with oiled, rock-hard bodies. He had seen Socrates watching one in particular.

He handed him the re-filled cup of golden wine.

"Let us find out," he said.

A FEW HOURS LATER, Elspeth pushed opened the door of Rango's and stepped unsteadily onto the pavement of the high street. She found the bus stop for Mile End and clambered to the top deck when it arrived.

There was a seat at the front and she slid onto it. Out of her pocket, she took the paper napkin from the bar and looked at what had been scribbled onto it, beneath the barman's number.

Give notice.

Clear out flat.

Buy ticket.

Sell everything.

Fly to Greece.

CHAPTER
FIFTEEN

"GOOD AFTERNOON, MR CORNWELL."

Caroline was wearing a high-necked cream blouse, which looked as if it was made out of tissue paper. The delicate front featured tiny mother-of-pearl buttons, shaped like stars. David pictured himself ripping the shirt in a straight line off her body. Below, her breasts would be spilling out of a cream satin bra, barely held by the material. He pictured himself biting into them.

"Caroline. How are you doing?"

"Dr Shapkin is glad you decided to come for another session. He was becoming quite concerned. You know, it's important to continue with the treatment once you've started it. Dr Shapkin's clients have to trust him to get better."

"Yes. Thanks, Caroline."

David tried to stop himself staring. Mother-of-pearl buttons. He thought that he could just make out the curved shape of a bra beneath the material. Cream satin. Porcelain. Heaven.

"You can go in now, Mr Cornwell."

"Ok. Thanks."

David dragged himself away from the buttons and the freckled nose and the blonde hair. He knocked, then pushed open the door of the office.

Dr Shapkin sat behind his desk. He was dressed in a sumptuous grey suit which looked as if the wool count was too high. His glasses reflected the gleam of the lamplight.

"David. I'm pleased to see you. Come and sit down."

David sank into the beige leather chair and crossed one leg sideways over the other, holding his ankle.

"Tell me, David, how have you been?"

AN HOUR LATER, David stepped out of the office and into the fresh February air. He had managed to talk for most of the session, and keep the shrink from bringing up anything about his childhood. That was a victory. And he had, in his pocket, another month's prescription for the meds which were working so well. All in all, it had been a good consultation. He could do this once a week. And hopefully, when everything had calmed down, he could start coming off the meds, get back to where he had been at the beginning of the year and straighten his head out once and for all.

He had meant to ask Dr Shapkin – without, of course, telling him anything concrete – about the decision he had before him, about what he should do and how it might affect him. But the subject hadn't come up. He still had two days before he had to give his answer, and since his run the previous morning, he had been leaning towards caution, towards the slow and steady route. It was what his father and Professor Baird would have advised.

Striding along, he felt good. He felt like a drink. He pulled his phone out of its case and found the number he wanted.

"David. What's up?"

"Danny, I'm walking down twenty-eighth and Lex right now. You wanna grab a drink in that bar on twenty-first? Are you finished up there?"

"Yeah, I'm pretty much done here. I could use a brewski. Gimme a few minutes to wrap this up and I'll come down. Or do you wanna meet in the bar?"

"No, I'll wait in the lobby."

"Alright, bud. See you in five."

Danny hung up the phone. A few minutes later, David crossed the road from Gramercy Park towards the entrance of the bank. It was a stunning landmark building – 1920s, he thought he had heard. Pre-crash, for sure. White marble paving and gleaming silver metal. Art deco? Is that what it was called? Or did that come later?

There were clusters of admin staff standing around the foyer, smoking and chatting, their hairsprayed dos and acrylic nails marking them out from the muted, clean-cut suits of the bankers. David studied them. He could find little similarity between the groups – it was as if they were part of two different sub-species. Lifestyles, behaviours, expectations, dreams, boundaries – all in separate planes of existence. Winners and losers, he thought.

A man holding a cardboard box pushed his way out of the revolving doors and into the foyer. The box had books and photograph frames piled on top. Someone had just got fired. David watched him cross the foyer to the taxi rank – the slump of his shoulders, his face below the short, banker's haircut, frozen in a look of fury, his eyes narrowed. He wondered what was going on in the man's head, beneath the anger. Was he freaking out? Mortgage payments and health insurance? A pricey girlfriend he'd have to lose? David gave a slight shrug as the man got into a cab and moved off into downtown traffic.

"Hey, bud. What's up?"

Danny slapped him on the shoulder and they started walking in the direction of the bar, a badly lit pub around the corner from the bank, the perfect haunt for an after-work drink.

Inside, they ordered beers and sat on stools, a bowl of salty peanuts between them.

"So, what's up?" Danny asked again, as the beers arrived.

"I've got this thing," David said.

"This thing?"

"Yeah," he said, and paused. He looked at Danny. "I've got to make a decision. And I'm not sure what to do."

"Well, what d'ya *wanna* do? You could start with that."

"I know what I want. But if I take that route, then there's a risk."

"Alright. And if you take the route that you don't want?"

"Then I still get what I want. But I get it slower."

"Hmmm."

Danny picked up his beer and took a swig. He threw a few peanuts into his mouth and chewed. In the corner, a band was unpacking microphones and guitars for a live set.

"By the way, I called my girlfriend. She's gonna stop by here in a bit."

"Alright. What's her story?"

"School sweetheart. From Jersey."

"What's she doing in New York?"

"Actually, she's still living in Jersey. But she was in the city today, so I told her to come along."

"Yeah, great."

"What about you, David? You still seeing that hottie?"

141

Danny had been at the bar the night Vanessa had let David give her his business card. He and the other guys had been impressed.

"Yeah. Actually, she stayed over a few nights back. First time."

"Oooooh. David getting in deep."

"Yeah, yeah."

"You like her?"

"Yeah, I guess so. She's kinda sweet. Pretty hot."

"Yeah."

They sat in silence for a few minutes, drinking the beer and watching the drummer constructing the drum kit.

"So, this decision you've got to make," said Danny at last.

"Yeah. I don't know what to do."

"Look, David, I've known you for, what, a year? Year and a half?"

"Something like that."

"Well, I've sat opposite you for a year and a half."

"Yeah."

"And if there's one thing I've noticed—"

"It's how good I am at my job?"

"Shut up, David. If there's one thing I've noticed, it's that you do not like to lose. At anything. Not in the office, not out of the office. It's like you turn into this major asshole every time there's a situation which is the least bit competitive, and you just bust everyone's balls until you've got what you want."

"Okay."

"I'm not insulting you, David. I'm just saying what I've seen. I think you're a good guy. I think you're smart. But you can be a real fucking asshole when it comes to competing."

"Alright. So what does that mean?"

"It means, be careful, man. It's your weak spot. That's as clear as hell to me and everyone else who's seen you work. You can't lose. You'd rather screw us all over than lose one step of the game."

"Wow."

"Yeah. That's pretty much how we feel. I mean, I told you, I'm not criticising. This is New York. This is pretty normal. I'm just saying, be careful. Whatever choice you're looking at, make the safe one. If you've got some risky situation and it starts going wrong, you're not going to be able to handle it, man."

A girl was waving at Danny from the doorway of the bar. Danny waved back and beckoned her over, then leaned across the counter and called for another beer. He put his head close to David's ear.

"Seriously, man," he said. "This could fuck you up. Be careful."

David put his hand on Danny's back. "Thank you. I appreciate it. That was really honest. Thanks, man."

"Yeah, don't sweat it. And you can stop being such an asshole while you're at it."

"Fat chance of that."

The girl had squeezed through the crowd towards them and Danny slid off his stool and kissed her. She had a round, pretty face and heavy eye make-up in a shade of aquamarine. Her hair smelled of chemical spray.

"David, this is Jenny. Jenny, David. David sits opposite me at the bank."

"Hi, Jenny. Good to meet you."

"Hi, David."

They shook hands, and David watched Jenny climb onto the stool next to Danny. She was wearing tight jeans which showed off her backside, and her off-the-shoulder sweater was the wrong size. She couldn't pull off that look. Not in New York, anyway. Maybe back home in Jersey.

"So, David," said Jenny. "How do you like working in the bank?"

THEY FINISHED the beers and ordered another round. The band had kicked off their set and the noise in the bar grew deafening with the live music and shouted conversations. David chatted to Danny and Jenny. She was a sweet girl, just as Danny had said. Not too smart, but not too dumb, either. A good choice for Danny. Her nails were painted in a kind of pastel which matched the aquamarine of her eye make-up. David could smell the hairspray when he leaned over to talk to her.

As he drank his beer, David felt something eating at him. He let Danny's words float through his head as he watched him nuzzling and kissing his New Jersey sweetheart. Jenny was stroking his hair with her acrylic fingernails. He pictured himself in Danny's place and felt a jolt in his gut at the thought. What a fucked-up picture. What was it? What was wrong with it? He tipped his beer bottle back and took a long draught. The image. The smell. Hairspray. Nails. Species. Shit.

The jolt in his gut.

It was everything Danny had said to him. Don't take the risk. Don't be so competitive. Accept the middle ground. Accept the mediocre life like everyone else.

The jolt in his gut again, and his mouth turned down in disgust. It was the epitome of everything he hated. This was exactly – *exactly* –

what he did not want to be, what he would never let himself be, what he rejected with every atom of his being. Mediocrity. Ordinariness. Acceptance of the middle ground. No fucking way. There was no way he would accept this. There was no way he would go for a wife with hairspray and a Jersey accent. And there was no way that Danny would ever be on the fast-track by thirty, or be a Director by thirty-five. That was the difference.

He picked up his phone and dialled a number.

"Hello?"

"Can you hear me?"

"David? I can't hear you. There's a really loud noise on your end."

"Babe, you wanna come round tonight? In about an hour?"

"Yeah, I'm free. I'll come in about an hour."

"I'll see you soon."

He hung up. He felt better. He picked up his beer and drained the bottle.

"Danny. Jenny. I'm gonna hit the road. Listen, thank you for all the advice, Danny. Much appreciated."

He put his hand on Danny's shoulder, then he took Danny's hand and shook it.

"Seriously, man. I mean it. Thanks."

"Yeah, anytime."

"Nice to meet you, David."

"You too, Jenny. Good luck with that project. See you tomorrow, Danny boy."

"See you, David."

BACK IN THE APARTMENT, David brushed his teeth, changed into a pair of jeans and waited for Vanessa. He switched the radio to a chill-out station and pushed all the files on his desk to one side. After a few minutes, the buzzer rang.

"Hey, baby," she said, walking into the apartment. She was dressed in slim-fitting black skirt and a sharply ironed white shirt beneath a black jacket. The skirt showed the outline of her perfectly toned rear. Not an inch of fat, David thought, remembering Jenny's ample backside crammed into her tight jeans. The image of New Jersey food shops came into his head – Carlo's Bakery, Marc's Cheesecake, Jimmy Buff's Hot Dogs – and Jenny stuffing her face with her eye make-up and big hair. His mouth pulled down again. It was a million miles from anything Vanessa was, or ever could be, thank god.

Vanessa put her green snakeskin handbag onto the kitchen counter and came over to David. She was wearing black high-heels. She put her arms around his neck.

"How have you been, baby?" she asked. Her dark straight hair fell towards his face and he could smell a heavy perfume on her skin; something oriental, exotic. He liked it.

"I've been missing you," David said. Vanessa was running her lips over his cheek, approaching his mouth. His arms slipped around her waist.

"I've been missing you, too," she said. "I've been busy at work. It's lay-off season."

"Yeah, I know," David said. He moved his face to meet her mouth, and slid his hands down over her backside, squeezing it with his fingers.

"David, you want me to..."

"Oh yeah."

They went through to the bedroom. Vanessa took off her skirt and white shirt and laid them carefully over the back of the chair. Underneath, she was wearing a white satin bra which pushed up her cleavage, and a white satin thong. It was just about what he had imagined Caroline wearing under that blouse, just a few hours earlier. David watched her undress, then kicked off his jeans and undershirt.

He lay back on the pillows. Vanessa climbed up onto the bed and moved towards him on her hands and knees. She was so fucking hot, he thought. It gave him an erection, just looking at her. She stopped next to his waist and ran her hands over his boxer shorts. Then she ran her fingers under the top of the shorts and pulled them down, slowly, before tossing them onto the floor. David gave a grunt of anticipation and shifted his body so that it was perfectly placed for her mouth. Oh, she was good. She was really, really good. Vanessa leaned down and started licking his penis gently, running her lips up one side and then down the other. She took the full tip into her mouth and worked her tongue over it. David grunted again. She leaned up on one elbow and stroked him with her hand.

"So successful..." she whispered in a low, smoky voice. "Such a successful man, such a rich, successful man... So powerful... Such a big, big man..."

She had his penis back in her mouth. David felt her tongue and her words circling in his head. He felt dizzy with pleasure. Big, big, big. His penis was rock-hard and Vanessa was trailing her wet lips up and down it, as if she'd been looking forward to this moment all day.

"So rich... So successful... Such a powerful man..."

David leaned forward and grabbed her head, and pushed it down hard onto his cock. He heard her gasp, and felt his penis surrounded by the hot, tight wetness of the back of her throat. He had to get it deeper. He had to. He held her head steady and shoved his cock as hard as he could up into her throat. *Oh my god.* He thrust harder and harder. It felt unbelievable. He could feel Vanessa's throat clenching and resisting, and that turned him on even more. He thrust and thrust, holding her by the hair with both hands and yelling out in deep gasps. He knew he was hurting her and it gave him a powerful surge of pleasure. He was going to come. He was going to come all over her. He was going to explode. He was going to break apart the whole fucking universe with his cock. BANG! BANG! BANG! *Oh my god.* Semen exploded out of the tip of his penis and into the back of Vanessa's throat, and he pulled back and thrust it in again and again until it was all gone, all spent. *Oh my god.*

He lay back on the pillow, covered in sweat. His head was spinning. Adrenalin was pumping so fast through his body he thought he might just take off. His heart was beating *hard*. He was panting.

He heard Vanessa get up from the bed and walk towards the bathroom. Was she alright? He'd make it up to her. He'd make sure she was alright. He caught his breath for a moment, then reached out a hand, half-rolled over, and grabbed the phone from the bedside table. He checked the display, then hit the speed-dial.

"Yeah?" a man's voice answered, loud, abrupt.

"Jeff. It's David." A pause. Silence. Heavy breathing. "I made a decision. I'm in."

NOŒ-BOUK LOWERED its form into the resting capsule and selected the highest level light setting. It drew its eyelids down and waited for the waves of sensation to begin.

"Admiral," it sent. "Admiral."

Before it appeared a sea, dancing and alive.

The sea gradually moved back and became two separate seas, and then further back, and *Noœ-bouk* was staring into the Admiral's eyes; into its face, with its faded features, and the grey skin like gathered moon dust somehow holding those globes of liquid within its impossible frailty.

"Admiral."

"You found what I communicated to be true. The cellular level?"

146

"Yes."

Waves of recognition flowed to *Nœ-bouk* from those barely contained waters. It could feel the Admiral's presence as clearly as its own. An awareness came to it that the Admiral was sharing the sensations of its physical body – that each expansion and contraction of its primary circulatory organ was simultaneously opening and closing within the Admiral's central chest area. The boundaries between them had weakened almost to nothing. Beyond its choice or control, *Nœ-bouk* had opened its emotions, physical processes and thought-state to the Admiral. It was something that *Nœ-bouk* had not previously been aware was possible.

"Then we are both *dead*."

The Admiral used the symbol block in its archaic form – *death* – which was not present in the active symbol blocks used on Home Planet. *Nœ-bouk* was familiar with the term. During its training in the early instruction centres, it had studied the lower thought patterns of non-unified planets in which the concept of *death* was a central parameter, however it had never known the term used before in an active sense.

"What is your meaning?"

"My meaning is: our bodies and minds from our Home Planet existence are no longer in activation. We are beyond the lifespan."

Nœ-bouk and the Admiral shared the resonance of this concept.

"I was given a symbol block," communicated *Nœ-bouk*.

"What was it?"

Nœ-bouk recreated the endless appearing and disappearing stars: *freedom.*

"Yes," the Admiral conveyed at last.

"What meaning do you draw out?"

"Do you share the sensations of my physical form? Do you read the thought strands which pass through my mind?"

"Yes. I share these processes."

"This is all unprecedented. Impossible. Our life force is merging into one single thread and we are within that thread. This is a field of pure essence. Here, anything could be. This is the meaning."

"*Freedom. Death. Essence.*" *Nœ-bouk* repeated the vibrations once again to the Admiral.

The Admiral did not communicate further, but it drew its image back in the visual horizon so that *Nœ-bouk* was able to view its entire being – the oversized head and eyes, the wasted limbs and emaciated trunk, barely supporting the structure – and *Nœ-bouk* was struck with the realisation of how little they knew of one another outside this

147

unprecedented experience, whether in details of physical form, or life-span memory or thought pattern. And yet the knowledge they did have of each other was on a deeper and more unified level than any informa-tion which *Noœ-bouk* had shared with other genus types on Home Planet through the exchange of thought waves and symbol blocks, or even physical gestures.

"What is the state of your cell deterioration?" the Admiral eventu-ally sent.

"It is stable, but at a level at which it should not be in active exis-tence. Minus twenty-four."

"My condition is similar. Minus thirty."

"Then you are correct. We are both *dead*."

The Admiral once again faded from *Noœ-bouk*'s vision field, and *Noœ-bouk* found itself in the light pod, with symbol blocks and thought strands circling within its mind space. *Freedom. Death. Possible and impossible.*

Why was it choosing to remain in a living state? *Death.* That was the symbol block the Admiral had used. The concept that a being, which identified itself primarily as a physical form, ceased to exist when the physical form completed its lifespan capacity. The concept was difficult for *Noœ-bouk* to understand. Yet now, surely, in these actions and choices, it was itself clinging to a physical form which had no practical application of any kind. In truth, it was not contributing to the vessel in a meaningful way. It had no skills which could benefit the ship or mission in a manner that other beings could not accomplish at an equally satisfactory level. It had been given permission to enter the vessel and remain on board as a reward for the task assignment it had completed. However, this should not have been authorised. The task assignment was the culmination of a logically planned and well-executed lifespan. There was no cause for rewards, or alterations to extrapolated logic-based conclusions. *Noœ-bouk* had fulfilled its lifespan contribution to Home Planet, and it should now move on from its phys-ical casing. It had made the decision to remain following a series of emotional reactions which had resulted from extreme physical deterio-ration. It should not have been permitted to make decisions in that state, nor based on such lack of established logic. The Council and the Admiral had made an incorrect assessment. *Noœ-bouk* would inform them of this. The very existence of the emotions it had been subject to should have acted as a deterrent. And now these emotions had deep-ened into a state of permanent negativity, almost to the point of separa-tion fallacy, and it was clearly following the recognised lower energy pattern of seeking a *love* experience in order to recreate the semblance of unity.

Noœ-bouk felt a strong urge to explain its mistake to the Home Planet Council and pass into the resting place. It was tired. It did not think it could exist without a logical basis to its actions or without any meaningful task assignment. This emotional unity with the Admiral was an experience which should be reported to the Scientific and Research Centre and studied as a newly observed side effect of two separate cases of extreme physical debilitation. It should not be taken as a new kind of truth. *Noœ-bouk* still retained enough extrapolation power in its thought process to be aware of that. But then it recalled the symbol block that the tentacled being had used. *Freedom.* And the Admiral; the way its entire physical form changed at the very vibration of its name.

Was it so wrong to experience these things which were archaic and which it had studied from a higher perspective as taking place in beings at primitive levels of development? No. This was considering the matter incorrectly. The physical deterioration had simply lowered its energy vibration to the point where this was the appropriate emotional state. Both it and the Admiral had clearly sunk below unity and, finding themselves in a paradigm of illusory separation, had created this *love* experience with which to raise up their vibration once again. *Noœ-bouk* could understand this.

The force of the Admiral's certainty, the symbol block of *freedom* which the tentacled life form had conveyed to it, returned to *Noœ-bouk* as it grappled with its doubt. It had never before been in a position where it had sought guidance from others in the matter of lifespan choices. And yet, it had no reference point remaining to check the validity of its reactions. *Noœ-bouk* allowed itself once more to visualise that folding star; repeating, repeating in endless variations. It lowered the thought shield.

ALISDAIR ENTERED the library and walked down the central aisle, breathing in the fragrance of the books and scrolls. The scent filled his body with anticipation, and he wondered if there were prototypes of all the different kinds of smells here, just as there were prototypes of the animals and plants in that fantastical garden. He imagined, in their purest form, the essence of cut grass, of cooking pancakes, of malt whisky. Flowering jasmine, brewing beer, the Scottish sea. The thought was wonderful. But the aroma he was breathing in right now was, beyond a doubt, his favourite – that musty, woody perfume of paper and the quiet velvet of ink, and the one he was convinced existed not only in his imagination, but in reality, too – the scent of hidden knowledge, waiting to be discovered.

He inhaled deeply and made his way towards the lectern with the carved dragons and griffins, which he had found on his first visit to the library. Straight up the steps from High Holborn, he recalled with a smile. There were figures seated at tables with volumes spread out before them and he marvelled at the thought of the lives they were reading, the knowledge they were drinking in. He found the lectern and saw that a book was already laid out on it. He touched the cloth binding with his fingertips, and then, on impulse, he opened it in the middle. There it was, on the page he had opened: the life of Socrates.

"Perhaps you would like to go into one of the viewing chambers?" said a voice beside him, and Alisdair turned to see a male librarian with tousled hair and a shabby suit, clutching a tall pile of books. "It is an interesting life," he continued, motioning his head towards the book. "It is often used for imprinting by those who intend to work with the law."

"Imprinting?" said Alisdair.

"Before they go back," said the librarian, "people often read lives which will be of benefit to the one they plan to live. They imprint them into their subconscious so that the knowledge is available to them. They can draw on it during their lifetimes."

"I was a lawyer," said Alisdair, "but I don't think I was familiar with this life."

The librarian narrowed his eyes. "Yes. You chose other lives to imprint. This one was not required for your last life. You were more involved with example and contribution to society, if I have seen correctly."

"Yes, that was the case."

"And do you not now remember your imprints? The lives you viewed?"

Alisdair paused to think. He saw flashes of panelled rooms, flushed faces and grand speeches; moments and inspirations which he now recognised had guided him throughout his years.

"Yes! Yes, I remember! I know what I saw – what I chose. Yes, these were most appropriate."

"Of course they were," said the librarian. "And I would think that many people will be using *your* life to imprint. It was very pure. You achieved what you intended in a direct manner. The Council must be pleased."

"Duncan, my guide, was pleased. I thought I could have done better."

The librarian smiled. "Everyone thinks that. It is all so easy with hindsight. And so difficult when you are in the middle of it all."

"Yes, I suppose so."

"Come, let me show you to the viewing room. If you prefer, you can always return to read here at the lectern."

"Very well."

Alisdair picked up the book and followed the librarian to the hidden door where Duncan had taken him for his review. There was the fireplace and the stiff armchairs; the panelled squares embossed with roses and thistles.

"It will be the same as when you reviewed your own life," the librarian was saying. "Enjoy it. I will come to see you when I have finished some of this work."

"Thank you," said Alisdair.

He sat down in the chair and laid the great book on the table. He looked around, remembering how his own life had appeared before him out of the shadows. Just as before, the chamber darkened to a muted dusklight, the flames of the fire rose and a woman with long, black hair took form before him, dressed in a loose robe and holding a baby to her chest. The image was holographic, as if the woman and the child were in the same room, and he stretched out his arm to touch them. The woman was whispering to the baby, and Alisdair understood the words she was speaking in ancient Greek.

"Socrates, Sophroniscus," the woman was saying. "Socrates, strong baby boy. You will grow up to be wise and productive like your father. He is so proud that I have given him a son. A strong baby son."

Alisdair could sense his spirit moving with the mother's words. He could feel the warmth of her skin, smell the cardamom and the rosemary drying in the corner of the room and see the strips of sunlight through the window and the oil in the mother's hair. He willed the scene forward, and he was a boy, throwing dice and knucklebones with his friends, catching birds in the trees and courtyards and transfixed by the world around him. The stars in the darkest night-times, the sun blazing in the day, the cycles of the seasons, the bud, flower and death.

Alisdair moved on again, and found that he was on the outside of a group of citizens, listening to a heated discussion. His mind was racing along with the words, tracing forward and back as each man spoke his turn, understanding the threads of logic and the motivations and the possible conclusions to each point of view. The questions burned inside his head as he gathered and sorted the words and felt the levels of understanding rising in him, opening into flower as the world revealed itself before him.

"Ah, Socrates!" A sophist had spotted him at the edge of the circle. "Our young friend has come to challenge us again. Tell us what you have understood. From what is the air truly made? Come, speak!"

Alisdair shifted the scene forward. He was on the streets of Athens and it was the procession of the Great Pan-Athenaea. It was four years since he had run from the Academy's altar of love to the centre of the city, naked and grasping a torch, racing his friends who that day had become men. Now the streets were filled with music, stamping horses, the smells of exotic foods, dancing girls and foreigners from surrounding cities bringing ideas, books, thoughts, models of the world, everything which thrilled him to his core.

Alisdair moved onwards, and he saw himself older now, his cloak thin, his beard thick and his body scarred from wounds and wars. Wherever he went, crowds of young men followed him, and he challenged them with questions and pushed them as deep as their intellects would go. Together they debated the great mysteries of existence, and Alisdair felt that he had never been happier, leading these discerning, interested minds beyond the accepted ideas of themselves, drawing out the knowledge, guiding them to the fulfilment of the men they must be.

And then Alisdair was walking in an olive grove. He had wandered alone beyond the walls of the city, along the Sacred Way, and the intense, sweet scent of spring was mixed with the wind from the Aegean Sea, and he was breathing deeply in and out. The ground was cool beneath his bare feet, and the birdsong in the air and the trees around him created a harmonious backdrop to his thoughts.

As he walked, his *daimon* – his personal spirit – came to him, and he stopped, frozen in his path, his body and face transfixed, his eyes blank and staring. As his body ceased to function, a vision appeared, an image of a place where everything was so exquisitely lucid, where every flower was a bright cut jewel and every leaf was hand-carved from emeralds. The place was so beautiful that it made everything on the Earth seem like a pale shadow, like the dullest reflection of a winter evening, like the palest semblance of the glory he saw before him. Socrates smiled as he looked around this place, as if he had seen it before, and he moved, in his vision, through this mesmeric garden, led by his spirit guides, and he felt the intense, true light which was shimmering around him as he walked, staring in wonder at the birds – the peacocks, the golden eagles, a white owl. For many hours, Socrates wandered through this immaculate garden, remembering from where he had come, and from where everything had come. In a state of pure bliss, he replenished the amphora of light which had guided him throughout his life, which had led him to seek and uncover the wisdom of the world.

At last, it was time to return. His *daimon* passed, and Socrates opened his eyes to the view of the olive grove before him and he gave out a deep and agonised groan. The silver-green trees were shrouded with grey, the tiny birds stirring up pollen were but shadows, the entire world had been wrapped in a winter cloud. He looked all around him and nothing seemed real. What he saw was the most apologetic remembrance of glory, the most piteous imitation of truth, the most awful joke played out upon the soul of mankind.

Socrates began to cry.

CHAPTER SIXTEEN

DAVID LOOKED AROUND THE FLOOR. This was pretty much how he'd imagined it would be. A big, crowded room full of cubicles, more or less same as his department. It was more worn, though; the carpeting thinned out and stained, the cubicle walls dented as if they'd taken a battering, and the desks messier than on the Leverage Finance floor. Piles of papers, candy wrappers, packs of cigarettes, photographs pinned haphazardly onto boards. He liked it. There was a lot of energy here. Fresh, masculine energy. Adrenalin. He nodded as he looked around.

A man in a navy suit came out of the MD's office at the end of the hall.

"David?"

"Yes."

The man beckoned him over and David walked down the row of cubicles towards him. The man had short-cut hair, and one of those intensely active faces that never seem to be still. Eyes full of movement and intelligence, plans and fast-shooting thoughts.

"So, you know the drill?" he said.

"Yes, I do."

"You'll be sitting over there." He pointed to a cubicle at the end of the furthest row. The cubicle next to it was empty, and it was in full view of the MD's office. They would be keeping an eye on him. Quite right, too, with something like this going on.

"That looks fine," he said.

"So, go and get yourself set up, then check back with me in an hour.

I'll be here all morning. The guys on the floor don't officially know what you're doing, so I don't want you shooting the breeze with them, alright? All they know is that you're on secondment and you're not taking a piece of their pie."

"Yes, sir." David doubted that there was anyone on the floor who didn't know exactly what was going on. After all, it was these guys who had acquired the junk-based derivatives in the first place. Oh well. Their fuck-up, his opportunity.

"The computer's all set up with the accounts. Have a look through them. I've had a list of target clients printed out for you. Word is, you're new on the floor and you've been given a couple of key products to help establish yourself with the clients. Easy sell. We've put a few sweeteners in there. Some real good ones."

"That all sounds great."

"But don't get ahead of yourself, you hear me? Just take it easy. This is a delicate job. Do you understand that, David?"

"Yes, sir. I understand that. I've got quite a lot riding on this myself."

The man smirked. His eyes flickered around the room.

"Yes. That's what I heard," he said. "One hour, then?"

"One hour."

DAVID BENT his head low over the outstretched body and began to lick across the skin in wide, wet strokes. He started with the navel, the movement of his tongue painting a blue and silver trail across its surface. The flesh tasted like birth to him, it tasted like soil. His nose followed his mouth along the trail, his own body responding to the scent, follicles rising and tensing. He worked his way over the centre and then across the thighs and down the porcelain legs to the feet. He took each small toe in his mouth and sucked it gently. The form did not stir but lay entirely still as the flesh changed colour and warmed beneath his mouth.

He moved up the legs to the genitalia, inserting his tongue as far as he could up through the bristles of hair and into the holes. He continued upwards, covering each of the breasts, the outstretched neck, across each shoulder to the arms. When the front was glistening silver, he turned the form and continued to run his tongue over the back, downwards to the curved buttocks and over the line of each leg. Turning again, he shifted to the face, carefully brushing the hair out of his way, silvering the closed eyes, slipping his tongue into each ear-shell, then the lushness of the nose and mouth.

When he had finished, he felt an enormous satisfaction. The form was now covered in a complete layer of membrane. He decided to move away so he could see who it was and, stepping back, he smiled. Of course. He had known all along. The flowing red hair and pale skin. It was Cassie. As this knowledge passed through him, he looked down and saw that he had a towering erection. He was ready for her. The membrane in which she was encased desired him. Her smell desired him. The smell of birth. He wanted to climb inside that smell. He wanted to become one with it. He brought his penis up to her glistening form and he pushed it inside her. The smell became overpowering. He pushed and pushed and she allowed him deeper and deeper until he was entirely inside her and she, covered in his membrane, was entirely inside him. He had come home. David ejaculated into the smell of birth, soil, woman.

He opened his eyes.

Very slowly, he sat up. He could not understand what was going on. He could not see properly. Grey light was coming through the window, but there was something wrong with his eyes. He felt a wet mass all over the bed. He wiped his face with the back of his hand and looked at his skin. It was covered in some liquid. Was he crying? He reached for a tissue from the bedside table, blew his nose, then rubbed his hands on the bedsheet.

There was something else wet. He looked under the covers. He had come in the bed – pools of semen were all over the sheets. He shook his head. It must have been ten years since his last wet dream. How could that have happened?

He climbed over the wetness and got out of bed. He wasn't wearing boxer shorts. Strange. He always wore them; he must have kicked them off in the night. He wiped himself with another tissue and dropped it to the floor. He'd clean it up later. He walked through the kitchen into the bathroom and rotated the silver taps to start the shower. Without thinking, he pulled down the seat of the toilet and sat naked on the lid. An image of Cassie came into his head. He had been making love to her, he remembered now. He suddenly felt an intense desolation, as if he had lost something unspeakably precious. It was as if Cassie were dead. Or as if the most treasured thing in his life had suddenly vanished. He put his hands over his face and closed his eyes. Total despair.

Steam from the running shower filled up the small bathroom. David sat with his hands covering his face, and he felt tears running over his unshaven skin. At last, he pulled himself up from the toilet seat.

He didn't bother to clean the tears away. He just stepped straight into the hot shower and let the water fall over his body, covering him in a glistening wave of liquid. He closed his eyes.

"YOU KNOW, I have a discretionary fund for doctorate students."

Professor Baird looked at David over his glasses. He was leaning forward across the desk, which was covered in chaotic piles of paper.

"It's an endowment fund, on top of the usual grant money, and it is entirely up to me, as the head of the faculty, whether I offer it to someone or not. A hundred per cent funding. Everything covered. You wouldn't even have to teach. It was designed to let us embrace any opportunity to improve the research quality of the department. David, you *are* that opportunity."

"Professor, I—"

"David, you have to understand. You have an exceptional intellect. I can say this safely because I also have an exceptional intellect. It can be a tiring job when you have so few people to relate to on an intellectual level. Usually, the only opportunities are at conferences or panels. But that's not what I'm talking about, David. If you take this opportunity, you can go in any direction you want. I mean, you wouldn't have to stay with economics. I know you have diverse interests and we would welcome research that moved in unconventional directions. This is where some of the most extraordinary breakthroughs have come from in the past, from linking seemingly unrelated fields. David, this opportunity could bring so much to you and the university. I really encourage you to think about it. You are the first person I've offered this fund to. In fact, I haven't even thought of offering it to anyone else."

"Professor, I—"

"David, look—"

"Professor. I got offered the job at Mercy Bank. I accepted it already. I start in Toronto, but I plan to get an MBA as soon as I can and go for a transfer to New York."

"To do what, David? What is there in New York except for money?"

"Well, money, sir."

"David, think about it. I am offering you a chance to make a difference. To make such a spectacularly big difference that any sum of money just doesn't begin to compare."

"Professor, it's an amazing offer. I really, really appreciate it. But I'm going to New York."

A SIGNAL HAD COME through to the Captain from two of the ships stationed in the *Tayr* vicinity. There had been an escalation of the energy imbalance in a certain area of the planetary orbit, and there was an urgent need to stabilise the locality.

The exploration crew of the landing creel had identified the new genus type on the living planet, and had extracted a genetic sample from it. While they were on the surface, several other anomalies had been recorded, and the scientific team were preparing a full report on the evidentiary pattern of irregular observations. The genetic samples extracted appeared to have originated from a living planet in the proximate galaxy, where expansion tendencies were known to be developing. This was the first clearly identifiable colonial excursion by the planet, and it would be referred to the supervising Councils. Energy shields might have to be placed over it, if the seeding was proven to have initiated there, in order to prevent further colonial attempts, until the lower energy had been dispelled and raised to a more federate level. In these situations, when an extra-planetary target of aggression was rendered inaccessible, it sometimes transpired that the lower energy became transposed into warring impulses within the planet of origin, and a period of own-planet warfare and destruction ensued. However, in these cases, it was advisable that the lower energies be contained within one planet, rather than allowing the continuation of aggression-based expansion, which could lead to negative repercussions throughout all of the proximate planetary systems.

The first vessel assignment had been completed successfully, and the mission statistics barely had to be run through the risk analysis system before the Captain sent out a symbol block of consensus, and the vessel's course was set for *Tayr*.

Noœ-bouk did not take part in any of the preparations for the new mission, and spent many inhalation periods resting in the light capsule and preserving its energy. It had not communicated directly with the Admiral since the holographic encounter in the light pod, but it had sensed, with every inhalation, the Admiral's life force growing stronger within it. Unfamiliar thought patterns and symbol blocks had been appearing within its mind space, and it had come to the conclusion that a state of permanent connection had already been achieved, which was resulting in them sharing their physical and mental processes. The sensation of the Admiral led to a continual flow of mild *kaiif* within *Noœ-bouk*. The Admiral was present in the universe; the state of *love* existed in the universe; and *Noœ-bouk* was tuned to one thought wave with the Admiral, in which, without overt communication of any kind, they shared with each other the experience of being alive.

"*Noœ-bouk*."

A thought wave was being sent to it.

"*Noœ-bouk*."

It came again. *Noœ-bouk* raised itself from the light capsule. A crew member, which *Noœ-bouk* had not seen before, had entered the resting chamber.

"The Advisory Committee has requested your presence."

Noœ-bouk was surprised. "Why did they not send a summons thought wave?"

"Respect," sent the crew member. "They desired to express their respect and consideration for your physical condition."

"I appreciate their consideration," communicated *Noœ-bouk*. "I will come."

Noœ-bouk followed the being along the curved, white corridors of the vessel, and into the compartments where the Advisory Committee were holding their sessions to prepare for the *Tayr* mission. The crew member stopped outside the sliding entrance of one of the chambers.

"Honour," it communicated. "I wish you well-being."

The doors slid open and *Noœ-bouk* entered the chamber.

Around a clear, white table were seated the Advisory Committee, including the Head of the Scientific and Research Centre, the Head of the Space Observation and Evaluation Centre and the Captain. These were the most senior members of the crew and *Noœ-bouk* understood that the issues they were discussing must be of the highest importance.

"We welcome you."

"Greetings."

"Enter."

Noœ-bouk approached the table and saw that there was a seat which had been allocated for it. It bowed to the beings at the table, and sent a symbol block of respect and anticipation.

The Captain initiated the communication.

"*Noœ-bouk*, we are in need of your consultation on the matter of energy-balancing."

"I will provide assistance to the best of my lifespan accumulation of knowledge."

The Head of the Scientific and Research Centre rose to standing position.

"There is an energy imbalance in the *Tayr* system," it sent. "If it is not resolved, it will cause extreme physical upheavals on the planet surface and subsurface. The upheavals will set back the planetary evolution by many million solar cycles, as it is measured on the *Tayr* plane. It is not advisable for this to occur. It may even be severe enough to affect other planetary systems. It is necessary for *Tayr* to ascend and enter the Federation."

"What is the cause of the imbalance?"

"The energy fields of the individuals located on the planet are not expanding fast enough. It was expected that the consciousness would have lifted to a more elevated level, but there have been factors preventing the ascension. The cycles of darkness and violence are deeply embedded into the overall field."

The Head of the Scientific and Research Centre paused, and made a physical gesture to the Committee, signifying critical importance.

"The planet has a limit of how much lower energy it can withstand before destruction will occur," it conveyed, forming thought strands in precise sequence. "It is extremely close to that limit. There are movements all over *Tayr* which are attempting to initiate ascension, and a certain rising is taking place. But it is not enough. Signs of damage are already beginning to manifest. It is necessary to bring in higher energy to balance it and prevent the planet from entering a phase of devastation and returning to a primeval state."

"What level of urgency has the imbalance reached?"

"Maximal level. If they do not rise, then the destruction will take place as it has before on this planet and other early development planets. But this event is neither advisable nor planned. It is necessary for them to rise. It is necessary for them to unite. The Federation is awaiting them. There are resources which only this planet can provide to the Federation."

"What about the Councils? Why do the Councils not have energy-balancing systems in place? How is it that we have been called into this situation?"

"The Councils have limitations on the levels of assistance they can provide. They supervise the beings who work with *Tayr*, but they are not permitted to control or change the energies. This is a unique situation in which permission has been granted to allow the participation of other planetary beings. By balancing the energy, we are keeping open the possibility of *Tayr* rising and joining the Federation. There is still a challenging and unclear path ahead, but in this single instance, we have been given permission to help. This is what has occurred."

"I understand. What is the energy reading?"

An assignee from the Scientific and Research Centre rose and projected a hologram to the side of the chamber, and the Advisory Committee turned to observe it. The hologram was a map of the solar system, showing the entire energy field of *Tayr* shimmering in many coloured layers. The assignee indicated a dark, convoluted pattern in one area of the field.

"This is where it has occurred," it communicated. "This is where the balance must be restored. Do you see the implications to the planet if it is not balanced?"

"Yes."

Noœ-bouk studied the map.

"This could be achieved with the channelling abilities of one being from Home Planet. One single energy-channeller could perform this."

"This is the conclusion we have also come to. We desired to receive your opinion to confirm the finding. We are considering whether to apply for an energy-channeller to be transported to the vessel."

Noœ-bouk stared again at the map. It would require a being of great personal strength and power, task-assignment knowledge and discipline. A being such as it had been.

A thought came to *Noœ-bouk*. It regarded the map. It experienced a shiver of recognition as it felt the thought simultaneously passing through the mind of the Admiral.

It felt another shiver as it received the Admiral's answer.

Noœ-bouk lowered itself to seated pose.

IT WAS many days before Socrates could bring himself to return to the city walls. He wandered in a state of depression, climbing to the peak of his beloved Lycabettus, where the clouds and the sunshine dwelt hand in hand, and yet he was unable to expunge from himself the feeling that something glorious, something utterly precious, had been lost. There was something which he now knew existed – which he had felt, experienced, touched – and the knowledge of which had cast into shadow everything around him. It was something the Gods had shown him, had chosen for him to know. Now the world seemed to him entirely lacking in beauty, in truth and purity. How could he bear to live? Was he, too, a pale shadow of reality? Was this all that his life of effort and toil and thought and teaching amounted to – the pale reflection of a truth, which he would never again be able to experience in its pure state? It was too much. It was unbearable. He had to think. He was not yet ready to return. He had to let his passions settle so that they would not cloud the structures which had at last begun to formulate.

In the distance were the high walls of the city, golden sunshine touching the surrounding hills. Athens. Protected by Athena. Protected by the owl. The greatest of all the city-states. A city epitomising the best of the virtues and the highest rank of thought. A place where men were not afraid to raise themselves up in pursuit of knowledge and understanding and excellence. His home.

Socrates seated himself on a flat rock, held his head in his hands, and concentrated.

CHAPTER SEVENTEEN

"SO, THE PROJECT'S GOING WELL?"

Vanessa reached over the table and picked up the enormous wine glass, in which half an inch of ruby-red, $150 St Emilion was glowing in the candlelight. She took a sip, then stretched her foot out under the table and ran it lightly up David's suit leg.

"As a matter of fact, it's going very well."

"You certainly seem upbeat about it."

"It's an opportunity. They were looking for someone to make some tough sales calls. I took the chance."

"That's fantastic, David."

"I've made over half the sales already. And it's only been a week."

"That's amazing."

"If it all goes well, I'll have got the project done within the month, and then it's bonus time."

The waiter, dressed entirely in black, with a white napkin tucked into his belt, approached the table and swept away the plates stained with Caesar dressing and scraps of romaine lettuce. He returned a moment later and poured some more of the wine into their glasses.

"How are you enjoying the St Emilion tonight?" he asked.

David nodded. "Delicious. Good recommendation."

"It's so soft," said Vanessa. "It makes me feel like I'm in France."

"I'm glad you like it," the waiter said. "Your steaks won't be a minute."

David leaned back and took another sip. He looked out over the marble balcony of the restaurant and down into the bustle of Grand

Central Station. Above them, the celestial green ceiling stretched out across the main hall; the entire spread of constellations, with each of the zodiac signs traced in delicate gold above the frantic rushing of New York commuters and office workers.

David loved the station. He loved it when he noticed someone looking up at the ceiling, pausing their hyper-speed day for just a moment. They would always stop. They would always be taken back a step, the crazy rushing of their lives instantly given a new perspective, shrunk down below that gold and green map of stars to what it actually was: a mindless, ego-fuelled, caffeine-buzzed stampede of human creatures from one place to another. He was part of this madness, and he loved that, too. It was something so strange and yet so necessary about the human race – this rushing forward. Seventy or eighty years of momentum, and then nothing at all. Silence. Somehow, the ceiling made that acceptable to David.

He put his nose to the thin edge of the wine glass, letting the scent waft up and fill his head. He took another sip.

"Bonus time sounds good."

"What's that?"

Vanessa was smiling at him. She had slipped off her shoes beneath the table and was running her foot up his leg again with her toes.

"I said, bonus time sounds good."

David gave a small cough and shook his head. He brought his attention away from the commuters below and back to Vanessa.

"Yeees," he said. "Yes, there should be a good package coming at the end of the project. Definitely something to look forward to."

"Any plans as to how to spend it?"

"Well, I'm thinking of taking a week or so off. Go somewhere hot. Bahamas. Hawaii. Somewhere with a beach."

"That sounds good."

"And I was thinking of maybe buying a ring for a lady I like very much."

"A ring? Anyone I know?"

David reached out across the table and took Vanessa's hand in his. He stroked her fingers.

"I like you a lot, Vanessa."

Vanessa licked her lips.

"I like you a lot too, David."

"You know, I didn't expect to meet anyone in New York. I thought this place was full of gold-diggers."

"It is. But not only—"

"So, you think this lady I know would be interested in getting a ring?"

"If she's the lady I'm thinking of, then she'd be pretty much over the moon."

"And what about a ticket to Hawaii? How do you think she'd feel about that?"

"I think she'd be ready to quit her job if they wouldn't give her the time off."

"Well, let's hope they give her the time off, then."

"Let's hope."

The waiter approached the table and set down two over-sized white plates.

"Kobe marbled beef," he said. "Best in New York."

A moment later he returned with several small dishes balanced up his arm.

"Creamed spinach. Scalloped potatoes. Fresh black pepper?"

"Yes, please."

They watched as he ground pepper over the steaks from an arm-length pepper mill, and then stepped back.

"You have everything you need, sir? Madam?"

"This is perfect," said David. "And the wine is really great."

"Thank you, sir."

David nodded to the waiter, then turned his gaze back to Vanessa. He had never seen anyone looking so hungry. He'd buy her a ring. He'd buy her a ring to assuage that hunger. He could work with that.

He raised his glass, looking into those eyes – hooded, mascara-blackened, simple in their desire.

"To that lady," he said slowly, every word filled with meaning, "and a ring."

"YOU'RE COMING OUT WITH ME?" David shouted from the bathroom. He pushed open the door to let the mirror un-steam. Vanessa was buttoning up her white shirt just beyond the kitchen.

"Yeah," she called back. "I'll take the subway home, grab a shower and then head in to work. There's still a ton of time. We don't work as early as you do."

David wiped the mirror with a towel and sprayed shaving foam into his hand.

"Nobody works as early as we do."

· · ·

BY 6:15, they were both ready. David locked the apartment behind them and they took the stairs down to the foyer.

"Just going to check the mailbox," said David. Vanessa pushed open the front door and stepped out into the cool pre-sunshine of the New York morning. She pulled her coat around her and went down the steps, turning at the bottom to look at a homeless man asleep in the corner of the canopy area, his body curled around sheets of newspaper. His bare head and hands were red from the cold, and appeared swollen.

Vanessa reached into her coat pocket and felt around for some notes. She pulled out a twenty and a five, leaned forward, and pushed the twenty into the man's hand, holding her breath against the stench of whisky and unwashed skin.

"Stay warm, mister."

The man made a low sound and lifted his eyelids a crack.

David swung open the front door of the building and came down the steps. He looked at the homeless man and the twenty-dollar bill in his hand, and then at Vanessa.

"Let's go," he said.

The man cleared his throat. He tightened his clasp around the twenty and pushed it into the pocket of his coat. He looked up at Vanessa.

"Thank you, lady."

"Let's go," David said again. He was trying not to notice the disproportionate size of the man's head to his body, and his eyes to his head. He wanted to look away but instead found himself staring straight into those eyes. They were grey, flecked with light, and an image of a tunnel came into David's mind, a grey tunnel, something to do with him. It was his tunnel. It was where he had to go.

"David." Vanessa slid her hand into his. "Are we leaving?"

David heard her voice and shook his head hard to break the line of vision. A tunnel. Stupid. Oversized eyes. Stupid. The guy was probably ill with some alcoholic disease which made him swell up in weird places. He started to walk down the street fast, dragging Vanessa behind him.

"Poor guy," said Vanessa. "I always feel bad for homeless people. I don't know why. I guess the winters here are so cold."

They were out on First Avenue now, just three blocks from the subway at 77th. The grey, cool light was opening out into a fresh, sunny morning. David pulled himself together. It was going to be a great day. He was going to buy Vanessa a ring. He was going to finish the project. He slowed down at the edge of the sidewalk and smiled at her.

"I'll take you to Canada sometime," he said. "Then you'll see what a real winter looks like."

Vanessa hitched her handbag up on her shoulder.

"You know, I'd rather stick to Hawaii and the Bahamas, if it's all the same."

"Yeah, yeah. Softie." David squeezed her hand, gently now. "I'll take you to Hawaii. Just as soon as I've got this project out of the way. I'll get the flights. And you can get yourself a bikini."

They had arrived at the subway. They slid their yellow passes through the machines and Vanessa leaned up to kiss him.

"I'll see you later," she whispered in his ear.

"I'll call you," said David, and he turned away from her as a crowded train screamed towards his platform. He strode up to it, checking his watch for the time, and stepped on.

IT WAS BEFORE THEM.

The planet most observed and vigilantly monitored in all of the universe. The most unstable, the most volatile and unpredictable planet.

Tayr.

Rai-bouk and *Nœ-bouk* stood on the main viewing deck with several of the other non-task-assigned crew members, and they watched as the vessel entered the planetary system. The vibration engineer raised the level of the ship so that it would not be perceptible to the powerful monitors and radar scanners located around the planet.

Nœ-bouk could see a surprising number of other vessels positioned in the vicinity, both large and small, each with its vibration level raised, or a sensory protection shield active. It was highly unusual for an independent planet to have so much external observation. It conjectured that the ships must be connected to the imbalance, present to manage the repercussions if the energy field was not stabilised. After all, a cataclysmic disaster on *Tayr* would affect all of this galaxy and many more besides, and any actions which could be taken to neutralise the impact in the initial stages would greatly diminish the eventual negative resonance on the home planets of the surrounding vessels.

Yet, even despite the multiple observers and the knowledge of the potentially catastrophic energy convolution, *Nœ-bouk* found the planet enthralling. The richness of the pulsing, living colour; the wilderness and oceans, peaks and frozen scapes which it represented; the much-studied plethora of life forms which inhabited its different environments caused *Nœ-bouk* to enter a state of wonder. It thought back to the barren rockscape of Home Planet, with its varying shades of red and pink light illuminating the dust and passive stones. The cratered moons passing overhead one by one. The underground dwelling chambers, and the central edifice of the planet – the mirrored pyramid where the logistical planning system was administered. Compared to the colours and profusion of life form and organic matter which were in abundance here on *Tayr*, it was a desolate environment for existence. It understood, as it never had before, how a being might choose to spend a lifespan on this planet, might elect the strange obligations of blindness and alienation from unity in order to know and see such diversity, and that particular element which was at the core of the *Tayr* experience: free will.

It had been easy to dismiss the wild and unpredictable choices of *Tayr* lifespans, when studying in the early development centres, within the elevated and logical thought structure of Home Planet. Now, however, standing beside *Rai-bouk* on the main viewing deck, it felt something inside of it move in a place which it could not identify and which had never been touched before. It was as if the gentlest fingertips had reached into its physical form and stroked some unknown organ, and in that touch, the organ had become alive. It was as if a new sense was awakening.

It moved its head towards *Rai-bouk* and observed on *Rai-bouk*'s features an expression with which it was not familiar. Its eyes were wide and it appeared as if it were in physical pain. *Nœ-bouk* would ordinarily have sent a thought wave to it, but now it felt an urge to share this experience in a different manner. It reached out its hand and tapped *Rai-bouk*'s fingers with its own. The touch was unusual – throughout its lifespan, there had been little requirement for physical interaction between genus types – and it was surprised at the warmth of *Rai-bouk*'s skin covering. It paused, after the gesture, and waited until *Rai-bouk*, without turning, shifted its hand and responded with a similar tapping on the surface of *Nœ-bouk*'s fingers. Their hands then remained still, resting, the skin touching, and together they looked out from the main viewing panel at the solar system and *Tayr*.

It appeared so lonely there. This planet, entirely cut off from other planetary beings and from the Federation, from other life forms, even from its highest ascension potential. Lonely and separated and in great pain. And yet such beauty was there. *Nœ-bouk* looked around the main viewing deck and observed that a silence had fallen over the crew, that not a single sound resonance or thought wave was moving on the deck. Life forms were leaning towards one another. Some were touching parts of their physical forms, fingers or sides, skin to skin.

Noœ-bouk had the thought, looking out at this planet which seemed so alone and vulnerable, unaware even that it was surrounded by multiple vessels which were monitoring its every energy shift, that it would willingly do something to create benefit for it. That it would be an act of the highest elevation to cross through that obliviating wall and bring a new energy to the planet, one which might give it that impetus to rise up, to balance, to open to the wonders beyond itself. To raise its energy high enough to make contact with the proximate civilisations and be the long-awaited thirty-seventh planet in the Federation.

To bring, at last, an understanding of unity, and to return the highest part of these life forms back to themselves.

To reunite that which was separated.

Rai-bouk's fingers moved over its own, and pressed down on the weakened grey skin. It was sharing *Noœ-bouk*'s thought waves.

"Only an extraordinary life form could achieve this," sent *Rai-bouk*. "We learned on Home Planet how many have tried."

"Yes," *Noœ-bouk* communicated. "Yes. But then one will succeed. One will channel enough light into the energy patterns of darkness. It will lift the planet. It will do a great service to the Federation."

Noœ-bouk used the thought wave which was transmitted by the Task Assignment Centre, when projects were apportioned: *the one with the highest natural ability and correctly applied discipline will achieve the maximum potential.*

The thought wave resonated between them as they shared the concept which had determined their own lifespans on Home Planet. The concept which held Home Planet on its trajectory of elevated achievement, for its inhabitants and Federation partners.

Noœ-bouk turned back towards the planet.

DUNCAN PUT his hand on Alisdair's shoulder and the city of Athens faded into a pale gold, and then into shadows. He watched as Alisdair returned to the chamber, drawing his presence back to the library, and to his guide. His brow was furrowed.

"Did you find what you were looking for?"

Duncan asked.

"I found what Socrates experienced," said Alisdair slowly. "He was in the garden. But I'm not sure if I have more questions now, or fewer."

"The life of Socrates was one of those few human existences that changed everything," Duncan said. "It is well worth exploring further. The threads of his mind and thought became woven into the fabric of all mankind after his death. He is everywhere. He is in everyone. It was a very powerful life."

"Yes. I always felt it to be like that. Of course it is."

The two men stood silent for a moment, in thoughtful reverence.

"Now," said Duncan at last, "it is time to leave this place and explore further. There are still many things I would like you to see before you choose a new life form."

"But what about Elspeth?" said Alisdair, suddenly remembering Eileen and the Earth Council. "I said I would be her guide."

Duncan nodded. "To be a guide," he said, "you need to understand what your subject is trying to achieve – what their goals are. Then you can see how best to help them."

"So, I should look in her book?" said Alisdair. "Is it allowed? While she is in the middle of a life?"

"For a guide, yes. Come."

The two men stepped out of the room, leaving the roses and thistles to fade into the shadowed embers of the fire. He followed Duncan to the familiar lectern, where a book was set out, a large tome bound in faded turquoise cloth and sewn with golden thread. Alisdair ran his fingers over the chipped wing of the griffin, just to make sure it was still there. He wondered who was giving lectures in York's Inn library in his place. One of his colleagues, perhaps. He smiled. He had come a long way since then.

He turned his attention to the book, stroking the cloth. He opened it at the beginning.

On the pages before him, he saw images of water, of liquid, of plant life. There was a sense of floating. Blocks of thought came to him, concepts of freedom, of development, of the desire to help, and a sense of the highest intelligence and the deepest curiosity. There was little physical movement.

He turned the pages forward and saw a barren landscape lit by dark-red light and underground tunnels. He looked further and saw unfamiliar planetary systems, physical and non-physical forms appearing; shifting, insect-like shapes, more liquid.

"Dear Elspeth! She's never been on Earth!" he exclaimed, turning to

Duncan. "Of course she doesn't know what she's doing. She's completely lost!"

Alisdair looked again, turning the pages. He saw a progression of varied and unfamiliar life forms driven by a curiosity almost similar to his own; a burning not just to know and understand, but to know everything *experientially*.

"She didn't go to Earth to *do* anything," Alisdair said. "She went there to *experience*, to spread some intelligence. Some different ideas. It was just... I'm seeing... curiosity."

Duncan nodded. "It is the most simple of all the reasons. Earth is a fascinating place. Advanced life forms like to go there, if only for a few cycles, to experience the beauty, the diversity, the free will. It is an entirely unique incarnation."

Alisdair suddenly looked worried. "But how can I be a guide to Elspeth if her soul is so different to mine?"

"You know how Earth works. You can help her to navigate. You can remind her that what she is doing is enough – just being present there."

"Oh yes," said Alisdair. "I can remind her of that. I can show her that her life is just right, that she is perfect. I would like to do that very much!"

Duncan laughed. "It sounds so easy. But you Earth people find *perfection* a hard idea to accept."

Alisdair turned the pages in the book, revealing shapes and landscapes of manifold variety. Duncan watched with interest, his half-moon glasses balanced on his nose.

"The advanced beings often get lost on Earth," he said thoughtfully, as they observed an existence of swirling, coloured gas. "They find it difficult to accept the idea of themselves as a single, fixed being. In other manifestations, it can be flexible – the idea of who or what you are. But on Earth, you need to believe that you are *someone* and convince others that you are *someone*. If you keep changing, or can't accept a single belief system, you can become isolated from the functioning community. You can find yourself in quite dire straits. And at the same time, it's difficult to connect with your own truth. It can be terribly hard."

Alisdair was nodding.

"The thought structures are oversimplified as well," Duncan continued. "Advanced beings use highly nuanced structures, and they find it confusing to simplify this into the Earth's binary and trinary system."

"I'm surprised Elspeth got as far as she did," said Alisdair. "I hope she has found some happiness along the way. I hope I was able to give her some good moments."

171

The beach and the flying sand came back to him, and he smiled. A moment later, he frowned.

"How do I do that?" he asked. "How do I show her what she came to Earth to do?"

"It's all about relativity," Duncan replied. "It's what I was talking about in the Earth Council meeting. The good and the bad. Goodness can't conceive of itself without the presence of non-goodness. You need to bring her into the presence of someone who is not on their path, so she can realise the truth that she has lived. This is how you teach it experientially, as a guide. An encounter such as this can give both souls the realisation they need to move forward. It will be beneficial for every-one. You can also create a meeting place where she is able to come to you when she is in a quiet or sleeping state. If she is open to the encounter, then you can use this to speak to her and let her know that you are her guide."

Alisdair looked relieved.

"Thank you," he said. "I will do all that. And more."

Alisdair drew his hand once more over the pages of the book, then folded over the heavy cover. A film of silver dust rose, twinkling from the turquoise cloth. He looked up. Duncan was smiling.

"You'll have to teach me that trick with the dust some time," Alis-dair said.

"Of course I will." Duncan cleared his throat. "But now there is more exploring to do." He gestured out of the library, towards the Prototype Garden.

"But the guiding? The meeting place?"

"It will all happen simultaneously," said Duncan. "Follow me. You are helping her right now, as we speak. You'll understand it as we go."

CHAPTER EIGHTEEN

"I GOT A CALL FROM MARTIN WALSH."

Jeff was standing over the side of David's cubicle, looking down at him. David dropped the dialled number and slid the phone back onto its base. He straightened up.

"Christ, I hope it's good news."

"As a matter of fact, he's pretty happy with you. 'A great fucking job'. Those are the actual words he used. A great fucking job, David. That's pretty high praise from someone like Martin Walsh."

"Wow. Really? He actually said that?"

"Yup."

"That guy is a legend. I thought he was going to bust my balls."

"Can't bust a guy's balls when he's doing a great job. Anyway, just wanted to stop by and tell you to carry on doing whatever it is you're doing. What the hell *is* it you're doing, by the way?"

David leaned back, smiling. He tapped his nose.

"Canadian charm, Jeff. You can't fake it."

"Yeah, yeah. Try selling that bullshit to the shareholders." Jeff reached out and patted David on the shoulder, then turned away and walked back to his office. As soon as he was gone, Danny swung round on his chair in the cubicle opposite.

"So ass-licking does pay off?"

"It's not like I haven't worked for it."

"And where's this mysterious place you're on secondment to? There are a lot of rumours going around, you know."

"M&A. And Equity Trading. I'm doing a double secondment. I'm setting up a bidding war for my salary."

"Yeah, very funny. Seriously, you're not gonna tell me what group it is?"

"No can do, man. Jeff put the word on mum. He doesn't want it to go public if I fuck up there."

"Whatever. Anyway, Jenny enjoyed meeting you. Said you were a lot nicer than she'd pictured."

"Jenny had pictured me?"

"Yeah, shut up."

"Hey, she was a sweet girl. You're lucky to have someone like that. Keep you grounded."

"I thought you had some girl waiting for you out there in your backwater?"

"Nah. That's old news. Listen. Gym? One o'clock? I've got my mile down to six point five."

"Yeah, you got it. Don't wanna get a paunch working the hours you do."

"See ya."

Danny swung back to his desk. David picked up the phone and looked for the number he had been dialling when he had been interrupted. It was SLC Corporation. Tony Morgan. Another happy client. Another big name for his portfolio. David nodded to himself as he waited for the PA to pick up. Things were looking pretty fucking good.

IN HIS DREAM, the two grey eyes of the homeless man expanded before him, growing larger and larger, until the wet spheres were the only things visible. The eyes appeared to have consumed everything as they grew: the homeless man's body, his head and all the surrounding space. The only thing remaining was their gargantuan presence looming over David, who found himself standing on his kitchen table back home in Kingston, dressed in a pinstriped suit, and no bigger than the stalk of an apple.

David tried to move to the left and the right, but on each side he was blocked by the huge, wet spheres, which were still expanding. They were going to envelop him. They were going to consume him. He was going to be swallowed alive by those monstrous pools of liquid. He crouched down on the table as the circles grew over him, and when they were almost touching him, when he was certain that he was going to drown in their bilious depths, he noticed that there was a kind of rim around them, a socket holding the vitreous in place.

He jumped up and balanced easily. There was a translucent film covering the wetness of the eye, which was protecting him from its water. Turning towards it, he discovered a network of silver channels, alive and buzzing with information. David dashed along the rim, following the pulsing lines, then darted back in the other direction. He could understand what was flowing in them. Zigzags of anticipation shot through his body – he was going to read it all! He was going to become a channel for that information!

He jumped upwards in his excitement and suddenly he was floating in front of the eye. This was just what he needed. Pushing with his hands, he swam through the air and followed the lines up and down the surface, absorbing everything. A sense of urgency came over him and he felt that he would die of thirst if he didn't drink down every drop of information as fast as he could. He swam wildly over the network of silver channels, directing his hands before him, his body gulping down the living, pulsing waves.

He drank and drank, and at last he was done. He relaxed his body and let himself float, gorged, on the air. Now, at last, he could sleep. "And, please," he whispered aloud, "please don't forget this again. It's too important."

DON'T FORGET THIS AGAIN.

What the hell did that mean?

David sat up in bed. He looked out of the window. It was still dark outside. That meant that it was before 5:30, when it started to get light. He rolled over and looked at the three clocks lined up on his bedside table. 4:15. That was alright. But there was the pain in his head again, the pressure pushing against his forehead. He thought that the medications had cleared that up.

He groaned and rubbed his hands through his hair. What did that mean, the phrase he had woken up with? *Don't forget this again.* Weird. And there was something in the dream about eyes. And that homeless guy. Maybe the medications needed changing. He'd talk to Shapkin about it. But right now, he still had the pain.

He got out of bed and went to the kitchen. He pulled the cranberry juice out of the fridge and took a long mouthful. Sour and cold.

That *feeling* again. Like there was a box sitting just inside his forehead and pushing hard against the skin. He put his hand up to his head, as if he could actually feel something inside it. Nope. Skin and skull bone. He knew what he had to do. He screwed up his eyes and held them closed for two or three seconds, then he went back into the bedroom. He sat down at the computer table and pulled out a pad of paper and a pen. He started to write.

AN HOUR LATER, David was ready for work. He took a last look at the annotated sheets of paper, then covered them with a file. He had tried to throw the whole pile into the trash several times now, but somehow he couldn't do it. He had considered taking them to the shrink, to see if Dr Shapkin could make anything of them, but he was still avoiding him. Although, if the dreams were coming back, that probably meant that the meds had stopped working. He'd give it a few days. Then he'd make the call.

He pulled on his coat and closed the apartment door behind him. He walked the five flights down to the lobby and checked his mailbox in the porch area. Through the glass panel of the vestibule he could see the homeless man sitting on the top step. That was unusual; he was normally curled up under that dirty overcoat at this time in the morning. David slipped the two bills from the mailbox into his coat pocket and pulled open the front door. As he walked down the steps, the homeless man reached out a hand and grabbed the bottom of his Canali suit jacket.

"Hey! Get off!" David jerked the cloth out of the outstretched hand. He turned around in fury to look at the man and saw the eyes incredibly close to him, grey and watery, folds of skin and veins and ragged beard surrounding them. The eyes were unusually large; shocking and repugnant within the broken face. David pulled himself away and stepped back onto the curb, nearly tripping over it into the road. He turned and started walking as fast as he could towards First Avenue, away from the building, away from the man.

This was Vanessa's fault. She shouldn't have given him that twenty. Now the guy was grabbing his jacket with his filthy hands. He'd be expecting money every time he turned up. David suddenly felt furious – at Vanessa, at the homeless man, at the building super for not clearing the guy out, at the people who were walking too damn slowly in front of him. He balled his hands into fists and squeezed them as tightly as he could.

He had to calm down, to stop being so angry. It was that stupid dream which had set him off, and then having to write that stuff down again. Why was that still going on? The medication was meant to have cleared that up. He was in the middle of the most important deal of his life and he was pissed and stressed over some stupid dream.

Calm down.

He was doing well on the deal. He had already covered half the sales and Martin Walsh was pleased and Jeff was pleased. Now it was going to get tougher, but he had plenty of sweeteners to add to the package: high-yield bonds, guaranteed futures. This was fine. He would be careful, and he would finish the job. And then he had Hong Kong waiting for him, or London or Tokyo. Wherever he wanted.

David breathed in as deeply as he could and checked his watch. Everything was fine. 6:25. He'd call Vanessa over later for some stress relief. He breathed out. It was going to be a good day.

"CAROLINE."

"Mr Cornwell."

"Is he available? Can I go in?"

"Go right in, Mr Cornwell."

David tightened his fingers around the handle of his soft, leather briefcase. He pushed open the heavy door and stepped into the familiar office.

"David." Dr Eugene Shapkin beckoned to him with an outstretched arm. David noticed a gold watch and a pair of cufflinks threaded through an expensive shirt. This guy was making some serious money.

"David, I'm glad to see you. Please, have a seat."

"Thanks."

David crossed the room and settled into the expanse of beige leather. He set the briefcase down next to him. He noticed Eugene Shapkin's hair was combed over a bald area on the top of his head and he saw a fat fountain pen sat in front of him on the table, alongside a medical report. It must be his report. There couldn't be much written there. He hadn't really said anything.

"So, David, how's everything going?" Dr Shapkin was leaning back in his comfortable swivel chair. He had picked up the fountain pen and was turning it in his fingers.

"Some things good, some things not so good."

"Let's talk about the not-so-good things."

David pulled the briefcase up onto his knees, opened it and took out a thin file. He closed the briefcase and stood up. He paused for just a moment and then walked over to Dr Shapkin's desk. He held the file out to him.

"I've been having dreams again." The shrink reached out and took the file. He laid it on the desk in front of him and waited while David returned to the chair.

"Tell me," he said.

"I wake up, early in the morning. Four or five a.m. And it feels like there's something in my head. Physically inside my head. Like a box. Like there is an actual box which has been put inside my head while I'm sleeping."

"I see."

"And it feels like it's pushing against my forehead, right here." David put two fingers up to his forehead and rubbed them across the skin. "And the feeling gets stronger until I just... sit down and start writing. And I don't know what the hell it is I'm writing. That's it in the file. I don't know what it is."

"But you want it to stop, David?"

"Yes. I want it to stop."

Shapkin didn't open the file. His fingers were resting on it.

"David, whatever it is you are writing down when you wake up from these dreams... that isn't important. What *is* important, as I told you in our first session, is that your subconscious is trying to alert you to the fact that there is something in there that needs to be taken care of. Something that needs to be examined and healed. The fact that these dreams are continuing, despite some fairly strong medication, tells me that your subconscious is *urgently* trying to get you to deal with what is hidden in there."

He tapped his forehead gently with two fingers, mirroring David's action.

"David, we need to find out what is really inside that box."

He finished his speech. There was a long silence. Eugene Shapkin looked at David, and David looked around the room, at the large palm tree in the dark-green pot, at the thick, beige carpet, at the cream, scalloped panels of the ceiling and walls. At last, he looked back at the psychiatrist.

"Change my meds," he said.

There was another pause, and the doctor cleared his throat.

"David, I've given you as much leeway as I possibly can. We can't pretend that we don't know what is going on here. You are clearly avoiding the issue. You are doing everything you can *not* to talk about what is really going on. And it would be unprofessional of me, it would be against the code of professionalism, if I supported you any further in this policy of avoidance. David, if I am going to change your medication to something stronger, something which would enable you to do your job with an entirely clear head without having to worry about strange dreams, then I am going to have to see some effort on your part. Some actual dedication to the healing process. I need to see that you are trying to deal with the underlying issue."

"What does that mean?"

"Three sessions, David. We will have three more sessions. And in those sessions, we are going to talk about your childhood, your parents, your life, your issues. You are going to stop avoiding discussing these things with me. If I am satisfied with your progress after three sessions, then I will prescribe you the medication which will make everything easier to deal with, while we get you better."

David caught Shapkin's eye and looked down at the carpet. He studied it for a long time – the thick tufts of wool, woven from multiple threads. The hidden knots below. The flecks of dirt. He looked up and met the shrink's gaze.

"I'll do it."

 LONG AFTER *RAI-BOUK* had departed to continue its task assignments on board the vessel, *Noœ-bouk* remained on the main viewing deck. It was mesmerised by the presence of the planet so close to them, and it alternated its position between the viewing pod, where it could study the landscapes in greater detail and precise beauty, and the shocking closeness of the living surface from the observation panel.

Within its mind space, it repeated its communication with *Rai-bouk*, and felt its desire growing to give itself to the wildness of the planet. To try – even if it should fail – to do what other elevated beings had not succeeded in achieving.

It felt a sound vibration in its head. It was the Admiral.

"You are sensing that I am drawn to *Tayr*," *Noœ-bouk* sent.

"I have stood as close to *Tayr* as you are now," the Admiral conveyed. "I have known the same desire. Your feelings are coming to me as an echo of a sensation I have experienced over many moon cycles. A sensation that has never left me."

"We can unite these desires," *Noœ-bouk* sent. "We can share a life-span on *Tayr*."

"It is the greatest challenge," replied the Admiral. "Few who incarnate there are able to fulfil their original intentions."

"We will incarnate together," continued *Noœ-bouk*. "Our presence will remind us of our work. We are sharing each other's minds and forms now. We will always carry this connection. It has been imprinted into our highest selves."

"I saw innumerable civilisations on my travels in the fleet," the Admiral communicated, "and yet no planet stayed with me as this one did."

Noœ-bouk drew a deep inhalation. "We will initiate a new lifespan together. Our combined energy will lift the planet. It will *reunite that which was separated*." It completed its thought strand with the familiar symbol block.

There was an extended thought space, as the concept resonated between them, and the heightened emotional state, which they were experiencing as one, lifted and dipped in waves of euphoric *kaiif*.

"Your desire is elevated," sent the Admiral at last. "I will share this lifespan with you."

Noœ-bouk's central circulatory organ was beating hard. It felt its skin tingling wildly with the idea of entering the planet before it as a participant. Of sharing this with the Admiral. Of experiencing love. Free will. Of attempting to reunite *Tayr* with its highest potential.

"And the channelling?" asked the Admiral. "What of the imbalance?"

"I will ask permission to perform this," conveyed *Noœ-bouk*. "If I have adequate form density then I will carry it out. It will be a service to *Tayr* before we begin our lifespan there."

"It will create much positive feeling," the Admiral sent. "It will be a highly advantageous manner to enter the planet, when such benefit has already been created for it."

The vibration of the Admiral began to fade, and *Noœ-bouk* communicated a final message, using the archaic symbol that the Admiral had once used.

"I *love* you."

The Admiral did not reply, but it opened up its mind space to allow *Noœ-bouk*'s vibration to reflect directly back to it, and *Noœ-bouk* considered what a beautiful way this was of expressing its response: as a mirror, to let its own vibration speak for the both of them.

The vibration echoed within *Noœ-bouk*'s thought space and then, at last, faded. In its place, a deep, urgent thrill began to rise through its form.

A lifespan on *Tayr* was ahead.

ELSPETH LOOKED DOWN from the window of the plane at the layer of grey cloud covering London. Whatever else happened, the weather in Athens would be better than the constant rain which had fallen for the past week. It had certainly helped her not to get sentimental about leaving behind the small life she had built. Selling everything she owned to anyone who would buy it; wrapping up the few ends there had been. Greece was hardly even far enough away to bother with goodbyes. She had only told her parents at the last minute, when she had already gone for leaving drinks with the librarians at York's Inn, when she had already moved out of her flat and had been staying the final few nights on a friend's sofa.

In her handbag, she had Plato's *The Symposium*, *The Republic* and *Phaedo*, all of them her grandfather's books. She had read *The Symposium* three times now. With each read, she seemed to understand something new. Not necessarily something about her own life, not something specific, but everything just seemed a bit clearer after she read it. It wasn't exactly a comfort level which improved, but it was something like that. It was like a sense of peace came to her while she was reading, and some of that peace stayed with her. It was a good feeling.

And now she was going to Greece.

The air steward approached and leaned towards her.

"White wine, please."

Above the grey layer of London cloud, the sunshine – which had always been there, hidden to the busy city-dwellers – shone through the plastic pane of the window. The air steward handed her a beaker of white wine and she took a sip and let the sunshine cover her face.

She closed her eyes.

In three hours, she would be in Greece.

CHAPTER NINETEEN

DAVID PACED UP and down the main hall of the station, his head jerking occasionally from side to side. He looked at his watch. Vanessa was late. He scowled at the watch. He felt his phone buzzing in its holder and pulled it out. He scowled again. It was Cassie. What did she want? He thought about ignoring the call, but then pushed the button.

"Yeah?"

"David?"

"Yeah, Cassie. Hey, how's it going?"

"David, give me a minute, okay? Look, I didn't even want to call. You've been acting like such an asshole since you went back to New York."

"That's a great start, Cassie."

"David, I'm worried about you. You're a logical guy. I know you. And you're acting strangely."

David felt a surge of annoyance. What damn right did she have to get worried about him?

"Strangely? How so?"

"David, put the facts together. You had a traumatic experience which you can't explain. It shook you up. And since then, your behaviour has been changing and you're refusing to acknowledge it."

David paused, letting the anger pass through him before answering.

"My behaviour has been changing? Maybe you just don't know me anymore?"

"You're very aggressive. You're not responding to logical

suggestions. David, we were in science class together. I know how you think. You're not being yourself."

David took a deep breath.

"Look, I've got a massive amount on my plate right now. My boss is on my case, I've got a major project that I really can't fuck up. I've got a lot going on. It's not like back home where nothing really matters that much. This stuff really matters. These are big fucking deals here."

"Seriously? Big fucking deals? If I was acting the way you were, I hope that you'd be on my case, making sure everything was alright..."

David could picture her. She would be standing at the payphone in the corridor of the research facility where she worked. Shiny linoleum floor and white doors with code entries. Her long red hair would be tied back and she would smell of coffee and lemon and maybe disinfectant. The image for some reason made him uncontrollably angry.

"Actually, Cassie, I do have some good news."

"Oh yeah? More big deals?"

"I got engaged."

There was a small noise on the other end of the phone. Then there was silence. That small noise for some reason made him feel very, very good. It somehow calmed his anger.

"Cassie? Listen, I wanted to tell you before I told anyone else. She's this amazing girl. She's so beautiful, she's so smart. I'm going to bring her to Kingston to meet Mom and Dad. Seriously, you're going to love her. Cassie? Are you there?"

"Fuck you, David."

"Speak soon, Cassie. Thanks for calling."

There was a click from the payphone. David's heart was beating hard. He felt inexplicably elated, almost high. He felt like jumping in the air. He looked around him. Where was Vanessa? He was going to buy her the biggest fucking engagement ring they could find. And then he was going to take her back to Canada and show her off to his mom and dad and Cassie. And then he was going to spend the rest of his life fucking her brains out. He looked around the station again and finally saw her coming towards him. He watched her, appraising her body and face against the other women in the station. No. She was the hottest. She was the prettiest. Nose job or not, she was hot.

"Babe."

She came up to him, leaned in and kissed him on the lips. His penis stirred with her kiss and he pulled away.

"None of that," he said. "Now, let's go and find a ring."

. . .

"I'LL SEE YOU LATER."

David kissed Vanessa on the lips, then went out of the apartment and closed the door behind him. Vanessa stood in the kitchen, her back against the wall. She touched her lips with one finger.

She was still dressed in the skimpy black baby-doll she had worn the night before, which just covered her thighs and pushed her cleavage up through delicate lace. On her finger was the ring. She held it in front of her as she had done every hour since they had bought it. The huge, incredibly expensive diamond. It made her hand look tiny, it was so big. Not Tiffany's, but absolutely as well-cut, as classy, as Tiffany's. She had never expected David to be so generous. He had changed in the last few months, and she liked all of the changes very much. She still had to call her parents and tell them the news. She'd do it from Hawaii, when they went there next month – she'd call from the hotel and let them know. She was going to give David the best holiday he had ever had in Hawaii. She was going to be the hottest fiancée ever. That would seal the wedding. She wasn't going to let anything fall to chance. Not this late in the game.

Vanessa raised her finger to her mouth and ran the diamond over her lips. Then, going back into the bedroom, she started to pick her clothes up from the floor and straighten them out. She'd grab a quick shower and then head into work. The suit was good for another day, but she'd have to start leaving some things here.

Hanging her slim, black skirt over the back of the computer chair, she glanced across the desk. It all looked ordinary. Files, stapler, pens, a financial calculator in a leather case. She ran a hand over the files and opened one at random, tilting her head to the side as she drew it towards her. She looked at the top piece of paper for a few seconds, then turned it over and looked at the next one. Eventually, she sat down at the computer desk and went through the papers in the folder one by one, studying the unfamiliar shapes and markings and the detailed diagrams. She remembered David talking about dreams and something about writing, but she hadn't imagined anything like this.

When she got to the end of the file, she started again from the beginning, studying each sheet of paper. There was a clear continuation from one page to the next; a body of information contained there, something extraordinary. There were some simple, repeated shapes – interwoven circles which appeared on most of the pages – but the majority of the drawings were complex diagrams, geometric arrangements or symbols from an unfamiliar alphabet. She felt a little stunned looking at the papers. She had never seen anything like this before. It was something beyond the scope of her ability to grasp, or more importantly, to control. She didn't like it. It was bigger than she was.

Vanessa got up from the table, leaving the file open, and stood above the papers, looking down at them. She glanced around the small bedroom. Any more secrets lurking? But then, David had told her about the dreams. He hadn't hidden anything. And if he had, then she'd find them soon enough.

She left the folder on the table and went through to the bathroom. Switching on the shower, she let the silk and lace nightdress slide to the floor.

AN HOUR LATER, she was ready for work. She buttoned her suit jacket carefully and checked her appearance in the mirror. Her lipstick was perfect, her eyebrows razor-thin. For a few moments longer than usual, she gazed into the hooded, mascaraed eyes, as if asking herself a question. Then she smiled. Glancing down at the diamond ring on her finger, she smiled again, this time with happiness.

She went back into the bedroom and leaned over the file. She flicked through the papers and removed a page with a diagram drawn on it. Further on, she drew another one at random, and then a third. She closed the file, laid it back in its place on the desk and straightened the pages. She folded them carefully in half, and then into quarters, smoothing down the edges with her fingertips. She took them through to the kitchen, opened her handbag and slid them inside.

One more check in the mirror and she was ready. Slipping on her coat, she walked down the carpeted stairs, the geometric angles of the perfectly cut diamond twinkling on her finger, and then out of the building, past the pile of newspapers and the homeless man asleep on the steps, and into the New York sunshine.

"WELL, HERE'S THE *MAN*."

Martin Walsh was striding over to David, who had just sat down in his cubicle at the end of the row, across from the MD's office. David stood up again and shook the hand held out towards him. Martin was dressed in a generously cut navy suit, with a gold tie laced with dark-red and a white shirt that looked brand new.

"Half the position down?" he said as he shook David's hand. "Half the position down in the first two weeks? Amazing. Unbelievable! I need guys like you on my team, David."

"I'm just doing my job, Martin."

"Well, you're doing a hell of a job. Hong Kong had better watch out, if you're going for the transfer there. And you're gonna get a hell of a recommendation from me as well. Great job, David. Really great job."

"I don't know how easy the rest of the position will be to move. I may have to make some pretty sweet deals to shift it."

"Just keep at it. We've given you everything you need to get it done. And you'd better know, the boys upstairs are on top of this. There are a lot of people keeping an eye on you, David."

David laughed. "No pressure, then."

"You got it. Alright. I'm on the thirtieth floor for the rest of today, but I'll catch up with you this evening. I want daily updates."

Martin strode up the aisle away from him, and over to the side of the room where his sales team was working the phones, coloured scraps of paper waved in the air and shouted expletives, a baseball moving up and down with hypnotic regularity. David saw Martin standing over one of his team, a hand resting on his shoulder as he listened to the call. He saw how his eyes scanned the cubicles, monitoring the work. The phrase came back to him.

There are a lot of people keeping an eye on you, David.

Eyes. He had been hearing the word everywhere lately. It seemed as if he had heard that single expression ten times in the last couple of days. Ever since the dream, which kept coming back to him in flashes. Small eyes, huge eyes, wet eyes, membranes, pupils, liquid spheres.

There are a lot of people keeping an eye on you, David.

He sat down at his desk and clicked the computer to active. He looked at the screen and skimmed over the sweeteners he had on his list, to add to the junk he was laying off. If all the easy-sell clients had gone, he would have to make the package sweeter and sweeter. He'd have to play this carefully. One mistake could lead to word getting out that they were unloading a junk position and that would be the end of the sales, the end of his chance. Caution, caution, caution. There were still two weeks before the financial results would be drawn up. Better to safely unload as much as he could rather than risk being left with half the position on his hands and panic upstairs.

He selected a client and checked the history before dialling the number.

"Yes, good morning. My name is David Cornwell, and I'm calling from the sales desk at Bullman Scout New York. How are you this morning?"

. . .

186

TWO MINUTES LATER, David put down the phone. No go. Not even a chance. Had the client known something? Could word be going round already? God, he hoped not. If it was, then the rest of these calls would be a waste of time. It was the first pitch he'd made that had been a flat "no". But there were always a few like that on a client list. He read up on the next buyer and dialled the number.

"Good morning, sir. My name is David Cornwell, and I'm calling from the sales desk at Bullman Scout New York. How are you this fine morning?"

It was a Midwest client. These were either the easiest or the most difficult, depending on any number of random factors; the main one, seemingly, how good a mood they were in. This time, the client was chatty, he was interested. His voice reminded David of Tony Morgan in Denver, and as he talked to the buyer, walking him through the different products he was offering, scenes of the trip came back to him: the view of the vermillion mountains from the plane as they were landing; the crowded bar and the tequila shots; Tony Morgan's eyes staring into his.

Eyes.

Suddenly, David saw a grey eye hovering in front of the computer screen. He blinked. The client was saying something. He was answering the client. He was explaining something. Interest rates, loan terms, risk portfolio spread. The client was interested. But before him, right there in front of his computer screen – not on the screen, but *right in front of it* – he was seeing an eye. It was the eye from his dream. It was wet, and there were silver channels like threads of electricity running over the white part of it. And it was growing bigger. The eye was expanding right before him. It was a hallucination. He knew that nobody else could see what he was seeing. He leaned back in his chair, away from it. Somehow, he was still talking on the phone. Could he touch the eye? He reached out his hand, then quickly pulled it back. If he could, then he definitely didn't want to. He moved his chair away. He couldn't draw his focus from the expanding wet mass.

He found himself studying the silver threads, just as he had done in the dream. They were giving him information. He was reading information from them. He started sweating. He had to get off this call. The eye was growing bigger. The room was getting darker.

Silence.

"Hello? Hello?"

"David, are you alright?"

"Hey, man. Is he alright?"

"Yeah, I don't know. David? You alright, buddy?"

David forced his consciousness back towards the voices. His heart was pounding and there was a high-pitched shrieking in his head. The voices sounded muffled and unfamiliar.

"Woah," he said, pulling himself up from the floor. His phone was lying on the desk, off its hook. Three of the sales guys were standing around him. The underarms and chest of his shirt were covered in sweat.

"Woah," he said again. "What just happened?"

"You fell off your chair, buddy," one of the guys said. "Here," he called out, "someone chuck me that towel from my desk. He's sweating like crazy."

Someone tossed a sports towel across the room. David pushed his face into it, then ran it around his neck. He loosened his tie.

"Well, that never happened before," he said.

"Do you remember which client you were speaking to?"

David leaned forward and clicked on the screen.

"Yeah. Right here. Wow. I'd better call back. Seriously, what happened? You just saw I fell off the chair?"

"Yeah. You were on the phone and then you just kinda slumped off the chair onto the floor. Must've passed out."

"Wow. Alright. Listen. Don't say anything to the big guy, okay? I don't know how that just happened."

"Yeah, no problem, bud. Sales floor stress. It's been known to happen. You're just not used to the pressure yet."

"Yeah, that's probably it. Anyway, thanks for coming and checking on me."

David held out his hand.

"David Cornwell. On secondment from Lev Fin."

"Josh Taylor. Trading team, Oil and Gas."

"Alright, then."

They shook hands. Josh walked back to his cubicle, and the buzz on the floor faded. David sat in his chair for a few minutes, breathing deeply and rubbing his face with the towel. He put the phone back on the hook and straightened up the files on his desk. He glanced at his watch and shook it. It said 5 a.m. Shit. It must have stopped again. He hadn't noticed it this morning. He thought it had been working when he put it on. He looked at the time at the top of his computer. 12:00. That couldn't be right, either. He'd only just got to work. It should be about 8:30 a.m. Had he just lost four hours? He stood up, his legs unsteady, and knocked his fist into the side of his head to clear it. He walked casually over to Josh Taylor's cubicle.

"Hey, man, what time do you make it? Looks like my watch has stopped."

Josh glanced down at his wrist. "Eight forty-five," he said. "Hey, you alright now?"

"Yeah, I'm fine. Thanks, buddy. And thanks again for the towel. Appreciate it."

He handed the towel back to Josh, who laughed and waved his hand away.

"Hey, keep it, man," he said. "You can buy me a new one."

"Yeah, alright."

David walked away as naturally as he could, and headed to the washrooms. He pushed open the heavy door and leaned over the sink. He flicked on the tap and looked at himself in the mirror. His face was deathly pale, his eyes bloodshot. What the hell was happening to him? He cupped cold water into his hands and pushed his face into it. He held it there, unmoving, just allowing the fear, anger and shock to pass through his body. At last, he pulled his head up and held paper towels over his skin to dry. He took off his watch and changed the time to 8:45. Had he seriously just passed out at work? Had he really just hallucinated that eye? This was turning into a nightmare. He would have to go and see Shapkin again. Damn it, he'd tell him whatever he wanted to hear. But he couldn't let this happen again. He was so close. So close.

NOŒ-BOUK LOCATED the Captain of the vessel in its private assignment quarters.

"Enter."

"Greetings," *Noœ-bouk* sent to the Captain, who replied with a symbol block of welcome and anticipation.

Noœ-bouk stood before the Captain. Their eyes met, and in their exchange, *Noœ-bouk* sensed respect and humility. It understood that it had become associated with the *other*, with occurrences of the *extraordinary*. The Captain was now viewing it as a being of a different cellular pattern. There was no evidence of the simple connection that was typical between co-genus types. *Noœ-bouk* was outside. It was *beyond*.

Noœ-bouk sent a symbol block of supplication.

"If you will gain permission for this event to take place, then I offer myself as the energy-channeller to perform the work on the region of *Tayr* which has become unbalanced. I have carried out the calculation and I have enough physical density to allow my form to execute the channelling. I would be honoured if you would seek permission for this to take place."

Noœ-bouk completed its communication with a symbol block of deference and respect.

"And when you have accomplished the channelling task assignment?" asked the Captain.

"Then my physical form will dissolve, and I will pass."

There was an extended thought space.

"I have seen your results from the cellular laboratory."

"Then you know that this is the most elevated action I can take. I can offer no other contribution to this vessel or the mission it is serving. I do not know if I can trust my formation analysis enough to benefit the Advisory Committee. I have been subject to previously unknown emotional impulses. I do not desire to exist on this vessel with no benefit to the greater mission."

"I have felt this vibration from you."

"I ask you to seek permission."

The two beings regarded each other. The Captain was not advanced in lifespan cycles, and *Noœ-bouk* considered that it might be drawn to a course of action with a lower risk assessment within its limited range of options if it had only a mid-range accumulation of knowledge as the commander of a space vessel. *Noœ-bouk* allowed the Captain to read its thoughts and eyes openly.

The Captain turned away and shifted its gaze to the main viewing panel of the compartment, and at the planet turning on its axis before them, its single grey moon twisting its path across the orbit line.

"It seems that *Tayr* is changing us," it sent to *Noœ-bouk*. "There is something I have experienced, being in proximity to this planet I have studied so much, which is changing my perception of events. I have no explanation for it, but I have made a report on this observation to the Supervisory Council."

It paused.

"I understand your request. I support your request. But I will be extremely careful in making this decision. In these moments, I am not secure in my own analysis. I open this to you, as you have opened your thought space to me. I have also been experiencing something similar to the emotional responses that I know to be a part of the *Tayr* vibration. I have reported this. There will be a Council meeting in the proximate moon cycle."

It seemed as if the Captain had finished its thoughts, and it turned its head away. But then it twisted back to *Noœ-bouk*, seeking its eyes, a contorted expression on its face.

"*Noœ-bouk,* your presence on the vessel…" The Captain seemed to be struggling to locate the correct thought strands. "At first I was not in favour of such an unprecedented…" It stopped, and started again, its eyes flickering back and forth from *Noœ-bouk*'s face to the planet surface and the single passing moon. "It was a direct order," it sent. "Yet, I have been on other ships, as a senior crew member and as Captain. Your participation has affected the experience within the vessel."

Noœ-bouk had never heard a series of thought strands from an elevated Home Planet being expressed in such a broken and discontinuous manner. It seemed as if, within the initial intention, there was both the desire to speak and to remain silent. The Captain continued.

"It has affected me also," the Captain sent. "I have seen – we have seen – that there are possibilities… beyond… Your choices on Home Planet were of the highest resonance and elevation. You are a *hero*. And now, your choices are *atypical*."

The Captain turned away to face the passing white moon. It brought its eyes to meet *Noœ-bouk*'s once again.

The final thought strand was clear and unbroken.

"I am grateful for your presence on the vessel," it sent. And then, "I will send a request for the Council to authorise the energy-channelling. I desire for it to be approved."

Noœ-bouk held the Captain's gaze for the path of an inhalation. It drew its head forward in a bow of respect. It sensed that the Captain's communications had been for the benefit of the Captain, rather than for *Noœ-bouk*. It felt a struggle behind the communication strands, and the atmosphere in the chamber was lighter; a relief was present now that it had been released into the open.

"I thank you."

Noœ-bouk bowed again. It turned away from the viewing panel and the hypnotic white moon and the Captain, and it moved out of the chamber. It heard the vibration ringing in its head once again; the vibration which had echoed back to it from the Admiral.

I love you. I love you. I love you.

Noœ-bouk moved along the corridor. It was ready to pass.

DUNCAN LED Alisdair out of the library and down the marble steps to the Prototype Garden. Alisdair caught sight of a tiger, ferocious with gleaming fur, flexing its powerful muscular form in the sunlight. The black and orange symmetry of its pattern was as bright as creation, and it snarled, pulling back feral gums to reveal dazzling, deadly teeth. Alisdair felt that he would willingly be eaten by such a creature.

Duncan turned away from the path of the tiger, and they walked down an avenue of silver birch trees with tiny emerald leaves and bark like molten metal poured freshly down the slender trunks. At the end of the avenue they came to the edge of a silver-grey lake, its centre and the far distance shrouded in a hovering mist. A boat was tied up to a wooden post. It reminded Alisdair of the Isle of Avalon, and the Arthurian legends, and he was about to pose a question, when Duncan interrupted.

"Come, come," he said. "Some of the stories were more symbolic than anything else. Although this really was the inspiration for Avalon."

"But they were just stories?"

"Many people on Earth have visited this garden in dreams or visions. Sometimes it is their guides who bring them. Sometimes their spirits become aligned with the vibration of original beauty, of perfection. There are many paths to this place. Many connections."

"But the stories—"

"Yes, they were just stories. But when something enters the human consciousness with such prevalence, there is usually a thread of truth to it. The source is pure. You can always feel the difference."

Duncan stepped into the boat.

"Unwind the rope, if you don't mind," he said, picking up the oars. Alisdair swung the end of the rope into the middle of the craft and climbed in. It rocked, then steadied as he sat down in the bow, facing Duncan.

"Where are we going?" asked Alisdair, as Duncan began to row.

"The library and the garden and the chambers you have seen contain the records of Earth lives," said Duncan. "We are going to travel to other places, to see lives which are not found in the books."

The boat moved through the water, and the sky around them – which had been of the purest, pigment-blue – faded to a muted silver as they entered the mist, and the water of the lake changed into a channel of grey. Instead of rowing across a lake, they were now floating on a wide stream which was leading them through some kind of emptiness. But before Alisdair had time to study the emptiness, a fiery-red planet came into view in the far distance, travelling fast towards them, and beyond that, a burning blue star, and beyond that, bodies and shapes he could not quite make out.

Alisdair watched them with interest. They did not appear unusual; he even felt drawn to them in some way. He still had the impression that they were rowing across a lake of water, and the impression had shifted only to the extent that the lake had become a galaxy, and the breeze had become the pull of stars and planets. It felt natural, as if it were all entirely the same thing; although the external circumstances seemed to have changed, it was as if nothing had changed at all.

Duncan looked around, clearly enjoying the journey.

"Choose one," he said.

"Choose what?"

"Choose a planet. Choose a star, a comet, a moon. Choose anything you see around you, and we will visit. Choose a supernova or a black hole. Choose the deepest space. Choose the centre of the universe. Choose anything."

"The centre of the universe!"

The boat disappeared and Alisdair found himself in intense darkness. He opened and closed his eyes but could see nothing at all. He put out his hands and felt around him, but there was nothing. He took a deep breath in and as he exhaled a sensation of peace came over him, almost ecstatic in its intensity, oracular in its living depth. It was a peace he had not known before. It was a peace which seemed to be poised in compressed motion, which was holding something inestimably huge within its attractor field, and at the same time, carrying everything within that field in directions or dimensions he could not possibly comprehend. It was not doing this with force of any kind, but with the pure expression of itself, with its own infinitely powerful resonance.

"The centre of the universe," Alisdair whispered into the nothing. And then he thought, *This incredible peace must be holding the universe together. It must be holding the threads and silks of all creation.*

As he thought this, he felt himself being drawn out of the darkness, and then he was back in the boat. He stared at Duncan, dazed.

"That was spectacular," he said.

"I should hope it was," Duncan said. "Next time, you can go to the centre of the multiverse. And after that, the centre of everything."

"The centre of everything. Is that not God?"

Duncan laughed. "Everything you see is God. You are God and I am God. This boat is God."

"Then the centre of everything—"

"Is simply the centre of everything doing its job as the centre of everything. It may have been one of your lives, you know, one of your experiences."

"To be the centre of everything?"

"Why not? Someone has to do it. You have a curious mind. I'd be surprised if you hadn't done one or two of the more unusual jobs."

"And you? What have you done?"

"The usual Earth progression. Gases, water, lava, rock, one cell, two cells, spirit-protectors, animals and then the run of humans, Neanderthal to yogi. I did the last part particularly fast. I was rather pleased. Although, of course, it makes no difference at all how fast you do it."

"And are you finished?"

"With the Earth, yes. Although I enjoy some of the other life forms now and again. Soon I will join the Earth Council. But mainly I am in this stage as a teacher and a guide. I take individual souls and prepare them for their next major level. Explain the rules of the game."

"Is that what you're doing with me?"

"Do you doubt it?"

"And the Scottish accent? The tweed? The name? If you have finished all the Earth lives, why do you keep them?"

"I keep nothing. They are entirely for your benefit, to make you feel comfortable. You are still close to your last life. The connections and memories are still alive in you."

Alisdair smiled. "Well, I'm appreciative." He sniffed. "There's been a smell of whisky all this time, hasn't there?"

"Well, I wouldn't be much of a guide if I didn't provide the full package. Now, let's see what else there is to discover."

"Hold on a moment," Alisdair was thinking. "You've said that before, about the rules of the game. What is the game? What's the point of going through the Earth progression? What are the rules?"

Duncan laughed. "It's the unity game," he said. "At least that's what I call it. And the point of the game? Its essence, I suppose, is to experience love in all its possible manifestations. To create every possible wild and magnificent expression of anything you can imagine. Good and bad, light and dark, just and unjust, simple and complex, single and manifold. Incarnate and spirit, in infinite dimensional variations. Every combination of everything. We're back to the tail of the lion, of course, but the lions are as many as there is the will, somewhere, to continue creating. Isn't it magnificent?"

"And in the end?"

"And in the end, to return. To bring all those experiences back together. To unity. To contract the pulse of life until it beats as one indescribably intense and compact kernel of everything that is. And then..."

Alisdair was nodding. He opened his arms wide. "Boom!" They both laughed. "The game begins again."

Duncan continued. "I know it seems intense when you're inside an Earth life – or most of the other incarnations for that matter – but it has to, otherwise no one would take it seriously. But it really is a game. You choose all the roles you want to play. You can do anything, you can be anything. It's entirely wonderful. The point is to enjoy it. Every different possibility. Live as rich, successful humans in the deepest bliss and contentment until you suddenly decide to try the opposite. Live as poverty-stricken geniuses. Live as women and men and everything in between. It's the most fantastic and wonderful game ever."

He paused and took a deep breath.

"I'm sorry. I get awfully excited when I talk about it. So few people ask, you know. You'd be surprised."

"So... in the game," Alisdair said, "every possible life is acceptable and they are all equal. But lives can still go wrong. You make a plan, broadly speaking, and you can get the plan wrong, and then it affects other people's plans?"

"Oh yes," said Duncan. "Lives go wrong constantly. Especially on Earth. Nobody is ever truly prepared for an Earth life because it's impossible to imagine not knowing everything that you know. Total oblivion. And then all that intense energy. The ego pulling you towards all sorts of things that are no good for you, and the emotions and desires and..." He paused and gestured wildly around him. "Just the range of temptations is astounding." He took another deep breath and exhaled with a whistle. "I mean, frankly, it's more amazing that any of the lives turn out more or less as intended. But then, that's why so many souls are eager to try the experience. You could say it's the ultimate challenge – to go through an Earth life on plan and not get side-tracked by all the things on offer. There's really a great risk of failure when you go there."

"But when it does go wrong—"

"Then that's an experience in itself. The important factor in those cases is bringing back the balance. The soul can become filled with guilt or start to believe that the lifetime is not worth continuing. Some event is usually needed to shock the soul back to their original path. It can be conscious or subconscious. Sometimes their guides can help."

Duncan glanced at Alisdair and noticed his serious look.

"But, come. That is not the situation with your Elspeth. Besides, you are there to help her now."

He smiled at Alisdair and motioned to the swathes of distant planets and coloured formations around them.

"Now that's enough about the game. We are here to explore. To experience. To enjoy."

He pointed again.

"What do you choose?"

CHAPTER
TWENTY

"WHY DO you keep looking at your watch?"

Vanessa stared at him.

"Was I?"

"Yes. You've looked at it every ten seconds for the last half hour."

"I hadn't noticed."

"Relax, baby. It's gonna be fine."

"I know, I know. I'm just thinking about work."

"Are you sure you want to do this?"

"Of course I'm sure. I want it to be just you and me. No relatives, no friends. Just us."

"Well, you look really handsome."

"You think so?"

"I know so."

"There's Danny. Wave at him. Can he see you?"

"Yeah, he's coming over."

Danny crossed the busy road from the subway station and made his way to them.

"Sooooo… Ready for the big day?"

Danny was dressed in a black suit and pale-blue tie, and his hair was slicked back with gel. He handed a bouquet of white roses to Vanessa.

"For the beautiful bride."

He leaned forward and kissed her on the cheek.

"Is Jenny coming?"

"She got called in on a work shift. She said to tell you guys she's really sorry. She would have loved to be here. She's going to join us this evening."

"That's a shame she can't make it."

Danny held out his hand to David, then pulled him into a hug, slapping the back of his suit.

"You must be terrified, man."

"Not a bit. I know I've got the right girl. And I know I'm not wasting thousands of dollars on a party for a bunch of people I hardly know."

"Yeah. That's right, you cheap-ass. Save the bucks on your own wedding. Very nice. Very Wall Street of you. Classy, David. Classy."

"You guys, cut it out!" Vanessa was laughing. She held her ring up for Danny to see. "Did you even see the size of my ring, Danny? You think David can afford anything after buying this?"

"And the wedding rings on top," added David.

"Woah, that's some monster!" Danny took her small hand and looked at the ring. "Seriously, that's some massive rock. How much did that set you back?"

"Nothing New York's finest credit system can't handle."

"Wow. Shit. Wow."

The three of them stood in silence for a moment, watching the lawyers and city employees scuttling up and down the steps of City Hall. The sun came out from behind a cloud and shone down on them. David reached out for Vanessa's hand and squeezed it.

"You ready?"

"I CAN'T BELIEVE you actually did it!" Jenny squealed from behind a frosted cocktail glass adorned with fruit and paper umbrellas.

"Congratulations!" She reached over again and hugged Vanessa, who was balancing a champagne flute in her newly ringed hand. Her tanned, angular shoulders rose out of a white Calvin Klein number, and a black, minimalist evening jacket hung over the back of her chair.

David watched the women hugging – the designer dress, the narrow shoulders, the diamond ring – and he felt good. With her hair smooth and dark over her shoulders, Vanessa could have walked straight off a fashion shoot. Except for the cleavage. Like a model, but with curves where they're meant to be. Damn, he was lucky.

He waved at the waitress, a girl with mile-long Hollywood legs and no visible skirt who looked like she was going to be the next big actress. She sashayed towards them through the crowd of roaring Friday night drinkers: bankers with loosened ties, girls with impossibly tiny waists and shining hair, martinis and credit cards, pent-up stress pouring out into the Manhattan evening.

"Another bottle of the champagne, two cosmopolitans and four tequila shots," David yelled to her, as the waitress leaned over their table. "All on my tab."

"Easy, tiger!" called out Danny, trying too obviously not to stare at the waitress's legs. "Not sure how much more I'm good for tonight."

"You're good until my credit runs out," David shouted back. "This is a wedding celebration, buddy. Rest of our lives, and all that. We're drinking until we are well and truly wasted."

"You said it," said Danny, lifting his champagne flute. "Now go and sit next to your smoking-hot wife. I want to give my girlfriend a cuddle."

"Oooooooh," said Vanessa. "And how long before we're coming to your wedding, Danny? I think Jenny's finger is actually burning up, she wants a ring on it so bad."

"Danny says he's got to get an apartment first." Jenny got up and slid into the seat beside Danny, kissing him on the lips before picking up a fresh cosmopolitan. She was wearing a silver off-the-shoulder dress and her hair was straightened into a sharp, New York curve. Danny put his arm around her waist.

"Apartment, or a big house in Connecticut. One of them," said Danny. "At the least, I want to be ready for a family. What about you guys. Have you thought about that?"

"We're not thinking beyond the end of this year right now," Vanessa said.

"Year?" said David. "I'm not thinking beyond *tonight* right now." He leaned over and slipped his hand behind Vanessa's head, drawing her towards him in an exaggerated kiss as Danny and Jenny cheered. He rubbed his face into her styled hair, smelling the jasmine and heavy spices of her perfume, and he bit the edge of her ear.

"With you," he whispered, "I don't need to think beyond right now."

NOŒ-BOUK STEPPED out of the Captain's private assignment quarters and moved along the curved white corridor. The Captain had received authorisation for it to carry out the energy-channelling, however there had been a minimum form-density level stipulated in order for the channelling to take place, and it was higher than the reading *Nœ-bouk* had received in its most recent scans at the cellular laboratory.

It was over. There was no possibility that *Nœ-bouk* could increase its density levels. Any attempt to do so would lead to an immediate release from its physical form. The imbalance would be resolved in another way, perhaps by another vessel, and all that *Nœ-bouk* had to do now was await the moment of transition. It would not be long. There was no reason for it to remain suspended in stasis mode. Neither for its own benefit nor for any wider cause.

Now that the impetus for remaining in lifespan activation had been removed, *Nœ-bouk* felt the heaviness of its recent experiences weighing upon it. The sheer quantity of new emotional stimuli, to which it had been subjected, was overwhelming, and the fact that *Nœ-bouk* had no comprehension of how to correctly respond to these stimuli created a sense of disorientation and vulnerability. *Nœ-bouk* was aware that on Home Planet, many of the states it had been processing had neither recognised existence nor even name allocation. On Home Planet, the concept of emotion as a response to a situation as simple as an inability to carry out a task assignment due to insufficient energy reserves would almost have been a cause for humour. Prior to embarking on the vessel, *Nœ-bouk* would have accepted such a result without further thought expenditure, aware that a genus type with the correct energy composition would execute the assignment to maximum task potential. And yet, what *Nœ-bouk* was experiencing now was a sense of helplessness, an impression of inconsequence, and an increasing desire to end the few moon cycles it had remaining.

It returned to its resting chamber and lowered itself into the light pod. It sent a thought strand to the Admiral.

"I am ready to leave."

The Admiral's vibration entered its mind space and *Nœ-bouk*, once again taken by surprise at the strength of the contact, felt the pressure of its central circulatory organ increase significantly, a sudden sensitivity of its face and neck covering, and what it attempted to describe to itself as a disintegrating sensation in its brain area.

"*Nœ-bouk*," the Admiral sent, and *Nœ-bouk* was so overwhelmed by the expression of its name by the Admiral, in combination with an intense longing for unity, that it was unable to reply.

"*Nœ-bouk*," sent the Admiral again. "We will pass. But before we pass, there is something that I choose to experience together. Are you in agreement? Do you understand what I am asking?"

Noœ-bouk, prone within the resting pod, received a symbol block from the Admiral, which once again rendered it unable to return communication. It was the symbol of desire on all levels, but most of all, of physical desire. It lay within the pod, the resonance of this extraordinary symbol block spreading throughout its physical form, adding to the heightened state that the vibration of the Admiral had already stimulated. It was many inhalations before the sensation had subsided enough for *Noœ-bouk* to be able to create a thought strand.

"It will be the end," it sent. "If we attempt this unity, then we will both pass. Our energies will not sustain it."

"This is correct," came the reply.

They both remained without communicating for many inhalations, the symbol block resonating between them. *Noœ-bouk* did not doubt that the Admiral could sense its physical and emotional responses as clearly as it was itself experiencing them. It knew. And the Admiral knew.

"Yes," sent *Noœ-bouk* at last. "Yes."

There was a long thought space, in which *Noœ-bouk* could feel the exchange of joy flowing between itself and the Admiral. The decision had been for unity.

"When we have passed," the Admiral conveyed, "we will meet again on *Tayr*."

"And if the challenge there is too great?" *Noœ-bouk* asked. "If you become lost within the currents of darkness? If I become lost?"

"Then we will find each other again," the Admiral replied. "We will use the language of Home Planet. Its pattern and symbols will be close enough to remember. It will bring us back to each other."

Noœ-bouk drew an inhalation. It felt a yearning for the planet. It felt its desire for the Admiral.

"My intention is to lift *Tayr* towards the Federation," it sent. "To bring it to a state of unity. To open the channels for the beings of Home Planet to be known and un-feared to *Tayr*."

"This is a task which has been attempted during many lifespans."

Noœ-bouk continued. "I will enter a form with the physical and mental capacity to achieve this result. The task assignments I have executed on Home Planet within this lifespan have been unprecedented. It is the same for your achievements. We will attempt this on *Tayr*."

"I will be there to assist you. To remind you. To know this experience."

"I desire this more than anything."

The Admiral sent a final symbol block to *Noœ-bouk*, expressing the most profound peace, and then nothing more had to be conveyed. They were ready.

Within its mind, *Noœ-bouk* created a life-size hologram of its physical form: frail, grey-skinned, emaciated; the small, pointed ridges protruding from each of its vertebrae; the delicate webbing of its feet and hands from which the scaled, claw-like fingers emerged.

Before it appeared a similar hologram of the Admiral, its body shrunken, its head oversized above the withered frame. The Admiral opened out its webbed hands, the clawed fingers stretched towards it, and *Noœ-bouk* reached in front of it and allowed the very tips of its fingers to brush against the Admiral's. This faint touch sent a shock of such positive sensation through its limbs and organs that its central circulatory organ began to pulse uncontrollably within its chest area and it was subject to an overwhelming dizziness, as if it was about to lose mind presence. It wondered, in the space of an inhalation, if this was the process of transition, but then it felt a pressure increasing on the skin covering of its hand and wrist, and its central circulatory organ slowed as it felt the Admiral applying a light touch to its pulse, calming its physical processes. The Admiral retained the grip on its wrist, and *Noœ-bouk* knew that it was necessary to look up. It raised its head slowly, and there they were. The waiting eyes that *Noœ-bouk* had fallen into a thousand moon cycles previously. The enormous, hypnotic eyes which were like dying universes, which were like the deepest and most convoluted oceans the infinity space had ever dreamed into creation. And *Noœ-bouk* again felt an entire arousal of its physical form and its emotional form, with waves of vibration flooding through it. It had no idea how to process these waves and so it simply allowed them to flow through it, flow, flow, flow, and it had the impression that the Admiral, who had not lessened the grip on its wrist, was controlling this process and knew what was occurring. And then the Admiral send a final thought wave.

"Your mind, your form, your being, *Noœ-bouk*. They are all here. They are present. I am going to enter them. I am going to enter you now."

"Yes. Yes. Yes. Yes. Yes."

ALISDAIR LEANED FORWARD in the boat.

"So, in this unity game – how do I progress to the next level? In fact, what is the next level?"

Duncan put down the oars and looked out at the suns and planets moving around them. Streams of fire in the darkness and circles of ice. Moons and comets, bodies of incandescent flame.

"The next level for you is to start combining your lives in physical form with a presence on a Council. You haven't yet achieved enlightenment as a human, where you would no longer require a body of any kind, and yet the lives you have lived have been powerful and pure. The perspective of a Council position would strengthen your journey."

"What Council would I join?"

"One of the Earth Councils would suit you. There are several which monitor the progression of different aspects of the planet."

"How far up do the Councils go? Is there an... ultimate, supreme Council that decides everything?"

"There are Councils going all the way to the highest levels. However, at the point at which re-merging with the source takes place, at the unity level, there are no more structures. The energy is stronger than any structure."

"And if I wanted to join a Council, is there anything I should do?"

"You should widen yourself to accept other life forms. Only in this context can you understand what is happening on Earth. You should see other planets and expressions of existence. Live some lives in different structures. Take part in the planning and seeding of civilisations on other planets. When you have done this, then you will have gained the breadth required to participate in the decision-making of a planet progression."

"Where are these other planets?"

"You can choose where to go. It could be this universe initially, but then we can go wider. Start with life forms that are not too far from human, and then progress to other dimensions, other universes, structures of energy that you cannot yet imagine in your current stage of development."

"How many lifetimes will it take?"

"There is no exact number. It depends how fast you progress. It could be dozens, it could be hundreds. You might choose more challenging lifetimes in order to learn faster. You may find resonance with a single planet and spend many lifetimes there, exploring different variations."

"But that will take thousands of years."

"That statement has no meaning here. Time and relativity as you have understood them do not exist beyond a few particular planetary environments. They are a construct used to frame an experience of physical incarnation. That is all."

Alisdair frowned. "I've heard that before. And I think I've been pretty open-minded about" – he waved his hand out to the side, taking in the swirling star clusters and distant planets – "all this. But time and relativity are just logical. We are here, now, in a single, specific moment. Before, we were in a garden. When we return, we will get out of the boat and be back in a garden. These are events which led to and lead from this place. They are causes and consequences. How can you say that this moment, and the moment before it, and therefore time, do not exist?"

Duncan smiled. There was a deep silence around them in the darkness and among the stars, and Alisdair had a strong feeling that something was going to happen. The sound of water floated to his ears, then the sound of a faint tapping, as of wood on wood. Duncan's eyes were focused behind him and he looked around.

Approaching on the stream of grey was a boat, and in the boat sat Duncan and Alisdair. Together, they were rowing the craft through the starlight. Duncan raised a hand to himself as the identical boat moved past theirs and out into the distance.

"What was that?" Alisdair asked, when he could speak. "What does that mean? The boat? What does it mean?"

They watched the craft disappear into the darkness, the tapping of oars on wood echoing in Alisdair's head. Duncan held his hands out wide.

"It means that there are no single moments which are separate from any other moments. It means that every moment that ever was, has already happened, and is happening right now. There are events, as you have described them, but those events do not happen in one moment in time. They are continuous. We can go now and step into any event which you think of as *past* or *future*, in any dimension on any planet in any life form, and it is existing right now. There is no *happened* or *will happen*. There is only *happening*."

"But if everything has already happened, then what's the point in me doing it again? What's the point in anything at all?"

"Yes," said Duncan. "What is the point?"

Alisdair closed his eyes. He became aware of a pulse beating inside him, something wider and more intense than his heartbeat. It was humming and throbbing within him, and then it was encompassing him as well, drumming in the space around his body, and within his body at the same time.

"Go deeper," he heard Duncan saying. "Feel your other selves there. The presence of your actions in different lives, now and always. Other parts of your soul in different expressions. Feel it."

Alisdair took a breath and tried to relax into the heart of the vibration. He saw flashes of his recent life in Edinburgh, on a windy beach; he saw a temple in Greece, white, a cerulean sea beyond; he saw himself at the Earth Council, standing before the turning globe. He felt all of this within the pulse and he nodded. It was just the beginning. He knew it.

"If you widen it further," said Duncan, "you can experience all of yourself, and then you can feel the lives of other people, until you feel within that vibration *all* of life. The pulse of unity. Right now, within that single beat. It's very addictive. Once you start tapping into it, you'll never get anything done!"

Alisdair opened his eyes, and the drumming gradually faded away.

"That was remarkable."

"It's a very liberating concept, once you get used to it," said Duncan. "It makes everything so much richer – that you can be experiencing and living and doing and being so much all at once. You've done well. It's often extremely difficult to shift to the new mindset after an Earth life. The Earth sphere is so very convincing."

"I think I prefer it this way," said Alisdair.

"Good. But those are enough new concepts for now. Shall we start heading back? It's time for you to choose a new life form."

Alisdair tilted his head.

"If I have understood our conversation correctly," he said, "considering that everything is happening at once, then we have already arrived back... and we are arriving back right now."

As he spoke, the garden materialised around them, and the boat clinked against the stones of the silver lake. After the muted starlight, the prototype colours dazzled.

Duncan chuckled. "Now you're getting the idea. I think you're more than ready to start something new." He passed the rope to Alisdair.

"Now why don't you tie up the boat?" He winked. "That is, if you haven't already."

CHAPTER
TWENTY-ONE

DAVID KNEW it had been the homeless man's eye. The one he had seen in the office before he'd passed out. The one in his dream. The one he felt could appear before him at any moment. The one that was driving him further into fear and paranoia.

He had to do something about it. He wasn't sure if the meds were contributing to the hallucinations or if they were preventing worse images from seeping into his mind. But they were definitely making him paranoid: compulsively checking his watch, hearing words that people weren't saying, imagining things in the corner of his vision. Eyes, owls, time. It was like three wires were buzzing constantly in his head, each ready to light up in a frantic wave of rage or frenzy at any moment.

The day before, he had called the apartment super about the homeless guy, who had laughed him off. Wasn't his job, he'd said. He fixed pipes, not social problems. He'd told him to call the police if it bothered him so much. But maybe he should call the landlord first? Call the rental agency?

David strode fast down Park Avenue, the multi-million, old-money high-rises on each side and the island of tulips running down the middle. He had decided to walk home tonight. The evening was warm, and Vanessa had flown back home to her parents in Minnesota to tell them about the wedding. She hadn't wanted David to come, which was fine with him. The last thing he needed right now was a bunch of in-laws. For that matter, he really needed to tell his parents, but he wanted to wait until this project was done. He knew they'd be pretty shocked, and his mom would be upset for a while. But they'd get over it. It's not like he lived there anymore.

He really had to calm down, though – he was far too much on edge. And the hallucination? That was really, really bad. Although the new meds did seem to be working. They'd cut out any dreams, at least for the moment. And it hadn't been too bad talking to the shrink. He'd mostly just followed the guy's suggestions. It wasn't too hard. He felt a little bad about what he had let be implied about his childhood, but still, this was probably the most stressful time of his entire life, and whatever it took for him to get through it, he was just going to stick it out. He wasn't going to let his future slip away just as it was taking shape before him.

He increased his pace until he was overtaking the other walkers on Park. Women in tight business suits with expensive briefcases, looking like they could fire entire departments with a word. Harassed analysts hurrying home to get some sleep before they would be hurrying back to the office in a few hours' time. He strode past them, one by one. He wondered how he looked through their eyes. He was always careful to dress well. Certainly not like an analyst or a VP. Probably a Director, he thought, or even an MD. No, not an MD. He was just too young. Okay then, Director. That was fine. If he didn't drop the ball, he'd be one in a few months.

He caught the glance of one of the suited women as he passed, and felt her eyes checking him out. He gave a half-smile, feeling her approval, before his head filled again with the image he was trying to block. *Goddam that homeless man.* He couldn't even look at a woman without those eyes flashing into his mind. Maybe he should go and knock on some doors in his apartment building? No. Then he'd look like a real asshole. Should he call the police, as the super suggested? They could come and move him one time, but that didn't mean he wouldn't be back. He wasn't going to call the police every morning.

Dammit. If Vanessa hadn't given him the twenty dollars, then the guy wouldn't have looked at him, wouldn't have grabbed his jacket, wouldn't have stared after him every time he came down the apartment steps; as if he wasn't feeling paranoid enough to begin with.

Twenty fucking dollars! It was far too much to give to someone on the street. He felt angry at Vanessa, but then pushed it away. No. It wasn't her fault. She was just about the one good thing in his life right now. His wife. His *wife*. Wow.

He thought of Cassie, and that he should probably call her. He remembered the last conversation, and for some reason that memory once again gave him a surge of elation. Yes, he'd like to call Cassie and tell her about the wedding and the Hong Kong transfer and promotion. Then she could stop acting like she still knew him. Like only she had the right to say what he should be doing in his life.

David turned off Park and onto Lexington. He had walked all the way uptown to 78th, and now he had to cut down through the avenues to his apartment. He passed the long storefront of a Papaya Queen, its display of fruit and flowers set out on the sidewalk under a plastic canopy.

He wondered if the homeless guy would be there on the porch when he got back to the apartment and, for a second, he pictured himself picking the man up and throwing him off the steps, hurling him out into the road, and out of his life. Doing it so hard and so violently that he would never, ever come back to the apartment building, to that block, to that street. Damn, that would feel so good. He felt a sudden surge of power. Solving the problem. That's what it was called.

"Who's going to solve this problem?" Jeff would ask the guys on the floor. "Who is taking responsibility for this problem?"

"I am!" they would yell.

"That's damn right!" Jeff would yell back. "Taking responsibility is the way to solve a problem."

Yes. He would take responsibility. This was his problem. This was his situation. This was his paranoid freak-out. And he was going to find a solution.

He was halfway down 78th now, coming out of 2nd Avenue. There was a blind alley leading off from the street, half-blocked by a cluster of green garbage cans and black bags. On an impulse, David turned and walked down the alley. He took a brief glance behind him, then reached back his leg and kicked one of the garbage bags as hard as he could. The bag flew against the wall. It felt good. He kicked it again, and again, bursts of adrenalin flowing through him. He kicked the bag over and over until it split open against the wall and a mass of paper, spoiled food and old bottles spilled out of the torn plastic onto the concrete of the alley.

David stepped back, breathing hard, and leaned forward with his hands on his knees. He felt good. Really, really good. He *was* the solution. He *was* taking responsibility. He inhaled and glanced up, wondering if anyone had been watching from one of the overlooking windows. He didn't think so. It wouldn't matter, anyway. They'd just see another stressed-out banker, another crazy New Yorker flipping over the edge, over that line where stress, pressure, bonuses, multi-million-dollar salaries, egos, face-offs, back-stabbing, dog-eat-dog, all those pure elements of man's rise to power and riches were balanced. Whoever crossed the line, whoever couldn't take the heat, whoever toppled or was pushed to the other side, was out of the game, finished. Doomed to a life of second-tier, middle-management pay packets and box-houses in New Jersey, Idaho, Kentucky. Whatever backwater they'd made it out of in the first place.

And which side of the line was he on right now? He wasn't quite sure. Leaning pretty sharply, that was for certain, but still just about holding on. At least he still knew the line was there. At least he could see it, and would know when to take a step back.

David straightened up slowly and brushed his hands over his suit, checking his shoes for garbage. He took a deep breath, then turned away from the spilled trash and walked back out of the alley and onto 78th Street.

He was alright. He was still on the line. The new meds were making him a bit weird, but he was holding on. And Vanessa would be back in a week. And his project would be wrapped up the week after.

He was going to make it through.

DAVID LEANED FORWARD over the body and began to draw his tongue over the tender, willing flesh. The skin tasted ripe and earthy, bursting with eagerness for his touch. Something in the taste seemed connected to a far-off recollection: if he could just push himself a little deeper with his tongue, then a door would open into the most marvellous memory, a pathway into a place of light and boundless happiness. He pressed his nose further into the flesh and breathed and breathed and moved his tongue up and down the limbs, tasting, drinking, losing himself in their smell. He knew what he was doing. He turned the form over – it turned easily, as if it were in water – and he covered the back with his tongue, claiming ownership over each cell of skin, bringing it alive with his glistening sheen of fluid. He licked upward to the back of the neck, then turned it again and licked the front, shifting to the face. When his tongue met a faint suggestion of hair, he was not surprised but continued in his work.

From the face, he moved downwards over the arms until, at last, he returned to the centre. He had completed his task. He had made this form his own and he had drunk in its scent of flesh and soil, and now it was time to finish.

He was aware of his huge erection. He had to take possession of what was his. He prepared himself to enter the form, his senses gathering and merging into a single flow. He was nearly there, he was poised. And then it occurred to him, as it had done before, that he should see who it was before he entered the body, before he claimed it for his own. He moved back from the form, glistening in its silver membrane, and he saw with surprise that it was not Cassie. It was a man. The man from the steps. That radiant man! And the man opened his eyes slowly, and from them poured out such a stream of love that David nearly released himself in ejaculation. No! He held himself back. He would wait. This sublime flow must be matched with the requisite physical act. He turned over the silver figure and prepared himself to enter it. His penis was enormous now. Erect. The perfect instrument to perform the ultimate union of emotion and matter. He reached forward to clasp the body in his hands.

A pain. He opened his eyes.

He closed them again, opened them.

He sat up, pushing the duvet off his chest. He felt as if there was a massive concrete block inside his head, crushing against his skull and skin on every side.

He couldn't possibly have dreamed that. He lifted the duvet and looked at his body. He was naked again, and his penis was hard and painful, aching to be touched. This was a new level of nightmare. The medications. Oh god. This was awful.

He reached down and wrapped his hand around his penis. He had to get this done. It was too painful. He focused and then thought of Caroline wearing the tissue-paper blouse. He pictured the beige-and-white office and imagined himself ripping the white tissue paper from top to bottom, revealing her cream satin bra.

Yes. This was working. He pulled the pins roughly out of her pale hair, letting it fall down around her neck. He ripped off her tight, grey pencil skirt and turned her around. She was wearing tissue-paper panties and he ripped them off, too. In a second, he had bent her forward over the desk and was inside her, pushing himself up into her. Thrust, thrust, thrust. It was the most amazing feeling in the world to be inside her, to be right up inside that tight, New England pussy. He was going to come so hard it was going to rip her in two, just like that blouse which had been driving him crazy. Caroline was moaning, her hair was flying everywhere. He reached round and rubbed her clitoris, and she screamed like a madwoman, losing every shred of dignity and control and uptight superiority; he was fucking it all out of her. She came, screaming, and he came, thrusting his cock right up inside her, and sending white streams of cum flying across the room. He thrust and thrust until there was nothing left but a trickle of semen and his hand clenched around a softening penis.

David fell back against the pillow, groaning. He'd have to clean that up, but he'd do it in the morning. He glanced over at the clock: 4:17. It was Sunday and he could sleep. He knew that something bad had just happened, but his mind had suddenly gone entirely blank. He would figure out whatever it was in the morning. For now, he was spent.

He closed his eyes, pictured Caroline bent naked over the desk, her golden hair spread out over her long, pale back. He slept.

 IT WAS an entire moon cycle before *Noœ-bouk* re-entered a state of active consciousness to find that it was still located within the resting pod. It must have been through many sessions of the light healing while it was in a state of non-presence, for its physical form felt restored. It felt potent. It felt vital.

Strange, *Noœ-bouk* reflected. It had expected that the experience of unity with the Admiral would lead to a dissolution of their physical matter, and yet here it was awake, conscious, present and with a feeling of replenished energy. It created symbol blocks for no one in particular: *Renewal. Wonder. Life.*

Pushing the symbol key of the light pod, the top slid open and *Noœ-bouk* stepped out into the chamber. It did indeed have a new vitality. It looked down to examine its entire structure and saw that the grey skin, previously almost transparent, carried an increased solidity and lustre.

It wondered if the Admiral was experiencing the same form sensations. It must be. This was evidently a new state created from the unity they had achieved. The act must have initiated a process of regeneration which had not been anticipated. *Noœ-bouk* decided that it would visit the cellular laboratory to request a reading. If this energy level could be maintained, then it might be high enough to perform the *Tayr* channelling assignment.

It left the chamber and moved along the curved, white corridors. It could feel that its facial features were in an uplifted position and its energy field was unusually clear. Other life forms it encountered on its way responded to it with a strong, raised vibration. It had truly achieved a state of elevated being.

"I have come to request a reading," it sent as it entered the cellular laboratory. The cellular specialists were located separately around the chamber, absorbed in a variety of tasks. *Noœ-bouk* observed the tentacled being – which had conveyed to it the symbol block of opening stars – in the liquid chamber, half hidden among strands of plant matter. Its tentacles were drifting in *Noœ-bouk's* direction, and it had the impression that it was being read by its intelligence.

One of the cellular specialists set up the scanning equipment for *Noœ-bouk* and it entered the capsule. It was aware of the attention of the tentacled being still fixed upon it, and it sent a symbol block: "Greetings and honour."

The life form did not reply, and *Noœ-bouk* blocked out the unpleasant sensation its gaze was creating.

The scan was complete. *Noœ-bouk* stepped out of the pod and awaited the results.

"Seventy above zero," came the reading from the genetics specialist. It was sufficient to perform the channelling task assignment. A flow of positive emotion moved throughout *Noœ-bouk's* physical structure. The genetics workers were sending it thought waves of accomplishment and satisfaction. They understood the significance of the reading. Something, however, made *Noœ-bouk* glance once again towards the tentacled life form. The being regarded it, but did not offer any communication. *Noœ-bouk* felt unsettled.

"What have you read from me?" it sent to the being.

For several inhalations, the life form did not reply, and then at last it opened a channel between itself and *Noœ-bouk,* and created an image block within that channel, which was visible only to them. The image block was of *Tayr,* pulsing in its living hues of light, its vibration balanced, its energetic flow smooth and natural.

"You will complete the energy balancing," the being sent to *Noœ-bouk.* "Farewell."

Leaving the Scientific and Research Centre, *Noœ-bouk* located the Captain's vibration on the main viewing deck and made its way along the corridors, the image of *Tayr* turning in its mind. The initial sense of positive sensation from the elevated reading should have remained, and yet the tentacled being in the liquid chamber had created doubt. There was something it wasn't understanding, something it wasn't seeing. Had it been subject to a genetic mutation that only an advanced life form was able to read? Had something else occurred during the unity process which had altered it?

Noœ-bouk reached the main viewing deck and reported to the Captain.

"I am able to perform the channelling task assignment," it sent. It transmitted the cellular reading and once again expressed its ability and intention to carry out the vessel's mission.

"Then it will be so," the Captain conveyed. "Let the preparations proceed. You will identify when the cycles are correctly aligned and inform me when it will be accomplished. I will report to the Council that this is taking place."

Noœ-bouk expressed respect and gratitude, and left the main viewing deck. The view of *Tayr*, turning in its orbit so close to them, was no less alluring and mesmeric than before, and it stirred something once again in *Noœ-bouk*. It wanted to share this sensory process with the Admiral; it would enter its vibration and allow it to experience the image of this animate beauty. It searched its mind for the vibration, but for some reason, it could not locate it. It attempted once more to find it, and once more could not. A sensation of fear passed through it. What could have happened? It tried sending a wider communication on the thought-channel of Home Planet, which would surely reach the Admiral. Again, nothing.

Noœ-bouk stopped in a curve of the corridor. Something was wrong. It conjectured for a short inhalation, and then it released a general Home Planet request for information.

"Where is the Admiral?" it sent.

As it projected the communication, it glanced down at its grey skin. The improved lustre, reflecting the new potency of its cells; the increased vibrational level which was enough to carry out the assignment it longed to complete.

As it sent out the communication, it suddenly knew what the reply was going to be.

It had achieved unity, and it had transferred its energy.

"The Admiral," the reply came to it, "has completed its transition. It has gone."

 THE WHITE COLUMNS of the temple reflected the bright sunlight of the morning. Beyond the pillars, down through the scattered olive trees, the sapphire Mediterranean Sea sparkled beneath a clear, seagull-flecked sky. Alisdair stood between two columns, facing out to the water, and looked down the cliff at Socrates, who was sitting on a crag of

rock, surrounded by the young men who had followed him out of the city.

Socrates was sweating; he wiped his beard and forehead repeatedly with the palm of his hand. His mind was still overcast by the vision the Gods had shown him. He had not yet found a way to form extrapolations from what he had seen, and it concerned him.

Alisdair felt another presence, and he turned to see a figure appearing at the other side of the temple. It was Elspeth. She was dressed in a long tunic, crossed around the waist with a loose belt. Her dark hair was pinned at the back of her head with a brooch of turquoise. Her feet were bare. When she had fully taken form, she looked around at the lofty interior of the temple and then down towards the olive grove and the shimmering sea where Socrates and his followers stood on the cliff face. She gazed at Alisdair with a slight frown, as if seeing him for the first time.

"Where are we?" she said at last. Her voice carried in a clear, pure note through the acoustics of the temple.

"We are in Athens," said Alisdair.

There was a long silence.

"Is that Socrates?"

"Yes."

"And is that Plato?"

"Yes."

"What language are we speaking?"

"We are not speaking a language. We are understanding each other."

Elspeth continued to regard him, then she picked up the hem of her tunic and walked towards him. Grey and silver dust stirred on the temple floor as she moved. When she reached him, she held out her hand, and he drew it to his cheek.

"*Ailspeth,*" he said.

"Where are you?"

"There isn't really a name for it. It's a place between other places."

"Why is my life such a mess?"

"You are defining your life using constructs that are not compatible with who you truly are," said Alisdair. "The ideas and thought system of Earth are not yours. If you want to be happy, then you must find out what it is you believe; desire; think – and then follow only that."

"But that's what I've been trying to do all my life."

"You've been trying to do it within the confines of the established belief system. You need to let that go. You need to open a space for your own ideas. Without any judgement or censure from what you have learned to be right or wrong."

"I was happy with you," said Elspeth. She tilted her head, lifted her arms up high and drew the shape of a pointed star in the ether. The outline hovered before them. She touched it with her fingertips and it started to turn.

"Why are my constructs true and the others not true?" she said. "Everyone else believes in them."

"Because they are *your* constructs. The ones you see around you are true for the people who created them and who believe in them. But they are not yours. Your thought system is your own."

Elspeth reached out and touched the turning star. It dissolved into the ether. She took a step backwards and twirled around, the skirt of her dress billowing over her legs and ankles. She drew another star and set it turning.

"What is this place?"

"It is a meeting point," said Alisdair. "It is a place that is between you and me. It is a place we desired to exist."

"I wish you hadn't left. I don't know what to do anymore. I just feel lost."

"Feeling lost is not something to fear."

Alisdair reached for her hand once again; he moved her palm against his face. The skin was covered in tiny silver bristles. Elspeth remembered her cheek rubbing against those bristles in her childhood, many years ago.

"Can you feel me?" he asked.

"Yes."

"I am always here. I will always be in this place if you need me."

Elspeth pulled her hand back and looked into her grandfather's eyes.

"Is this for real?" she asked. "Will I remember it?"

"No."

"Then what is the point?"

"I wanted you to know that this temple is here. It will return to you when you need it."

Elspeth looked out over the shimmering sea.

"I am happy here," she said, and then her form faded until there was only pure sunlight shining between the columns.

Alisdair smiled. She had come. She had followed the book he had left her. Beloved Elspeth.

He gazed out to sea for a long time, watching the motion of the waves and the light; the seagulls diving down and then up, sometimes with a flash of silver; the fishing boats caught on the white surf waves. He turned and made his way down the cliff slope to where the young men were gathered around Socrates. He could hear his voice ringing out.

"From what is our understanding of the world constructed? When the Gods represent to us a brighter, clearer truth, how can we claim that what we see is real, or possessing any value at all?"

Alisdair found a flat rock and sat down, brushing the dust from his ankles and feet. He tilted his head to listen. In the distance was the sound of the sea, and a seagull calling out, and the falling sunshine.

CHAPTER
TWENTY-TWO

"DAVID."

"Martin."

"How did it go yesterday? Any progress on the position?"

"Yeah, a little. It's slowing down, though. Just as I thought it would."

"Well, this is where it's going to start taking a little more skill, isn't it?"

"Yes, sir."

"I heard there was some kind of an incident yesterday?"

"Martin, look, it was nothing. I got a little dizzy when I was talking to a client. Some of the guys got worried. I think I've been pushing a bit too hard."

"How about the client? You made the sale?"

"Yes, sir. I made the sale. A hundred of the target and some of the twenty per cent bonds to ease it through. Not a bad sale, all in."

"Very nice, David. Well, just watch yourself. We don't need you pushing too hard and then not finishing the job. Like I said, I've got my eye on you over here."

"Yes, sir. It's all absolutely fine."

"Alright then, David. See you later."

"See you, Martin."

"HEY, Cornwell, what's wrong with you today?"

Danny was leaning over the wall of his cubicle.

"Hey, Danny. What's up?"

"I've hardly seen you since the wedding. How's everything going? Jenny had a really good time."

"Yeah. It was a great day. I'm going to get you some of those pics when Vanessa gets back."

"So what's up with you?"

"Nothing. What d'ya mean, what's up?"

"You're jumpy. I just watched you put the phone down three times. And what are you doing here, anyway? I thought you were on your mysterious secondment during the day?"

"I had some client stuff to catch up on. Can't drop the ball, right?"

"Right."

Danny looked down at him.

"David, you want to get a drink after work? Seriously, you're on edge there. You're twitching."

"Yeah, thanks. Let me think about it. I've got a bunch of stuff on today, but if I can, I'd like that. Tell you the truth, it's pretty high pressure working two jobs."

"Man, I bet it is. It's hard enough working one. I think you're crazy for agreeing to it. But then you can't turn that stuff down, right, Super-Competitive Boy?"

"Right."

Danny reached out to put his hand on David's shoulder.

"Woah!" David jerked away, his hands shooting up on each side, his muscles flexed in a furious response.

"Woah, man, take it easy. You are on edge. Alright, I'm gonna go back over there. Get a grip. It's just a frickin' job, alright?"

David brought his hands down onto the desk, trying to pull himself together.

"Shit, I'm sorry man. You're right. I'm going to take a breather. Shit."

David got up and stepped over to the main corridor which led to the washrooms, walking deliberately and holding his breath inside his chest. His hands were shaking and he fixed them close to his sides as he walked, tensing his fingers to keep them steady. He reached the washroom door and paused outside it. He didn't really want to go in, but there was nowhere else for him to hide, short of leaving the bank, and he had too much work on right now for that. Some emotion or chemical was pulsing through him after Danny's touch. A kind of wild fury, an urge to reach out and smash Danny right in the face. What the hell had he been playing at? Frickin' guy should keep his hands to himself.

He pushed open the washroom door and went in. It was empty. He ran the cold water and held his wet hands over his face. He seemed to be doing a lot of this lately. Maybe he just couldn't handle all this shit. Ever since he had woken up, he had felt the weight again. Not the weight where he had to write something down, but a pushing against all the parts of his brain, against his skin and his head. A weight which was cutting off his air supply and slowing his brain function, forcing him into a smaller and smaller space where there was nothing to breathe.

He knew what the weight was. It was a classic stress symptom; the one that led to a heart attack at forty-five. And there were other symptoms. Over the last day or two, he had hardly been able to carry out simple tasks. It was as if his brain was losing connection with the rest of his body. All he could do was somehow get through each minute of the day, second by second. Try not to punch someone, or start shouting or kick garbage bags in back alleys. Maybe he really was losing it.

He glanced at his watch. How long had he been in the washroom? Two minutes, he reckoned. He was sure Danny was keeping an eye out. He'd go back after one more minute. He checked his watch again. Half a minute. He hadn't let himself think about what had happened the night before. The dream. Licking *that*… and then waking up with *that*… oh god, he wasn't going to go there right now. Then having to do *that*. Even if it was Caroline he thought of in the end, there was still the dream. There was still the reason he needed to think of her at all.

No. There was no way he was going to let himself go back to that memory. No way. And there was no way he was going to tell Shapkin about it. He'd have a field day. Who knew what sick theories he'd make him confess to if he told him about the dream? But he should probably tell Shapkin about the anger. About kicking the garbage bags. Well, maybe not about that, but he should tell him that he was feeling angry a lot. That might have something to do with the meds. There might be something he could take which would keep his head clear and counterbalance the effects.

But hold on. He was on the new meds. He had been on them when he'd had that dream the night before. The thought stopped him in his tracks. These *were* the new meds; the ones Shapkin had warned him were extremely strong, but that would ensure he could do his job. And if these weren't working? Then there was no hope. Nothing was going to work. End of story. He would have to find his own solution to what was going on. Just as always. It was David against the world and he was on his own. *He* was responsible and nobody else. He felt a little dizzy from the thought, and he waited a few moments for the implications to sink in. He took a deep breath and looked at his watch again. Somehow, he felt better. Somehow, he felt liberated. He would not have to go back to Shapkin. The guy had done everything he could and it had done nothing at all. The problem began and ended with David. He would take responsibility. He was the solution.

He turned and looked at himself in the mirror. Already, his face seemed a little less haggard, the heavy bags a little less dark. He stared into his eyes.

I am the solution, he mouthed to himself in the mirror.

He pulled his shoulders back, straightened his dark-red tie and brushed down his Canali suit jacket. He gave a nod to his reflection in the mirror, and walked calmly out of the washroom.

THE CROWD WAS GOING INSANE. It was game four of the division finals. Who the hell knew where Professor Baird had got the tickets, but he'd got them, and he and David were sitting in the lower bowl, watching the Maple Leafs get thrashed by the Detroit Red Wings. David loved the Maple Leafs, but at least he wasn't from Toronto. Those guys went mental when they didn't win.

"Another drink?" yelled Beardy.

"What?" David could hardly hear him over the din of rock music blasting through the venue, and the yells and shouts from the fifteen thousand hockey fans crammed into the Maple Leaf Gardens.

"Another drink?" Beardy shouted in his ear.

"Yeah, I'll get them."

David pushed to the end of the aisle and up to the top of their section to the concession stand. He joined the queue of fans, all dressed in the Maple Leafs' white-and-blue jerseys, many wearing bright-blue wigs with their faces striped in the team colours.

David bought two oversized plastic cups of Coke and carried them back to the seats. The third period was just about to begin. He handed a drink to Beardy, who took a silver hip flask out of his jacket and poured a long measure of whisky into each of the cups. He took a draught and wiped his beard with the back of his hand.

"I love hockey," he yelled in David's ear.

"Oh yeah?" David shouted back.

"It keeps you real," Beardy shouted. "Stops you getting lost in academia."

"Yeah!"

The game began again. Rock music and announcer voices swept out across the stadium, to wild hoots and cheering. The puck shot over the ice, and the huge, helmeted giants went tearing after it. Within a minute, sticks were flying and one of the players was down, and then another on top of him, and the crowd started to scream, "Fight, fight, fight!" and, "Go, Leaves, Go!" Moments later, the sticks were gone and the players were punching each other with gloved hands. A referee skated over to break them up, and the crowd booed as the players pulled away.

A moment later, the puck was sent flying. One of the Maple Leafs players chased it across the ice and smashed it past the goalie into the net. A frenzied wave of cheering rose around the stadium, and every one of the fifteen thousand Maple Leafs fans jumped to their feet, hugging each other and whooping as loudly as they could.

"I love hockey, too," David shouted over the din.

Professor Baird had finished his whisky and Coke in the two minutes since play had begun, and his beard was glistening wet. He wiped it with his hand.

"The Canadian dichotomy," he yelled at David, waving his fist in the air. "One of the most peaceful nations on Earth, and the most blood-thirsty when it comes to hockey. I'm gonna write a paper on it some day."

"Yeah. Something like that," David shouted back. The last thing he wanted to do was analyse the game. Just let them play, dammit. Let the guys do their thing, and let the crowd enjoy it. No analysing. No intel-lectualising. Just feel the emotions. Feel the life.

"So, have you changed your mind yet, David?"

Beardy turned round in his seat to face him, and David could see the creased forehead and the desire in his eyes. He leaned away and brought the plastic glass up to his face. The professor was speaking.

"We'll keep a place for you if you ever change your mind. You can work a year or two at Mercy Bank and then bring that experience back to the university. We want you, David."

David drained the plastic cup and closed his eyes for a second. The roar of the stadium was perfect. The whisky in his head and the job offer and the life ahead of him. He felt elated, carried on the noise, the happiness, the excitement of the game.

He opened his eyes and turned to Beardy. "I really appreciate it," he said. "But I've made my choice."

· · ·

AFTER THE GAME, David found a payphone covered in beer, and called Cassie.

"Babe, you gotta come downtown. We won the game."

"I know you won. Three-one! We've got a TV on in the dorm. You're *at* the game?"

"Yeah. This professor took me. He's trying to get me into his doctoral programme at the university. Hundred per cent scholarship and faculty job at the end. It's full-on bribery."

"David, that's great. Why don't you take it?"

"I wanna see how many Maple Leafs games he'll take me to first. Anyway. Get your butt downtown as fast as you can. We're gonna be out the whole night. You don't have lectures early, right?"

"I don't have anything tomorrow. I told my supervisor I've got some independent research."

"Even better. So get going. I'll pay for a taxi. Come on, you can be here in thirty minutes."

"Actually, the guys here were talking about heading downtown. Maybe we'll share a ride."

"Even better. It's insane here. The bars are going to be open all night. They're probably going to make it a national holiday."

"Okay. Let me talk to my friends. I'll try to make it."

"Who are the guys, anyway?"

"You don't know them. They're teaching assistants. Post-grads."

"Should I be jealous?"

"Jealousy isn't logical, David."

"Just make it down here as soon as you can."

"Alright. I'm on it."

"Hey, Cassie?"

"Yeah?"

"I love you."

"See you soon, David."

"Alright. See you soon."

AFTER IT HAD UNDERSTOOD what the Admiral had chosen to do during their unity experience, *Nœ-bouk* had gone to the main viewing deck and entered one of the observation pods. For many inhalations, it had remained within the capsule, looking out at the turning

222

planets and feeling the emptiness caused by the lack of the Admiral's physical presence in the universe. The fading vibration when it sent a thought wave; the non-resonance when it created a symbol block; the constant sense of dizziness, and the inability to register the meaning of any expression of existence within any point of relativity.

After many inhalations, *Nœ-bouk* succeeded in calming its emotional processes to a more neutral stasis point. It focused its thought patterns on the Admiral, and how it would be preparing itself for the incarnation on *Tayr*.

The path they had agreed on, the shared lifespan within the darkness of the separation state, seemed more distant and strange to *Nœ-bouk* than anything it had ever contemplated, and yet it also seemed to be a natural progression from the events which had been unfolding since the moment in the Cellular Genetic Centre, when the red-mouthed being had suggested it make the choice to live.

It knew that the challenge of lifting the energy of the planet, and initiating the connection of *Tayr* with the Federation, had been attempted many times in the course of the planet's history, and yet it had felt drawn to the task. It had sensed the possibility of being able to access the skills it had accumulated during its lifespans on Home Planet, and apply them on *Tayr*. It would need to choose the correct physical body. It would be necessary to identify a structure which could sustain the flow of energies required for processing information at elevated levels and in multiple streams. It would need consultation and careful selection.

Observing the planet before it, *Nœ-bouk* attempted to imagine what the experience of non-connection would be like; of not knowing, of separation from the surrounding life forms. A chamber devoid of light and energy flow, perhaps; similar to Home Planet when the largest moon was almost crushing the surface and the red-tinged sunlight had been blocked out entirely. An oblivion of all but the knowledge of individual sensation and own-being mind waves. *Nœ-bouk* felt a wave of fear at the thought, and recalled the Admiral. They would be together. They would be sharing the fulfilment of what had been initiated during the recent moon cycles. They would break through the oblivion using the process of *unifying love*.

Nœ-bouk initiated a final attempt to identify the vibration of the Admiral on the Home Planet stream. It was possible that traces could be remaining, as the Admiral's presence had held such a high level of prevalence within the Home Planet consciousness. The vibration faded out, finding no connecting wave. The unity experience had caused the entire dissolution of the Admiral's physical being.

It was done. It would not attempt to seek the vibration again. It would not think to the next lifespan. The Admiral would already be initiating the stages of incarnation, and the agreement between them had been made. There was no benefit in expending its attention capacity on unknown scenarios. It was of greater importance to preserve its energy for the channelling task ahead.

Noœ-bouk activated the thought shield, blocking out all mental waves, and prepared to leave the viewing capsule. It had few moon cycles remaining before the correct conditions for its final channelling assignment would be aligned.

It had no more need for thought.

"ARE YOU READY?"

Alisdair nodded.

"There is just one more place for you to go before you begin your next incarnation."

"I am ready."

"Release yourself."

Alisdair tried to open his eyes to look around, but he had no eyes to open. He experienced a moment of panic, but then Duncan's voice reassured him.

"Release yourself. It is different. Experience it."

He stopped trying to open his eyes, and tried to take a deep breath to relax himself. But then he realised that he had no mouth, and that he was not in a place where there was air. No eyes, no mouth; not in human form. Did he have a body? Now he was interested. What was he using to process this situation? His mind? Did he have a mind? What intelligence was he using to understand and question?

"Your consciousness." Duncan's soothing Edinburgh accent. "It is what you have always had. It is you experiencing yourself. It is just energy. Relax. Explore."

Consciousness. That felt right. Alisdair left aside the question of whether he had a body or a mind, and focused on getting an impression of what was around him, although he wasn't sure how the awareness was coming to him without the use of his sense receptors.

He became aware that he was in a place of great freedom – there were no limits he could perceive. There was an expanse of blue colour around him. It could be water. It could be sky. It was open and unlimited; fluid, or simply free. He tried again to determine what form he had, but he couldn't picture anything. He was simply here, existing in this blue, fluid state. He was within it, but still somehow himself. There was no division that he could find between the self he now was and the environment – neither his own consciousness nor the surrounding blueness had any clear boundaries. He could not identify if there was any physical element present, or any element relative to anything else.

As he explored the concept of his new reality, an awareness of tremendous potential began to come over him. He felt that the environment could somehow transform, that the combination of his consciousness and this fluidity could fuse into anything at all. His thoughts, his will, his desire; they could all create shapes from the blueness.

He began to play with the idea of creating something out of the expanse around him. He sensed the possibility of form, and his passing thoughts gathered a density within the colour. The more he directed his perception towards them, the more they appeared to actualise out of the surroundings. He was not perceiving shapes, but it was as if he were gaining an impression of their possibility or non-possibility. He somehow became either more or less aware of their presence within the proximity of his consciousness.

Alisdair was enjoying himself. Duncan had known where to take him. He focused his thought into the blueness, and began to imagine.

CHAPTER
TWENTY-THREE

"DAVID, what's the score today? How are we doing on the position?"

"Martin. It's all good."

"So what's the score down to now?"

"I'm building up to a big one, Martin. The clients I'm working with are more careful. I'm just feeling how sweet I have to go."

"That's the way to do it, David. It's an art. A delicate art. You've got to *feel* the thing. It's different with every client, how far you can push. When do you think you'll make the deal?"

"I'm hoping tomorrow. I don't want to give them the weekend to change their minds."

"Yeah, that's the way. Good job."

Martin reached forward to pat David's shoulder, and David immediately braced himself, drawing the muscles of his body tight to avoid pulling away from the hand. Martin felt him flinch.

"You okay, David?"

"I'm fine, Martin. I just got in early this morning to check my Lev Fin clients. Didn't get much sleep yesterday."

"Yeah, okay. Well, keep it together, alright? We're watching you."

"Thanks, Martin."

David took a deep breath. Okay. He had not punched Martin Walsh. He had not punched Danny. Now, he just had to keep it together. He hadn't made any sales today; he'd barely been able to call up a client. Twice this morning, he thought he had seen an eye in his peripheral vision; he had turned, and there had been nothing there. He felt on edge just thinking about it.

Another deep breath. He was holding it together. He was not losing his mind. He was in control. He was going to win this one. This was not going to take him down. Not now. Not here. Not like this.

I am the solution, he mouthed. *I am the solution.*

He looked at his watch.

THE RAIN WAS JUST STARTING as David stepped out of the bank. He opened his umbrella and looked around from the edge of the marble foyer. Bankers in expensive dark suits were sprinting the few blocks to the subway, or scurrying into the line of waiting yellow cabs hugging the curb. David wanted to walk. He needed to clear his head and get some fresh air, figure out what he was going to do. Vanessa would be back the day after tomorrow and he had a week and a half to complete the sales. Martin had been pretty easy on him today, but he knew there was a lot he hadn't said. This was the second day in a row he hadn't made a sale. In fact, he'd barely been able to pick up the phone. He wasn't going to risk passing out again on the floor. He'd be taken straight off the project. His career would be finished.

David wondered what was happening to his head. On the one hand, he had this incredible weight pressing down on it, so that he could barely think straight. And not just on his head. On his shoulders, on his back, on his chest; this constant sense of being more and more trapped.

And on the other hand, he had these outbursts he couldn't control. The aggression. The anger that would rush up in a split second, consuming him. As if the whole world was against him and he needed to lash out so hard, using all his physical power and aggression, just to save himself. Just to keep himself alive.

God, he was feeling it again, it was starting through him again. He quickened his pace and breathed deeper. *Breathe. Breathe. Breathe.* He was going to figure out a way to handle this, to get through it. One of Vanessa's blow jobs would help, but that was still two days away. And what if he had another of those dreams when Vanessa was around? The homeless guy. *Oh my god.* He had tried not to think of it, but now the image came back to him. He had been about to… about to…

Holy shit. He remembered the sweet taste of skin in his dream and a quick flow of saliva rushed into his mouth. He turned against the wall, sucked the body of liquid to the front of his lips and spat it out onto the pavement. Disgusting. What the hell was this *licking*? And those eyes. He had seen those eyes in the dream, and he had liked them. He had felt happy when he'd seen them.

David shuddered. The rain was falling heavier now. What the hell was going on? Ever since Vanessa had given money to that guy on the steps, he hadn't been able to get him out of his head. His eyes, his face, those dreams. It was as if *they* were somehow the source of all his problems. If he could just make them disappear, then all this stress, all this weight, all this nightmare would disappear with them, and he could get on with his life. He could get on with his work, his career, his new marriage. He could go on honeymoon; he could get the transfer to Hong Kong. He could claim the total happiness which was so close to him, and which, right now, he felt was slipping out of his grasp.

A pair of eyes. A pair of eyes he couldn't get out of his mind; which he had dreamed, hallucinated; been constantly in the back of his head for longer than he could remember now. How do you get rid of a pair of eyes? Well, there was the obvious way…

He pushed the thought back down. It was a ridiculous idea. It was an irresponsible, ridiculous thought. And yet, it was a solution. It would solve his problem. It would enable him to snatch back the happiness that was drifting away, and let him grasp it once again with his outstretched hands.

For one entirely lucid moment he saw the solution before him, so perfect and so clearly laid out that he was stunned it had never occurred to him before.

He pictured himself, just yesterday, kicking the rubbish bags. He recalled his rage and his reflexes today when Danny and Martin had tried to touch him. He thought of his tongue licking warm, male skin. He felt a revulsion so strong that he thought he was going to vomit right there on the pavement. The taste on his tongue. His stomach muscles contracted and his biceps flexed in furious disgust.

He knew that he could do it.

THE HOMELESS MAN was sitting on the step, sheets of newspaper spread out around him. The rain was pouring down by this time, and some of it was running off the edges of the dark-green canopy which hung over the sidewalk of the apartment building. Within the sound of the rain you could hear a hammering of drops on the canvas, a rushing of drainpipes, a swoosh of tyres in puddles, streams of water flowing off rooftops into alleys and interior courtyards.

The homeless man was wide awake and in a half-sitting position, leaning back on the newspapers. As David approached, he saw the man get up from the step and start to shuffle away into the storm and down the street, one of the newspapers held over his head.

"Hey!" David shouted at him.

The homeless man didn't turn around, and David followed him. He saw the man's hair hanging down, long and dirty, and his oversized suit and jacket.

"Hey!" David shouted again.

The homeless man shuffled across the street, starting up the overpass which crossed the FDR, heading towards the East River. David walked fast behind him, glancing down at the frantic, speeding cars below. The evening was dark by now, and orange streetlights lit up the rain in chaotic swirls. In the distance, a car alarm was wailing out its warning siren. The sound of the downpour was beating in David's ears.

He made it across the road and looked around for the man. He had somehow crossed the overpass and was already on the narrow running track beside the river. David could see him hurrying along. He strode after him, stepping in streams of water, soaking his shoes and socks. Now the homeless man was in front of him.

"Hey, stop!" he called out, but the storm was raging so hard that his words spun out behind him into the wind and the water. He ran forward until he was level with the man, and he reached out his hand, but then drew it quickly back. He couldn't bear to touch him. He quickened his pace until he was a little ahead, and stood in his path.

"Stop," he said. "Stop!"

The homeless man looked up at him from beneath the dripping newspaper; David was just a few inches away. He had never been this close, but he could smell him now, through the rain, the wetness of his body, his skin, his hair, the unwashed clothes, armpits, urine and whisky. It was the same smell from the dream. It was the smell he had tasted with his tongue, which had given him unspeakable, erotic joy. He almost retched.

He pulled himself up, and for the first time, looked directly into the man's eyes. Something in him moved. The eyes were full of tears, as if they were raining. The homeless man was crying, and as David looked into his eyes, something in the deepest part of him responded; something so deep that, for a few moments, his body was unable to comprehend the world around it. For a few moments, it was as if they were sharing the same tears, as if the tears flowing from those eyes were his own.

David felt himself drifting from the scene. He knew that he had separated from his physical body. He somehow had no more connection with the actions taking place. From a distance, he saw the grief he was sharing with this homeless man, and from that grief he saw the rising flow of rage and fear and revulsion passing through him, building steadily until it became all that he was: an animal, closing off everything within him, everything good; an animal, overtaken by the purest and most lithe darkness.

He saw his body move within that darkness. He saw his limbs move to its dance, to its music, to the beating of the pouring rain, to the flow of the night-time river.

Shove. The man stumbled and fell onto the concrete.

Kick.

Ribs.

Kick.

Head.

Kick.

Blood ran out onto the walkway; its redness against the stained grey filled David with the utmost relief. The blood was the solution to everything. The way through the darkness. The way to happiness. The man curled himself around. David drew his leg back and aimed a perfect kick at the man's head.

Smash.

The sound of skull. A quiet, grey trickle.

It occurred to David that the man was not crying out. The thought flashed past. The homeless man was twitching now, his arms and legs jerking outwards. His eyes were open.

Two more kicks. To the ribs, to the stomach.

David pulled his leg back and smashed his shoe into the man's skull, summoning every ounce of paranoid, terrified rage within him.

Smash.

Crunch.

At last, there was more blood. David breathed in and breathed out with a sweeping euphoria. He had never, never, never in his life felt a release like this before. He was flying. He was soaring. He was hurtling through the universe, a vessel of limitless power. He had done what needed to be done. He was a winner.

The darkness pumped through him, cradling him in its night-time embrace.

In a place beyond euphoria, beyond ecstatic release, as he watched himself transformed, powerful, animal, David knew that he had lost everything.

THE CHAMBER WAS READY.

Noœ-bouk had performed a final genetic scan before initiating the preparation stages of the channelling, and it had maintained its positive level of form density. The solar orbit positions and the planetary component levels had been calculated and a chamber partitioned for the task ahead.

For almost an entire moon cycle – even now, *Noœ-bouk* processed its thoughts in Home Planet systemology – it had remained in the adjoining chamber in a deep, meditative state, gathering the waves which would be required for the channelling assignment, and aligning itself with the source field. When the solar orbit positions and planetary component levels reached the point of maximum compatibility, it would be carrying within its physical form a combination of powerful and malleable energies.

Noœ-bouk had always been able to do this. It was one of the reasons for the exceptional results it had demonstrated throughout its lifespan. It had the ability to draw waves into its attractor field from the spacescape around it, and to charge or combine them until it had attained the exact composition necessary for each task. It had been trained for many moon cycles on Home Planet to achieve this with increased efficiency, but the truth was that it had always been able to carry out these assignments with ease. Its physical and energetic make-up were ideally suited to the work.

For this assignment, the Captain had made a request for *Noœ-bouk* to accept the assistance of two members of the vessel crew. Although *Noœ-bouk* had previously worked without the participation of other beings, it had on this occasion agreed, out of respect for the Captain, and as a concession to the risk-level of the task.

It sent a symbol block of readiness to the two beings, who entered the compartment with their vibrational shields activated, to avoid dispersing the energies that *Noœ-bouk* had consolidated. They led *Noœ-bouk* to the adjoining chamber, where a circular platform had been positioned in the centre of an otherwise empty surface area, and waited while *Noœ-bouk* took its place.

Noœ-bouk regarded the beings: vital, mid-cycle genus types. From the raised platform, it lifted its arm and made a small motion of its clawed hand towards them. The gesture signified to the two crew members that they should leave the chamber, and that everything had been correctly prepared to a satisfactory level. And perhaps, had the beings possessed the capacity to interpret a physical gesture made at a particular moment in the lifespan of a being whose existence had become a wildly veering pivot between ecstasy and destruction, it might have signified to them, and to the vessel, and to its physical presence within those endless, turning cycles: *farewell*.

The assistants left the chamber. The door panel slid shut. *Nœ-bouk* drew a deep inhalation and lowered the lids over its eyes. It raised its arms up on either side of its form and ran a check over the energies it was carrying. They were all correct. It was perfectly prepared. It was ready for its transition.

With its eyes closed, and entering once again into the meditative state, it moved aside the physical confines of compartment, vessel and space, until there were no boundaries remaining between the energy field of the planet and its own physical form. Sinking deeper into a trance, as everything but the assignment became invisible to it, *Nœ-bouk* gradually widened its presence, reaching out and sensing the living pulse of the planet, the areas of positive flow, and the weakened areas which were open to the more convoluted waves and causing the increasing imbalance.

The energy field of *Tayr* was something *Nœ-bouk* had never experienced before. Its tasks on Home Planet had been carried out in the clear and calm spacescape, where it had negotiated the attractor forces of the three red moons, and the weaker forces of distant bodies in the solar orbit. The field it now entered was violent in its turbulence. The gaping darkness of the sections out of balance and the intensity of the areas which flowed smoothly. It sensed in the surrounding waves the passions of the *Tayr* beings: the aggression and blood; the joy of temporary unity and the pain of separation; the striving to discover that which was always there. All this was contained, reflected and intensified in the expanse in which it now found itself.

It took *Nœ-bouk* many inhalations to acclimatise to these new conditions, and it held the energies it had gathered close, protecting itself from the upheaval of the *Tayr* flux and flow. At last, it was prepared. The waves it carried were in perfect malleable form, ready to be merged into new streams. It had sought out and identified the areas of imbalance. The components for achieving the task were at the point of maximum compatibility and the solar orbit position of *Tayr* was within the correct range.

With a final, deep inhalation, *Nœ-bouk* located the darkest and most convoluted area within the *Tayr* field and moved aside the spatial and temporal barriers between itself and the imbalance, so that it could enter the place entirely with its being and become, in free form, a part of the turbulent flux. Using the waves which were contained within its holding sphere, it transformed itself into a bridge between the area which carried the correct vibration and the area which was out of balance, and it stretched and moulded itself to that space, until the unbalanced section was filled up with its being and its vibration. It then opened itself into a channel and created an attractor pattern, willing the new, positive waves to flow through it, superimposing themselves over the unbalanced area and overriding it with their stronger vibration. The unbalanced energy, little by little, was caught up and dissolved into the pure source-stream that *Noœ-bouk* carried, and was replaced by the waves which were surging across the bridge.

Slowly, the new movement filled the gap, filled the space, and at the same time, *Noœ-bouk* began to experience a weakness in itself, a weakness of form, both real physical form in the chamber, and essential energy form in the *Tayr* vibrational field. Through the deep meditative trance, *Noœ-bouk* understood what was occurring. There must have been an error in the calculation of the energy required for the channelling. Perhaps it had been computed without taking into consideration the additional stages of adjusting to a denser, unfamiliar environment. If *Noœ-bouk* was not able to maintain its physical integrity until the positive stream had been established, the energy would revert to the chaotic flux that it had first entered and the planet could be lost. The flux could even increase in power and enhance the violence of the end result.

Noœ-bouk willed the stream to gather momentum, and as it did, the weakness it was feeling became a sensation of loosening, as if the components of its construction were coming apart, as if the bonds holding them together were dissolving. It felt more and more of the *Tayr* energy moving through it, moving through those widening gaps within itself, and it knew that it no longer had the ability to control the process, that the point where it could alter the event sequence had passed. *Noœ-bouk* struggled to remain in consciousness within the field, as the molecules and bonds and force which held it together grew weaker and drew further from its cohesive centre. It envisioned before it the turning globe, with flowing, smooth energy – the image sent by the tentacled being in the cellular laboratory. *Noœ-bouk* focused on this single point of vision, as its consciousness, gradually, thread by thread, faded into the surrounding ether.

And then, at last, it felt a sudden rush of new energy passing through it, and it was the natural, positive movement of the *Tayr* stream; and then another wave passed through it, a stronger one, and the knowledge made its way to the very last strands of *Noœ-bouk*'s comprehension, that once it had dissipated, that positive stream would continue to gather force and would override all of the imbalance into its natural flow.

And then that knowledge merged into an intense wave of peace. *Noœ-bouk* experienced a single last surge of pure source energy moving through its form, and in a sensation so extraordinary, that it was impossible to say whether it was the most exquisite feeling of perfect completion or the most agonising experience of unity separating, *Noœ-bouk*'s energy dissolved entirely into the *Tayr* field, and its physical form, at the very same moment growing rapidly fainter and fainter, disappeared from the platform of the chamber.

 ELSPETH FELT her way carefully through the orange grove. The night was the deepest black, but the stars above shone like a carpet of silver thread. Everything was utterly unseen, even the sea of white blossoms which lit up the grove during the day. Elspeth walked with her hands out in front of her, feeling her way between the trees. She had a torch in her small backpack, but she didn't want to spoil the perfection of the darkness.

When she estimated that she was in the middle of the orange grove, she ran her hands over the bark of one of the trees before sliding down the trunk to the ground. She breathed in deeply. The fragrance of the blossom was extraordinary. Heightened by the darkness and the stillness of the grove, the intense scent seemed like a physical presence there with her. It felt as if she was sucking it into her body as she inhaled; an intoxicant, something which could transform her with its elements. She felt dizzy and a little high.

Elspeth stretched out on the ground below the tree and slid her rucksack under her head. There. That was perfect. She had a bunk she was renting at a hostel in the town, but for the past few nights, she had come here and slept among the orange trees. She loved it. She felt in a state of absolute peace lying here; free, in this secret, mystical place where nothing and everything was real. All she owned in the world was the bag beneath her head and the clothes on her body. And if she wanted to, it would be the easiest thing to get rid of these items and to have nothing at all. She could leave her bag at the hostel and walk away, owning nothing. She would have total peace. She breathed in.

The sound of a thousand night-time cicadas clicked and hummed around her to the vibration of the concentrated heat. Elspeth tried to clear every thought from her mind and just listen to the air moving in and out of her lungs. She counted as she inhaled, one, two, three, four, five, and then she exhaled. She remembered something she had heard in a yoga class, that each human is allotted a certain number of breaths in a lifetime, and that the slower you breathe, the longer you live. Not that she particularly wanted to live a long time, but it felt good anyway, to be conscious of your body like that. Elspeth looked up into the carpet of stars, and she breathed. The scent of the orange blossoms filled her and she drifted into dreams.

All of a sudden, she was entirely awake and alert. There had been a noise. Her limbs were rigid and her skin had hardened into tiny bumps. She lay still, resisting the urge to sit up and look around. The noise she had heard was footsteps. She prepared herself to leap up and run if a light appeared.

She listened. The steps were coming in her direction. They were slow and she could sense a weight behind them. There was no torch, so she imagined that the walker must be moving as she had done, with their hands out in front of them to feel their way. The footsteps drew close, and then, just a few feet from her, they stopped, and there was the sound of a body lowering itself to the ground.

Elspeth held the air in her lungs. This was awful. She should have called out, or coughed, so that the intruder would move away. The person was so close, she thought she could feel the heat from his body. It had to be a man – the weight of the footsteps, the heavy breathing. He was making a lot of noise now, shifting and rustling, but what would happen when he was quiet? He would hear her breath. And in the morning when the sun rose? Who could he possibly be? And why had he come to an orange grove in the middle of the night?

She couldn't let herself sleep now. She wanted very much to sit up, but she couldn't risk it. Perhaps if the man fell asleep, then she could tiptoe back through the grove, although she could easily get lost and the area was huge. At least she would find her way out of sight of the stranger, and then as soon as it was light, she could leave. That was a good plan.

"Is someone there?"

The deep voice startled her out of her thoughts, and she drew air sharply into her nose and held it there. He couldn't have heard her. The cicadas were louder than her breath.

"I heard something. I'm sure someone's there." The voice came again. It was a deep voice, with an accent. There was something gentle and ragged about it, as if it had suffered a lot.

"Please," the voice said. "I have a flashlight. I can take it out."

"Don't," Elspeth said quietly. The single note of her voice trailed out like a living thing into the space between them, and hung there, watching them both. It demanded attention and a readjustment of their relative states.

At last, the man spoke again.

"I'm a Canadian," he said. "I just came here to think. I'll leave if you want. I must have scared you."

"What do you need to think about?" Elspeth spoke softly, but again her voice seemed to take on its own shape and form in the darkness. The man was so close to her.

"I had a breakdown," the man said. "My life fell apart. I've been in a clinic." He paused. "When I left the clinic I couldn't go back to what I was doing. I came here to find some answers."

"Why did you have a breakdown?" asked Elspeth.

There was a very long silence. She listened to the man's breath hissing in and out and she looked up at the stars. She thought that they could be floating right now through space, side by side, just floating, asking each other questions, and she thought that they could be two sparks of consciousness, without any bodies, just floating side by side, exchanging questions and answers.

"I killed someone," the man said.

Elspeth felt her entire body draw inwards and the hairs on her arms rose in a single movement. Her hands started shaking. Should she run away? Was this about to turn into an indescribable nightmare? A heavy white mass entered her head. She thought she should get up and start running.

"It was the most terrible thing in the world," the man continued, in a low voice. Elspeth heard his words trembling. "I did it, and six months later I had a mental breakdown. I was in a clinic. I have never told anyone what I just told you."

"Who did you kill?" Elspeth was shocked by her question. Her body was still incapacitated by fear, and she had no way of judging how the situation was going to play out. Terrible scenes flashed into her head. If this man had never told anyone what he had just told her, surely she would have to be the next victim?

"I killed a beggar. In New York City. He used to sleep on the steps of my apartment building."

Elspeth heard ragged breathing. The man was crying.

"I was under terrible pressure at work. I was taking a lot of medications. I had this... unbelievable anger. This man, there was something about him that was setting me off. It's impossible to explain. At the time, it seemed so real. Now, it seems impossible. I have no way of understanding it. I can't understand how I could have done it."

"How were you not caught?" asked Elspeth.

The man took a deep breath. "I don't know," he said. "There didn't even seem to be a search. Maybe it's so common in New York. They don't waste time searching if someone won't be missed."

"That's awful," said Elspeth.

There was a silence again. "Why didn't you tell anyone?" Elspeth asked. "Why didn't you go to the police?"

"I moved away shortly afterwards," the man said. "It had all been planned. The move, I mean, not the... the..."

"And then?"

"And then it got harder and harder. I pretended it hadn't happened. I was on a lot of psych drugs. I was dealing with so many things. I'd just got married."

"You'd just got married? And you killed someone?"

Another silence. Elspeth again pictured them together floating through space. They were here, among these stars, just these questions and these answers.

"It sounds insane. It was insane. I don't know what to do. I don't know whether to tell someone. Would that help? Would that help if I went to jail? Would that help anyone? Would that help me? I spend most of my life in jail and then I come out and I'm broken? I'm broken now. Is that my punishment? Is that enough? Who decides what is enough? Oh god."

Elspeth didn't say anything. Together, they floated among the thick carpet of stars, the questions, trailing out in silver threads, searching for their answers, searching for the symmetry to complete them, the stars around them rising and fading, held by precise mathematical equations to the moving, living universe around them.

CHAPTER
TWENTY-FOUR

THE HOMELESS MAN lay on the concrete, his eyes wide open. It was quiet now, except for the falling rain. The sound of blows had gone. The sound of crushing bone had finished. It was calm.

He looked up into the sky, in each of his eyes a hidden universe collapsing. Slowly, very slowly, the drumming of the rain grew softer, merging with the flow of the river, and then with the flow of the night-time, and then with the flow of the darkness.

Silence. The eyes were gone, and the two universes were still.

IN THE SCIENTIFIC and Research Centre, the assignees monitoring the energy flow around *Tayr* watched in a heightened state of amazement as the convoluted area of imbalance was transformed before their eyes into a smooth, positive flow. They had observed such energy work in localised situations on Home Planet, yet watching it performed on a highly populated living environment, with the threat of cataclysmic, multi-planetary side effects, was a valued experience. Even the tentacled beings remained still at the base of the liquid chamber, moving their thin antennae to follow the results of the channelling.

"Wonder," one of the Scientific Analysts sent a symbol block into the chamber.

"Yes," responded its colleagues.

They remained for many inhalations after witnessing the planetary rebalancing, carrying out readings and checks for all the relevant criteria. They created a hologram of the event and together they observed it from different dimensional perspectives. When the results had been confirmed, the Head of the Scientific and Research Centre went to find the Captain, who was on the main viewing deck with other members of the senior crew.

When the Captain had received the symbol blocks, it gave a gesture of acknowledgement and thanks. It then sent a communication which could be read by all the crew members on the vessel.

"This assignment is being acclaimed a success," it conveyed. "I am being congratulated by all of the proximate vessels, some of which have monitoring equipment superior to ours. It is a positive outcome for the *Istina*, on its first voyage. We have achieved great benefit for *Tayr*. I thank you."

The Captain turned back to the Head of the Scientific and Research Centre. Together, they examined the effects of the channelling and compared them to the results transmitted by the surrounding ships.

"In the next solar cycles, the aggression on *Tayr* should weaken," the Captain communicated. "The energies will be resonant with the peacemakers, and conflicts may be resolved. If the rising were to continue, it is possible that fear would cease to be the dominant force on the planet."

"This is an outcome that has been studied and desired for many moon cycles," the Head of the Scientific and Research Centre replied. "If this has been achieved, then our voyage will be recorded in the annals of *Tayr* and examined for generations of lifespans."

"Yes," the Captain affirmed. "I did not expect such a mission so early into our voyage." It paused. "I must make a report to the Council now. Many systems in the universe have been affected and they are waiting for task-completion confirmation."

It conveyed a final symbol block of thanks and partnership.

The Head of the Scientific and Research Centre left the Captain, and made its way to the chamber which had been set up for the channelling work. The two assistants were waiting near the door.

"We were instructed not to enter until a thought wave had been received," they sent.

The Head of the Scientific and Research Centre pushed the symbol key for the opening to slide back, and it stepped into the muted white compartment. The assistants remained outside.

Inside the chamber, it observed the empty platform in the centre of the six white walls, and detected the unmistakable trace of source energy present in the inhalation particles.

It stood a few steps from the platform and recalled the form of *Nœ-bouk*: its strange, translucent skin, as if it was not quite existing in its physical body but somehow beyond it; the fact that it had carried out extraordinary work for both Home Planet and, now, for this distant planet, with which it had no affiliation. It had chosen to end its lifespan performing the task assignments for which it had the greatest natural ability, and which created the widest possible benefit. It had extended this tenet of Home Planet philosophy to its maximum possible expression. And yet, in that expression, the Head of the Scientific and Research Centre found, in the place of a validation – a doubt. A challenge. A shadow left by this strangely translucent form, now dissipated into the energy flow around *Tayr*.

It wondered whether, once the Home Planet vessel had left the vicinity of the planet, this doubt would also dissipate, along with the unfamiliar thought patterns created by the chaotic influence of the atmosphere. And then it wondered, before it exited the chamber, if it truly wanted that doubt to disappear.

It turned and pressed the panel. The doors slid open.

DAVID TURNED to Cassie and aimed a kick at her long, bare leg.

"Dare you," he said.

Cassie smiled at him, her red hair shining in the sun. She tilted her head, her grey-green eyes meeting his. Then her fingers were unfastening her short dress and she pushed herself off the end of the wooden pier and into the lake. She whooped as she swam out to the centre with powerful strokes.

"It's awesome!" she shouted. "It's freezing. Come on!"

David stood up on the pier. He kicked off his shorts, unbuttoned his shirt and prepared to dive.

"You can't catch me!" she yelled, and swam towards the middle of the lake in a fast, steady crawl.

He caught up with her quickly and dived underwater to catch her legs and pull her down. She struggled, and under the surface he released her legs and held out his hands; she took them, and they found each other's eyes through the distorted mirror of lake water and blew out streams of laughter. They rose to the top with their hands locked, and trod water, facing each other, squinting against the slanting sunshine.

Then David drew her body close to his, holding both of them up with one hand, and he kissed her wet face on the cheeks and the ears and the nose, his tongue tasting sweet, fresh water and the hotness of her mouth.

"Don't forget this summer," he said to her. "Don't ever forget it."

LATER, they sat on the edge of the pier in their underwear, letting the afternoon sun warm their skin and hair. Cassie's pale body was at last starting to go brown, and her hair had lightened to a golden red. She had a handful of stones to skim across the water.

"Look," said David, reaching into her palm. "You do it like this. You have to make it bounce so that it ripples. If you do it properly, it goes right to the other side."

Cassie sent a flat pebble skimming lightly over the top of the lake.

"Hmmmm?" she said, watching it bounce five, six, seven times, before sinking beneath the surface.

"Not so bad," David said. He leaned over again to her palm and selected the longest, flattest stone.

"Has to be the biggest!" said Cassie, touching his chest with her fingers.

David took it in his hand and shifted sideways, away from her, to get the correct angle. He squinted against the sunshine, moved his arm back against his chest, and sent the stone twisting over the water. It bounced once in a low, long trajectory, and then again and again, far out into the centre of the lake.

They watched in silence as the ripples moved outwards and outwards and outwards, growing smaller, until it was impossible to tell where the faint ripples ended and the almost-invisible movement of the surface became a single, constant flow.

David closed his eyes.

THE ADVISORY COMMITTEE had gathered for the final review of the *Tayr* channelling and to reach a consensus on the next assignment for the *Istina* to pursue.

The Captain was present, and it observed from the far end of the white table as the hologram of the planet was projected and the Head of the Scientific and Research Centre demonstrated the results of the channelling from different planetary and dimensional perspectives.

"*Tayr* has been brought back from danger of cataclysmic destruction," it sent. "There is no imminent risk now to the proximate planetary systems and civilisations."

"And the rising?"

"We do not have authorisation from the *Tayr* Council to assist beyond the work that we have done. *Tayr* must lift itself towards the Federation. Only those incarnated into the planetary environment can cause this to happen."

"Then our work in the vicinity is complete."

"Yes."

The hologram of *Tayr* faded, and *Rai-bouk* rose to standing position to present the variations proposed for the next assignment. The convoluted ring structure surrounding the black holes was identified as the highest level of risk, combined with the possibility of new scientific knowledge which would benefit both Home Planet and the Federation. The Head of the Scientific and Research Centre was a proponent of the task.

It was decided.

The Captain sent signals of partnership and prosperity to the vessels positioned within the *Tayr* vicinity, and the Home Planet ship once again started on its course, tracing its original path between the planetary orbits and the asteroid fields, returning to the black holes it had passed in the initial stages of its journey.

As *Tayr* grew fainter in the distance, *Rai-bouk* stood alone in one of the viewing compartments at the stern of the vessel and observed the fading hues of colour, the clear energy field around the turning sphere. It thought of its co-planetary being, its energy now merged within that field, within those waves of green which rose and fell in endless rhythmic movements, and it raised its arms in the motion of a channeller, and held them poised, as if imagining a different existence, one where anything was possible, where there were no limits, a state beyond the parameters of accepted logical conclusions.

After a few inhalations, it drew the lids down over its eyes, then raised them again. It lowered its arms and turned away from the viewing panel, and with the slow, restricted movements of its elongated limbs, it made its way towards the Scientific and Research Centre and to its next prescribed task assignment.

CHAPTER
TWENTY-FIVE

ALISDAIR ROSE from where he was sitting among the craggy rocks of the cliff face, and climbed back up the slope towards the temple. Between the columns, he stood to catch his breath, looking out at the pigment-blue sea drawing and folding in rhythmic lines before him.

He raised his arms and drew a circle in the air. Within the outline, the rows of an orange grove appeared, a woman and a man lying side by side beneath silver, night-time blossom. He could hear the thunder of cicadas, the quick beating of their hearts and the stream of breath drawn in and released. He made a motion with his hand, and a wind passed through the grove, rustling the blossom. White petals floated down onto the heads of the woman and the man. The woman opened her eyes.

Elspeth's shadow-form brushed the petals from her cheeks and then stood, feeling out the edges of the circle with her fingers.

"I took a life," said the man. "I am a murderer."

Elspeth reached down and touched his face. He opened his eyes and his shadow-form stood. She led him to the edge of the circle and they stepped through, their fingers entwined. They emerged from the darkness into a white temple and bright sunshine.

The fragrance of the orange blossom mingled with the drifting sea salt. The man looked around him, at the startling blue of the sky beyond the temple columns, at Alisdair, at Elspeth, and then up to the roof of the temple.

"I have broken everything," he said. "I have lost myself. I cannot find the way back."

He looked at Alisdair, with a pleading expression.

"Where do I go now?"

"There is nowhere to go," said Alisdair. "There is nothing broken."

"What does that mean?" said the man. "I am a murderer. What I did was real. It can't be changed. I am broken."

Alisdair moved his hand in an arc around the man, and white petals fell on his hair and his shoulders.

"You cannot be broken," he said. "You are not something that can be broken. It is time to release the part of you that committed the act. It is time to make a new choice."

"And I?" said Elspeth.

Alisdair smiled at his granddaughter. "You are here to show him how to do that. Remember the constructs that are true for you."

The man looked expectantly at Elspeth. Elspeth started to laugh and she swirled around in the temple, her long dark hair flying out behind her.

"I don't know anything," she said.

She turned again, the skirt of her tunic moving around her body, her hair lifting and flying. "I don't know anything," she repeated, turning and turning. "I don't know anything."

She kept spinning, faster and faster, and the space in the temple around her took on the shape of a white spiral, moving upwards and downwards, with Elspeth's form circling steadily in the centre.

The men watched as Elspeth whirled within this spiral, then gradually slowed as the vortex faded.

Eventually, her body came to a stop, and she breathed deeply in and out, and looked at her grandfather and at the man.

She tilted her head, then circled it one way and repeated the movement in the other direction.

"We make it all up," she said. "It's all just a game. It's extraordinary."

She lifted her arms, and on each side of her, small white birds appeared. She held out the palms of her hands and they alighted on her fingers and arms.

"Look," she said to the man. "Look. I'm creating them."

The man watched her, shaking his head.

"How could I have killed a human being?" he said. "How could I have done that? I can't understand it."

"None of it is real," said Elspeth. "We created all of it. All this!" She waved outwards to the temple and the sea beyond, the white birds rising from her arms, then settling again. She pointed at the man. "You, me, this place, everything we thought, everything we believed. Our lives, our bodies, our worlds. It's all made up. But we can make up anything. Anything at all."

The man shook his head. "I was not a bad person. I was a good person. I was not a bad person."

His words echoed around the temple interior. Elspeth started to laugh. The birds rose from her hands and flew up to the ceiling.

"That has no meaning," she said. "It's nonsense."

Her laughter went on and wound upwards. Small white feathers fell from the ceiling onto their heads.

Elspeth moved to stand in front of the man.

"Let me show you," she said.

She lifted her hand and passed it in front of his eyes so he was caught in the brush of her attention.

"You believed the world around you," she said. "You believed someone else's dream. Now you must believe something new. Something of your own."

The man tried to look away, but he was held in the path of Elspeth's hand.

"It is time to believe something new," she repeated. "That is where you will find your forgiveness."

Neither of them spoke. A wind blew up and the sound of waves crashing onto rocks entered the temple and grew louder. White birds appeared and circled the man and the woman, their wings beating in heavy pulses of air. The man could hear his own breath leaving and returning through his nose. The sounds grew louder and echoed inside his head until he felt they were going to crush him. Birds' wings beating. Breath. Crashing water. He was pouring with sweat and his arms were shaking uncontrollably. A seagull shrieked and the man felt as if the noise was tearing into his skull. Images flashed before him. Murder. Blood. Eyes. Money. A flash of red. Something soft. A smell of lake water. A ceiling of stars. A dream of lifting. Exploring. Opening.

He could hear the water now, rolling onto the stony lake shore in the fresh wind. He could hear the voices of teachers. Then a softer voice, eager, intelligent; and later – loving.

He heard the whisper of the girl, as she released his gaze. "Now, create."

The man looked at the white birds. He looked upwards. From the ceiling of the temple, drops of blood fell down. He held out his hands.

Elspeth watched him. "Try again."

He took a breath. Again, drops of dark red blood fell over him, onto his body and hair and clothes.

"Again."

The man's face twisted in frustration. The drops of blood ran down his cheeks and dripped onto the temple floor. He closed his eyes and squeezed his hands into fists, focusing the thought into one single point of his body.

Through the rain of blood, a scarlet bird appeared, beating its wings. Then another flew down. After a few moments, the air around him was full of crimson birds, and the blood was gone. They sat on the man's shoulders, arms and head.

"Again."

An expression of hope appeared on the man's face. He focused once more. Over the birds, a new rain started to fall, in grey droplets. It fell over the crimson birds and they rose and flew out of the temple. He lifted his face and felt the wetness on his skin. He closed his eyes.

"Now," said Elspeth. "The space is open for your dream."

Around the man, the air seemed to darken, and tiny flashes of light appeared in the ether. There was a sound of water blowing over stones and a smell of summer leaves. Then the darkness grew more intense, and there were only the tiny points of silver to light the man. He lifted his arm in the air and drew a shape in the darkness. He drew other shapes, and then a mathematical equation. He turned, surveying the patterns and symbols he had created.

"Yes," he said. "Yes."

The darkness faded and the man found his eyes resting on Elspeth. They held each other's gaze and she smiled.

Alisdair stepped towards them. "You must go back now," he said.

He led them across the temple to the circle, barely visible in the sunlight, and they stepped through it. Alisdair watched as they returned to their bodies in the orange grove. He closed the circle and looked down at his granddaughter; her strained, tired face; the small rucksack beneath her head.

"Beloved Elspeth," he said.

Elspeth turned her head towards the voice. There were tears in her eyes. She reached her hand out to the side, and found that a hand was held towards her. She touched the fingertips.

"What's your name?" she said, very, very softly.

"David," came the reply.

· · ·

ALISDAIR STEPPED AWAY from the circle and climbed down the cliff-side to where Socrates was sitting alone, gazing towards the sea. Alisdair clambered among the rocks and took a seat beside him.

"I need your help," he said.

 THE EARTH COUNCIL was being summoned.

The individual members of the Council drew their consciousness into a central, focused point and allowed an image to flow through it, growing stronger and more detailed, until their intention and thought were merged into a single, constant flow. In the space surrounding them, a blue light began to emerge and intensify, forming a columned ring, and the figures took shape one by one, around the inside of the circle.

As the Council members exchanged salutations, a new outline began to appear within the temple. Its energy pattern was not from the Earth spectrum, and the Council watched with interest as the frame acquired definition. It was tall and a silver-grey colour, and was oscillating at a high magnitude, which gave it a shimmering appearance. Its head was large and disproportionate to the slightness of its body.

It was the Admiral.

The twenty-one Council members turned towards it, and several leaned forward in a motion of respect and recognition. The Admiral approached the centre of the chamber, and they opened up a space in the circle for it to join them.

"Welcome, *Ba-hutá*," they spoke.

The Admiral took its place among them, and together they observed the turning globe, around which they were gathered. Constantly changing patterns of energy moved over its surface, growing lighter and darker, clearing then gathering.

"I have come to ask for help," the Admiral sent to the Council. "A lifespan on *Tayr* is not being completed according to intention. There is destruction where the objective was unity."

"Let us look."

A woman with hair the colour of starlight opened her arms. Above the turning sphere, she drew a carpet of threads, moving and weaving and glowing brighter and fainter.

The Council looked at the map.

"This is the current life," she said.

They examined the map more closely, and saw the connections lit up between the souls who were participating in the lifetime. They saw the intended pathway in a clear line, then traced the adjusted course of actions, which twisted further and further from the initial thread, forming into denser and darker clusters.

"He has forgotten," the Admiral sent. It turned to create a supplication block to the Council, opening its arms wide. "Our agreement was clear."

The woman with starlight hair continued to study the map and brought her hands over a point on the surface.

"And yet you are present in this life. You are incarnated."

The Admiral signified assent. "I am present. But the attachment between us has weakened. It has lost the ability to return him to his initial intent."

"Your being is more advanced. It is able to retain its integrity in this unfamiliar environment."

She turned to look at the Admiral. "Have you attempted communication with this being?"

"I have done everything which is permitted, within the planetary Council laws, to bring assistance. I have created a channel of contact to remind him. It has had the opposite effect. It has led him to further block out any connection, any resonance. He is changing his thought patterns and receptors with chemicals. This path of action has failed."

"Why can you not summon his oversoul here, to join in this discussion?"

"His soul is not yet at the stage where it can be present in multiple dimensions."

The Admiral paused. It looked around the twenty-one Council members and sought them with its eyes. It opened its arms wide in supplication. "Our intentions and agreement for this lifespan were elevated and founded in the desire to bring knowledge and benefit," it sent. "In the preceding incarnation we experienced an unusual... an extraordinary... unity. We chose to manifest that unity on *Tayr*... on Earth." The Admiral struggled to complete its communication. "Our love was..." It stopped. "I ask for your help."

The Council members bowed their heads in reverence at the unusual emotion displayed by the Admiral. Signalling willingness to one another, they leaned over the map and traced the patterns being created. They examined the original life plan, in which a pulsating gold ran through all of the connections, and the energy over the entire globe lifted into a gentler, lighter flow. The Council exchanged quiet words and formed images that appeared and then faded.

At last, they turned to the Admiral.

"There is a possibility," said the woman.

"I am grateful for any assistance," sent the Admiral.

"There is a human located close to him," she continued. "He is preparing to leave Earth and complete the transition." She paused, checking that the Admiral was following her. "If you desire, you can enter the form and attempt to contact him in a new way. Without symbols. Through physical remembrance. Through your presence. It may be enough to bring him back."

"When is this being preparing to leave?"

"It is leaving now. You must decide if you choose to enter the body."

"Is it permitted, to be present in two physical forms, within one lifespan?"

"You had an agreement to share the life with him. It is permitted for you to be present in more than one physical form."

"Then I will do this. I will go."

A man, whose skin was tinged a faint blue colour, spoke: "The man you seek to help has already moved far from his initial purpose," he said. "It will be a task of the highest complexity to return him to his original state. You must understand this. Even for a being as advanced as you."

He leaned forward slightly in respect and opened his hands to show the intention of his words. The Admiral lifted its arm in a returning gesture.

"I understand," it sent. "I will go."

There was a murmuring among the Council as the decision was accepted and processed.

"Admiral. We honour you. We wish for your success in this endeavour. We have the highest respect for you and for the beings of your planet of origin."

"I thank you."

The woman with starlight hair laid out the new map of the life the Admiral was to begin, and together they traced the lines of possibility and connection. It was simple, made up of just a few threads.

The Admiral raised its arms and crossed them over its chest area. It drew a long inhalation into its mouth opening, and as it released the inhalation, its form disappeared from the chamber, leaving only a faint haze of silver within the resonant blue of the circle.

. . .

WHEN THE ADMIRAL WAS GONE, the woman once again opened a soul map over the turning globe. She moved her fingers outwards over it and the map drew into focus, and then closer until the distant, flashing points of a city were discernible, and then closer as the web and threads of buildings became clearer, and then closer so that the outlines of humans could be seen moving among the static peaks and geometric points and shapes. At last, the man they sought was visible, among the orange-lit, night-time streets, surrounded by a confusion of desires, twisted waves of thought and a constant pulse of fear, streams of images and distortions. Owls, symbols, stars, all blurred within a haze of medications.

The Council observed the man, tracing how his vibration touched and spread to those around him, and was in turn changed by those whose presence he encountered. They perceived the energy of the planet shifting in response to his decisions, the convolutions growing stronger and more unbalanced, the mantle gathering the darkness into itself.

"This being did great service to Earth in a different lifetime," the woman spoke. "I do not see what has happened."

The man with blue skin interjected. "The vibration of its form was too pure," he said. "It was not adequately prepared for the adjustment in density and thought structure. It had never before incarnated on a living planet. The risk was high but it had decided to go."

"Was it the right decision of its guides to permit the incarnation? It is causing much chaos and disruption."

The man with blue skin opened his hands to the Council.

"Many have failed," he spoke, "and some have failed and caused great harm and chaos. We have observed this pattern in those who know the experience of unity. They desire to bring the energy to Earth. The Supervisory Council has given permission for these intentions to be honoured. There is great risk of failure."

He stopped and looked around the Council. There were gestures of assent. The woman with starlight hair leaned forward.

"There will be a time when a being is successful in this intention," she said. "A state of unity will be achieved. Earth will rise and join the Federation. Then the decision to allow this will be vindicated."

"But not now."

"Not now. But more are coming. Permission has been given."

The Council was agreed. A final blessing was passed among the members and the Council dissolved the image of Earth. The pillars of the temple faded and the twenty-one beings released the resonance which drew them to one another, and disappeared into the surrounding space, leaving only a faint trace of blue shimmering within the emptiness.

CHAPTER
TWENTY-SIX

THE ORANGE GROVE turned and turned within the darkness, a vast sea of white blossom created by thought and dream and desire.

Elspeth lay within the darkness, beneath the falling white petals, and she looked up through the canopy of leaves and stars and wondered what place she would create for herself, and what world.

David lay beside her. He looked up through the canopy of leaves at the tapestry of stars, and he felt the beginning of acceptance. He felt the beginning of himself.

Her hand reached out to his, and his to hers, and their fingertips touched.

Socrates walked into the grove. His face was bathed in tears.

"It is the cruellest joke," he said. "For man to know the true nature of good, and then to be returned to a place where there is no possibility of good. A place of shadows."

He saw David and Elspeth lying side by side in the darkness, beneath the trees. He looked up and saw the heavens rushing past and heard the sound of the stars singing wildly. For a moment, he forgot the tears on his face and watched in amazement.

Elspeth stood up. She felt drawn to this man. She reached her hand to his face and stroked the tears from his cheeks. She put her arms around his neck and held her night-time body against his. He smelled of oil and undiluted wine and sweat. His beard was pressed against her hair.

Socrates allowed the woman to embrace him. He was transfixed by the stars. It was a dream.

"I have taken a human life," said David. "I am trying to find my way back."

Socrates turned to look at the man, lying on the ground.

"Then you must give back what you have taken," he said. "Your soul must make a journey through its own death before it can return. It must know the pain it has created."

"How would that change anything? I cannot continue to live after what I have done. What I did was unforgivable."

"Your soul will be able to return when you have made this journey. Everything must be brought to balance. You will be able to continue the life you had begun."

"My soul will return to what?"

"To itself."

Elspeth moved her head around to face Socrates, and kissed him gently on the lips. He pushed her away and she fell to the ground beneath an orange tree. She lay there, discarded, on the white-scented soil.

David stood up.

"Take my life," he said to Socrates.

"It is worth nothing to me," Socrates replied.

David moved closer and put his arms around him. Socrates took his head and kissed him tenderly on the mouth.

"You make the choice which is just," he said to David. "There is no other way. You must experience your own death."

"I am afraid."

"There is nothing to fear. The only place to return is to yourself."

He pushed David away. He fell to the ground beside Elspeth, among the white petals and the dry earth.

Socrates took a root of hemlock from his tunic and threw it on the ground next to David.

"Everything passes," he said. "Do not be afraid. Death is the brightest of all realities."

He stood above them, looking down, the stars ringing out into the darkness. He faded into the light of the stars.

David took the hemlock in one hand and reached out the other to Elspeth. Their fingertips met and rested against one another.

The pathway widened in the darkness above them.

David's shadow-form rose and stared into the opening. He could see a faint glistening of gold, a distant rising sun over a desert plain.

"I am ready," said David.

He stepped into the opening.

. . .

WITHIN THE FORMLESS expanse of blue, Alisdair was gaining an understanding of his surroundings, sensing the possibility of shapes within the blue. He traced them with his consciousness, exploring different combinations, and when one of them created a resonance within him, he focused his perception on it and began to fill it, drawing the surrounding colour into the outline of a form, and moulding it into density within the frame.

He understood that it was more a passive than active process, this gathering of form. It was a recognition and acceptance of the initial vibration, and then, simply, an allowing; holding his consciousness present as the process took its natural and inexorable course. He could perceive that the blue was transforming into something deeper, increasing in density, until he became aware that physical matter was gathering around him, and that more and more of the colour was being drawn into the initial shape and forming itself into cells and structures and consciousness. Alisdair remained in his state of passivity as his awareness performed this task within the surrounding expanse. He didn't know what was being created, but he knew that he had found resonance with it, and that whatever would emerge from the process would be a part of his desire and a part of his imagination and a part of himself.

It was done. Alisdair sensed a completion. He was still immersed within the colour, but now he had become a separate entity within it. He found that he was able to move this relative part of himself. He expanded his consciousness around the new shape and found that it was massive and smooth. He could propel himself through the blueness using elements of the structure. He felt a pressure building up in his centre, and then an incredible release as the pressure moved at a vast speed and a substance was expelled from an open point.

The relief was extraordinary. It was dizzying and wonderful. He was plummeting downwards now, into the deeper blueness. Alisdair gathered all of his awareness into the frame and spread himself around it, seeking to understand. At last, realisation came to him. He knew what he had created. He knew what his thought and desire and curiosity had drawn into physical form. With an intense joy, with wonder and excitement in equal measure, and feeling the pressure once again building within the centre of his massive structure, he swam upwards.

 DAVID LOOKED DOWN at his feet. The thongs of his leather sandals were biting into his skin, and he felt scorched and filthy. The skirt of his tunic was covered in dust and he wanted to drink something. The sun was relentless and there was no shelter other than the sparse branches of the olive trees scattered across the arid ground.

He took a breath of the hot, dry air and walked onwards, shading his head with his hand. He knew that it had to be here somewhere. Far behind him was the orange grove and the girl. Ahead of him was... what? What was it he was looking for? He did not know. But he knew that it would bring him help. Redemption? No. That word was too big, too far away to allow him to enter the realm of hope. He did not dare to look for that. But something had to return. Some part of him had to return what had been taken, before his life could continue.

David walked on. Behind him were the shimmering hills of the city and the sparkling blue sea. Behind him were temples and mountains. Behind him was paradise. Ahead of him was desert and olive groves stretching out for a hundred miles. He had no water with him. Each level of thirst and pain was bringing him closer. He walked without hurrying, placing one foot in front of the other, repeating, with every step, his chosen mantra: "I am a murderer, I am a murderer, I am a murderer."

His life in New York, his life in Canada, the existence which led him to become what he became, to commit that act, seemed so far away now that David was unable to understand how much of it was real. The only thing he knew for sure was that he had taken a life, and this single event he now remembered with such keen sensory detail that every time it entered his mind it was as if he were repeating the act over again. The trajectory arc of every kick, the taste of the wind, the sight of blood, the rush of force as his foot met with the flesh of the man he was killing. He felt again the incredible excitement and relief, the thrill that from this single act his life was taking off, that from this act everything good would arise around him. He had succeeded. He had overcome. He had won.

The thrill rose in him and fell again with each repetition of the words. They rose in pure form, then joined with his despair, then fell again. With each rising, the reality, the events that occurred before and since, became more uncertain, more dreamlike. His memory and under-standing of actions, of times, of thoughts, became shadows which he merged into realities. The haze of colour and medications, the inside of a clinic, an orange grove in darkness, a girl and a boy staring up at woven stars on the shore of a summer lake. He threaded them into a narrative, and then they were gone, and the only thing left was the rising thrill, the blood, and the sinking down again. His life had become one single, infinite action.

David shifted the tunic around his shoulders. His head and face were burning in the sun. It did not matter. Let his skin burn off entirely, if it would bring him any peace. He would gladly suffer the hunger and thirst and pain offered by it. He glanced around again. What was he looking for? It would be a kind of opening. A cave. Or a tunnel. It would be a place where he could find the final threads of a narrative with which to complete this stage of the journey. He would be conscious, or his body would have collapsed beneath the unyielding sun; it would make no difference. He had at last released that tenuous threshold between his dreams and his waking. He could exist now in the long, single moment of his own destruction, without trying to avoid or hide it, until the end came.

And he would be patient.

CHAPTER
TWENTY-SEVEN

"SO THIS IS VANESSA?"

David's mother came towards them with her arms held out wide. Vanessa got out of the car, wearing a tight pair of jeans and a hooded Maple Leafs top she had borrowed from David. She hugged his mother.

"I'm so pleased to meet you," she said.

David stepped out of the car and kissed her on the cheek.

"I'm sorry we rushed it all like this," he said. "It was a kind of spur-of-the-moment thing. And then I had to finish up a major project at the bank before we could drive up here to see you."

"It's your life, darling," his mother said. "Did you finish it up? The project?"

"Yeah. It all went well in the end. I got a major promotion to celebrate. And the Hong Kong move. Well, I told you that much on the phone."

"Well, everyone's excited to see you, darling."

"Are we all set up for the party tonight?"

"All ready."

"Is Dad home?"

"Of course he is. He's dying to meet Vanessa. Now come on into the house."

"CASSIE!"

David waved to her from the other side of the garden, where the guests were standing in groups, holding bottles of Molson and tumblers of Crown Royal. Cassie glanced up, but then looked down again quickly. She was wearing a black shirt with flowers and her hair was pulled back into a long, severe ponytail. She looked older. She looked like a scientist. David walked across the garden.

"Come and meet Vanessa."

She looked up, her green-grey eyes meeting his for just a moment before looking away again.

"Cassie..."

"David, I'm not staying long. I've got to get back to work. I just came here to bring you something. It's from my parents – and me. We wanted to get you something for your wedding. And to say good luck in Hong Kong. That's where you're going, right?"

"Cassie, I wanted to talk to you. We're heading off in a day, on the honeymoon. Cassie, these things have been happening. Maybe you—"

"Shut up, David. Okay? I've got this present for you. And then I've got to head off."

Cassie walked towards the house, and David noticed that she was thinner than he had ever seen her. Even her hair looked thinner. He suddenly wondered if she was alright, if there might not be something wrong with her. He felt an urge to smell her, to push his nose into that childhood scent again. He followed her into the kitchen, where there was a large box wrapped in silver paper on the table.

"Open it," she said.

He looked at her and tilted his head.

"Cassie?"

"Just open it."

David pulled some of the paper from the top of the present, then tore down the sides to reveal a wooden box.

"What is it?"

"Open it and see."

He prised the top upwards and looked inside. It was a large, black instrument. He knew at once what it was.

"It's a telescope," he said.

"You always wanted one."

"Cassie, how could you even afford this?"

"I'm highly paid at the faculty. Big bucks, David."

"Wow."

David turned towards her and moved forward to give her a hug. He caught a trace of fragrance as he leaned over, but it wasn't the lemon and whisky he had wanted to smell; the autumn morning and lake air.

It was a new scent: stronger, more chemical. Some shop perfume. He immediately hated it. Cassie stepped away from him.

"David, we were very close once," she said. "I wanted you to have this. I wish you good luck. But don't get in touch with me again. I'm going to go now."

"Cassie…"

He stared down at her, and at last she brought her face up to meet his, the hair pulled back from her forehead, and instead of the anger and hurt he had expected, the hatred and betrayal, there was just a simple love in those eyes, unhidden and unbroken. The grey, flecked with threads of green, looking both at him and beyond him; a look that had always made him feel safe, loved, understood and known.

She held his gaze for the duration of a breath, and then she closed her eyes, and he wasn't sure if it was because tears were coming or because she had shown him what she had wanted him to know. She opened them again, but now she was looking away. She was looking at the telescope on the table, and at the kitchen floor, and at the doorway behind her where the party was going on in the garden beyond.

"Goodbye, David," she said.

She didn't meet his eyes again. She spoke the words into the space of the kitchen, as if it were empty, as if he wasn't in it. Then she turned and went out of the room and he could see her through the doorway as she passed among the crowd of his family and friends, and out of the side-gate which led towards her house, towards the lake, towards the islands where they had lain beneath a vast, starlit sky, beneath the enormity of their unknown futures, on a single turning planet, hand in hand.

WHEN THE HOUSE WAS ASLEEP, David slipped out of bed and made his way downstairs. He took a clean glass from the cabinet in the living room, poured himself a large whisky and added a handful of ice from the freezer. He turned the key in the back door and stepped out onto the porch, looking at the garden where the party had been. All those people from his life. He had a sudden feeling that he might not see any of them again. Except for his parents. And Cassie.

He took a long drink and looked up into the stars crowding the deepest night sky. These were the stars he had fallen in love with in his childhood. These incomparable Canadian stars which seemed to have a life of their own, glistening alive and white and utterly brilliant up there in the universe. Even now, they sent a thrill through him. He wondered what the stars would be like in Hong Kong. He doubted if he would be able to see any from the city, with the barrage of light. But there must be places on the island where it was dark enough. He tried to calculate which constellations would be visible in that part of Asia, but then gave up. He would have been able to figure that out a few years back. Beardy could have done it in three seconds flat.

David drank down the last of the whisky and went back into the kitchen. He picked up the wooden box with the telescope and carried it to the bottom of the garden, to his father's tool shed. Setting the box down, he took out the telescope and laid it on the grass. Then he went back into the shed and came out with a black-and-silver hammer. Calmly, he squatted on the ground next to the equipment. He brought the hammer up and then smashed it down onto the long, sleek instrument, shattering the main lens. Shards of black plastic and bent metal fell to the ground. He brought the hammer down again and again, until the telescope lay in pieces in front of him, twisted and mangled.

It was done. He stood and stretched his legs, rubbing his hands over them. That was better. He felt much better now. He put the hammer into its place in the tool shed, then gathered up the pieces of the smashed telescope and put them back into the box. He carried the box out of the side-gate and down the street to the dumpster, where he slid it deep down into the mass of waste. He returned to the house, poured himself another large whisky and drank it on the porch, breathing in the fresh, lake-blown Canadian air.

From the window of the guest room above, Vanessa pulled the curtains closed, walked back across the soft carpet and climbed into bed. They would be in Hawaii the next day. Hong Kong in a month. Far away from this backwater. She closed her eyes, picturing New York, skyscrapers, diamonds, city lights and David beside her. She slept.

 THE ADMIRAL LOOKED DOWN on the physical form it was preparing to enter. It was in a state of sleep, and the primary being, whose time it was to depart, was beginning the process of transition. The figure lay curled around an empty whisky bottle, huddled behind a large green trash can in an unlit alley. The body was worn, damaged, with little strength remaining. The primary being was ready to leave. It sensed the Admiral close and sent a greeting. The Admiral approached.

The being moved out of the body and waited while the Admiral entered. It drew further away from the physical form, trailing a thread of silver, until it had passed through the barrier of light, and the human thread was severed. It was gone.

In its place, a new thread was forming, as the Admiral attached itself to the casing and felt around the sleeping figure. The internal organs were functioning at a minimal base level, and there was damage and disease and inefficiency. It could not be sustained for many more inhalations. It would have to make some adjustments to maintain the viability of the form. The Admiral could feel something slipping away, and its thoughts became increasingly muddled. It closed its eyes as a sensation of dizziness eased it into a deep sleep.

WHEN THE HOMELESS MAN AWOKE, it was late in the morning. His hand was still clenched around the whisky bottle and he held it up to the light to see if there was anything left in it. No. It was empty. He rolled it behind the trash can and began the painful process of getting to his feet. He would have to begin the usual rounds of the city, making his way to the food collection points which made New York one of the best cities in the world in which to be homeless and jobless. Endless, quality free food. You just had to find enough money to keep the supply of liquor running. But even that wasn't too difficult. Lots of money. Lots of guilty consciences. You could get a five, a ten, even a twenty sometimes.

The homeless man got himself to his feet. He didn't much feel like making the rounds this morning. He felt like trying out somewhere new. Maybe the East River. He had a hunch he might find a good place to sleep there. Maybe one of those fancy entrance halls which were well-heated in the winter and cool in the summer. He would try it. There was nothing to lose.

Within an hour, he had gathered his belongings and made his way, shuffling and swearing, to Houston and over to the East Side. He didn't think while he was walking; he just had a feeling, and while he had that feeling he moved forward. He stopped off at one of the homeless missions and was given a box of stale pastries. He sat on a park bench and ate, throwing pieces to the pigeons with whom he had always felt a kind of bad-tempered affinity. Tolerated, unwanted creatures. He belched and continued on his journey.

By nightfall, he was walking parallel to the East River. This would be a good change, to sleep somewhere he could hear the water. He was tired. He finished the pastries and washed them down with a cup of coffee, handed over by a hurrying passer-by. He wanted to sleep. He turned up a street from York Avenue, making sure he could still hear the water, and found an oldish-looking apartment building with a green canopy. This would do. He was beat. Tomorrow, he would find one of the soup kitchens nearby. Maybe a church. There were always some places. But now, he was going to sleep.

He made his way up the first couple of steps, then eased himself onto the tiles of the porch. It was comfortable, he was out of the way of the canopy lighting, and he was covered, in case of rain. This was good. It was better than the alley. And tomorrow he'd score a quart of malt. He took out some of the newspaper he carried and spread it over himself. It smelled of whisky and the alley he had slept in. He stopped thinking at this point and closed his eyes. He adjusted his body to a more comfortable position against the steps, and fell quickly into a deep sleep.

Beyond the murmur of traffic and water, the distant sirens and horns, the electrical hum of the pulsing New York night, as the Earth turned calmly in its orbit, held by a precise mathematical equation within the moving, living universe, the Admiral lay curled within the porchway, sleeping, oblivious, and waited for David.

CHAPTER
TWENTY-EIGHT

ALISDAIR MOVED his form through the immense space of blue. He felt powerful and free and without limit. He sensed other creatures in the vast liquid expanse around him and he heard their calls and responded with his own sound, without thinking. He saw dolphin-like mammals and flashes of tiny fish in schools, innumerable colours passing around him. He discovered that he could sense the other creatures in the liquid; he knew their presence far down in the darkness, and around him, and in the lightness above.

He came to the realisation that his form, and the living liquid, and the light flowing through the liquid, and the plant life and the seen and unseen within the expanse were all connected into one song, and he was at the centre of that song. It was an incredible feeling. It was a feeling of knowing his place beyond all doubt within the structure of everything around him; of understanding his role in the song and how to perform it in a way that wasn't possible for any other living being.

He had the awareness that he would consume the creatures around him to maintain his survival, and that the creatures would feed on each other, and that the entire expanse was changing, always changing, and he understood that this was the very nature of the expanse: this constant change. The movement of his fin. The flash of silver from a darting fish. The haze of colour passing within the blue.

He felt the pressure gathering once again within his centre, and he pulled it to him, drawing that feeling of wonder and music and release, and he rose to the surface and pushed it all out of him and it shot up, up into the unseen sky and sunshine far above.

"Come." It was Duncan's voice.

Alisdair felt his consciousness moving out of the creature's form, and up over the liquid. Duncan was there, a faint outline of light, and together they observed the planet, the layers and shapes of blue, and they looked at the fish flying out in silver dozens, the dolphins jumping in precise arcs, and the whales as they rose to brush the surface with their vast shadows.

"I would like to stay here," said Alisdair.

"You have already been here," said Duncan. "This is where many beings choose to incarnate for the first time. It is simple in this place to move from consciousness to form. You remain as pure energy within the blue, until you are ready to create. You have had many lifetimes here, at the very beginning."

"The very beginning?"

"Your very beginning. There is no universal beginning, as such."

"Then—"

"No answer I can give you can explain this. It is something you must come to know. You always have been. You always will be. There is nothing at all except for now. This moment. And it is eternally changing."

"This moment."

"The eternally changing moment."

"So right now—"

"You are everything you ever have been and everything you ever will be. Look."

Duncan reached up into the surrounding blue and gathered a ball of sky with his hands. He moved it slowly apart, revealing a skein of silk. Hundreds of different shapes moved within the silk: men and women, children, animals, life forms he had never seen before. And at the end of the skein of silk, there were shadows and flickers of light, and Duncan threw the silk into the air so that it merged into sunlight, and faded into nothing.

"Come," he said.

The silk was gone. The blue planet was gone. Alisdair and Duncan were back in the jewelled garden.

"It is time for you to return," said Duncan.

"And Elspeth?"

Duncan reached forward and touched Alisdair on the forehead, and Alisdair saw Elspeth in the orange grove, smiling in the morning sunlight.

264

"You will be with her whenever you both choose to be. But your work with her is done."

"Then I can move on."

"I am also moving on."

"Where are you going?"

"I am taking a place on the Earth Council."

"And I?"

"Follow your thought. You have already decided where to go. I will see you soon."

The eyes of the men met, and they smiled, and in the smile was understanding, and thanks, and friendship.

"Then I will see you now," said Alisdair.

"Yes. I will see you now," said Duncan.

Alisdair felt a strong pull leading him somewhere, an urging, and he followed it. He was being drawn through energy fields, and he felt the layers of his selves falling from him as he moved. He saw flashes of himself in a chamber, discussing life-paths with groups of souls, and he knew that he had been there while he had been with Elspeth, while he had been on the blue planet, while he had been with Duncan, deciding life contracts, paths and agreements. He knew that he had made his choice.

He had the feeling, moving through the light planes, that he was both disintegrating and gathering form at the same time. And then he was simply disintegrating, and it was the most exquisite feeling he had ever experienced, and he released himself to it entirely, as he felt his consciousness moving at a speed unimaginable; past the light, through the light, as the light, and at last, away from the light.

And then he slowed, and he stopped, and he was somewhere. His essence was somewhere, although he could feel no form around him, no physical place, no space of reference. It was as if he were existing as nothing within nothing, but at the same time, it was something, he was somewhere. He sensed a web-like structure – something mathematical, something liquid, perhaps gelatinous – and he felt a confusion creeping over him, and at last, understanding nothing, with no desire beyond a strand of simple curiosity, he opened his eyes.

DAVID WALKED FORWARDS. He was no longer sure where or who he was. He had been blinded by the heat and the sun. The skin of his body was covered in red-and-white blisters, his eyes felt as if they were burning in their sockets. He knew that he must draw the strength to put one foot in front of the other, and then again. One foot in front of the other. He did not know his own name. He did not know whether he was alive or dead. He did not know anything.

It was the end of the day, and the light was fading. The blisters on his body had stopped their liquid bubbling, and had settled into raw, open sores, creating a constant pain all over him. His cheeks were wet, and he understood that he had been weeping, though whether from sorrow or from the relentless sun, he did not know.

He hallucinated that the pain was the stinging burn of ice and that the bright light around him was the white of swirling snow. He was confused by the vertiginous blizzard and dragged his feet forwards through the unbearable cold, blinding winter, his body burning over every part of its surface.

David blinked. Where was he? He looked around. The desert was gone. The olive trees were gone. He looked down. In his hand was the root of hemlock given to him by Socrates. He lifted it up and looked at it. He sniffed it. It smelled bitter, unpleasant. He imagined a cup, with the root ground and correctly mixed; but this was all he had. He took a small bite. His throat tried to reject it, but he forced it down. He took another bite. He swallowed. He dropped the hemlock to the ground.

He stepped forward. He looked to each side of him and found that he was walking through some kind of cave. The walls were glowing in fiery red and gold and throwing shadows onto the floor of the enclosure, like dancing figures. He turned to look behind him and he saw that the hemlock had gone. Beyond just a few feet, he could see nothing; the path he had trodden had been drawn into a haze of darkness.

David felt very calm. He felt the pain all over his body; the searing blisters where his skin had been scorched and melted. It was a total, smouldering pain. It felt wonderful. For the first time since the euphoria of the act had worn off, he felt a kind of peace, the very beginning of a realisation that it might be possible to accept himself, to accept what he had done. The pain had somehow opened a door back into himself; a door he thought had been closed forever.

David took a deep breath. He knew that the road he had travelled had brought him, over hundreds of lifetimes and experiences and sorrows, to this place, to this moment here, to the inside of this glowing cave; and he accepted it. He accepted the pain of his skin and the pain that he had caused. He accepted the guilt and the forgiveness. He accepted, with deep joy, that everything would return.

He fell down in the cave and his soul stepped lightly out of his body. He stood, looking down at the burnt flesh for a few moments, and then walked away from the discarded form, up towards the opening of the tunnel, towards what seemed at first to be a burst of bright light. The silver thread which held his soul to his body trailed faintly behind him as he moved through the light, and he passed out of the cave opening and found himself in a garden, where there were fountains of tumbling water with droplets like cut sapphires, and animals in incredible hues: tigers, peacocks, a white owl. A figure approached David as he was looking around, and held out its hand.

It was the Admiral.

David lifted his arm to accept the hand. He felt his selves shifting into previous, parallel and future existences, and for a few moments, with his hand clasped in the Admiral's, the two became first one, and then a multitude of lives and images and selves and possibilities, a single bright light burning in the stillness of the garden.

David's self shifted into the form of *Noœ-bouk*, as the Admiral transformed to Cassie, a glow of red hair, and beyond and beyond, to the previous and future incarnations through which the thread of their love had been woven. At last, the homeless man appeared before him, and David met his gaze and held it, understanding at last that nothing was broken, and nothing could ever be broken.

Then, something was gone. A heaviness. A darkness blocking the expression of natural joy. The Admiral released his hand and David found himself being drawn back, away from the dazzling garden, away from the Admiral, back towards the pathway which was still open for him, the pathway leading to an orange grove, turning, turning in the darkness, and the sleeping forms of a man and a woman, side by side beneath a canopy of falling petals.

267

ELSPETH AWOKE as the first rays of the colossal Athenian sun drew light over her sleeping body. Before her skin was able to register the morning chill, a scent of the sweetest orange blossom came to her, and she breathed in as deeply as she could.

A moment later, she opened her eyes and levered herself onto her elbows. She rubbed the dirt from her arms, brought her knees towards her and pushed herself up from the ground. She hopped from one foot to the other a few times to loosen her body. Her limbs were aching and cold, and her neck was stiff from the awkward angle of her rucksack, but she had some kind of sense, which she had not had before, of happiness. It felt as if something had changed during the night, as if a missing piece of her had somehow been returned.

She rolled her neck round one way and then the other, and then she pulled her rucksack up onto her shoulders and prepared to leave. She bent down to smooth the dirt, so that nobody would see that she had been sleeping there, and she noticed another indentation in the soil, next to where she had been lying. A feeling came over her. Could she have slept in two places? Could she have rolled over? She compared the shapes of the pressed earth, but it was impossible to tell. Something inside her, a memory, a dream, seemed ready to come rushing to the surface and into her mind, and she sought it, she tried to hold it. But then there was the squawk of a seagull overhead, and the sensation was gone. There was no memory, there was no feeling, there was only the sunshine warming her hair and skin, and the shadow of the seagull's wings passing over the white blossom.

Elspeth brushed dirt over the two strips of pressed soil with the palms of her hands, and then she straightened up and looked around her. Beyond the orange grove, there was a cragged mountain. It was the opposite direction from the city and it looked a few hours' walk away. As she stared up at the peak – challenging, unassailable – she suddenly felt wildly happy. She was going to climb it. For no reason. For no reason at all other than the pleasure of the climb, the sunshine on her skin, the view from the top, the feeling that she could fly! She started to laugh. It was enough. It was really enough, this feeling. There was no more search, no more discontent, no more jarring with the world of other people. There was this mountain. There was this sunshine. There was her.

She started to walk.

DAVID OPENED his eyes as the Athenian sunshine spread over the coverlet of his single bed. It must be late morning. He reached his arms up above him and stretched, pulling his weakened muscles into pain. It felt good. He lay flat, his hands behind his head, and looked at the stripe of sunshine lying across the cover. He felt better this morning. The single line of gold seemed to represent a kind of hope. Something new. Something possible.

He sat up and pushed the coverlet from his chest. He touched his face. When had he last shaved? He must look like a down-and-out. He probably looked like he didn't have a place to get a decent shave. He'd sort that out this morning. He'd clean himself up.

David got out of the bed and dropped to the floor for push-ups. There was a time when he did this every morning. Fifty. Seventy. A hundred. He forced himself to ten, his arms and chest feeling the strain of his weakened body, then he lay flat for a few moments on the floor. He'd build it up again. He'd train back to fifty. To a hundred. He could do it.

He stood up and went to the window and pushed the curtain back. It wasn't much of a view. The grey city in a haze of sunlit fog, the din of cars and motorbikes and shouting. He slid open the balcony window and stepped outside into the sunshine. His phone was in his hand. He didn't remember picking it up. He looked at it, and smiled. He flipped open and clicked through to his contacts. She wasn't even there. From memory, he dialled the number into the phone.

He stared out over the balcony at the golden haze as the phone connected and started to ring. An owl flashed before his eyes. The image of a white owl. He welcomed it.

There was a click.

"Hello?"

"Cassie."

Breathing. Sunshine. The sound of traffic.

"It's David."

THE WOMAN BEHIND THE WATERFALL

LEONORA MERIEL

Seven-year-old Angela is thrown into confusion when she sees her mother crying in the garden one day. As she attempts to discover what is wrong, the spirit of her grandmother comes to guide her through the trauma of discovering the truth of her own past and her mother's dark secrets. Full of magic and beauty, the novel captures the innocence of the child, the struggles of a mother and the wisdom of a grandmother – and the lessons they can learn from each other from beyond their generational roles.

A classic literary fiction tale of three generations of women in a Ukrainian village and the joys and sorrows they experience and share. The book is a celebration of Ukrainian culture and was written to showcase the beautiful Ukrainian land, language and customs to a worldwide audience.

"A literary work of art" – *Fiona Adams, Richmond Magazine*

"A strange and beautiful novel" – *Esther Freud*

"An intoxicating world" – *Kirkus Reviews*

Available in hardback, paperback, e-book and audiobook.

AND BREATHE
LEONORA MERIEL

On a silent meditation retreat deep in the Thai jungle, a Brazilian feminist, a neurotic French scientist and a ruthless Ukrainian oligarch are struggling to find peace. As the world around them falls silent, their inner voices become louder, clamouring for their attention, seeding doubt and dysphoria. Over the course of ten mosquito-ravaged nights and ten achingly uncomfortable days, their deepest fears begin to overpower them.

With each character written in the first person, the reader is able to experience the most intimate voices of these three, and to share their terrors and traumas. As each one of them is transformed by the meditation, the reader is also challenged to face their own fears and change alongside them, as the power of the ancient *Vipassana* meditation technique makes itself known.

"Enthralling to the end... a grippingly intense, yet beautiful read" – Emma Carmichael, author of *Driving Tito*

Available in hardback, paperback, e-book and audiobook.

MBAQUANGA NIGHTS
LEONORA MERIEL

1989.

The African Jazz Pioneers are in full swing. Coltrane's club is hopping. Glasses and plates are pushed aside as the room dances.

What's so special?

Look around. The faces are black, brown and white. It's Durban, South Africa. It's apartheid. It's illegal.

When a pair of young music lovers decide to follow their dreams and open a jazz club to showcase the musicians whose irrepressible songs they have grown up with, they have little idea of what stark choices they will be facing as the political situation heats up and riots tear through the surrounding townships.

With an epic tale that starts in the depths of a Ukrainian shtetl and winds its way back and forth across oceans, history and memory serve to create a personal story of individual choice – and the fate of nations.

"A wild ride that stretches through jazz and history" – Zoe Mcleod

CPSIA information can be obtained
at www.ICGtesting.com
Printed in the USA
LVHW040852290622
722311LV00009B/87/J